Vanessa's Curve of Mind

a novel

Kirk Smith

To my very good friends for many years, Lee and June
With best wishes
Kirk Smith

OLD HEAVY DUTY PUBLISHING

ISBN-13: 978-0-9890010-0-7
ISBN-10: 0-9890010-0-8

Library of Congress Control Number: 2013905530

Old Heavy Duty Publishing

is an imprint of

Northwest Navigation Company
P. O. Box 1431
Bellingham, Washington 98227

NorthwestNavigation.com

Cover painting by D. W. Miller.
Calabi-Yau manifold graphic by Nick Henscheid, based on a Mathematica program by Andrew J. Hanson.

Albert Einstein, "The Motives of Researchers," by permission of Albert Einstein Archives, Jerusalem, Israel.

To my mother Frances,

who loved words and music.

FORWARD

In a single year at the beginning of the twentieth century, Albert Einstein started a scientific revolution. While still a graduate student without a PhD, he published four papers that changed the face of physics forever.

His first paper, in March of 1905, shook up our understanding of the nature of light and later won him a Nobel Prize. In April he finished writing a paper on the size of molecules but saved it for his dissertation instead of publishing it immediately. His May paper showed that Brownian motion was observable evidence for the existence of molecules. One of his most revolutionary papers—the first statement of the special theory of relativity—appeared in June. Finally, he submitted a note to the editor of *Annalen der Physik* that appeared in September showing that relativity implied $E=mc^2$. Early in 1906 he at last defended his dissertation and became Herr Doktor Einstein.

Could a graduate student with a mind as brilliant as Einstein's repeat his achievement at the beginning of the twenty-first century in the emerging field of cognitive neuroscience? Especially if she were a woman whose nude photos were still available on the Internet?

Man tries to make for himself... a simplified and intelligible picture of the world and thus overcome the world of experience, for which he tries to some extent to substitute this cosmos of his. [The] painter, the poet, the speculative philosopher and the natural scientist... makes this cosmos and its construction the pivot of his emotional life, in order to find in this way the peace and security which he cannot find in the narrow whirlpool of personal experience.—Albert Einstein (1918) [English translation, 1934].

CHAPTER 1

Vanessa Trippett, the graduate student at the other end of the long table, had fastened her cobalt blue eyes on Stan Harte when he began his lecture and refused to release him, even it seemed, when she blinked. And he appreciated what that kind of attention from Vanessa Trippett meant. He'd heard the rumors about her—how behind the pale mask of her perfectly proportioned face burned a brain like an intellectual forge, how in her single-minded quest for understanding she had asked his colleagues exactly the questions that exposed logical flaws in their thinking or gaps in their knowledge of their own specialty.

Stan was starting to worry that it was about to happen to him. For more than a decade, he and his colleague Paul Kovick had given guest lectures to each other's graduate seminars at the University of Washington in Seattle. It was Stan's turn to talk to Paul's psycholinguistics seminar. In the students' minds, his expertise should exceed their instructor's, at least in the subspecialty of this lecture, which was the role of meaning in the psychology of language. In fact, Paul had warned him about Vanessa the day before.

Paul came to Stan's office, closed the door, and sat down. He looked ill at ease, which surprised Stan because they were longtime friends and usually supported each other in the political wrangling in the psychology department. He was a patrician blend of virility and urbanity that attracted bright young women like iron filings to a magnet, especially women in the first-year graduate class. Years of sedentary living had not completely erased the evidence that he'd been a star football player in high school, and the trace of gray in his black hair conferred an air of scholarly authority.

"I assume you're going to cover multidimensional scaling again this year?" he began.

"Why? I thought that was one of the reasons I was talking to your class."

"Right. That's why I came by. To tell you that my student Vanessa will almost certainly ask you a lot of questions tomorrow."

"I hear she's embarrassed quite a few of our colleagues with her questions."

"You don't know the half of it. Be forewarned, buddy! She'll ask an innocent-sounding question… and follow it up with another… and another… until she finds a hole you can't fill."

"Sounds like good clean academic fun." Stan smirked to hide a ripple of anxiety. For a forty-four-year-old full professor with a string of publications and a reputation as an accomplished scientist, was there anything more emasculating than being shown that you don't know what you're talking about? Especially when your error is exposed while you're lecturing to a graduate seminar on what you supposedly know better than anyone else in your department.

Paul scowled. "I'm not joking, Stan." He slid his chair forward and leaned toward Stan across the table. "The stories you've been hearing aren't exaggerated. With the kind of intellectual horsepower she possesses, she can destroy you without realizing what she's doing."

"She's not doing it to show off?"

"She's not trying to prove anything. She doesn't need to: The exams and papers she writes are head and shoulders above the rest of our students."

"I gathered that from reading her comprehensive exam last fall." Stan recalled the answers that read like journal articles rather than off-the-cuff responses to test questions.

"Her questions aren't malicious, either. Or in any way calculated." Paul shook his head. "I think the problem is that she believes everyone around her is as smart as she is, so she assumes the fault is her grasp of what someone has said. Her questions come from a passionate desire for knowledge and clarity. She's so bright, she doesn't realize someone else doesn't have the answer to her question—or worse, that no one has it. She alw disappointed as her target is chagrined to find out eems as forthcoming."

"Hard to believe." Especially coming from the pe wer's knew her better than anyone else in the department. Sh living with Paul almost a year now, in spite of the r someone would file a complaint under the inappropriate st faculty relationship policy.

"I know. I know." Paul groaned unconvincingly. "You t I'm overdoing it, like I usually do. But it's hard to portray accurately without sounding like a raving fanatic."

"So what are you saying about tomorrow? That she'll make me look like an ignoramus in front of your seminar?"

Paul smiled sympathetically. "I've watched every one of my guest lecturers this year get squashed. But like you said, academically it's good sport. The other students stand to learn from these exchanges, and that's what seminars are all about, right?"

"Thanks for your concern about my welfare, pal." Stan leaned back in his office chair, trying to cover up his growing trepidation.

"Look, I'm sorry. But I'm trying to educate the *rest* of the class. She already knows more than they do. She knows more than *I* do on a lot of topics. Please, don't let her drag you into answering her questions about the nuts and bolts of extracting dissimilarity scales. If you do, everyone but Vanessa will spend the rest of the seminar lost in a thicket of incomprehensible symbols."

"I don't know, Paul. That's hard to do without seeming completely superficial." Stan prided himself on his ability to teach the mathematical details of psychological scaling. He was convinced that understanding where the numbers came from demystified the results.

"Listen," Paul said. "She knows more math than the whole goddamned psychology faculty could muster in an emergency. And if the math department ever finds out about her, they'll be over here en masse trying to recruit her."

"You don't have to tell me! I tried to read a paper she wrote describing her theory." Stan remembered it with a cringe. A dozen pages of equations filled with unfamiliar operators and intervening text that read like a mathematical proof using words he'd never seen before. About all he could gather from the introduction was as proposing a seven-dimensional model of what she “mind-brain continuum.” From references to elliptical y and Calabi-Yau manifolds, he figured out that the tools derivations were drawn in part from differential geometry. when he reached the last page, his feelings of intimidation had en way to a mixture of awe and disbelief.

Vanessa was trying to solve the mind-body problem, the Holy Grail of contemporary cognitive neuroscience, an enigma as old as the Greek philosophers who first posed it more than two thousand years ago. He'd had a strange premonition at the time: This might be the first draft of the most revolutionary theory in the history of psychology—and very likely medical science as well. If so, he and his colleagues would have to learn the math he'd just skimmed over. And he wanted to be the first in his field—after Vanessa, of course—to master it. What a boost that would be for his faltering career!

“Yeah.” Paul let out a long breath. “It's a ridiculously ambitious theoretical project. If only I could get her to focus on a project of practical scope, she could be finished with a master's thesis in a month.”

After a moment of silence, Stan said in a gloomy voice, “Doesn't sound like it will do me any good to prepare for tomorrow.” He laughed tonelessly. “The condemned man should eat a hearty dinner.”

“I'll call an ambulance to come get you afterward.” Paul didn't smile. “Good luck,” he told Stan as he stood to leave.

Well, here he was in Vanessa Trippett's crosshairs, and this guest lecture wasn't as much fun as it had been every other time he'd done it. Vanessa's presence had changed everything. In fact, he was starting to sweat like an advanced graduate student giving his first paper to a scientific meeting where all the big guns in the field were out there in the audience, a jury deciding the fate of his career and his chances of getting a good job in the next year or two. The pressure *had* sharpened his mind, forced him to organize his sentences better and make his explanations clearer.

At the same time, he had a heightened awareness of his own behavior and its effect on the other students. They were watching the growing tension between him and Vanessa. And as he came to the end of what he planned to say, he realized that he had spent most of the time looking at Vanessa—as if he were talking only to her. He was sure the other students saw it, too, and the realization brought the heat of a blush to his face.

Sure enough, when he said, as he always did at the end of these presentations, "So... questions?" Vanessa's exquisitely shaped hand shot up. "Yes, Vanessa?" He felt his heart rate skyrocket, and the stern face of his ninety-year-old father's cardiologist flashed through his mind.

There was another source of Stan's febrile apprehension. He had seen photos and videos of Vanessa on the *Playboy* website three years ago and been enthralled by her sensuous body and exotic appearance. It was just his luck that he was away on sabbatical at Stanford the same year she entered the graduate program. When he returned in the fall and saw her, he was flabbergasted. But when he checked her *Playboy* photos, she was clearly the same woman.

Although he later heard from colleagues that she had chosen Paul Kovick as her major professor and was now living with him, Stan had been looking for an excuse to get better acquainted with her because he had always wanted to talk to a *Playboy* model. And after reading her paper, he couldn't see why she was working with Paul. His interests and expertise were much less compatible with hers than Stan's.

This lecture might be his only chance to capture her attention, impress her, and start her thinking about him as a better advisor than Paul. At the same time, being caught out by a woman like Vanessa in front of a bunch of graduate students would be a waking nightmare.

"Dr. Harte, you've presented semantic theory entirely in terms of binary features, variables that can take on two values, zero and one. Is that correct?"

"Yes. As I said, binary features have a long history in linguistics." An elementary question—harmless enough. Was it a good setup for asking a question of clarification? Or a lure to extract a statement that would crumble when the rotten logic hidden underneath it gave way?

Vanessa nodded intently. "On the other hand, the work on multidimensional scaling of meaning is based on the assumption that concepts are organized in an *n*-manifold with a continuous metric. How is that metric derived from binary distinctions?"

A good question. And not even close to any of the various possibilities spinning through his head in the seconds between his answer and her question.

"Vanessa…" Paul's warning sounded like the growl of a peeved bear.

Stan looked at him in surprise. What he saw startled him. Paul's face was crimson, and the blood vessels stood out and pulsed in his temples.

"No, Paul," Vanessa said without raising her voice. "This is a crucial question. Why not posit continuous scales from the very beginning?"

Stan's head rotated back to Vanessa. There was a straightforward answer, but already he saw the precipice where she was taking him. Stan hesitated, staring at the abyss of theory he saw ahead of them, a bridge she expected him to describe, a bridge he was pretty sure didn't exist.

Suddenly, Paul leapt to his feet. "Vanessa," he shouted at her, "you ask every speaker I have in here the same goddamn question!"

In shocked disbelief Stan's head swung back in Paul's direction. Never, in the hundreds of seminars he'd participated in, had he seen such a violent display of emotion. He glanced around the table at the other students. They were acting like it had happened before. Brad Holmes was actually smirking.

Vanessa completely ignored Paul. "Why not provide a quantitative underpinning for explaining why people dichotomize meanings, instead of start—"

"Vanessa, shut up!" Paul grabbed the marker for the whiteboard. "You've missed Stan's whole goddamn point."

At the word "point," he stabbed at her with the marker. It flew out of his hand and fell in a steep arc halfway down the table, where it bounced three times like a loose football. His whole body toppled as though his torso was following the trajectory of the marker. There was no cry, not even a grunt. His head missed the edge of the table by an inch.

Vanessa was on her feet even before the muffled thud of his full weight hitting the floor. "Paul!" she cried out. "What's the matter?"

As she rounded the front corner of the table, the student sitting there stood and moved into her path. She shoved him back against the table and in another step knelt at Paul's side.

"Paul!" she shouted, shaking his shoulders roughly. "What's wrong? Can you hear me?"

She rolled the unresponsive man onto his back and with her thumb on his chin tilted his head back. Leaning over him, she turned her head with her ear practically touching his mouth. Then she grabbed his wrist and straightened up, scanning the faces peering down at her. "Scott," she said pointing to one of them. "Call 9-1-1!"

The student took out his cell phone and flipped it open as he stepped out of the circle of students who had gathered at the front of the room.

"Emily," she said to one of the women. "Go to the office and see if they have an AED."

The woman looked confused.

"I'll go," said a second woman.

"Quick, quick!" Without standing up, Vanessa shed the flannel work shirt she wore as a jacket and flung it in the corner. Stan couldn't stop himself from staring momentarily at her breasts under the pink fabric of her T-shirt and the soft bra whose outline he could clearly see.

Vanessa bent over Paul again and, with her mouth on his, blew hard. She shook her head, then clamped his nose with her thumb and fingers and blew twice more. Each time his chest rose and fell a little bit. She scrambled sideways and began pumping his chest using her full weight while she counted aloud: "One and, two and, three and…"

Up to this point Stan had been rooted to the spot where he was standing when Paul fell over. Now, he knelt at Paul's head and timidly placed his fingertips along Paul's throat. "I can feel a pulse… when you…" he said to Vanessa, who nodded.

He felt thoroughly inadequate watching her work like a heroic expert. She had complete control of the situation and herself while he—the only faculty member in the room—was just an incompetent bystander.

He glanced up at the ring of students jostling for a look. The sound of Vanessa's steady counting masked their murmurs. Her hair was so close he could have counted the individual strands. The fruit blossom fragrance he smelled had to be her shampoo.

"...fifty-seven, fifty-eight, fifty-nine, and sixty, sixty-one..."

Still counting, she lifted her head, anxiety scrawled across her face. Droplets of perspiration were forming on her forehead. Her hot breath, reeking of garlic and stale coffee, assaulted Stan's nostrils.

"...ninety-eight, ninety-nine, and a hundred!" She slumped back on her heels. "Still?" she asked Stan between gasps.

"No, the pulse is... uh... gone."

She rose on her knees, hands locked on Paul's chest again.

"Let me help with the compressions." Stan moved on all fours opposite her. Trying to imitate her, he laced his fingers and gingerly placed the heel of one of them on Paul's chest.

"Thanks," she said gratefully. She reached out and forcefully moved his hands a little higher on Paul's chest before creeping back next to his head.

"A hundred?" Stan asked her.

She looked at him like he was a slow-witted child. "Yes!" She jabbed her forefinger into his arm. "Go!"

He pushed cautiously on Paul's chest. Ribs crackled and crumbled under his weight.

"Harder!" she shrieked. She rose on her knees and started moving sideways to where she had been before.

Stan hesitated. "I'm breaking his ribs."

"I already did!" A wail of desperation tinged her voice. "Here, let me."

Before she could yank his hands away, he began furiously pumping Paul's chest.

She placed her hand on top of his as if to gauge how much force he was exerting. "Better," she said softly. "Seven, and eight, and nine—"

"And ten, and eleven," they chanted in unison. Her voice faded to a whisper, until only her lips moved with his. She took her hand away.

Roger Zhrudsky, the psychology department's chairman, appeared at the door with a red canvas case under one arm. It was about the size of a large, thick cafeteria tray. He hesitated, scanning the room, then pushed his way through the students. "I have the

AED!" he shouted. He knelt next to Paul's head and unzipped the stiff canvas case.

Vanessa pointed to the device he pulled out. "Press that button."

"Remove backing from pads and place on the chest of the victim as shown on backing," a mechanical voice intoned.

Vanessa sat up and shoved Stan so hard he almost toppled over backward into the students standing behind him. She clawed and scrabbled at the blue shirt on the inert man until she had pulled it out of his trousers. Grasping the loose tails of the shirt, she ripped them apart, tearing the buttons loose. Then she tugged his T-shirt up to his armpits.

Roger was looking at one of the pads. Vanessa grabbed the other, glanced at the backing before jerking it off and slapping the adhesive side onto Paul's bare chest. She turned and reached for the other one, but Roger already had the backing off. She pointed instead to the side of Paul's ribcage toward which Roger's hand was already moving.

As they worked, Stan stood and backed away until he bumped against one of the students. "Sorry," he mumbled, barely glancing over his shoulder. The sight of Paul sprawled unmoving on the floor made him momentarily dizzy. Was he really going to die? Right here in front of them?

"Analyzing heart rhythms," the metallic voice said. "Stand clear." For several seconds everyone froze, holding their breaths. "Shock advised."

"Stand back," Vanessa said looking around the tight circle of faces. She pushed Roger away from the AED. "Everyone clear!" she shouted, glancing around again. She stabbed another button on the AED.

"Administering shock," the mechanical voice intoned. "Stand clear."

A moment later Paul's body jerked and shuddered. He gasped and his eyelids fluttered.

"Analyzing heart rhythms. Stand clear."

"Wait!" Vanessa spread her arms to hold back the people who pressed forward behind her. There was another tense silence.

"Heart rhythm restored. Put patient in recovery position and call 911." Heads swiveled in search of the graduate student Vanessa had dispatched.

"We already have," Roger announced.

Vanessa was kneeling again and turning Paul on his side. His eyes were open now, and he seemed to be struggling to get up.

"Wha' hap'n?" he slurred.

"Take it easy, Paul. Just relax." When he pushed back on her arm, she bent over him and said softly, "Don't try to get up yet."

"I'm okay." He pushed on Vanessa's chest.

"Please, Paul," she crooned. "You fell down."

His eyes darted left and right. He struggled to push himself up.

"Just take it easy," she said, almost in a whisper, moving closer to his ear. "The doctor will be here in a minute."

"Wha' happ'nd?" he asked again.

"You hit your head. You knocked yourself out, so we called 911."

"Where'm…?"

She bent over his ear, her mouth almost touching it, and murmured something only he could hear. He seemed to relax.

Stan stared at Paul lying on the floor—and Vanessa hovering over her lover. But he was thinking about what would happen in the coming weeks. Unless this was much less serious than it looked, Paul wouldn't be able to act as Vanessa's sponsor. Someone would have to fill in temporarily, and Stan was the logical candidate.

Then it hit him like a kick in the face: *Jesus! Paul almost died right here at my feet, and I'm thinking about taking his student away from him? What the hell is the matter with me?*

CHAPTER 2

Outside, a distant siren sounded.

"Okay, everyone not helping with this, out of here." The new voice resonated in the small, crowded room. It was Jim Forrester, whose office was three doors down the hall from the seminar room. He was a stout man with a full beard the fiery red of Viking warriors.

"Come on. The EMTs are going to need as much room as possible." Jim began pushing the students who had been in the seminar toward the door. When several took one or two steps backward and hesitated, he pointed. "Out. You're in the way."

"Easy, Jim," Roger intervened. "They saw it happen, you know. They're worried about Paul, too."

"But we need the space, Roger."

The students began filing out, with backward glances at the man lying on the floor. They grumbled as they drifted into the hallway, where they formed clumps of three or four. Several faculty members, who arrived as word spread, pushed through the students into the seminar room.

Stan suddenly felt alienated, maybe because Vanessa had pushed him aside, maybe because it was clear she cared so deeply for Paul. And Stan hadn't contributed anything to saving Paul's life. It had been Vanessa's show from beginning to end. Besides, he wasn't really needed here. So when Jim turned back to watch the proceedings, Stan followed the last student into the hall, stopping just outside the door and standing there like a gatekeeper. He got a couple of curious stares from the students. Snippets of their conversations echoed in the narrow hallway.

One booming voice carried above the din. "Shit! I thought old Kovick was finally going to squash that fucking bitch."

"I'm surprised she even tried to save the guy."

"I thought she was fucking living with him." The first student's voice could be heard easily above all the other conversations seething in the echoing hallway.

"A little lover's spat, perhaps?" A third man's voice.

"One thing's fucking certain. Kovick's out of the picture."

"What makes you think that, dude? She's been sleeping with him for nearly a year. She's not going to drop him just because he can't have sex for a few weeks."

"Don't be too sure, dog. I fucking know her type."

"Her type?"

"The Playmate type, man. They sleep around a lot."

Stan stole a glance to confirm who the loudmouthed braggart was. Brad Holmes. Rumor had it he had slept with half the women in the graduate program.

Vanessa didn't deserve that kind of abuse. The last thing she was doing was sleeping around. She and Paul hadn't been hiding their affair, but they were very discreet around the department. Since Stan had returned from his sabbatical, he'd once or twice seen them arrive together for department receptions. But they didn't hang around together and never held hands, as Paul had done with most of his previous young and usually gorgeous girlfriends.

He'd seen her in Paul's office occasionally, but that was not unusual for a doctoral student and her advisor. Now that he thought about it, he couldn't remember seeing any show of affection between them. The only incident he could think of was the morning he'd seen them coming into work together. They were acting like good friends enjoying a joke.

Because nearly everyone believed they were living together, there had been some grumbling among a few of his colleagues about their affair violating the spirit of the university's policy on student-faculty relationships. But in the absence of a complaint from one of them, the circumstances didn't technically violate any explicit regulations. It was a potentially explosive situation, but from what Stan had gathered from the rumors he'd heard, it might be difficult to determine who was exploiting whom.

Michelle Davidson came dashing around the corner. She was a plump, energetic woman in her late thirties who wore her blond hair in a sensible bob. A tiny nose punctuated her round face. She taught the graduate statistics courses and consulted with both faculty and students on the statistics they used in their research. Excusing herself as she pushed through the students, she paused next to Stan and peered past him into the seminar room through the open door. "What happened to Paul?" she asked.

"He had a heart attack. We... Vanessa saved him with CPR."

"How's he doing?"

Stan glanced into the room. "Go on in. We're waiting for an ambulance."

"Thanks, Stan." She slipped quietly into the room.

Stan overheard a woman nearby say, "Well, there goes Vanessa's master's thesis."

"Jeez, Kim! Kovick almost died in there."

Stan took a quick look in the direction of the voices. None of the four women noticed him.

"What the hell is she doing in this course anyway? She knows more than he does."

"What's she doing in this program? She already knows more than most of the faculty."

"And now she's made us all look like slackers, standing around while she saves the guy's life. As if being a goddamn genius isn't enough."

"As if being an Einstein in a Playmate's body isn't enough."

"As if she was hiding that body by wearing baggy jeans and flannel shirts."

"...which she doesn't button so her boobs play peek-a-boo for the guys."

Stan turned to stare at the four women. When one of them looked around and caught his eye, he glared at her before turning away.

Behind him, he thought he heard her say, "Lookee over there at who's got the hots for her now."

The sound of pounding feet on the stairway made everyone turn toward the end of the hall. When a man in a blue uniform appeared, Stan pointed at the open door. A man and woman with a stretcher followed him. Half the students crowded into a tight cluster behind Stan to peer in the open doorway.

The EMTs examined Paul briefly. When he tried to crawl onto the gurney, they insisted that he let them lift him. As they started to roll it toward the door, Roger turned from watching the EMTs. "Vanessa, don't you want to go along in the ambulance?" he said quietly.

Still on the floor where Paul had been, she looked up at him for an instant as if startled by the sound of her name. She shook her head like a frightened child. "No… it's okay."

Roger shrugged, then turned to follow the others through the door.

Stan watched the EMTs roll the stretcher out the door, past where he was standing. He caught only a glimpse of Paul's chalky white face as they passed. The EMTs rolled the stretcher onto the elevator. As soon as the doors had closed, the students rushed back into the room to collect their notebooks and other belongings. They stared with brazen curiosity at Vanessa, who was now sitting on the floor with her back against the wall and her arms wrapped around her knees.

The students all hurried out again and headed down the stairway so they could watch as Paul was loaded into the ambulance. From the vitriolic comments Stan had overheard, he had a shocking new understanding of why Vanessa had no friends among them. He took two halting steps into the room.

Michelle was kneeling at Vanessa's side and patting her shoulder. "How are you doing, Vanessa?" Her voice was soft and calm.

Vanessa didn't move. Her face looked drained, and she stared at the room with unseeing blue eyes. Stan wanted to take her in his arms. Why hadn't he stayed with her and Paul? He could be the one consoling her now. He couldn't hug her the way he wanted to, but this would have been the perfect time to establish a personal relationship with her. As always, he'd blown an opportunity to connect with a woman who attracted him.

"You did the right thing," Michelle said. "You probably saved Paul's life."

Vanessa nodded without looking at her.

"Would you like to talk about it?"

Vanessa shifted her gaze for the first time but didn't meet Michelle's eyes. "No… but thanks. I'll be all right."

Michelle withdrew her hand from Vanessa's shoulder but stayed kneeling on the floor beside her. "I'd be happy to spend some time with you, even if it's nothing more than you telling me what happened."

Vanessa nodded but gave no sign she was going to move.

"I've never had to do CPR on a real person myself," Michelle said, "but I think you should talk to someone." She glanced around the empty room. "I shouldn't leave you here by yourself."

"Okay." Vanessa let Michelle put her hand under one arm and help her to her feet. "Thank you."

"No problem. Do you have a purse or notebook?"

Vanessa nodded and walked to the other end of the table. She closed a thin laptop and slid it into a blue backpack she retrieved from the floor. She smiled wanly. "Okay."

Stan stepped aside so the two of them could leave the room. Michelle's eyes met his as they passed. "Thanks," he whispered.

Michelle nodded. As they walked side by side down the hall to the double doors that led to the stairs, Michelle put her arm around Vanessa's shoulders. Watching them Stan felt a pang of envy.

He returned to his office intending to look at his notes for class the next day, but instead he sat and stared out the window at the branches of a fir tree that extended well above his second floor window.

Vanessa was truly an improbable woman. Beautiful enough to meet *Playboy*'s standards—how many women between eighteen and twenty-five met that criterion? Smart enough to outstrip most of her birth cohort as an undergraduate—in advanced mathematics, yet!—and now, as a graduate student. Seemingly, a *Playboy* model with Einstein's brains. *What are the odds of that? One to how many billion?*

No, wait! Hypatia of Alexandria. The leading mathematician of the fourth century, widely recognized for her contributions to astronomy and Platonistic philosophy as well. And every historical source suggested she was also known for her beauty. Stan imagined Vanessa in the priestly white robes Hypatia likely wore.

All right, so this improbable confluence of genes happened once in human history. Twice was at least conceivable. But beyond her stunning appearance and her spectacular performance as a student, what he knew about her added up to very little.

He'd had only one brief conversation with her. A week ago she'd stopped him after a departmental colloquium talk. Without preliminaries she'd asked, "Dr. Harte, are there any theories of mental space that are integrated with brain anatomy?"

He could think of nothing sensible to say to her except, "I can't think of any offhand." His expertise ended at the boundary between cognitive psychology and neuroscience. He felt like he'd been caught not knowing something an expert on cognitive theories ought to have at his fingertips—and he was supposedly the department's specialist.

Since he didn't have an answer for her, he'd said, "Why do you ask?" He'd hoped her answer would give him a chance to recall any gossip about a similar development in neuroscience that he'd heard at a recent meeting in Boston.

She hadn't given him a chance to think. She'd launched into a description of a theory so concise and mathematical that it made his head spin. She'd spoken in complete, grammatical sentences, not quite rehearsed—but close. It had reminded him of his one face-to-face meeting with the linguist Noam Chomsky, whose off-the-cuff answer to Stan's question sounded like something you'd read in a scientific journal. The trouble was, what Vanessa had said sounded like a plausible challenge to every psychologist and neuroscientist in the world—and it rang with the arrogant authority of unassailable logic.

And when Stan had finished his roundabout response that added up to an admission that he'd never heard of anything so ambitious, her clipped parting was, "Thanks, anyway. If you think of something, let me know." She'd then spun around and headed for the door.

"Vanessa?" He'd followed her out into the hallway.

She'd halted and faced him again. "Yes, Dr. Harte?"

"Have you put any of this down on paper? A term paper or something?"

"Not a term paper. A rough draft for a journal article." She'd frowned. "I could email it to you, if you like."

"Would you, please? Maybe I'll think of something when I can see more details."

"I will. And thanks, Dr. Harte." With a skeptical smile, she'd turned again and scurried away down the hall.

Beyond that one conversation, he'd rarely seen her around the department the way he did most of the other graduate students. The only time he'd seen her tête-à-tête with anyone in the halls was the morning he passed her and Maria, the woman who came around and emptied the office wastebaskets. They were chatting away in animated Spanish punctuated by frequent giggles.

Vanessa couldn't have looked more different from the woman he'd talked to previously. For all that she seemed intently focused on the conversation, he also sensed that she saw him and deliberately avoided acknowledging him as he walked by.

Then there was that conversation with Paul the day before: Stan had asked, "I'm curious. When you advise her, is she as confrontational as she apparently is with everyone else?" What Stan really wanted to know was whether she was as aggressive in her private life as she was as a student. But Paul had never divulged much to Stan about his many short-term romances with young women.

"You don't 'advise' Vanessa Trippett about her research." Paul had grimaced. "I tried that early, and she lit up my office like an incendiary shell. We have a moratorium. She keeps her symbolic artillery off the battlefield and I don't ambush her with my linguistic cavalry.

"My role as sponsor has been to provide the resources she needs to go her own way. I just wish she'd settle on a simple empirical thesis project and get on with it. She could have a master's thesis written in a month or so—if she wanted to."

"Sounds like a student from hell, complete with fire and brimstone."

Paul had come out with one of his enormous belly laughs. "She's exhausting to live with, Stan. You can't imagine what a dynamo of relentless, focused energy she is. She's considerate and eager to help out with the household chores, though. When she first moved in with me, one of the first things she said was, 'If I'm going to live here, I have to contribute something.' And it's more than just 'something.'"

"That sounds like the opposite of 'exhausting.'"

"Until you find out that she has a one-track mind. Whatever we're doing, wherever we are, she wants to talk only about the mind and the brain. You've heard her, so you know that a conversation with her is like being a student in an oral exam on topics you haven't studied and probably wouldn't understand if you tried."

"You mean because of the math?" Stan had said.

"The woman seems to think in equations."

"And speaks like she's reading from a journal article?"

"Yeah, right. Except it ends with a test question you can't answer." Paul had shaken his head as though it had just happened to him. "I sometimes think she has some atypical form of Asperger's. She's like a kid who can't stop talking about dinosaurs."

"Huh." Stan had shared Paul's bewilderment.

"And Stan, her patterns of work and sleep are little short of maniacal. As soon as we finish cleaning up after dinner, she sits down with whatever she's working on and instantly becomes oblivious to the world. She doesn't even hear her own cell phone with its Beethoven ringtone. Between the time she sits down and the alarm the next morning, it's utterly unpredictable whether she'll be working or asleep.

"She's compulsively stealthy about getting out of bed in the middle of the night when I'm sleeping, but when I get up to piss, I see her in her study completely unaware of everything around her. And she seems to need no more than four or five hours of sleep."

What he'd said explained a lot. A student who could concentrate like that would likely digest huge amounts of material. She'd be able to write the kind of incisive and synoptic answers Stan had read on her general exam. But usually someone who spent that much time at a desk didn't stay slim and look fit.

"It sounds unhealthy, Paul. How does she keep that figure of hers?"

"Amazing, isn't it? The only thing I can figure out is that except for an occasional dinner out, she eats like a mouse. And she walks everywhere. You know where I live? In Wallingford?"

Stan had nodded, guessing it was a little less than two miles.

"She walks it, every day, both ways if she can."

In retrospect, Stan's conversation with Paul yesterday was even more mystifying than it had been at the time. He'd never heard Paul talk about his personal life, especially his constantly changing girlfriends. But what he'd said about Vanessa didn't fit with any of Stan's previous ideas about her. He still couldn't rid his mind of her *Playboy* photos.

As an early subscriber to the online version of *Playboy*, he'd followed her career as a nude model, both in print and online. Her photos and videos had created the feeling that he was already familiar with her body—intimately familiar. He'd also heard her vaguely immature voice on an interview video and laughed at her acerbic yet droll answers to an interviewer's raunchy questions about her sex life. She had seemed like an empty-headed model, trying to make it in either the fashion or the movie world.

He sat a few more minutes watching a mental slideshow of some of her photos he liked the best, especially the ones in which she had her head turned so she looked into the camera out of the corners of her eyes. Soon he had an erection straining at his pants. With a sigh, he swiveled away from the windows to face his desk. He'd have to review the notes for his class at home.

Collecting the sheets scattered on his desk into a pile, he tapped them into alignment and dropped them into a folder, which he slid into the battered green backpack that smelled faintly of sweat from years of use. He phoned a Thai place and ordered take-out for his dinner. When he hung up, he wasn't hard anymore. He headed for home, a collage of images of Vanessa, clothed and unclothed, whirling in his head with a soundtrack compiled from his recent memories of her voice.

Memories of the events in Paul's aborted seminar followed him home, fragments recurring in a jumbled order intercut with mental replays of Vanessa's *Playboy* videos, flashes of her photos, and bits and pieces of his two recent encounters with her. More than once he caught himself with chopsticks poised over his Pad Thai, unable to say how long he'd been motionless. His bottle of Ting-Tao was lukewarm by the time he finished eating.

He went to his study where he reviewed his notes for his lecture on theories of metacognition. Then he woke up his computer and fired up the program he used for slide shows.

"No playing around this time," he said to himself in a barely audible voice.

He had a folder containing six *Playboy* photos of Vanessa, either head shots or fully, if somewhat provocatively, clothed. As he studied these one by one for a minute or more, he mentally compared her appearance to what he remembered of her in person.

He was not naïve about *Playboy* models. They were elaborately made up for photo shoots. He'd already realized that her skin wasn't really as unblemished and translucent as the white marble from the Greek island of Paros. And the blue highlights in her hair were probably due to tint and lighting. In the classroom earlier, they had been mahogany, even chestnut, just as they were in some of her *Playboy* photos that he'd forgotten.

He kept returning to two photos. One, from her first appearance on *Playboy*'s website, had made a deep impression on him. She reminded him of Falconet's statue of Galatea, to which a prankster had added an unlikely crown of obsidian hair and far-fetched blue eyes. The other was a head shot he'd cropped from a close-up that originally included her breasts. Like all the photos, her eyes drew the viewer's attention like sapphire meteors in the night sky. Yet even the startling eyes in the photos did not capture the bottomless blue depths of the Arctic Ocean he'd seen in her living eyes earlier today.

The photos from the last shoot were his least favorite. The makeup artists had exaggerated her exotic coloration, turning her skin almost blue white and giving her jet-black hair with lapis highlights mirroring her eyes. Candy-apple red lipstick made her thin pink lips seem full and voluptuous. They'd transformed her into a Jo No Kabuki dancer, the one who portrays the ghost of a noblewoman—or a concubine.

A few of these photos were the most revealing of all, however. Just remembering them aroused him so much that it required a single-minded focus on each mouse click to shut down the program. The effort left him staring blankly at the screen cluttered with open text and website windows. He gazed unseeing until the screen dimmed and the astronomical screen saver took over.

When his erection had subsided, he stood and stretched. It had finally happened! After more than three decades of looking at nude models in *Playboy* magazine and later on the website, he had at last met one "in the flesh." But in all those years of fantasies, he'd never fabricated anything like the complicated woman he'd met in real life.

The situations and conversations he conjured with the models he saw on his computer were never embarrassing or complicated. Yet he knew from his experience with real women that he would be intimidated by a *Playboy* model's beauty and sensuality. Vanessa raised the intimidation factor to the fifth power. He couldn't imagine a comfortable conversation with her that led to an intimate relationship.

He paused in front of a window that looked out onto his shadowy backyard. The leaves of his rhododendron bushes glistened faintly. It had started to rain. What must it be like, he wondered suddenly, to have sex with an Einstein reincarnation like Vanessa?

He pictured her on top of him pumping away on his penis while explaining tensor calculus—instead of talking dirty. Just as they were about to come—simultaneous orgasms always happened in his fantasies although they had been rare in real life—she asked him one of her test questions instead of moaning or screaming. The video in his head evaporated and with it the erection it had stimulated.

He wandered into the living room and sat down. The academic question, raised by Paul's temporary absence from the scene, was why he was advising Vanessa in the first place. Although he was an authority on the psychology of language, he made no pretense of expertise in the broader field of cognition and thought. And he knew less math than Stan did. Clearly Stan had a real shot at taking Paul's role as Vanessa's advisor, just as he would probably be taking Paul's place in the classroom.

Why shouldn't he take over as her major professor permanently? Realistically, who else would sponsor her? Michelle Davidson? Maybe. But for all her symbolic facility, Michelle's substantive specialties were gender differences and genetic influences. Vanessa wanted to work on a cognitive theory, and damn it, that was his specialty!

A student like Vanessa might be exactly what he needed for a career that had stalled in middle age. She'd bring a fresh direction for him to pursue. Indeed, she'd put him on the frontier of cognitive neuroscience—a field he could barely teach at the moment, let alone steer a research project.

Vanessa was aiming for a goal he'd never dared to pursue. As her advisor and mentor, he'd likely bask in her reflected glory—even share authorship of some of her papers. She was headed for the stars, and he could join her expedition, be a part of her brilliant achievement. If he could just understand her vehicle, the damn math.

And as her advisor? He'd be spending a lot of time with her—and soon. They'd be working together on her thesis, going over methods and design or, if he was lucky, revising her drafts. Several meetings a week at first. Later he'd be coaching her for the oral defense of the thesis. They'd be collaborators, allies against the criticisms of the other two members of her committee. And unless she was completely different from his previous students—a very real possibility from all he knew about Vanessa—they'd become good friends.

Sooner or later he could casually suggest they continue their meetings over coffee, a little later drinks in a bar near campus or dinner, depending on how things went. In a more relaxed atmosphere, maybe she'd exchange answers to personal questions, and he could ask her why she posed for *Playboy* and how she felt about being naked in front of a photographer and his crew, knowing that her photos would appear on the Internet. He'd always wanted to know how naked models felt during a shoot.

Just as his heart rate began to rise with excitement, a whiteboard full of differential equations and triple integrals flashed before his eyes. Wasn't it hopeless? And not just because his background was woefully inadequate to be her advisor. Women had never been attracted to him the way they were to Paul. Why should Vanessa be any different? And he was so hopelessly insecure—not to mention a total loser—when it came to enlarging a friendship into an intimate relationship with a woman.

He'd never once succeeded in hooking up with someone for a one-night stand, and he could count on one hand the number of short-term relationships he'd had. The two long-term relationships in his life—six months with a girl in college and ten years of marriage—had ended in humiliation when his addiction to pornography had come to light. True, the divorce also involved infidelity on Heidi's side, but not on his, unless you counted his many imaginary hook-ups with *Playboy* models in front of a computer screen. The best he could hope for was a platonic friendship with Vanessa based on a role as her academic advisor.

He fell asleep fantasizing a one-night stand with Vanessa following a meeting with her in his office in which he had somehow—it seemed magical—fully understood her theory and proposed a brilliant innovation in her mathematics.

CHAPTER 3

As Michelle accompanied Vanessa to her office, she began to wonder if she had made a mistake. What qualifications did she have to debrief someone who had just done CPR on… her lover? The CPR classes she'd taken hadn't covered debriefing.

Would Stan have been able to help out? She hadn't thought to ask him as they walked out. It would have been nice if one of the clinical students in the class had offered. But from what she knew, most of them were probably afraid of Vanessa.

She stole a glimpse of Vanessa's face as they climbed the stairs. It was drained of all color and expression, and she hadn't said a word since they'd left the seminar room. The contrast with the Vanessa she knew startled her. Usually when they were together, Vanessa ignited and fueled spirited exchanges about an unfamiliar statistical test she'd come across, a derivation that was giving her trouble, an error she'd found in a journal article, or an idea she wanted evaluated. A conversation with Vanessa was always like diving into a mountain lake that still had chunks of ice floating in it.

Michelle unlocked the door to her office and gave it gentle push so Vanessa could walk in ahead of her. She hoped the sanctuary she'd made for herself would have a healing effect on Vanessa after her harrowing experience. As the door swung open, the smell of a garden after a spring rain wafted over them. There were plants everywhere in pots on flat surfaces and in hanging baskets. Michelle had painted the walls herself with a sunny shade of yellow to cover up the original institutional gray. And she had sprinkled them with posters of Paul Klee's fanciful paintings.

Without saying a word, Vanessa went straight to Michelle's worktable, where she slumped into a straight chair.

Michelle circled the table and was about to sit down in her swivel chair at her desk across from Vanessa, when she realized that Vanessa was staring at the wall with unfocused blue eyes. All at once she was frightened. Should she call one of her clinical colleagues who had crisis management experience? With effort, she said as calmly as she could, "Do you feel comfortable just telling me what happened, Vanessa?"

Vanessa's eyes darted around the room, as if the events of the last half hour were hidden in one of the Swiss painter's childlike creations. "Paul just fell over… No—it was… I'd just asked Dr. Harte a question…" She closed her eyes and took a deep breath. "I can't remember, Michelle."

"It's okay. Take your time…" Michelle felt her insecurity begin to drain away. "Would you like some coffee?"

"Uh, sure… thanks." Vanessa's voice was dull.

Michelle began a ritual that the two of them had shared every Thursday afternoon of the previous academic year. She filled her coffee machine from a gallon jug of water she kept under her desk. Vanessa was silent so long Michelle looked up from scooping coffee beans out of a squat plastic jar into a small coffee grinder. Did Vanessa's vacant eyes mean she'd lost her train of thought, or was something else going on?

All at once, Vanessa's face came to life. "Oh, I remember now! Dr. Harte had described several versions of semantic feature theory. Then he asked for questions. I asked him…" She finally looked Michelle in the eye momentarily. "You know me." She didn't smile the way Michelle expected her to.

"You always ask hard questions."

"Yeah… So anyway, Paul jumped out of his chair and told me to stop asking the same—you know, he said, '…the same damn question of every speaker I ask to talk to the class.'" She grimaced. "I think he was throwing the marker for the whiteboard at me, Michelle." She shook her head slowly. "But he just kind of keeled over instead."

Michelle was shocked, but tried to keep her emotions to herself. She shook her head sympathetically. "Did he put out his hands to catch himself, or did it seem like he was already unconscious?" She screwed the lid back on the jar of coffee beans.

"Like a sack of wet cement and rocks, Michelle. It was a horrible squishy thud."

"And he didn't move after he fell?"

"When I got to him, I… I rolled him over and I could tell right away that he wasn't breathing. So…" Vanessa looked at her hands folded in her lap. "I don't actually remember what happened then. It's all a blur."

"Excuse me a second." The whine of a small motor and the clatter of coffee beans filled the room.

When Michelle looked at Vanessa again, she seemed visibly relaxed in spite of her empty stare.

"Where I grew up…?" Vanessa paused again.

"Orion Station?" Michelle prompted. "I remember your telling me about it—in Eastern Washington—near Yakima, right?"

"Yes. Kind of a commune of astronomers, astrophysicists, mathematicians, and a few stray artistic types like my dad. We were at least thirty minutes from the closest hospital in Yakima, so the rule was that everybody who lived there had to learn CPR.

"The first thing we kids were taught was where we kept the AED, even before we were old enough to understand what it was. We just memorized the letters. It was stored in a box even the smallest of us could reach, and we had to practice dragging it—the thing felt like it weighed a ton—to where someone was pretending to be sick. I must have been six or seven when I first watched the adults practice compressions."

"Well, apparently your training accomplished its purpose."

"I must have gone into autopilot… because the next thing I remember is feeling so happy when Dr. Zhrudsky came in with the AED. We were taught to continue compressions because they keep the blood circulating and—"

"The idea is to get oxygen to the brain, if I remember my CPR training."

"Yeah, until you can get a defibrillator to start the heart again."

The coffee machine's private musings turned to snorts and coughs. The aroma of fresh coffee overwhelmed the smell of soil and plants in the room. Michelle stood again so she could pour coffee into two white mugs with childish clown faces that her two daughters had painted in primary colors. Vanessa waited until Michelle pushed one across the table toward her. The coffee was too hot to risk even a sip yet. Reenacting their long-standing ritual, they raised their mugs and spent a few seconds inhaling the vapors.

Vanessa gingerly set the mug on the table in front of her. "You probably wonder why I didn't go along with Paul to the hospital."

"I suppose I did, yes. Roger certainly seemed surprised."

"We had a big argument this morning... It probably had something to do with..."

Michelle studied Vanessa's face for a moment. "I doubt it. He's under a lot of pressure right now. When the deadline for a grant renewal approaches, there are always conflicting demands on a person's time."

"It wasn't that. We've been fighting about my thesis for weeks now. Before we left home this morning he told me he'd resign as my sponsor if I even talked to another faculty member about forming a committee. Then, right before the seminar, I stormed into his office and said I didn't give a shit what he did. He threw me out."

"You don't mean literally?" Michelle was appalled.

"He shoved me toward the door and told me to get the hell out. And he slammed the door in my face."

Michelle had never seen Vanessa this agitated before, nor seen tears begin to form in her eyes. Michelle quickly pulled a box of tissues out of a desk drawer and set it on the table.

"Michelle, his face was redder than I've ever seen it. And the veins were standing out all over his forehead." She took a tissue, blew her nose on it, then fell silent.

Unable to think of anything appropriate to say, Michelle took a long draught of her coffee. In the space of less than ten minutes, she had seen several sides of this young woman that hadn't emerged in more than nine months of regular conversations.

Their first meeting had begun as an oral exam to determine whether Vanessa could receive credit by examination for Michelle's course in statistical methods, a course that all first-year graduate students in psychology were required to take. As an undergraduate math major, Vanessa had taken a yearlong statistics course from mathematicians. Later, while she was taking psychology courses for a minor in that subject, she had audited the graduate course in statistics. The purpose of Michelle's exam was to verify that Vanessa's background was at least equivalent to the course Michelle taught.

Within the first ten minutes of the meeting, Vanessa had derived the Kolmogorov-Smirnov test from a Brownian bridge and then proceeded to show Michelle how to apply it to a set of data she'd given her. It wasn't the kind of answer Michelle had expected. Few PhDs in psychology possessed that kind of deep understanding of the mathematical underpinnings of statistics.

Michelle had approved Vanessa for the nine hours of credit the course was worth and signed her up for an independent study. Throughout Vanessa's first year, they met once a week for hour-long sessions that often stretched to two. Michelle taught her as much as she could about the uses of statistics in psychology, while Vanessa enriched Michelle's knowledge of the mathematics behind it all. Michelle readily admitted that she had learned more than Vanessa did. They had become friends, and Michelle made no apologies for treating her as an equal.

Without warning, Vanessa caught her breath loudly. "I just hope he…" She blotted her cheeks with a fresh tissue and kept it wadded in her hand. "I won't have a sponsor now, no matter what."

"I'm sure something can be worked out, depending on how Paul does."

Vanessa looked down and said nothing. After more than a minute, she spoke without looking up. "I think I'd better find someone else. Paul was already exasperated with me, and…"

Michelle waited for her to go on. She had no idea what would come next.

"I told you earlier, I'm not interested in language by itself. It's only part of what I want to understand. An important part, but far from the full story—the mind."

"Yes, I understand that much of your theory."

"But it's too grandiose for a thesis, right?"

Michelle had long since learned that Vanessa defended herself with virtuoso defiance. The best strategy was to deflect her counterattack with a subtle diversion. "If I understand the papers you've shown me and what you've told me, I'd call it challenging."

"You mean I made Paul *insecure*?"

Michelle nearly dropped her coffee cup. She was used to conversations with Vanessa that moved with dizzying intellectual leaps, but she'd never seen her vault emotionally charged chasms before. "You put us all on the defensive, Vanessa."

"Not Paul. He's the most self-confident man I've ever met. That's what I liked about him from the moment I met him. He wasn't intimidated by my looks the way so many men are, and he didn't seem to be the least bit threatened by my brains, like ninety-nine percent of the men I've talked to—at least at first."

"I've wondered why you got into a relationship with him."

"A lot of people immediately concluded that I was trying to sleep my way to a PhD. I've gotten used to everyone assuming that about me." When Vanessa's eyes met Michelle's, they seemed to spit fire. "I'll tell you why I've been living with Paul Kovick. When he came on to me, I was excited. He was someone I could talk to as an equal. He knew more than I did about language. He knew more linguistics than Traynor, the guy I took linguistics from last year." She stopped suddenly.

Michelle was chilled by her look of impatience.

"Sure, Michelle. Don't be a prude. He's sexy. And he's great in bed. And I love sex."

Michelle felt betrayed. "I'm no prude, Vanessa." she said angrily. "I like sex, too. I just…"

"But only with your husband, right?"

"That's personal!" Some debriefing this was turning out to be. At least she'd gotten Vanessa back to her usual combative self.

"My relationship with Paul is personal, too. But I'm not promiscuous, like everyone seems to infer from my nude photos." Vanessa wasn't shouting, but Michelle was sure people in hall could hear what she was saying through the closed office door.

"I've never thought you were."

"I like sex with the man I care about—one man, Michelle. One man who doesn't play around with anyone else. And every single man I've ever wanted to stay with—" She started to cry again.

Michelle's hand shook when she gave Vanessa another tissue She felt completely out of her depth. She liked this complex woman so much. And, with the fierce determination of a mother, she wanted to see Vanessa realize her incomparable goals. But she had lost her way in this conversation.

"I drive them away, Michelle. I always want more than they will give me. Or they get tired of me. I don't know." She shook her head dolefully.

Michelle suddenly felt exhausted. She had to find some way to calm Vanessa's eruption of emotion. She wondered fleetingly whether it might help her to ask her about an especially knotty statistical analysis a colleague had recently brought to her for advice. She opted for a more practical problem.

"I don't think what has happened is your fault. And I don't think you can plausibly blame yourself for Paul's heart attack. But we need to find you an advisor." She stopped herself before she said anything about how long the advisor would serve.

"No one else around here wants to."

"I believe you're wrong."

"How about you? Will you sponsor me?"

"I've already told you I don't know the cognitive literature well enough to do you justice."

"But you understand—"

"The math? No, I don't have the time to master the foundations of what you're doing."

"But that's just a matter of—"

"Vanessa, let me finish."

"I'm sorry. I always do that."

"I know." Encouraged by her smile, Michelle went on. "Do you have something written up? A proposal or something?"

"I have a thesis. I mean, well… I don't know for sure what's wrong with it. Our fights started back when I gave Paul this draft and said I wanted to use it for my master's degree."

Michelle sipped her coffee pensively. "Would you be willing to let me look at it?"

"Oh, sure." Vanessa's voice was almost expressionless.

"Suppose you attach it to an email, and send it to me right away? Then maybe we can meet again tomorrow and talk about it." Michelle wanted to check up on Vanessa again as soon as she could.

"All right. When?"

"I'll be in my office here after two tomorrow," Michelle said. "Can you make it between then and five?"

"Okay." Vanessa hoisted her backpack to her shoulder and stood up.

"Maybe by then we'll know how Paul is doing."

"I hope he's okay." Vanessa hesitated. "I mean, that he doesn't… isn't… that he recovers right away."

"So do I."

"Thanks for your time, Michelle. I'm glad you insisted we talk."

"I am, too."

Michelle watched her as she went to the door and disappeared around the corner. She couldn't ever remember seeing Vanessa with her shoulders hunched over. Michelle was still very worried. She hadn't liked it last fall when she heard about the affair with Paul. But she'd kept her mouth shut. Later, she was glad she had when she saw that the relationship was going to last longer than Paul's usual dalliances.

When she thought about it, she wasn't especially surprised that the relationship had gone aground. If Vanessa was going to be happy in a relationship, she was going to have to find a partner nearly as smart as she was—a stratospheric criterion—and as focused and intense. As much as Michelle appreciated Paul's intellect and scholarship, he was no match for this extraordinary young woman, no matter how good he was in bed.

Michelle's assessment of Vanessa had changed after their first year of weekly meetings dictated by the independent study. The meetings had continued, but the focus of the conversations had changed. They talked less about statistics and mathematics as Vanessa began to formulate for herself a theory of singular originality and breathtaking scope. Michelle couldn't follow the mathematical techniques, but she could see the potential. And it scared her to see it coming from Vanessa.

If a senior scientist with Vanessa's talent had told Michelle about such an intellectual enterprise, she would have believed she was in the presence of the leader of a scientific revolution, a paradigm shift in psychology and neuroscience as conceptually shattering as plate tectonics in geology or relativity in physics.

Vanessa wasn't even a young Turk yet. She was a student, whose ideas would be dismissed as naïve, even laughable. Editors and readers of scientific journals only made an effort to understand a theory as unorthodox and difficult as Vanessa's when the author was well-known and respected in the field.

Vanessa would face another frustration—a barrier as daunting as the Great Wall of China. Michelle had been attractive enough as a student to know how men in general and powerful gatekeepers in particular could taunt and tease, refusing to treat anything other than sexual attraction seriously. It was true that things were better now than when Michelle was starting out. But she hadn't been a stunning beauty like Vanessa, and she certainly hadn't had a history of nude modeling dogging her.

Michelle had seen plenty of evidence of Vanessa's intelligence and glimpsed her determination and fortitude. But she feared that the gods guarding the scientific establishment would whip up a storm to smash Vanessa's ship of fragile genius on the rocky shores near the very beginning of her extraordinary voyage of discovery.

> 2008-11-05 13:18:27:
> Dr. Harte, Dr. Davidson suggested I talk to you about my master's thesis. I'll be free this coming Friday afternoon, and Tuesday and Thursday after 2 pm next week. Vanessa Trippett
>
> 2008-11-06 08:42:52:
> Vanessa, Next Tuesday at 2 would work for me. Do you have a proposal or anything else written up? If so, it would be helpful if you could get a copy to me before we meet. Stan Harte
>
> 2008-11-06 08:45:06:
> Dr. Harte, I'm attaching a draft of my thesis as a PDF file. This makes it look like a published paper and is a little easier to read than a manuscript with figures and their captions on separate pages. Let me know if this doesn't work for you; I can make a hard copy in the format you prefer. Vanessa

The file was indeed easy to read—at first. So easy that Stan gasped as he skimmed the abstract. She had apparently found a way to measure awareness with a surprising amount of precision.

Awareness—or consciousness—that slippery idea that we know when we see an object or hear a sound, that we can tell when we've had an idea or come to a conclusion, just as we sometimes realize that an object we overlooked or a sound we missed has influenced what we've done. Vanessa boldly claimed that she had devised a way to turn that mysterious quality of individual perception and thought into numbers.

He rushed on, the opening paragraph flowing smoothly, almost *too* smoothly for such an amazing achievement. Her method was a very simple extension of the priming experiment. Show people a photograph followed by a word and ask them to make a straightforward decision, such as whether a first name, JOHN or JANE, is a man's or a woman's name.

Vanessa had flashed photos of faces, men's or women's, just before names. Like many studies before hers, she'd found that it took a fraction of a second longer to decide the gender of the name when it didn't match the face—a man's face followed by woman's name, for example.

What was different in Vanessa's experiment was that sometimes the faces were barely visible or even completely invisible, hidden by an ingenious technique of her own invention. A cleverly constructed diagram made it clear at a glance how she'd atomized the pixels of a photograph into several frames, so that the faces were hidden from the viewer.

The results were summarized in two graphs so densely packed with information that Stan spent several minutes studying each one. Yet as he did, both of them burst into blossoms of understanding before his eyes. There it was—priming with faces people couldn't see, the decision whether a name belonged to a man or woman taking milliseconds longer when the gender was mismatched. And the number of milliseconds increasing as the number of pixels per frame decreased.

A simple demonstration of priming was startling enough by itself, but Vanessa hadn't stopped there. Continuing her experiment seven days a week over six weeks, she had demonstrated that the faces and names became associated, even the hidden faces people didn't realize were there—evidence for unconscious learning, learning without awareness.

The coup de grace, however, was finding with invisible faces a phenomenon first reported by a German psychologist named Hermann Ebbinghaus at the end of the nineteenth century. When she repeated a hidden face and a name over and over, it took longer to learn than when she put other pairs in between the repetitions.

By the time he reached the end of her paper, the organization was so clear, the design so complete, the results so elegant and the logic so tight, the conclusions appeared beyond doubt. It was all too facile. He felt like he had just watched a master magician at work. Except that this performance had sawed in two his understanding of how the brain perceives the world and reassembled it as an altogether different creature.

It was only when he went back to examine the details that he realized how much information was buried in the figure captions and the notes at the end of the text. Suddenly the intellectual terrain of her paper was filled with steep, rocky ravines. Everything was there, but only a patient specialist would be able to dig out all the minutiae necessary to evaluate the validity of her results.

There was one detail that was almost hidden—not quite deliberately omitted, but stated so indirectly that it escaped Stan's notice for almost the entire hour he spent poring over Vanessa's text on his computer screen. She had tested only one subject—herself. When he finally confirmed this improbable detail, the whole backstory of her conflict with Paul Kovick fell into place. Of course Paul wouldn't let her take such a deeply flawed and curiously unsophisticated report into an oral defense meeting, even for a master's thesis.

Almost from the beginning of research on human perception and learning, it has been a given that because investigators are biased when they test themselves, their results are automatically suspect. It was now a canon in scientific psychology that to be valid, all procedures must be repeated with at least a dozen people who don't know how the scientist wants the results to come out.

Beneath all the layers of Vanessa's sophistication was a naïveté so paradoxical it left Stan dumbfounded.

CHAPTER 4

Long before Stan became a faculty member himself, he discovered that professors' office doors served a significant social function. Most faculty members had private offices. Only two or three of Stan's colleagues had a key to his. And the door had no window. This perk was valuable when discussing confidential matters, of course. But it opened the possibility of harassment charges, especially when he had to meet privately with a female student. The door was also an effective barrier to interruptions when his work demanded sustained concentration, but only, he had discovered, if it was used properly.

When deadlines loomed, he resorted to a "do not disturb" sign. But most of the time, he wanted to be available when a colleague or student truly needed to talk to him. An open door invited all comers. A closed door eliminated some unimportant visits, but it encouraged people to knock—a serious intrusion. But a door open an inch or two seemed to work best, especially because Stan's desk faced the wall, so he sat with his back to the door. Anyone who peeked through the crack saw him working and hesitated long enough to consider carefully the purpose of their visit. He often heard people coughing or shuffling their feet behind him, but they had to knock or say something before he responded.

He'd left the door open about two inches, so when he heard a knock at the door and swung around expecting to see Vanessa framed in the doorway, he was surprised she wasn't there. She waited until he said "Come in" before she pushed open the door and hesitated, still in the hallway outside.

"Have a seat." He waved toward a straight-backed chair.

He had also given a lot of thought to the arrangement of his office furniture. He had a worktable attached at right angles to his desk so the surfaces formed an L. Students usually sat opposite him at the table with his library, a nearly solid wall of books, behind them. He'd discovered over the years that staring at the orderly shelves of books aided his memory, while the unpredictable shapes of the conifer outside the window helped him think through vexing problems.

She ducked her head and said "Thank you," as she crossed the room. Lowering her backpack to a chair, she turned but didn't sit down or even raise her eyes.

Her indecision puzzled him. "Please sit down. It's good to see you again in more normal conditions."

She ignored his invitation. "I owe you an apology."

"Why? What for?"

"Emily Gallagher told me I almost knocked you over—into the people standing around."

"You did give me a good push, Vanessa." He chuckled. "But your mind was on other, more important matters. You certainly don't need to apologize."

A mousy smile brushed her lips, but she still didn't look up. "I remember tapping your shoulders gently, so I wouldn't bump you when I…"

Suddenly her startling blue eyes met his, sending an electric shock spreading through his body.

"I'm sorry, Dr. Harte. I remember very little of what happened. My brain must have disconnected from my mind. I just did what I'd been trained to do. I do know you helped me, though. Thank you very much."

"You were incredible, Vanessa. Paul Kovick owes his life to you."

"I just hope I started soon enough to keep him from losing too many brain cells." She seemed to relax as she finally slid into one of the chairs across the worktable from him and lowered her backpack to the floor in one motion. "Was the PDF file okay?"

"Very helpful."

He was about to ask her about the strange way she had chosen to write the report, but she began talking before she was completely settled in the chair. "As you know, I no longer have a sponsor—at least for a couple of months."

"Paul? He's scheduled for surgery this week, I gather."

"Bypass surgery. Michelle said the prognosis is good."

"But he won't be back to work for some time—that's clear."

"Yes."

Her response was so laconic, he had to think for a second how to go on. "You're in your second year." And those damn *Playboy* photos of her breasts weren't helping his thought processes. "Is that right?"

"Yes. I guess it's more or less obvious that I'm here to ask whether you'd consider…?"

"…sponsoring you? Michelle mentioned that. However… I'm not clear where you are in the graduate program. Have you started your master's research program?"

"Six months ago. The paper I sent you is a draft of my thesis."

He couldn't help raising his eyebrows. "Really? It's taken you that long to write it up?"

She shook her head vigorously. "No, no. I finished collecting the data and wrote it up three months ago."

It was the perfect opening for him to find out why she thought it was appropriate to collect the data entirely on herself. "That was a question I had."

"It required about a hundred and fifty hours. At four hours a day, six days a week, it took six weeks."

"You spent that much time in the lab?"

An impish smile flickered on her previously somber face. "It's how I spent my summer vacation."

"That's mind-boggling."

"I also prepared for comps. The lab time was a good break from studying, and vice versa." From the sudden disappearance of her smile, she wasn't being facetious.

"I'm impressed," he said. He'd missed his opportunity to bring up what he saw as the fatal flaw in her thesis. The silence grew awkward. She looked away when their eyes met.

He'd fantasized so often about making love with her, but now he felt panicky with her so close he could see the stray strands of hair on her forehead. He wanted to reach out and touch her hand resting on the table so badly he could almost feel the softness and warmth of her skin beneath his fingertips.

Finally, he came to his senses. He decided to confront her. "So this was a hundred and fifty hours of testing… yourself?"

"Yes."

They stared at each other.

"But—"

"Is there something wrong with that?"

He took a deep breath. "I assume that when you studied for comps—"

"I passed, Dr. Harte. With commendations. Including the specialty section on cognitive psychology."

He remembered again the answers she wrote. They read more like review papers than something composed without notes and under the pressure of a time-limited exam. "So you are certainly aware that no one does research on a single subject—on themselves, particularly. As a matter of fact, I can't think of a single paper I've read in the last fifteen years…"

She waited to be sure he'd run out of steam. Then she said calmly, "Ebbinghaus covered the entire field of human rote learning. He—"

"But that was the nineteenth century, Vanessa. No one—"

"Most of his important findings have been repeated and verified many times since. Thousands of papers have been published in the last hundred-some-odd years, and they're all mere footnotes to his book."

He let out a long sigh. She had him.

"Should his book have been turned down for publication?" she went on.

"Publication standards have changed."

"For the better? How many papers report results showing that an effect can be replicated a dozen times over the course of forty days?"

He was mentally out of breath from the pace of this exchange. How could Paul keep up with this fireball? How could anybody? "Okay, but—"

"These one-shot, forty-five-minute experiments—what do they have to do with cognitive processes acquired and practiced over a lifetime?" She had become the woman he'd seen in the hallway a week ago, except now she was speaking English and she wasn't giggling.

"I have to admit—"

"I see cognitive psychology as part of biological science, Dr. Harte. And one of the most striking properties of living things is that they vary from one individual to another. Obviously, that's true of people. But it's also true of rabbits. It's true of trees... and spiders... and rotifers. When you focus on how all rabbits—or people—are alike, computing means across different rabbits and treating the variation among them as noise, you're not going to see how the components of the nervous system fit together inside a single rabbit."

The wattage of her eyes was blinding. "I'm interested in how the pieces of the mental machinery work together to constitute the human mind, Dr. Harte. You learn about that by computing means over time for one individual."

She stopped abruptly. Her gaze dropped and her nearly transparent skin suddenly flushed bright pink. "I'm sorry," she said. "I get carried away on this issue."

She turned her head aside. He thought she was going to cry, but when she continued, there was no change from the soft but steady voice in which she had apologized. "You see, Paul and I have been arguing about this since he got back from vacation last fall and found out what I'd been doing—I mean, all summer. It got pretty violent." The rosy color that had begun to fade from her face returned. "I meant, heated."

"No need to apologize, Vanessa." If she could argue this coherently off the top of her head, he decided, she deserved a hearing. The real question was whether there were at least two other people in the department willing to listen to her in a committee meeting. And, ultimately, to acknowledge that her position was justifiable. "I have to concede you have a valid point, Vanessa."

"Thank you for listening to my rant. Would you like to read a paper I wrote trying to defend this idea for Dr. Zhrudsky's philosophy of science seminar?"

"What was his reaction?" He wondered momentarily whether Roger was a possible candidate for her committee. Then he noticed she was looking at her hands again.

What was going on in this woman's mind? There was absolutely no way he could predict what was transpiring behind that enchanting face.

"He never saw the paper," she said. "I wrote another one on a different topic because… Well, we discussed single-subject research like mine before the end of the quarter. I made my arguments, and he…"

"Yes?"

"Can I be frank with you, Dr. Harte?"

"Certainly. I'll keep what you say to myself."

"He… refused to take my comments seriously." She smiled forlornly. "I have a reputation for offending faculty members, in case you hadn't heard. You probably don't want to have me as your student."

It was a bizarre comment to interject into their conversation. And he could see that her fleeting smile hinted at months of frustration. "Actually, you've made a good case for what you've done. I'm almost persuaded." He smiled to encourage her. But did he really want to wrestle with this intellectual Amazon? His body said yes; a voice in his head whispered, *You'll regret this.*

The smile she returned and the tilt of her head suggested skepticism. "What would it take to close the deal?"

He laughed at her off-kilter business metaphor. "To begin with, you'll have to re-write it in a more conventional form."

"Why do I have to follow that arbitrary format? Isn't the point of writing a thesis to report an original research finding?"

"Yes, of course, but—"

"So why not write it up so it's ready to send to a journal editor?"

"Because—"

"I know. Because some old fogies in the graduate school are still living in the twentieth century, or worse, have never published anything worthwhile since they left graduate school."

"Vanessa, stop!" Even as he raised his voice, he thought, *My God, no wonder she gave Paul a heart attack.*

"Yes?" She stopped. Her face flushed crimson. "Sorry, I'm going to make you angry with me, and you haven't even said whether you might take over for Paul and sponsor me."

He took a very deep breath while she was speaking, then said, "I think I know what you're capable of achieving." *Steady now! This isn't a bar pick-up.*

"But—"

"Stop interrupting, will you?" He couldn't say it sternly. The conversation was laughable. With a start he realized they were smiling at each other.

"See?" The instant she said it, she clamped her hand over her mouth. It hardly seemed possible her translucent skin could turn any redder.

"If you mean, do I see why so many of my colleagues are annoyed with you, yes. Yes, I do."

She nodded but kept her hand clamped over her mouth.

"Now. I was saying. You're an extraordinary student. Everyone around here knows that. Stop shooting yourself in the foot and act like you're only an above average student. Do what every other student has to do—in public. Offstage, you can conquer the world."

She still had her hand over her mouth, but she nodded. He thought he detected contrition in her eyes but wasn't sure. *Is she mocking me? Or playing mental footsie?*

"You're not a very good actress, you know. You're pretending to be penitent, but you can't fool me."

She frowned.

The hand business was getting to him. He frowned back. "I will sponsor you until Paul comes back, okay? Then we'll decide: If you think I'm what you want in an advisor and I think I can handle your rambunctious ambition, then I'll sign on officially as your major professor. Is that an acceptable contract?"

She lowered her hand just enough so he could see her lips. "Thank you."

"You're welcome." He let out his breath between his teeth. "I agree to listen to you rant and rave about the state of our discipline. I'll also try to understand your mathematics—but don't get your hopes up on that. But you must agree that in public, you will act like you're a very, very bright, highly disciplined student, who intends to blow through this program like a gold medalist in the steeplechase."

She had let her hand drop to rest on her collarbone. "That means I jump all the hurdles?" she whispered.

"That's exactly what it means. Do you agree?"

She placed the hand over her heart. "I promise."

Her smile sent a thrill through his whole body. They seemed to be making a very personal connection, a great deal more than he'd hoped for. If he was going to have a chance with this sexy ball of intellect, he now had to put the full weight of his experience behind his punches. *You aren't after her body—not yet anyway. It's a battle of minds.* And that he understood well enough to win—for the moment.

"Okay, cut the drama. You're the public Vanessa for the moment. No more outbursts. I want to discuss another practical issue."

"Good." She reached into her pack on the floor and pulled out a notebook. She plucked a pencil from her shirt pocket and poised it over an empty page.

"Have you considered doing a small study—say, twenty subjects, to show that your invisible faces can prime people's judgment of name gender? Just that, and nothing more?"

"I've already started one. If I treated it as a footnote in my thesis, would you consider sponsoring it?"

"Yes, I suppose. But do you understand, that's my minimum condition for agreeing to take you as a student?" He worried that he was overdoing the stern tone in his voice.

She cocked her head. "Are you saying that the study you just described won't convince you, even if it comes out the way I predict it will?"

"Would it change *your* mind if it came out the other way?"

"Good question." Her eyes shifted and focused inward. "If it were a simplistic study, like you suggested?" She waited until he nodded. "It's the same idea Paul had, in fact."

He nodded again.

"The answer is no, but if it were a parametric, within-subject design, then yes, it might."

"How about… let's say you add the little study to this paper," he said pointing to the now black screen where her draft had been earlier. "Not as a footnote, but as a pilot study, okay?"

She tilted her head again and the faint smile returned. "And something else?"

"And you must promise me—and later, your committee—that you'll do that big, multi-subject parametric study for your PhD."

"Beggars can't be choosers, can they?"

"Vanessa," he said, trying to keep his exasperation out of his voice, "if you want to pursue your single-subject research in this graduate program, you're going to have to jump through some hoops. And if you expect someday to turn psychology upside down, you have to get a PhD—following the rules of the graduate school—and..." When she scowled, he frowned as severely as he could. "Hear me out, okay?" She nodded indulgently.

"To even get a hearing in science today," he continued, "you have to have a decent academic job—not a ninety-hour-a-week teaching post in a junior college. That's just the way it is."

"Understood." She was on her feet suddenly, hefting her backpack in one fluid movement. Her condescending smile had become unmistakably ironic. "I told you I've rubbed a lot of faculty the wrong way. I guess I've rubbed you the right way. Thank you."

She scurried out of his office and was gone before he was able to react. But after she left, he shivered momentarily.

"Knock, knock!" It was Michelle's voice. When Stan turned around, she was standing in the doorway with her usual cheerful smile. "You've talked to her?"

He nodded. "Less than an hour ago."

"Well?" she said.

"Well... I have a new student."

"Good."

"I think."

She squinted at him, still smiling. "You think it's good, or you think you have a student?"

"Both."

"'I think,' as in not sure—and worried?"

"Yes."

She laughed. "Want to talk?"

He nodded her toward a chair.

She dropped a stack of notes and papers on the worktable and pulled a chair around it, so they faced each other with no table between them. "What do you think of her?"

He tilted back in his swivel chair. "Everything about her is strange. She must be from a whole different planet. Neither Venus nor Mars—maybe outside our solar system."

"I'm more interested in your reaction to her work." She chided him with a chuckle. "Presumably, that's independent of your reaction to her personality."

"That's what I was talking about. Her work—the study and the way she wrote up the report. They're even stranger than she is."

"C'mon, Stan. Stop beating around the bush."

He sighed deeply. "Okay, first the report. The write-up is completely non-standard, right? At least for the cognitive literature. You know the style guidelines she followed?"

"*Science*, wasn't it?"

"Right. As if she thought it was good enough to be one of the few papers they take in cognitive psychology."

"She not your usual grad student, Stan. She told me recently that she cares more about publishing than getting a PhD."

Stan raised his eyebrows. "That *is* unusual. But still—*Science*? Does she really think anyone outside the field would be interested in her work? An astrophysicist? An archeologist? Like the *New York Times* science reporter's going write it up as a big breakthrough?"

"From what I've seen of her, her ambitions match her intelligence."

Stan had to reconsider what he'd said in light of Michelle's calm rejoinders. She evidently knew Vanessa in an entirely different way than Paul did. "I have to admit," he continued, "that once I got used to the way it's organized, I realized her paper is very well written, almost too concise."

"I'm really interested in what you thought of the results."

"You would. Anyone would." He shook his head. "What can I say? Her study is original, impressive, and naïve all at the same time. What did you think?"

"I had an advantage, Stan. Last spring she and I began studying statistical analyses of time-dependent trends within highly intercorrelated systems, like repeated measures designs on the same person. There are actually quite a few established approaches out there in other fields. It was unfamiliar terrain for both of us, but she went through it like a mathematical buzz saw."

Michelle pushed a strand of hair away from her face. "Vanessa worked through the underlying logic of the existing methods and on her own derived a couple I think are completely original."

"I'll have to take your word for it." He shrugged.

"Did she present her arguments for testing only herself?"

"That's an understatement. Does she do that to everyone?"

"Well, you, Roger, and I make three," she said. "Two of us were impressed. How about you?"

"Roger? She told me he squelched her in class, and—"

"He feels lousy about blowing up at her."

"Really?" Stan's was taken aback. "How did you know that?"

"He came to talk to me about her after what happened to Paul. He volunteered the incident in his seminar."

"He wanted to talk to you about that?"

She suddenly looked like the Cheshire cat perched on a tree limb across from him. For someone who never repeated gossip, Michelle usually knew more about what was going on than the department's rumormongers.

"No," she said, "he was concerned about who was going to sponsor her with Paul out of commission for a while. When I asked him if he knew that Vanessa had written another paper for his course and hadn't handed it in, he was incredulous. She'd never mentioned it to him, and I don't think anyone else knew."

"Have *you* read it? The paper, I mean."

"Vanessa had told me earlier what happened, and I asked if I could read it. You should, too, if you're going to sponsor her. It's impressive, like everything she writes."

"Has Roger looked at it since you told him about it?"

"I told him I'd ask Vanessa to give him a copy," she said. "What took him totally by surprise was the fact that she'd written two papers for his course."

"Yeah, we're lucky to get one good one out of most of our students." He was beginning to get a fuller picture of just how much better she was than any student he knew of, either at UW or anywhere else for that matter.

"He told me the one she did turn in on mathematical modeling was extraordinary."

Stan shook his head again. "You know, Michelle, what worries me most is that both times I've talked with her, I've come away feeling like I'd just lost a wrestling match."

The metaphor had popped into his head from nowhere, or so it seemed. He hoped Michelle didn't pick up anything on his face that revealed the image of nude wrestling that had flashed through his head.

"Get ready to lose a lot more matches, Stan. That doesn't bother you, does it?"

"It's pretty hard on a male ego."

She patronized him with a smile. "That's a guy thing, isn't it?"

"Of course." He squirmed at the thought that she could see the video clips in his head.

She looked him straight in the eye. "From everything I know about you, Stan, I think you're the best suited to work with her."

"Is that a compliment?" If she thought he was less vulnerable to Vanessa's erotic allure than the rest of his male colleagues, then she wasn't reading his mind, after all.

"Of course it's a compliment. And I think you should prepare yourself to take over as her sponsor permanently."

"What?"

"She's mentioned several times, even before Paul's heart attack, that she thought she'd made a mistake choosing to work with him. When she started, she thought language was the key to the mind. But I've watched her horizon widen immensely. You're the obvious choice for her in this department, don't you think?"

"I suppose." Stan tried very hard not to betray the sudden jolt of pleasure he felt.

"You know you are, Stan. You share her interest in a theoretical approach and from what I've seen of you, you're much more open to treating students as equals than Paul is. You just have to think of her as a female Einstein, who'll revolutionize psychology, but needs a patron to shepherd her to a degree and a good job."

"All right. Let's say she and I agree with you. You know her a lot better than I do. Give me some advice about how I'm going to 'shepherd her to a degree,' as you put it."

"Simple. Aside from seeing she meets the requirements, work with her the way you'd work with a post-doc. Give her advice on her research if she asks for it. Be ready to defend your suggestions, but don't be upset if she doesn't follow them. Support what *she* wants to do in any way you can. And above all, don't make the mistake of issuing any ultimatums."

"Whew! So I have to have the wisdom of Solomon and the patience of Job?" Stan knew Michelle's husband was a Lutheran minister and she was, as far as he could tell, a devout Christian.

She laughed. "Two excellent role models for you. Let me say that I quickly discovered she was *more* than my equal in math. I learned more from her than I could teach her. And you will too if you think of her as your partner."

"Partner?" He wondered again how it was possible that she saw no trace of the images in his head, where he was dancing with Vanessa, who was wearing nothing except high heels.

She gave him a sardonic smile. "Your partner in getting her through grad school and placing her in a good job, Stan." The smile became a stern glare. "Don't make the same mistake Paul did."

"I get your point." He tried to look as serious as he could. "In any case, it looks like I've already grabbed the tigress by her tail. Do you think Roger would be open to serving on her committee?"

"I do. I think the three of us are her committee—for the moment, at least. The question is, can she use that unorthodox text she gave us to read?"

"I've already told her she has to run a small, between-subject experiment and include it in a rewrite that follows department thesis guidelines."

"What was her reaction?"

"She quoted me the 'beggars can't be choosers' proverb. But she agreed to do it."

"That's a good indication you're the right person for her." She pulled her stack of papers toward her and stood. "But she won't have to beg you for anything. Just watch her. You're going to enjoy this student, Stan. Take my word for it." She smiled mischievously. "Good luck," she added as she left his office.

CHAPTER 5

Michelle had carefully planned what she would say to Stan, anticipating more resistance than she had encountered. As she returned to her office, she reviewed their conversation to be sure she had covered everything she thought was important.

As she let herself into her office, she concluded that Stan's reaction had been more positive than she'd hoped. He seemed even more open to Vanessa's radical and ambitious goals than Michelle had expected. And he'd found a way to impose some discipline on Vanessa's unbridled assault on what was by any measure a monumental scientific challenge.

She lowered the folder and book in her arms to her desk, picked up the book and slid it back into its place on the shelf above her desk. Then she pulled up her chair and sorted the folders into three piles. Spinning the chair around she took each pile and filed it in a different drawer of the steel cabinet behind her. She followed this routine mindlessly, her thoughts on the conversation with Stan continuing.

There had been that odd moment when he seemed embarrassed by his choice of the wrestling metaphor—something she'd seen in his face and eyes. And why had he blushed slightly when she suggested he treat Vanessa as a "partner"? Was Stan under the same spell as the rest of the men in the department? She supposed he was.

She long ago gave up trying to imagine how men's sexual fantasies played into their interactions with female colleagues and students. Her husband Karl had convinced her they were a reality.

She had to assume that her male faculty colleagues' meetings with Vanessa were at least occasionally accompanied by mental images of the nude photos of her they'd seen.

Stan, however, wasn't a womanizer like Paul. That was a plus for Vanessa. But since Stan and Heidi had broken up, Michelle had noticed a change in Stan's behavior around women he didn't know, especially attractive women. He seemed more embarrassed or ill at ease. His genuine shyness puzzled her.

Maybe it was just her bias toward men with a lighter complexion, but she thought sandy-haired Stan was more attractive than Paul, whose hair was the color of onyx streaked with gray. Wiry and athletic, Stan was a runner and biker, an avid backpacker in the summer and cross-country skier in the winter. She knew he regularly lifted weights at home and at the gym on campus. His strong jaw wasn't hidden by facial hair, and his lively brown eyes sparkled with intelligence and honesty. *Why hasn't he attracted a woman to replace Heidi?*

Whatever the source of Stan's personal problems, there was no way of predicting the chemistry between him and Vanessa. She had surprised Michelle by moving in with Paul last year. Michelle was even more surprised when the relationship lasted more than six months and completely confounded when she learned from Vanessa the intensity of their recent arguments.

Even if striking Vanessa's steely intellect against the flinty bedrock of Stan's patience and experience sent up a shower of sparks, he was the best person in the department to guide a student like Vanessa through the graduate program.

Brad Holmes had been both fascinated and frustrated by Vanessa since that day back at WSU when she'd appeared in the undergraduate perception course he was taking. Drawn immediately to her obvious physical assets and titillated by her *Playboy* nudes that appeared soon after, he managed to get off on the wrong foot immediately.

She was polite. She wasn't unfriendly. She just wasn't interested in anything he was, and she was adroit enough in conversation to deflect any segues into territory outside their studies. He didn't get many chances to try again. She didn't hang out with the other psych majors, but he saw her in faculty offices all the time, especially Greene's.

To his immense surprise, she'd shown up in the graduate program at the University of Washington less than a year later. They'd even been assigned to the same office, if you could call it that. Four graduate students stuffed into a ten- by twelve-foot room. Each of them had one of the battered desks, some steel, some wood, which were lined up on each of two facing walls, each with an unmatched, broken-down chair. A large wastebasket at the far end of the room always seemed to contain the rotting remains of someone's lunch.

Brad and his friend Shawn Engle liked to hang out in the office drinking coffee and socializing. Although other students with offices elsewhere dropped by frequently to join in, their officemates, including Vanessa, rarely stayed more than a few minutes, using their limited space to park the books, notes, and papers they didn't need at the moment.

He'd tried once asking Vanessa a question about a statistics assignment. Everyone knew she was a whiz at the subject. The word was Davidson had let her skip the stat sequence. God only knew what they talked about during their weekly sessions, but whenever he passed Davidson's office when Vanessa was there, they had the whiteboard covered with math gibberish.

Vanessa had taken one look at the problem and begun asking him questions. It took her less than a minute to show him that he didn't understand shit about some pretty basic concepts. She was unrelenting—kept asking simpler, more basic questions, until she finally uncovered something he had a handle on. Then she started building, step by step, until forty minutes later, she at last got back to his question, which he could now answer for himself.

True, he never forgot what she'd taught him. Yet it felt like she was stomping on his dick the whole time. The damnedest thing was, she hadn't once looked surprised or impatient when he acted like an ignoramus again and again. But neither had she smiled—even once.

Still, he could not get her out of his head. Collecting as many of her *Playboy* photos as he could find only frustrated him more. Especially when she smiled for the camera once in a while. He liked those shots because she never smiled at him. But his favorite photos were the ones where she looked like she was getting off playing with herself. He had most of them on his laptop screensaver. Her body was fucking awesome.

He and Shawn were in their office shooting the shit about Erika Wennerstrom and her hit song on the Heartless Bastards' latest album, when Vanessa walked in.

"Hi," she said, barely looking at them. She shrugged out of her pink raincoat and hung it on a coat rack with a permanent list. With three coats and rain parkas hanging on it, it looked like the mast of his family's sailboat heeled over in the wind.

"Hi, yourself," Brad said. "Looks like it's raining out there."

"Not that much." She glanced over her shoulder at him, where he'd perched himself on the edge of his desk. After a second she turned back, her eyes fastened on the screen of Brad's laptop sitting next to him. Suddenly, a look of recognition came over her face. Her eyes flashed like blue pyrotechnic bursts more brilliant than the daylight sky.

"Get those photos off that screen." She pointed. "This is a workplace, and those photos are totally inappropriate here." Her usually quiet voice was strident.

Brad couldn't help himself. He exploded with laughter. "Inappropriate? Shit, you posed for them."

Shawn had his feet up on his desk and was leaning far back in his ancient wooden office chair. "I think they're awesome anywhere." He looked languidly at Brad for confirmation, then guffawed so vigorously it looked like the creaky old chair was going to split under the weight of his bulky body.

She glared at Shawn, then turned back to Brad. "If you don't do it… now… I'll get rid of them for you." She pulled back Brad's empty chair in front of the screen and sat down.

"What the fuck are you talking about?" Brad's voice boomed as he slid off his desk and stood over her, clenching his fists.

Ignoring him, she began deftly stroking the trackpad and clicking icons on the screen.

"Hey!" His shout reverberated in the hallway outside. "Stop that, bitch!"

She didn't look at him until he gave her a shove on the shoulder.

"I told you to stop, you skank. Those are my fucking photos, and I can fucking do whatever I fucking please with them."

She stood so forcefully the chair tipped over behind her. "Then you do it while I watch. Either you wipe them off your hard drive, or I file a harassment complaint."

"Get away from that machine, you fucking whore!"

Vanessa picked up the back of the chair and tilted it upright again. "And don't lay a hand on me again unless you want to answer an assault charge, as well." She sat down without looking at him.

"What the hell is going on?"

Brad jerked his head around to see Jim Forrester's bulky body filling the doorway like Erik the Red looking for plunder and rape. Behind him he heard Vanessa go back to fucking around on his computer. He pointed at her without looking. "She's fucking with my computer."

She spun out of the chair pulling it aside so Forrester could see the screen. One of the photos she was about to erase filled the entire screen. In it she was lying on her back on a rumpled bed, legs parted for the camera.

She pointed at Brad. "This jerk was using photos like this as his screensaver." She shifted her pointing finger to the photo. Her soft flat voice seemed barely audible after the men's shouting. "He was leaving it running for every passerby to see."

It was obvious that Forrester was having trouble focusing on anything beyond the photo of the naked woman. When Vanessa stopped talking, however, he was finally able to get his full attention on the clothed counterpart, who had addressed him. "What were you doing to his laptop, Vanessa?"

"Erasing the offensive ones, Dr. Forrester. With your permission, I'd like to finish."

There was an excruciating moment of silence in which everyone except Vanessa seemed to be holding his breath. Then Forrester said, "Yes, go ahead." His voice lacked its usual blustery self-confidence.

"Thank you." Vanessa sat back down and returned to the task she had started.

There was another moment of silence broken only at irregular intervals by the audio icon of a miniature toilet flushing. The three men stood immobilized, watching Vanessa's back.

Forrester broke the silence. "Do you plan to file a complaint, too… uh, Vanessa?"

"No," she said to the screen, "as long as I don't see these images in this office again."

Forrester turned back to the two men. "Consider yourselves lucky she's cool with having them gone, okay?"

Brad shrugged dismissively, but Shawn said in a meek voice, "We do. Thank you for—"

Forrester jabbed his fleshy forefinger at Brad. "And I want this door left wide open any time one or both of you are in here. If I ever see those pictures, or ones like them, again, you're toast. Understood?"

Brad barely tipped his head, but Shawn began nodding his head like a trained seal. Forrester glared at them for another second. Why was the motherfucker so bent out of shape over Vanessa?

The legs of the chair scraped the floor when Vanessa stood without warning and scooped up her backpack. Forrester stepped aside so she could get through the door.

"Thank you for your help, Dr. Forrester." She swept past him and disappeared down the hall.

Forrester examined Brad and Shawn with disdain. "Cool it, you slobs." He stalked back to his office across the hall.

2008-11-13 08:24:09:
Dr. Harte, I'm attaching a draft revision of my thesis in UW-psych format. Also note that I've included the small study we discussed in the introduction. The results are from 27 participants out of the 32 I plan to test. I have the remaining participants scheduled this week & early next. Vanessa

2008-11-13 15:12:41:
Vanessa, Your draft looks good enough to take to a committee. Nice work! Can we meet again next Tuesday at 2:00 to discuss setting up your committee? Stan

This time she pushed open Stan's door immediately after knocking. He had turned to look for a reference lying on his worktable, so he saw her before she greeted him. When she turned to close the door behind her, he knew something about her was different. It wasn't until she sat down that he saw what it was. She always wore her silky raven-hued hair in a ponytail with the end tucked up and pinned so it didn't flip around. Today it swung loose in sensuous arcs when she turned her head.

He was so preoccupied with the change that he missed his opportunity to tell her to open the door again as he did with all female students, graduate or undergraduate. After watching several colleagues get into trouble with sexual harassment complaints by women far less perilous than Vanessa, he knew the risks and was half out of his chair intending to open the door himself, but an errant impulse halted him. He sat down again, filled with indecision.

To suppress his discomfort, he launched immediately into the first and trickiest subject of their meeting. "I talked to Paul last night. In the hospital."

"Yes?" She leaned forward tensely.

"He's doing very well after surgery. I was surprised how chipper he seemed to be."

She leaned back, and tension he hadn't noticed before was visibly leached from her body.

"I'm so happy to hear he's okay. I've been worrying that something else would happen to him. That he might even…" Her voice faded into silence.

"I think you can rest easy. From what he said, it sounds like his surgeon is confident he'll recover quickly."

Stan had been worrying, too. The thought of losing a colleague like Paul troubled him, and not because of the staffing problems. He'd already arranged to take over Paul's seminar and finish out the quarter with material from his own cognitive seminar. They'd sort out the handoff back to Paul when he could handle it.

In spite of the mixture of feelings Vanessa had stirred up in Stan, Paul was a real friend, although they rarely socialized outside of work. But after Paul's close call, Stan had realized that of all his colleagues here at UW, Paul was the one he most enjoyed spending time with. That didn't make it any easier to keep his promise and deliver the message Paul had asked him to give to Vanessa.

"Paul desperately wants to see you, Vanessa. He asked me to tell you that the arguments were all his fault and the way he treated you was unconscionable."

"Really?" She sounded like she didn't believe what she'd heard. "That isn't right. I was a stubborn bitch. It was all *my* fault."

Stan was amused. "Sounds like it would be good for both of you to see each other. But you must promise me that you won't let your visit turn into an argument over who's to blame."

She slouched a little in the chair and vacantly studied her hands. "No, I guess you're right. There's no point assigning fault as long as I at least get a chance to say I'm sorry."

"So you'll go as soon as you can?"

"Maybe tonight."

"Paul would like that."

Although Stan had done what Paul asked and it seemed to have had the effect he'd intended, he wasn't sure how to change the subject. He turned his arm and glanced down at his watch. "Unless you want to talk about Paul some more…"

She shook her head. "We should probably talk about my thesis now."

"Yes." What a relief to have that successfully behind him. "I looked at the data you sent me yesterday. Clearly the results are no different from what was in the draft you sent me last week."

"No, it barely changed the numbers." She had been holding a folder, and as she now handed it across the table to him, he caught a faint whiff of crushed cloves.

"The complete set of data is included in the final draft," she continued. "I printed this one out for you. I'll send you a DOC file you can mark up with comments for me."

"It's in excellent shape as it is, Vanessa. Let's not worry about a final version until we have an official committee."

"Michelle already told me she'd be on it. Is that okay?"

"Yes, she's an excellent choice. And she and I have also discussed who might be an appropriate third committee member."

"It's going to be difficult finding another faculty member who isn't annoyed with my behavior in class." She giggled softly, the pitch no higher than her speaking voice.

"Both Michelle and I think Roger Zhrudsky would be an excellent addition…" She started to shake her head, but he held up his hand to keep her from interrupting. "No, no. Wait for me to finish." He needed the extra time anyway. Her bobbing ponytail had seriously distracted him again.

"Dr. Zhrudsky's expertise in the perception and attention area will be extremely helpful, and—"

"But he's resolutely against single-subject research. He—"

"Hold it. There's something you don't know." She searched his eyes, shaking her head doubtfully. "I told you I talked to

Michelle. What I don't think you know is that Roger went to talk to her about finding you a new sponsor."

"He did?" She frowned as if she didn't believe him, and her head continued to shake.

"Yes. In the course of the conversation he volunteered that he regretted stomping on you in class."

"He remembered our argument?"

"And he was even more impressed when he found out you'd written a second paper for his class on a different topic. He'd like to read the first one."

"Really?" Her tone conveyed disbelief, but her expression betrayed her pleasure.

"Yes, and I'd like to take a look at it, too. Okay?"

"Sure." She hesitated. "But shouldn't Dr. Zhrudsky see a copy of my thesis first, if I'm going to ask him to be on my committee?"

"No, let's wait a week or so on that. Don't dump too much on him all at once. Let me give you two pieces of advice about talking to Roger. First, keep in mind that he's an administrator, and there are big and continuous demands on his time. He only takes on one student of his own at a time. Second, he rarely agrees to serve on any other student committees. However, he's already promised that he will be on yours. So don't be pushy."

"I'm very grateful to you, Dr. Harte. I'll try to remember my mendicant status."

No wonder she annoys everyone, he thought. *Mendicant status*? "Don't overdo it, Vanessa. Both Michelle and I are sure he'll agree."

"I understand what you're saying." She looked and sounded honestly contrite. "Really I do."

"And please…" His heartbeat surged. "…call me 'Stan,' okay?"

She searched his eyes warily. "If you prefer." Her timid voice was so soft he could barely hear it. "That's very nice of you."

"It's my preference."

Their gaze held for several seconds, at least it seemed that long to Stan. He looked away first, a little edgy.

She rescued him from his rising self-consciousness by changing the subject. "You haven't said whether the results of the small study convinced you the data on myself are real."

It took him a moment to shift gears and formulate his thoughts. He looked out the window reflectively. "I'm in a tough spot here. There's nothing I can say rationally. You've made a convincing case." He had been talking to himself so far, but as he reached a tentative conclusion, he faced her again. "As far as it goes—and that's the problem."

"I thought you'd say that."

"It's a gut feeling, Vanessa. My instincts tell me the brain just doesn't work the way your study implies."

"The brain?" She waited for a nod of agreement. "Not the mind?"

"Well, of course. Both."

"I'm glad you agree with me that cognitive science is really the study of the mind-brain continuum."

"Yes, yes. That's a given, Vanessa. But there are two issues. First, there are absolutely no phenomena remotely like yours in time scale." He held up his hand again when she started to break in. "No, let me finish; the two issues are related. There are no theories that imply, so far as I know, that the brain should work this way."

"Except mine." Her thin lips pouted—a big surprise.

An image of her with the same expression and no clothes flashed before his mind's eye.

"I didn't make that clear in the theory paper I gave you, did I?"

A sudden sinking feeling swept through him. He was going to have to admit he couldn't follow her paper.

But she continued after the briefest of pauses. "That paper requires a lot of work to read, Doctor— uh… Stan. Everyone I've given it to has said the derivations interfere with what I'm trying to say. But I didn't mean what I wrote to be a put-down."

"That makes me feel better. However—"

"However, you won't be persuaded until I finish the parametric study and replicate at least some of the results from the data on myself, right?"

"No, look." He struggled to find the best way to explain his misgivings. "Try to put yourself in the place of a reader like me—a skeptical reader. My first thought is, 'These findings are so astonishing she can't be measuring people's consciousness. There has to be another explanation. Something about the stimuli or procedure is causing these incredibly orderly results. There has to be an artifact here.'"

"Oh, I see."

"Yes, my perspective is different from yours. I'm pretty sure that if and when you publish this, everyone in the field is going to rush in hoping to demonstrate that your effect isn't real—or at any rate, doesn't mean what it seems, doesn't mean what you're claiming it does."

"So I need a different kind of experiment?"

"Exactly." Her challenge was the perfect opening for him to voice his main concern about her findings. "You need a design that will begin to rule out at least some of the obvious counter-explanations."

"Which are…?"

This challenge stopped him momentarily. "I'm not sure… I don't know," he said, stalling. "We have to put our heads together and come up with some." His metaphor interfered with his train of thought. "Maybe your committee can help us. That's what often happens during good committee meetings."

"Doct— uh, Stan? Would you change your mind if you participated in my experiment yourself? If you experienced changes in your own private consciousness while looking at my hidden faces and then saw that your results fit mine, would it change your gut feelings?"

He looked out the window at the fir tree, mulling it over. "I'd never thought of it, but no, I doubt it."

"I think there's a good chance it might. Would you be willing to give it a shot? Be a pilot subject in my single-subject experiment? It's all set up, any time you want to…"

"It would be in Paul's lab, right?" Why was he hanging back? Ordinarily, he insisted on being a subject in any new procedure they tried in his lab, whether it was one he'd thought of, and asked an assistant to implement, or in this case, something a student had come up with. Experiencing what the participants will see and do cleared up any misunderstandings and gave an investigator an intuitive basis for judging an experiment's validity.

"Does that make a difference?" she asked.

"I don't know." It seemed different. "I guess you can test anyone you like… as a pilot subject, at least." Of course, they would be alone together in a dark room behind a door with a do-not-disturb sign on it. Yet he'd done it with all his students, male and female, graduate and undergraduate. Indeed, he required it. And really, could it be done any other way?

"I want you to look at your own data," she said, "and judge for yourself whether my results are valid."

"I suppose it's the same as your testing another grad student." But this was very different, and he knew it. It wouldn't be what actually happened in Paul's lab. It would be what some people might imagine would happen between a forty-year-old divorced professor and a former *Playboy* model—if someone found out they had been in a lab together alone.

She tilted her head, so her inscrutable eyes looked aslant into his. "I gathered from what some of my professors in cognitive psychology said—Joel Greene back at Wazzu was the first—that it's pretty much standard procedure for investigators to be subjects themselves first. Am I wrong?"

"No." Whose side was she on, his superego or his id? "You're right."

All these years he'd been gawking at photos of naked women and fantasizing about what it would be like to make love to them. But how to meet such women? And he'd never been any good at small talk and the mating dance that came so naturally to men like Paul. And now, here he was, not just acquainted with a woman who avoided small talk in favor of discussing what he knew best, but... Could he even hope she was making an overture? Handing him an invitation to the dance without his asking first?

He spun around in his chair to look at his calendar. "What about a week from today, same time?"

"That's great, except we'll need to start a little later next week, say, 3:45?"

"How long will it take?" He was thinking it was kind of a late start.

"A couple of hours."

He looked at his calendar again. "All right. Next Thursday at 3:45 it is." Now that they seemed about to walk onto the dance floor, his feet were turning into blocks of ice. He didn't know the steps. Or did he? An idea sprang out of the sea of his uncertainty, and before he could scrutinize it, the words were coming out of his mouth. "So, we'll be done by six? Uh... maybe we could have dinner afterward?"

"That would be nice, but then I should treat you, shouldn't I?"

"No, I invited you first."

She smiled and cocked her head to one side. "Okay, thanks, uh… Stan."

"Besides," he said. "I know what a graduate fellowship pays. I can afford it, so save your money."

"All right then." She rose, pack in hand, in a single flowing motion. "I'll see you next Thursday, and I'll try to talk to Dr. Zhrudsky between now and then."

CHAPTER 6

In the six years that Roger Zhrudsky had been chair of psychology, he had learned a great deal about how to lead and manage a department of between fifty and sixty faculty members, all of whom considered themselves independent academic empires. For example, a carpeted office with soft, indirect lighting tended to cool tempers and stimulated rational arguments and an inclination to compromise. The imposing desk of real walnut placed at an angle to the walls automatically gave him a position of authority. And the tastefully displayed books on a wall shelf and on the credenza behind him lent an air of academic authority to the room.

The book he had edited on the role of attention in color and shape perception occupied a prominent position in this tiny professional library along with the widely used textbook he had written with two other well-known people in the field of perception.

The meeting that Vanessa Trippett had requested would be the first time they'd talked since working together to revive Paul Kovick. Zhrudsky had signed the formal letter of appreciation from the department, expressing gratitude for her quick thinking and skilled handling of the medical emergency.

He still couldn't get out of his mind the impression left by her decisive orders and the way she commanded everyone in the situation—even shoving poor Stan out of the way after he'd helped her. Nor could he account for her sudden collapse when the crisis was over, the nearly catatonic state that overwhelmed her, and her refusal when he'd suggested she go with Paul to the ER.

He felt tense and uneasy, partly because their academic contact had been so confrontational in the past and partly because she had become such an explosive topic of discussion throughout the department. He knew from talking to Stan, and earlier Michelle, that Vanessa would ask him to serve on her master's thesis research committee. From his two colleagues, he knew something about her work, and given her acknowledged brilliance, he was looking forward to participating.

Her soft knock at his door belied her sometimes cutting substantive questions. Her deference was really unnecessary, since Cathy had already announced her over the interoffice speakerphone.

"Good morning, Dr. Zhrudsky." Her voice was as soft as her earlier knock had been. "Thank you for seeing me now."

"Not a problem, Vanessa," he said. "It's a real pleasure to talk to you under less stressful circumstances."

A smile flashed on her lips. "I've also hoped to talk to you—and thank you for bringing the AED so quickly."

"I'm convinced that CPR training should be universal." This comfortable topic didn't relieve his apprehension about what he needed to discuss in this meeting.

"I agree, Dr. Zhrudsky. I started when I was, maybe three, being taught where our AED was kept and how important it was to get it to someone who could use it."

"That sounds impressive." He was intrigued, wishing it were an appropriate place to ask her more about her background. Looking at her alone here in his office, he fully appreciated why the men in the department were so fascinated by her.

But he had to move on to the most difficult part of the meeting—for him at any rate. "Well, Vanessa." He shifted a folder to and fro by quarter inches on his desk pad. "Michelle tells me that you wrote a second paper for my seminar, but never turned it in. Did I understand correctly?"

"Yes." She hesitated. "What happened was, I… we discussed the topic—single-subject designs—in class, and I changed my—"

"Because I got so irritated with you objecting to every point I was trying to make, that I… I lost it, quite frankly. And I want to apologize, Vanessa."

"No, no. It was my fault. I shouldn't have kept butting in. Especially interrupting other students."

"Actually I was specifically annoyed because you were tearing my arguments to shreds." His smile appeared to have the desired effect on her.

Her reserve melted ever so slightly. "After writing a paper—working through all the arguments, both pro and con, I concluded that single-subject research was being underestimated. I was already working on a research project for my thesis using that approach, so I had a lot invested in my arguments. I suppose I felt threatened. I didn't need to be rude though, and I'm sorry."

"Interesting," he said. "Well, we all become invested in our theories. And it's to your credit that you know how to defend yours. In any case, I'd like very much to read your other paper, the one we're talking about."

Vanessa bent over to unzip her backpack. When she pulled out the paper, the staple caught and pulled a second paper with it. Confused for a moment, she flipped back and forth between them and then, holding one in each hand, she stood up. "Michelle told me you might like to look at it." She took a step toward his desk and put one of the papers in his outstretched hand.

As he reached to take it from her, he caught a whiff of cinnamon that took him a second to interpret properly. He concluded that it must be her shampoo or hand lotion; it wasn't as strong as perfume.

When she quickly retreated to her chair, he swiveled halfway to one side, tilted back in his chair and lifted the title page on top. After spending a minute reading the abstract on page two, he said, "I see," softly to himself.

Vanessa fidgeted, unable to relax and sit back.

Zhrudsky began turning pages, obviously skimming the text. He paused once. "Good point." After flipping rapidly through three more pages, he stopped again, closely reading the conclusions.

He swung back facing her again. "It looks like a good paper, Vanessa," he said, placing it on his desk in precise alignment with the folder. "May I keep it to read more carefully?"

"I was hoping you would, Dr. Zhrudsky." She smiled shyly. "I asked to see you because I wanted to talk about my master's thesis." She pointed to the paper on his desk. "This one presents a more complete and logically coherent philosophical foundation for the research I've done."

"All right."

She plunged on, speaking faster. "Would you consider—have the time, that is—to serve on my master's committee?" Her voice rose in pitch. "I know you're very busy, but I think your expertise in attentional processes would be invaluable to me." She caught her breath.

Zhrudsky smiled at her again. "Stan and Michelle already alerted me to the possibility you'd ask. However, they were both a little coy about what you're working on."

"It's single-subject research. At least the most interesting part is." Her words tumbled out. "But I've just completed a small conventional experiment—a pilot study really."

"Right," he said, "but tell me more about the processes you're studying and your research paradigm."

"I think I've found a way to measure consciousness. I discovered how to vary the amount of information in a visual display and observe its effect on awareness."

He stifled an urge to exclaim, "Wow!" If she had succeeded—and both Stan and Michelle told him Vanessa's work was promising without revealing its aim—then she was already showing more promise than most young scientists. Recovering his balance, he said, "That's too abstract, Vanessa. Can you be more specific?"

"Think of a photograph of a face on a monitor, okay? It's composed of a couple of million pixels, right?" She paused, as though waiting to be sure he wasn't going to stop her. "Now, we know that showing all the pixels for a tenth of a second or more results in what we call conscious perception. More than that, we can measure the degree of awareness with *d*-prime."

A fleeting smile moved across her lips. "I know you understand signal detection theory well enough to appreciate that *d*-prime is a quantitative variable with an absolute zero. Similarly, the number of pixels in a photo is also a ratio scale… you wouldn't argue with that, would you?"

"I'll give you that for the moment."

"Suppose then, that we take random samples of those two million pixels, and show each sample one at a time at the rate of seventy-five frames per second. I'm investigating the function that relates the size of the samples to *d*-prime. Does that make sense?"

"Not entirely." He was both amused and indulgent. "But you've certainly stirred up my interest." And his envy of Stan. If only a student half as good as Vanessa showed up next year when he'd be out of this job and a full-time faculty member again.

She looked puzzled. "Shall I go on then? Or do I need to clarify something?"

"Why don't we proceed as follows: When you have something written up, leave a copy with Cathy, and I'll read it. Then—"

"I have it right here, Dr. Zhrudsky." She held up the other paper she'd kept in her lap.

"Really? You have a thesis written already?"

"Could I give it to you now?" She stood again and took a step toward his desk but kept the paper against her chest. "You're sure you aren't too busy to…?"

"I'll find the time to work it in." He held out his hand and took the paper from her, knowing it committed him.

It surprised him that she seemed to appreciate that he had very little time to do what he'd originally hoped to do in an academic career. He was tired of the politics of administration and the sheer triviality of what he spent most of his time doing. His longing for the excitement and rewards of research were to the point of pain, as his last year in office crawled on interminably.

He placed the paper on the palm of his other hand, judging its length by its weight. "I understand you have a shorter version of this."

She looked at her empty hands, now resting in her lap. "It seems I write two papers for every assignment."

Her remark made him laugh involuntarily. "So I gather."

She looked up with a faint smile. "Not really." Her face was instantly serious again. "I didn't bring a hard copy, but I can get one to you later today."

"Good. Email it to me. We can print it out here in the office if I need it."

"Thanks, Dr. Zhrudsky." She stood. "I appreciate your time."

She snatched up her pack, the zippered top gaping open. She was at the door, her hand on the knob, before he had time to speak to her again.

"Oh, and Vanessa?"

She looked back over her shoulder, still holding the knob. "Yes?"

"About what happened last week. The screensaver?"

"Uh, yes?"

"Dr. Forrester told me..."

"I—" She let go of the knob and turned to face him.

"Next time, please don't take things into your own hands. I'd appreciate it if instead, you brought complaints like this to me. Do you understand?"

She nodded slowly. "Okay." She thought for a moment. "Yes, I understand. I'll try not to act precipitously again."

"Thank you."

She turned, grabbed the knob and left as quickly as she could.

Precipitously? He recalled that the sheer size of her vocabulary was the first thing he noticed about what she said in class. He soon came to appreciate the precision of her choice of words as well.

Paul Kovick had had it with this life in the hospital—if you could call it a life. No, he wasn't able to function completely on his own yet. But he wasn't about to move into a so-called "transitional facility." He wanted to be back in the familiar surroundings of his own apartment. He could pay for whatever in-home services he needed. He'd finally gotten his surgeon to release him to house arrest tomorrow... or the day after, for sure.

Paul had gone through at least three phases of yearning to get out. At first, he'd pictured himself returning to his previous life. Well, not really to the frantic pace of it—maybe life at a much slower tempo. But above all, he wanted to return to a life shared with Vanessa.

Reality quickly intruded on this fantasy. He could barely keep up with her voracious sexual appetite before. Now, if he did go back to his condo, which he'd been sharing with her for over a year, he wouldn't be able to have sex with her at first. Maybe, he was told, in two or three weeks.

What would he do alone there with Vanessa—without sex? And what would they talk about? No matter how they started out, his imagined conversations with her always flashed back to the awful fights they'd had over her master's thesis and the ludicrous way she'd spent the summer testing herself. Gradually, his pipe dream of spending the next few months in quiet companionship evaporated.

The more he turned over his memories of their life together, the more ridiculous it seemed to him. Those crazy sleep habits of hers and her hyperactive intelligence were more than he could stomach at times. He was almost glad when she said she wanted to stay in Seattle during the summer to study for comps and fine-tune her master's project, even though he offered to pay her way to accompany him to Provence. Not counting those six weeks he'd spent in the south of France, the nine months they'd been together had been a manic whirlwind.

He'd had no idea what he was letting himself in for when he suggested she move in with him. But the tornado had actually struck earlier—the first time she walked into his office. She told him straight out she'd picked him as her advisor because she believed that language was the key to understanding the mind and the brain. In the next breath she admitted she'd never taken a course in linguistics and was "...determined to master the subject."

Master it? How was he to know that she could learn more linguistics than he knew in her first year? Since she couldn't get credit for an undergraduate course in linguistics, he suggested she sign up for three hours of independent study with him, thinking it would be a convenient cover for the linguistics course and wouldn't be much work for either of them. Damned if it didn't turn out to demand more work from him than teaching a regular graduate course.

She showed up the following week having read all the stuff he'd assigned for the next two weeks and the entire text for the linguistics course. He shouldn't have asked her if she had any questions. She immediately drilled down to the limit of what he remembered from the readings he'd assigned. For the next few weeks, it was all he could do to keep up with her. Before long, he realized they'd reversed roles. The only way to salvage what was left of his pride was to ask her questions and accept that he'd become the student.

If he hadn't been obsessed with the prospect of seducing a *Playboy* model, he would have bailed out at the end of fall quarter last year. But by then his campaign was well on its way, and he couldn't stop himself.

He'd begun the way he always did, suggesting coffee in the afternoon a few times, then dinner in a nice restaurant, then a play or a concert, depending on her interests—and he could be very pliable when it came to entertainment, light or serious, and music, grunge or classical. Whatever she enjoyed, he could, too.

This strategy didn't work so well with Vanessa. She agreed to coffee but kept right on talking about linguistics—and asking questions like bullets that turned a walk to a coffeehouse on the Ave into a hazardous game of dodgeball. And the very first time, she complained about not having a whiteboard to help her explain things. For a week or two, he was stuck with seeing her in his office. But then he found a weakness.

After a long session where she had run out of steam temporarily, he suggested a glass of wine at a quiet enoteca. She accepted, and he discovered she was fond of good wine. To his surprise, she enjoyed getting a little tipsy, although she never lost control of herself.

After a couple of dinners with her, he stumbled on another chink in her armor. She was very unhappy sharing an apartment with two other grad students. Later he found out they didn't care much for her, and once she was around his place, he understood why. She didn't seem lonely exactly. But then, it seemed that to be her friend you had to keep up a constant scientific conversation. He could be extremely flexible when it came to seduction, so he planned and prepared for debates with her on topics he learned interested her.

On a Friday afternoon early in December, it started to snow. When she showed up for a meeting they'd scheduled, he took a chance. Waving at the deluge of large snowflakes pouring past his window, he said, "I don't know if you've heard that Seattle turns into a disaster zone when it snows."

"Really? Why?"

"The hills. Plus it doesn't happen that often."

"Do you want to cancel our meeting? That's fine with me."

With his heart beating like a drumroll, he said, "What would you think about canceling our reservation this evening, and—?"

"I was thinking about that too." She seemed to regard their date as unimportant.

Not what he was hoping for, but he forged on undaunted. "Would you consider joining me for dinner at my place instead?"

She scrutinized his face, but she was also smiling. "I'd consider it, yes."

He put his elbows on the table between them and leaned forward. "I like to cook, and…"

"Yes?"

"I have a good wine cellar," he whispered.

She laughed. "You know my weaknesses, don't you?" She managed to smile and frown at the same time. "But how does that help if we get snowed in tonight?"

He took a deep breath. "I've got a spare bedroom with a desk for a laptop—wi-fi, if you need it."

"Oh." The way she said it was exquisitely ambiguous. Did it mean "I know that line" or "Tell me more"?

He leaned closer, trying not to smile lecherously. "What I meant was that you could spend the weekend working at my place."

"Uh-huh."

"I promise not to interrupt you, except…"

"Except for?"

"Well, you're going to want something to eat tomorrow… Aren't you? I mean, if you stayed over… have to stay over, that is."

"You promise?"

"What, to feed you?"

"Not to disturb me." She planted her elbows on the table one at a time and leaned toward him. "Except for meals?"

"That's the deal." He couldn't keep his face muscles under control. "Well?"

He didn't realize how close they were to each other until she stretched toward him and grazed his lips with hers. "You can't fool me." The playful smile that followed was unreadable.

He was so baffled by her mixed signals that he momentarily forgot his plan. "What?" he asked.

She waved at the window without taking her eyes off his. "Shouldn't we get started?"

She took his arm as they walked to the bus stop and, when he put his arm behind her on the seat back, she snuggled against him. She helped him make the salads, chop the vegetables and set the table, took the bottle of Saint-Emilion he selected, pulled the cork and poured it while he arranged the coq au vin on their plates. As they worked together, she finally began to talk about herself and ask him polite questions about himself.

It continued to snow through the night. She stayed until Sunday afternoon. Before she left to spend the Christmas break with her mother, she moved her stuff to his place.

The weeks between early January and Valentine's Day were a middle-aged man's erotic daydream. He'd never been more sexually satisfied in his life, although even during those early days with her, she sometimes ran him ragged. When he really lacked interest and she wanted to make love, she paraded around the condo naked until he gave in. She begged him to try new contorted positions. Strangely, she was the only woman he knew who fell asleep before he did after they made love.

She was such an energetic partner, it was no wonder she looked fit and nubile—that and all her walking. By the time he left for Europe in June, he'd stopped initiating sex altogether and was still getting more of it than he wanted. Even he couldn't keep up with her without a respite of few weeks.

Reflecting on the hectic life he'd been leading for most of the past year, he reluctantly concluded that he should probably follow his surgeon's suggestion and offer to pay for an apartment for her, at least for the rest of this school year. It wasn't fair to expect her to take care of him, even if he hired someone to clean the apartment, fix their meals and manage all the other mundane tasks for them. She was still taking courses and should be finishing up her master's thesis. Without him.

Always when he got to this point in his train of thought, the nightmare of their last two arguments—the first when he nearly knocked her over getting her out of his office and the last, when he blew up at her in class—flooded back to haunt him.

The arguments had started much earlier. He'd enjoyed the first intellectually challenging discussions. But then she began rejecting the master's projects he suggested. She was losing interest in language, she told him. When he tried to convince her to do a "quick and dirty" experiment on semantic processing that he was sure would make a good thesis, she shifted to directly attacking his own field of psycholinguistics. Language, she argued, was just not that "pivotal to thought," and her justifications were razor sharp and sometimes impossible for him to counter effectively.

The first proposal she wrote for him was beautifully crafted, elegantly written—and ridiculously impractical. Over a thousand hours of lab time to collect data to be analyzed with statistical tests he'd never heard of and others she had invented herself. Michelle had later confirmed their originality and told him she thought the derivations were valid.

When he challenged the motivation for Vanessa's fanatical focus on quantification, she responded by presenting him with a theoretical paper, a salvo of mathematical firepower even Michelle couldn't fathom. And with this paper, Vanessa began talking about a theoretical thesis.

Nothing he could say or do persuaded her to tackle a realistic master's project. In desperation, he asked her to scale back her first proposal to a practical scope only to find in his inbox a proposal for a single-subject experiment that she refused to believe was methodologically unsound. Then she wasted the entire summer running it on herself and, in the fall when he returned, issued an ultimatum: She was going to form a committee, period—with or without him.

What always drove him over the brink into an uncontrollable rage was the cold, brutal way she argued with him, never raising her voice, never interrupting him, then answering with incisive logic, rich in details of published research he hadn't read or had long since forgotten. And, when he finally lost it completely and started bellowing at her, she walked away and refused to talk to him until his incoherent rage subsided. After he regained control of himself, she would be as receptive to making love as discussing their disagreements further. He couldn't remember winning even one of these battles.

No, she was the student from hell, and living with her now would be worse than hell for him. His only problem was figuring out how to persuade her they had to "separate" for at least a few months. Sadly, he realized that it probably wouldn't be long before she found another victim to move in with. "Victim?" The word "succubus" appeared in his head one day like a fly that sneaks into the house and lives there the rest of its life. He had started dreading the moment he saw her again.

CHAPTER 7

2008-11-20 09:42:01:
Vanessa, I dropped by to see Paul yesterday on my way home. He's looks really good and his doctor is apparently happy with his progress. Practically all we talked about was you and why you hadn't been to see him. I'm sure your fears about making him worse are incorrect. He needs to see you. I think you have to go see him, TODAY! Michelle

2008-11-20 10:23:09:
Michelle, Stan said almost the same thing. I'm still very uneasy about seeing Paul again after what happened. Would you be willing to go along with me to visit him in the hospital? Only this first time, okay? Please—I desperately need your support. Vanessa

2008-11-20 10:28:36:
Vanessa, I'd be happy to go along, but it will have to be late this afternoon. Traffic will be a nightmare, so maybe we should walk? Meet me around 6:20 outside 318 PAA. Michelle

In spite of Paul's foreboding, when Vanessa rapped lightly on the door and peeked in, the whole barren room filled with sunshine and a breeze off the ocean fluttered the curtains, sweeping away the alien smells of disinfectant and medication.

"Hi! It's me. Can we come in?"

He stretched out both arms to her without trying to stand up from the chair next to his bed. "Vanessa! Yes, yes, come here."

Holding a bouquet at arm's length, she rushed around the bed and bent over to kiss him on the cheek. As she did, her pack unexpectedly slid off her shoulder, knocking her off balance. She shuffled her feet and caught herself on the arm of his chair.

Taking advantage of her momentary instability, Paul took hold of her shoulders and pulled her lips to his. Their kiss was brief and sloppy.

She stood up, laughing nervously. "You must be okay."

"I've missed you terribly, honey. And I knew it was my fault—your staying away."

"It was only because I was afraid I'd make you angry with me again."

"How could I be angry with someone who saved my life?"

"I have a knack for it. Making people mad, I mean. I do it all the time. Even people I really like."

He noticed Michelle for the first time. "I see you brought a chaperone." He gave Michelle a wry smile. "Hello, Michelle. Good to see you again."

"How are you doing, Paul?" Michelle had seated herself in a straight-backed chair in the corner of the room opposite his.

"Not too bad. Can't wait to get out of this prison, though." He waved his hand in a vague arc.

"Oh, I forgot." Vanessa held out the bouquet to him "Dahlias. Our favorite restaurant."

"Too bad we're not eating there tonight."

"I knew it was the wrong thing—flowers." She laid them on the bed.

"I didn't mean it that way. Living in a damn jail cell has gotten to me."

"Yeah, sorry." She lobbed her backpack to a soft landing on the foot of the bed and boosted herself up between it and the bouquet. Her feet didn't quite touch the floor.

"Don't fret about it. I've needed something tangible to remind me of you."

There was a moment of silence. She swung her feet back and forth like a child.

Having her here in the same room again, smelling the jasmine fragrance of her skin lotion made him vacillate. He should discuss their future—if they had any together. But the thought of his life without her loomed like a bombed-out city at nightfall.

He grasped at a practical straw floating by on the turbulence of his emotions. "So… I understand you have a committee."

"Maybe. Michelle will be on it for sure." Vanessa glanced behind her.

"She can count on me, Paul."

"Of course. You two speak the same language."

"The same language, perhaps." Michelle lowered her eyes and shook her head slowly. "But sadly, not the differential geometry dialect."

"Don't be so modest, Michelle." He didn't take his eyes off Vanessa. "It's Stan I want to know about. He's taken my place?"

"Yes. He agreed to chair my committee, but—"

"And he's going to let you use your data on yourself for a thesis?"

"Not exactly. He still doesn't believe my results are real, but he thought they were provocative enough to justify forming a committee."

"Don't worry, honey, everything you do is provocative."

"He thinks it's some kind of artifact. But he's agreed to be a subject himself, and I'm pretty sure that will convince him."

"I'm sure he'll see the light. I know firsthand how persuasive you are. Not that I ever found it irksome." He looked pointedly at Michelle. "Like some of our colleagues. Quite the opposite. I found it, ah, refreshing… invigorating… intellectually, of course."

He smiled at Michelle. "It was her theory I couldn't hack." He turned back to Vanessa. "I assume Stan can handle it?"

"Not really, Paul. But I never seriously thought I could make a thesis out of my theory."

"I understand Roger will be the third member?" He felt his body sagging as the energy drained out of it.

"I'm not sure. I just talked to Dr. Zhrudsky on Monday. I think he's interested."

"Roger will make time for you. He'll tell you how much work it is being department chair and play hard-to-get. But he'll find you—and your work, of course—irresistible. He was hooked even before you asked. I heard about him and your two papers for his seminar."

"That was the strangest experience, Paul. He never said a word to me in class after stomping on me that one time. Not a hint that my comments made any impression on him. And then, six months later Michelle tells him about that paper and, when I go to his office about my committee, boom!" She clapped her hands. "The next thing I know, he's apologizing to me about it."

A motion behind Vanessa drew his attention away. Michelle was on her feet and quietly opening the door.

"So you have a sponsor and a committee," he said. "I won't get to share a little of your glory, but at least I don't have to worry about keeping up with you for a while."

When the door clicked shut, Vanessa turned to look. Then she glanced at the chair where Michelle had been sitting. With an embarrassed giggle, she looked back at him. "You sound like I'm your daughter, and you just married me off."

She turned to unzip the top of her backpack. "Listen." After digging through the contents, she pulled out two ten-by-thirteen-inch manila envelopes. "I've been paying some of the bills that have come in, but my account is empty and my credit card is maxed out."

She held up one of the envelopes. "These are the ones I've paid so far." Lifting the other, thicker one, she said, "These are due soon."

"I'm glad you brought up the subject." He searched the room with his eyes. "Hell, I don't have my checkbook here."

"I have it." She riffled through her backpack again and came up with a commonplace check wallet. "I wouldn't have thought of it except it was lying on the counter on top of the unpaid bills." She handed it to him, with an indulgent smile.

He patted his chest, then looked at her again. "Okay, and you have a pen, of course."

"Of course." She pulled one out of her shirt pocket.

He supported the checkbook on his knee and wrote awkwardly. "This ought to be enough to cover things till I get home." He tore out a blue check and handed it to her.

"Paul! Five thousand's ridiculous. There aren't that many bills."

"Pay off your credit cards, honey." He smirked. "And…"

"And what?"

"No, I won't say it."

"'Keep the change,' I suppose. That's insulting." The smile didn't fade from her lips.

"A good line, honey. But I wasn't going to be rude. Just thinking that you'll maybe have to take care of stuff like this for a week or two, even when I get out of here."

She held up the check. "Well, I'm keeping this only until you can write your own checks. But believe me, I'll keep track of the checks I write and you'll get the balance back."

"We're sounding like an old married couple." He laughed to himself. "Bickering about money."

"Paul, that brings up something—"

He held up both hands, palms open. "I know what you're thinking. You're far too busy to play nurse, right? Well, I wouldn't even consider asking you to."

"It's not that exactly. It's—"

"No, no. I have it all worked out. I met with a social-worker type here in the hospital, and I've already signed up for a complete package of home care—transportation, cooking, housecleaning, the whole schmear. And all you'll have to do is come home and keep me company every night."

"That's good, Paul. Thank you." Unruly muscles in her face gave away her anxiety. "But..."

"What now?"

"Paul I feel terrible about this. Not telling you, or giving you any—"

"Shit, Vanessa. You haven't already moved in with Stan, have you?"

She stared at him. ""What? Are you saying I slept with you—moved in with you—to get ahead in grad school?"

He lowered his eyes. "No, I'm not. I'm sorry I said that." He put his hands on the arms of the chair as though he was about to stand.

She pushed herself off the bed and took a step toward him with her hands raised to stop him. He let himself drop back into the chair.

She put her hands on her hips. "Why would I still want to have sex with a perverse advisor like you?"

"Perverse?"

"An advisor who wanted to hold me back, not help me move ahead more quickly?" She was turning the bright pink he'd seen dozens of times since they'd first clashed over her thesis.

"Vanessa, honey. I was doing everything I could think of to get you to focus on a project you could finish in a reasonable amount of time and get through a committee."

"I finished collecting data and wrote up my project more quickly than all but two other students in my class." She began pacing back and forth in the Lilliputian space at the opposite end of the room. "What did you ever do to facilitate my research except let me use your lab when you didn't need it for your research?"

"Vanessa, you know that isn't true." He realized he was speaking loudly enough the nurses could hear him. How did she manage to keep her voice level—cold and hard as a steel blade?

She turned at the opposite wall and stopped. "So why didn't you ever let me test you as a subject, Paul? And did you ever, just once, encourage me when I wrote proposals for you? No, God damn it. Besides carping about sticking to something manageable, you picked my sentences apart, sent me back for rewrites, went out of your way to quibble over flaws that anyone with brains could find freckling everything you've ever written."

"Calm down, Vanessa. I admit you're right. I—" He glanced at the door. Where were the fucking nurses now, when he needed real help—instead of lectures on anger management.

"No, *you* calm down and listen. Because I have an appetite for uncompromising criticism, I thought at first you were trying to help me. Good criticism makes my work stronger, brings out the best in me. But your nitpicking was aimed at holding me back."

"How can you say that? I barely changed a sentence in your—"

"I'm talking about raising methodological objections."

"You mean single-subject research?" He felt a dull pain in his chest. Wasn't this what his surgeon had warned him about? He'd said point blank, "It nearly killed you, buddy. That lioness will finish you off if you go back to living with her."

"That, and the theory paper I wrote to explain my results." She went back to pacing. "You wouldn't even admit you didn't understand it. Just dismissed it without reading it and told me I'd never get it through a committee."

"Ease up, Vanessa, for God's sake. I'm not supposed to—"

"Oh, shit! I knew this would happen." She reached for the doorknob.

"No, wait," he whimpered. "I'll be all right. Just forgive me. I'm a bastard, just like you've been saying—and worse."

She rushed across the room and knelt by his chair. She reached out and touched his cheek. "I just can't—"

"Nor can I." He pushed her gently away. "We can't go on like this. I want you to move out before I come back to the condo."

She stood again. "I already have."

For a moment he stared at her blankly. This was supposed to be his doing. "You have?"

"I found a place of my own. A one-room apartment in an old house on Twelfth near Forty-second. I can work and sleep when I want and not disturb anyone else."

"I'll pay the rent for you—"

"No, you won't. That's the whole point. My only responsibility will be not disturbing the other residents." She suddenly smiled. "You can't complain I'm too noisy, can you? Except when we make love—and my tiny twin bed is far too small for that."

"I'm actually glad you found a place, Vanessa." *Relieved* would have been more accurate. "I was going to suggest it, but I couldn't bring myself to say it to you."

"It was pure luck on my part. A Jordanian student had his visa cancelled and had to go home. I walked by just as the manager was putting up a sign."

"I'm glad." He sighed. "It was fortunate for both of us."

"I intend to keep checking on your condo. Taking in the mail. Paying the bills that come in—until you can."

"Thank you, honey. I really appreciate it." Whether it was fatigue creeping up on him or simply a growing resignation, he leaned back in the chair and looked at the ceiling for a moment. Might as well tell her now. Clearly it was inevitable. And she'd already taken care of the part he had dreaded telling her. "Please don't try to help me out any more. You have to move on. I'm very sorry I held you up so much already. Maybe Stan…"

"It wasn't your fault, Paul. I know how hard I am to live with, and—"

"Don't say that. I enjoyed—"

"No, you didn't. I can be a bitch sometimes. I'm better off with my own place." Suddenly her face lit up like the rising sun. "Besides, some of my habits are pretty weird."

"They aren't, but I understand what you're saying."

"Paul, I'm really sorry. But our relationship—"

"—wasn't working, you mean?"

She bit her lip. "Under different circumstances…"

"It wouldn't have lasted."

"No, I suppose not."

They both fell silent. For the first time he became aware of the foot traffic and muted voices in the hallway outside the closed door of his room.

She was the one who broke the spell. "I have to go, Paul." She hauled her backpack onto her shoulder and held out her hand to him.

He took it and pulled her toward him. "One last kiss."

She lowered her backpack gently to the floor and moved alongside his chair. Her lips lingered on his, tremulous and hesitant. Full of sadness and longing, he released her.

"Thanks for coming, Vanessa," he said as she stood up. "Good luck."

"Get well quickly, Paul." She slung her pack over her shoulder again and left without looking back.

Vanessa came to Stan's office on Thursday afternoon as they had agreed. When she walked in, he was so taken aback that no greeting came out of his mouth. She was wearing a tailored navy business suit with narrow lapels that converged just above her waist. The startling hot pink blouse underneath had a tiny mandarin collar. The skirt fit tightly and came an inch or two above her knees, showing off her long legs. But what left him gasping was her wavy, blue-black hair, which cascaded to her shoulders. He'd never seen her without a ponytail.

She paused for a moment not quite posing. Her pale skin grew pink as though seeking to match the hue of her blouse. She lowered her eyes and smiled apologetically. "Ready?"

His answer was slow in coming. "Yes. Yes, I am." *Oh, hell! I'm turning red. She'll guess what I was thinking.*

As he pulled his office door shut, he asked, "So, how did your meeting with Roger go?"

"Pretty well, I think, although he wanted to talk about the CPR thing first."

"That's no surprise."

"Then he asked about my second paper for his seminar."

"You gave him a copy?"

As they rounded the first corner, he saw two graduate students standing in the hall talking. Both had been in the seminar when Paul had had a heart attack. Brad Holmes was Vanessa's officemate, and Stan was pretty sure Vanessa had shared an apartment with Emily Gallagher and another grad student before she'd moved in with Paul. Both of them glanced up, did a double take, and scrutinized both Vanessa and Stan.

Vanessa and Emily said hello, but Brad said nothing. He was too preoccupied with Vanessa's blouse and skirt—the kind of male look that displays a little boy's longing for x-ray vision.

"How's it going, Brad?" Stan said.

Brad looked at him reluctantly. "Not too bad, Dr. Harte." His eyes flicked back to Vanessa and then met Stan's again, full of insolence. "How 'bout you?"

"Fine, thanks!" Stan could feel the two students' eyes following them as they walked on without stopping. *By god, I just made Brad Holmes jealous! I can't believe it!*

When they turned the next corner and approached the door to the laboratory complex, Stan's colleague, Hank Cavanaugh, reached the top of the stairway from the first floor. He glanced up and stopped, one foot still on the last step. He stared openly at Vanessa, who ducked her head and made for the door, pulling out her keys.

"Hi Hank," Stan said. "How's it going?"

Hank mumbled, "Fine, thanks." He smiled sheepishly when their eyes met. He started down the hallway past Stan, who noticed that as he went by, he swiveled his head to catch another glimpse of Vanessa as she pulled open the door for Stan.

All the labs were in the core of the building and accessible only by two locked doors in the hallway. Between these two doors was a narrow corridor lined with black acoustic tiles except where recessed lights shone dimly in the ceiling. Ranks of doors spaced at intervals along the walls opened into a total of eight suites of rooms.

Vanessa waved Stan past her, but he didn't know which suite it was.

"No," he said, "Go ahead." He was surprised to feel his hand resting lightly on the small of her back. The fabric of her suit coat felt warm under his fingertips. When he exerted a slight pressure to urge her forward, her body yielded gracefully to his touch. Their faces were within inches of each other, and in the instant she passed him, the fragrance of her shampoo filled his nostrils like she had waved a bouquet of apple blossoms through the air between them.

"Thanks," she said over her shoulder.

She turned and led the way down the twilit corridor. Behind them, the door to the outside hallway closed with a sigh and a muffled click. She stopped at the second door on the right and, after briefly fumbling with her ring of keys, opened it. It swung inward, and she snapped a light switch as she entered. A feeble light came on behind a partition in a far corner of the room.

Although it gradually grew a little brighter, most of its output was absorbed by the flat black paint on all the walls, the partition, and even the tabletops. Two office chairs were also black. The carpet was mottled dark gray. Paul's lab space was laid out the same way as Stan's, but was even smaller, with one room large enough for at most two participants and a second, tiny control room.

"Wait," she said softly when he started to close the door behind him. She squeezed past him leaving him enveloped in a breeze downwind of an apple orchard in bloom.

She hung a white sign on the door that read, "Experiment in Progress: Do Not Disturb." She reached behind him for a four-inch white box with a slot on the back for a doorknob. She slipped it over the knob with a metallic click. When she closed the door quietly, Stan knew that there was almost no chance someone would unintentionally open the door on the cramped room where he faced her in barely enough light to make out her features.

CHAPTER 8

When she turned toward him, he felt her hand lightly on his arm, urging him in the direction she was pointing with her other hand. "Have a seat, Stan, and I'll talk you through the procedure."

They pulled up two chairs to the table, and he stared at the screen, which was a uniform gray that glittered with constantly changing hints of color. When she clicked a mouse nearby, a faint cross in a darker shade of gray appeared in the center of the screen.

"Your task in this first part will be to focus on the cross until a face appears briefly." She was clearly reciting the instructions verbatim. "Then, a given name will appear below where the face was—like this." She clicked the mouse again.

For less than a second, a woman's face filled the region where the cross had been. It disappeared almost before he saw it, and the letters J-A-N-E appeared, below where the face had been.

"All you have to do is decide whether the name matches the face: yes or no. Could the person whose face you saw be named Jane?"

"Yes."

"Right. Now, hold one of these clickers in each hand." She held out two plastic remotes the size and shape of iPod nanos with a single button on them. "Go ahead, press the button on each one." They emitted a faint tick when the button was depressed. She glanced at the screen. "You're right handed, aren't you?"

"Yeah, how'd you know?"

"You pressed the right one first. So right will be yes, okay? And left, no."

"Yes... no..." He pressed them one after the other. "Yes... no..."

Her little trick gave him the spooky sensation that this procedure was going to reveal his thoughts to her, although he knew that was nonsense.

She pointed to the words on the screen. "These reminders will always appear along with the name to help you remember which side is which answer. Any questions so far?" She paused. "Okay, let's try a few."

After five times through the procedure, she stopped the display. "Good. From now on you may or may not see the face. Or you might think you saw one but not be sure. One will always be there, but we expect that sometimes you won't be able to see it. When you don't know or aren't sure whether a name matches the face, guess. Try these. Ready?"

A face flashed on the screen so briefly that he saw nothing but a smear of flesh color. He clicked yes with his right hand when MIKE appeared. He did five more. Twice he plainly saw a face, once, only a flash of color, and twice, nothing at all. He began to settle into the routine, following the slightest inclination when he guessed.

"You're doing well, Stan." She lightly patted his shoulder.

Her gesture profoundly distracted him. *Is the way to this woman's heart through her research? What? Where'd that come from?*

She let her hand rest gently on his shoulder. "One more thing. You have to respond before a deadline. This time, I want you to wait and not press a clicker. Just watch and see what happens."

He saw nothing after the cross except the letters B-I-L-L lower on the screen. He waited. In less than a second, the words, "Please respond more quickly," appeared in two lines at the top of the screen.

"Any questions?"

"No." He hesitated. "Can I practice a few more?"

"Certainly. Except that I'm going to start you out and let you settle in as I collect data."

A dialogue box appeared in the lower right corner of the screen. On the keyboard in front of her, she typed his name, the date, and several letters and numbers that meant nothing to him. Then the box disappeared, and she stood. "Ready?"

"Okay… if I have questions?"

"Just say something." She laid her hand on his shoulder lightly again. "I'll be right over here behind the partition." She moved a sliding door partly closed and then open again. Her eyes hesitated on his for a second in the semidarkness. Then she pushed the keyboard aside. "Okay, here we go." She clicked the mouse and disappeared behind the door.

He turned to the task, which quickly became a boring routine. Everything was mechanized: Messages on the screen at intervals reading, "Take a one-minute break." A minute later, a beep and on the screen, the words, "When ready to begin again, press both clickers at the same time." After about ten minutes, "Take two minutes this time—stand up and stretch if you'd like to." After two more minutes, a beep and another ready message. And finally, "First block complete. Call the experimenter for a longer break."

"Vanessa?"

"Great, Stan. I'm tracking your performance in here." She appeared silhouetted in the doorway. "Five minutes this time. You should get up and walk around. Let's get out of here and get a drink of water—or take a bathroom break, which is where I'm heading."

He hurried to the bathroom and stopped only briefly at the water fountain so he could be certain he would be waiting outside the door to the labs when she returned. The five minutes were nearly up when he saw her approaching. He quickly unlocked the door with his own key and held it open for her.

Just before he had his hand on the small of her back again, she paused in the open doorway. "Anxious to get back to work?" Her lapis eyes glittered when she grinned at him.

They were so close together he felt self-conscious about his hand and let it drop. "Challenging work." He returned her ironic smile. "Hope I don't fall asleep."

She replied with a soft laugh and led the way back down the dimly lit corridor. He took his place in front of the screen, and she stood on his right in front of the sliding door.

"We need to give your eyes a chance to adapt again. I found I could only work for a half hour at a time without a break to wake up. During the summer, I'd start first thing in the morning, use the first break to start a pot of coffee, the second for the first half a cup, the next to finish it, and the fourth for the inevitable trip to the bathroom." She giggled.

"God, you're disciplined! You did this even on clear, sunny days?"

"Eight to ten o'clock, six days a week. Then I'd go for a walk for forty-five minutes to an hour, and when I got back, put in another two hours. I also used the breaks to eat my lunch. Five minutes is just right for a sandwich, I discovered."

He shook his head in admiration. "That's real devotion to science. Makes me feel like a slacker."

She glanced at her watch. "Time to get to work!"

As he picked up the two clickers, she pointed to the screen and clicked the mouse. "Everything about the procedure will be exactly the same as before. We'll start with six warm-up trials, okay?"

He nodded. It took only a few times through the procedure, and he was back in the groove. By the next one-minute break, the boredom had returned. He began to appreciate how much commitment and discipline it had taken for her to spend six weeks at this.

"Break time!" Vanessa called out as the message appeared on the screen in front of him. She slid back the door. "Let's get out of here."

As she reached for the doorknob, he said, "Wait," and touched her forearm, feeling the vitality of her body again. "I didn't expect to see so many people around the building this late."

"Neither did I." She kept her hand on the doorknob so he didn't lose touch with her arm.

"Let's take the outside stairway and go out into the PAA plaza."

"Good plan." She led the way.

For some reason having to do with emergency evacuation, Guthrie Hall had brick-enclosed stairways that were completely isolated from the rest of the building. Each had an exit at ground level. They encountered three students they didn't know in the short time it took to reach the doors to the stairway. The stairwell was deserted. They didn't speak until they emerged into the gloom and fine mist of a November afternoon in Seattle.

"Oops!" She abruptly halted in from of him, and he raised his hands to keep from knocking her down. For a split second he held her by the shoulders—a moment he would relive dozens of times in the week to come.

"Sorry," he said, although he was elated.

"No, my fault. I thought it was raining." She held her hand out palm up beyond the overhang. "But it's just a little moist air."

"Let's hang out in the PAA lobby." He pointed across the plaza.

Inside the brightly lit entrance to the Physics and Astronomy Building, they found a corner out of the stream of students. Their eyes met.

"Stan, I can't tell you how much I appreciate this. In all the time Paul was my sponsor, he never offered to be a subject for me. He kept finding excuses to put it off."

"Really? I always insist my students test me before they start working with volunteers."

"I thought Paul did, too. But I discovered he only does it when it's part of his own research projects. Students are on their own, I guess." Her eyes drifted off to the passing foot traffic.

So what did all these little hints and gestures mean? Clearly, Stan had scored some points with her by agreeing to this session today. But should he get his hopes up? Women were so damn hard to read, and this one gave off more confusing signals than the Enigma Machine.

Suddenly, her eyes whipped back to his, catching him gazing at her perfectly balanced features. "Stan, is my outfit appropriate for tonight?" She swept her hands from her shoulders to her knees. "You didn't say where we were going, and…"

"It's perfect! 'Dressy casual,' as they say in the guide books." His eyes had followed her hand. When they came back to her shoulders and she flipped her hair back, he noticed the delicate silver butterflies with filigree wings fluttering from her earlobes.

"I'm not big on fashion, you know. My usual clothes are… might embarrass you in a nice restaurant. Actually, I can't afford stuff like this. Paul insisted on going shopping for clothes with me." Her face turned pink. "He picked it out and paid for most of it."

At close range he realized that her blush had brightened her lips to a rosy hue no lipstick could imitate. "You look very elegant, Vanessa. I'm enjoying Paul's largesse—and his taste, although I'd never tell him that."

"I maybe shouldn't have brought it up, but I'm actually kind of embarrassed dressing like this around the department."

"Don't be. You look great!"

"But you saw the way Brad looked at me—and Dr. Cavanaugh, too." She shook her head. "My reputation around here gives me enough problems. Dressing like this just encourages gossip. I even went home after class this afternoon and changed, so I wasn't wearing this all day."

He was at a loss to respond. He wanted to say *thank you for dressing up for me*, but he wasn't a hundred percent sure she had. Were her feelings about their friendship similar to his? *Don't be too hopeful*, he told himself. *Don't overinterpret what appears to be happening.*

Out of the corner of his eye he saw a trio of undergraduates talking to each other. They were standing so all three could stare at Vanessa. He felt himself standing more erect that usual. It was all too easy for him to imagine being in the shoes of these three guys—and Brad and Hank, for that matter—filled with envy. Even if nothing more happened between him and Vanessa, he'd treasure today's testosterone high.

She stole a glance at her watch. "Time to get back to work."

After another block of gender judgment trials, he was pleasantly surprised by a message on the screen that read, "Please stand by for instructions about the next block of trials."

When he glanced up, Vanessa had already turned on dim room lights and was standing in the doorway. "We're almost done. I'm testing you exactly the way I tested myself the first time. I was so eager to see if I was unconsciously learning anything that I ran name recall and name recognition tests on myself at the end of my first session."

She slid the keyboard she'd been using in front of him. "You can put the clickers on the table and use this. When you press the spacebar, you'll see a face on the screen. Please type a given name on the keyboard followed by the return key. Each of the faces you'll be seeing was paired earlier with the same name every time it was shown, although you might not have actually seen the face.

Therefore, you should type in a name you remember seeing earlier, guessing when you think you don't know the right name."

She grinned when he glanced up at her. "Just go ahead and type the first name you remember that comes into your head. This phase of the experiment is also a test of how many of the names you've learned so far. Any questions?"

"No, I guess not. I remember this test from your reports. There's a recognition test coming, right?"

"Yes. We'll go through the faces again in a different order, show you two names and have you pick out the one you think goes with the face."

"Okay. Let's go."

The recall trials were frustrating. He was surprised how many names he seemed to remember, but mostly he was guessing about which names went with which faces. The recognition trials were less discouraging because one of the two names often "felt" like it belonged with the face more than the other one.

At the end of the recognition trials, Vanessa turned up the lights and opened the sliding door. "Come in here and take a look at how you did." She had a big smile on her face.

At the far end of the narrow control room, there was a deep shelf at desk height. It was littered with papers. Large binders in blue, green and red were lined up against the wall. A book lay open under a goose-necked lamp. In the corner was a wide-screen monitor displaying two graphs side by side.

"Your results and mine." She pointed first to the right side and then the left. "The ordinate is a *d*-prime that measures priming. Think of it as the degree to which the face that precedes a name facilitates the gender judgment. When the face matches the gender of the name, it makes the decision easier—*d*-prime goes up. When it doesn't, it makes the decision harder, and *d*-prime goes down."

"And the *x*-axis?"

"Rate of presentation. The four lines in each graph are four sample densities."

In spite of the fact that hers had swarms of dots like spiral nebulae viewed side on and his only a sprinkling of dots, the patterns were the same. He guessed that the axes of the plots had been derived using her theory, but he was too intimidated to ask more. Every time her theory came up, he realized his math background was more inadequate than he'd thought it was.

"They're remarkably similar, aren't they?" he observed.

She tapped an arrow key. "Here's a table of our learning data at the end of the first session. You recalled fewer names than I did." She looked at him solicitously. "Of course, I originally selected both the faces and names. You'd expect me to do better. As for learning the pairings—which name goes with which face—you recalled only three percent correctly to my five. Close, and not very impressive for either of us."

"I felt I was just guessing."

"Me too, at this stage. But recognition went better, didn't it?"

"Still not as good as yours," he said, looking at another table on the screen.

"True. But mine are based on six weeks of data, remember. Yours are for just one session."

He glanced at his watch. "We'd better be on our way. They'll probably hold our table for half an hour on a Thursday night. But let's not press our luck."

He'd decided to take her to Nell's, a three-star restaurant on Green Lake. Was he being overly optimistic about the evening when he chose a place in the neighborhood where he lived? No, he told himself. It was because he went there just often enough that the staff recognized him and knew where he liked to sit. When he made a reservation, they would see that he got one of his two favorite tables. And it was the kind of place he'd take his daughter for a special occasion.

In the car, Vanessa seemed more relaxed than usual. She began telling Stan how the data from her hidden photo procedure were central to her theory of the mind-brain continuum. By varying how the photos were presented and measuring when people were aware of them, she could locate where the mental event of seeing a face was located on one dimension of the mind. This axis unified the physical world of the brain with the mental world of the mind.

She called it the psi-axis, using Greek letters for mental variables, and compared it to the property of temperature in the physical domain. It was, she said, a measure of life itself, stretching from the absolute zero of inanimate material through the entire evolutionary scale to human consciousness.

He'd been preoccupied with negotiating the traffic and only half listening. But when she began this particular flight of fancy, he understood enough to ask an intelligent question. "So even bacteria have minds? Even viruses?"

"Yes, but only to a tiny degree. The point is, using my consciousness axis we'll ultimately be able to assign a number—a very small number, in this case—to the consciousness of a virus."

"We'll be able to say we're a million times smarter than viruses?"

"Precisely. I'm guessing, though, that the ratio will be many orders of magnitude bigger—a hundred trillion, or more."

"Pretty audacious for a mere theory of the mind, I'd say!" He stole a glance at her.

"A theory of the mind-*brain* continuum, Stan."

When he had pulled into a parking place and shut off the engine, he turned to her. "I'd never realized the sweep of your theory—its implications for biology. I mean, it encompasses the evolution of thinking and pathologies of thought and emotion like schizophrenia. The causal explanations of them, and a lot of other big questions, are in your theory, just waiting to be worked out. Have you… thought about anything like… any of this?"

Her sphinx-like expression struck him as indulgent. "You think I don't dream of stuff like that? A theory like mine would change the way people think about themselves and others—and science, as well. Imagine what it would be like to look at an online display of what's happening in a patient's brain and know what she was thinking or feeling."

"Then you have—?"

"But Marie Curie wasn't trying to find a treatment for cancer, and Einstein certainly wasn't looking for a bigger, more destructive bomb."

"That's true, but—"

"Look, I don't know where my ideas are going to take me. But I've always gotten my kicks out of mastering the first principles of a science, the ones that explain how nature works. Someone else can figure out how to solve the world's problems."

He decided he had nothing to add. She hadn't left much room for disagreement. "I don't know about you, but I'm starving." He slapped his hands on the steering wheel.

"Me too. I was wondering when we'd get around to that."

The big open room of the restaurant wasn't full, but there were enough occupied tables so the noise level made it difficult to eavesdrop. Stan had her sit on the side of the booth where she could look down on the activity in the kitchen. She immediately immersed herself in the menu, while he studied the wine list.

After he'd ordered two glasses of prosseco, she peered at him over the top of her menu. "I can't decide between venison and pheasant. Any suggestions?"

"Pick one. I'll order the other one. You can try mine, and we can switch if you change your mind."

"You're far too accommodating!"

"I've had both, but everything here is excellent."

"Pheasant, then."

"I have the perfect wine for both. How about the Cloudline pinot noir from Oregon?"

Her face lit up in smile that left him giddy. "How did you know pinot noir is my favorite red?"

So far the evening appeared to be proceeding the way he'd hoped. She seemed still more relaxed than in the car, even flirty—a good sign. He was not without misgivings about what he was doing. She was the first graduate student he'd seriously considered in romantic terms. Such relationships are always complicated ethically. But how many of his colleagues had he watched do the same thing? And in his case, there was no marriage to break up. Earlier he'd envied Paul Kovick getting her into his bed. Had Paul's misfortune… dropped her into his, now? His head spun at the thought.

And how was Paul going to feel if things continued the way they seemed to be going? Paul was his friend. They were scientific allies in the usual internecine warfare among the subspecialties within the department. More than likely Paul would view Stan's stepping in to sponsor Vanessa as an encroachment on his professional territory. And what if he also took Paul's place…? Yet he had to wonder how Paul managed to keep up with her intellectually. Stan considered himself better equipped than Paul, but he had to admit that she could be hard on his ego at times. Would she be as bad for his health as she apparently was for Paul's?.

CHAPTER 9

After a ceremonial clink of their tulips of bubbly, she tilted her head and looked at him aslant. "So, what do you think, Stan? Did being a subject and seeing how closely your results match mine convince you?"

She was back on her research again. And she was trying to pull him that way by flirting with him! It wasn't about her theory, though, so he knew he'd be able to hold up his half of the discussion. That encouraged him a little.

"You know," he said, shaking his head, "It still has an aura of sorcery. I'd like to believe it. But this little voice in my head keeps whispering that the whole phenomenon is counterintuitive. Like space being curved, or time slowing down when you approach the speed of light."

She sighed. "I need a perihelion shift to predict."

"What?"

"Sorry. The general theory of relativity predicts that the orbit of Mercury, which is elliptical, slowly precesses—that is, rotates—around the sun. Completely counterintuitive in Newtonian physics, but easily derived from gravitational field equations."

"I thought you were a math major as an undergraduate."

"That's a long story."

"We have time."

He'd nudged her back onto something personal. And if he could keep guiding the conversation in that direction, he might eventually find out why she'd posed for *Playboy*.

"Okay." She rested her elbows on the table and her chin on her folded hands. "I come from a long line of astronomers and mathematicians. My great grandfather was an astrophysicist, my grandpa and his brother were astronomers, and my mom's a mathematician."

"Wow, what a lineage!"

"Yeah. Well, I'm the black sheep. An aspiring cognitive neuroscientist, or something like that."

"What led you astray?"

"A psychology course. Taught by Joel Greene. A fantastic course that began with the history of the mind in philosophy and ended up with a synthesis of psychology and neurology. I began dreaming then of a theory that would formalize that synthesis."

"A formal mathematical theory? Like that paper you gave me?"

"Exactly. That's when I changed course." Her eyes were no longer on him, but focused on some distant realm. "I took stock of the courses I'd taken up to then—the end of my sophomore year—and decided I was further along in math than in physics and astronomy. So it was the logical major for me.

"I'd been taking upper level math courses since I started college. My mom thought I was a genius, so after I was accepted at WSU, she took me to Pullman and saw to it that I got credit by examination for most of the courses in the first two years of the math major. I'd learned most of it from her and my uncle."

She paused to taste the octopus appetizer they had decided to split. After another bite, she said, "I like it." She gave him a look that made his whole body tingle.

"I'm glad you're enjoying it." He finished off his prosseco. "So you added a major in psychology?"

"No, it became my second minor. But I'm only now getting a handle on the brain. I'm making huge gains in Dr. Forrester's class. I'm reviewing every study I can find with quantitative data and trying to fit it into my theory. I'll email you a copy when I'm done."

There was a pleasant interlude between the octopus and their wild game, during which he ordered the bottle of pinot noir. He'd wondered if she'd shy away from small talk, but she seemed to enjoy answering his conversational gambits: How did she like the weather west of the Cascades? She hated it. Living in a big city? Apparently, she was indifferent.

Her preferences in music? Rarified, as he guessed they would be. She liked Beethoven, especially his late string quartets and last six piano sonatas. She gave him a short lecture on another one of his late compositions, the Diabelli Variations, which he'd never heard of.

"I'll play them for you sometime," she said. "On a CD player, of course. I don't play the piano… I wish I did."

So she didn't spend all her time thinking about her theory and research. Had he penetrated her armor? He certainly hoped so. But he was beginning to wonder what real intimacy with her would be like. She was so different from other younger women he'd slept with—so much more her own person, leaving aside her intelligence and knowledge. She was also very different from Heidi, his ex, who was a smart and dedicated academic but had nothing like Vanessa's intensity.

He couldn't help imagining what Vanessa was like in bed. Did she ever stop thinking about her research long enough to make love? He could almost hear her explaining the hardness of his erection in topological terms: "It's the intersection of two surfaces, your penis and my vagina."

When the main courses arrived, Vanessa began a spontaneous game in which each of them tried to outdo the other in describing the flavors of their food as they passed their plates back and forth across the table. He was surprised by how much wine she drank and the playful mood it seemed to induce in her.

"The sauce," he said of the venison, "tastes of black pepper with a suggestion of red currants."

They exchanged plates.

She cut a tiny morsel of meat and stirred it in the sauce while looking up at him playfully. Then she turned her head and touched the tidbit to her tongue so that he had a fleeting image so suggestive he felt his penis twitch.

She chewed slowly, closing her eyes in concentration, before swallowing it. "Now, there's a little heat to be sure, but also the distinctive taste of juniper berries with notes of alpine honeysuckle." When he started to challenge her on the existence of such a plant, she held up her hand as though she still held the gustatory experience in her memory. She continued in an artificial, high-pitched voice, "And, just an innuendo of oil-cured Adriatic olives." She giggled.

It made him want to hug her like a small girl. "I wouldn't even consider trying to match that flowery, outrageous description." He realized they hadn't talked about her research or theory for the last half hour. It was the perfect moment to introduce a new topic. Yet he hesitated. Since he'd first found out that Vanessa Marie, former *Playboy* Coed of the Month, was a student in the graduate program, he'd wondered why she posed and how she felt when she took off her clothes for photos that would appear on the World Wide Web. *The evening is going so well. Will I ruin it, if I ask her?*

She gave him a coquettish smile. "What? Are you off in some fantasy world?"

He felt trapped—his face had given him away. He had no idea how transparent he was to her. "Okay," he sighed. "I have another question for you."

"I'll try to answer it."

"It's a little more personal. Don't answer if—"

"No, it's fine, Stan." Her smile reminded him of the way adults smile at small children's questions. "Go ahead."

"Do you have Hispanic forebears?"

She gave him a puzzled frown. "Yes… but why…?" Her face suddenly lit up with a smile. "Oh, I know what you're—"

"I saw you chatting with Maria—in Spanish, and I wondered how—"

"I thought you were going to ask about my freaky combination of skin, eye, and hair color."

"I'd like to know about that, too."

"Okay. I'm this outlandish mixture of Finnish and Irish, with a great-grandfather from Spain and a grandmother from Mexico. My Grandma Trippett told me I was a throwback to her mother, a Finn with the same eyes, skin and hair. But I learned Spanish from Maria when I was a kid."

"From Maria?"

"Uncanny, isn't it? Orion Station hired lots of Latinos from Yakima to help with everything from construction to childcare. Like many of the other Latinas, Maria brought along her daughter, Doncia, every day and took care of both of us. I learned Spanish from them both and helped them improve their English, more or less. All the Orion kids played with the Latino kids." She grinned and giggled like she had in the hall. "I can also speak Spanglish. And know how to swear in Spanish, too."

"But how did Maria—?"

"She moved to Seattle a couple years ago—to be close to Doncia, who's a nurse at Swedish Hospital, now."

"God, I wish I'd had an opportunity like yours. I hated every required credit hour of French I took and flunked my French language exam for the PhD—twice." As he said it, he realized he'd never admitted that to any of his present colleagues.

"I didn't know how lucky I was until I got to Wazzu and tested out of the language requirement. I took Spanish literature courses instead of English. It was wonderful. I'd never read any of the great Latin American authors—like Neruda and García Márquez."

He shook his head. "If all the hippies had started communes like your Orion Station, the sixties would have transformed the country."

She squinted over his shoulder as though she was recalling faint images from her childhood. "They were uncommon people, my grandparents—stargazers out to change the world beginning with their own square mile of unpromising sagebrush and a vision of a citizenry of scientists. What dreamers they were."

Was it time to cast his dice? Would it shatter her reverie? He knew so little of her moods, not to mention her feelings about modeling. It could be a part of her life she preferred to avoid—even hide.

"You really wanted to ask about something else, didn't you?"

"Well, yes." How did she read his thoughts so acutely? Now, he was cornered—left with no choice but to plunge in. "You don't have to answer."

"Let me guess. Why'd I pose for *Playboy*? How'd I start?"

He felt myself flush. "Yes. How'd you know?"

"Every man asks, sooner or later."

"Well, I'm not insisting on an answer."

"For the money."

He looked surprised.

She nodded. "It was that simple. I had a four-year National Merit Scholarship, but it didn't pay for everything. I was sick of living in the dorm. I wanted an apartment off campus, and having one to myself was expensive—not least because it meant I also needed a car."

She looked down. "My family—the Orion Station community, really—was giving me a spending-money allowance, but I felt that changing my focus to psychology was a betrayal of sorts. Part-time jobs in Pullman didn't pay much."

She broke off when the waiter appeared with dessert menus. She refused even to accept one. "I'm so full I don't want to look."

"How about some coffee?" Stan asked her.

"Yes, by all means," she said enthusiastically.

After the waiter left, he considered whether to press for the additional details he wanted. She was staring into the ruby red wine remaining in her glass.

"I'd like to hear more…"

She looked up at him without shifting her head. "There's not much more to tell."

"If you're okay with telling me, I'd really enjoy hearing exactly what happened."

"All right." She looked off into the distance again. "I saw an ad for a *Playboy* casting call: 'Try out for *Playboy*'s "Girls of the Pac-10" feature.' I'd posed nude before…" Her eyes flicked to his face, then darted away self-consciously. "Art classes. But they didn't pay very much either. I assumed, correctly as it turned out, that *Playboy* models did better. I went, took off my clothes and they liked what they saw."

The line about 'art classes' didn't ring true. He was certain he saw it in her eyes. Or, had she realized after she said it that he might be bothered by the image of her standing naked in the center of a group of undergraduate men gawking at her voluptuous body that would soon appear on *Playboy*'s website? In fact, he did envy their leisurely, brazen inspection of her body, but that was *his* problem. Did she sense his resentment?

He almost asked, but he wasn't sure how she'd react to such a probing question. "I'm not surprised they were turned on. You were beautiful—you still are."

She grimaced. "My body just happens to fit the current cultural norm for beauty—or did then. You might not think so now, Stan."

"I'm sure—"

"No, don't compliment me for something I have nothing to do with. The *Playboy* photographers made my body look erotic. My photos sexually aroused you, Stan. End of story." She sighed when he blushed. "You're giving yourself away, you know?"

He chortled. "Yeah, but you're so comfortable about it, I don't really feel embarrassed."

"I've never felt uncomfortable about posing naked." She seemed to catch herself. "The *Playboy* photographers and staff were very professional. They said I had potential and offered to pay me for a shoot in Pullman. I sized up the deal: It was a one-time proposition, but I figured out the hourly pay was better than anything else in town.

"They ran photos from the first shoot on *Playboy*'s website, where I appeared as a Coed of the Week. Then I was voted Coed of the Month, and those five sessions pretty much paid for the car and apartment for two years. Six months later, when I'd begun seriously trying to save money for grad school, they offered me the Special Editions Extreme gig. It gave me a cushion in the bank that left me with enough to get through the first few months here."

The waiter interrupted her again with their coffee. After a microscopic sip, she grinned. "Even the coffee's good. Thank you, Stan. This has been a wonderful dinner."

"I agree." The coffee was clearly too hot to drink. He glanced around and realized that the customers had thinned out. Still, the conversations of the remaining ones protected their intimacy.

"I hope you won't be offended." He felt himself turning red again. "I watched your modeling 'career' develop, as it were."

"That's fine with me, Stan."

"I've had a subscription to *Playboy* since before you were born probably. I hate to admit it." His laugh was self-conscious but she joined in. "I was an early adopter of the *Playboy* Cyber Club."

"You saw my very first appearance, then?"

"I'm pretty sure I voted for you, too. I can see why they kept asking you to pose."

"I sometimes wish now I hadn't. So many college girls model nude. I wonder if it haunts them the way it does me. Apparently, enough people disapprove to make it a real pain."

"It's none of their business," he said emphatically. "They don't have to look."

"Unless… you've heard about the screensavers, haven't you?"

"Brad Holmes is a jerk and a troublemaker. And from what I've heard, he's not that great a student, either."

"I feel sorry for him. He's smart enough. But his interests are so limited and shallow."

The waiter discreetly slipped the bill onto the table near his elbow, but he ignored it.

"Stan, I have a question for you now." She cradled her chin in her hands. Her eyes twinkled roguishly. "You've given me an idea for a design that I think will persuade you my findings can't be due to anything except awareness. It's very different from what I ran on myself and depends on an element of surprise. It would require two more sessions like the one this afternoon. Would you consider it?"

He couldn't keep her mind off her research for long! Clearly, it was an obsession with her. But there could be no doubt. She loved what she was doing as deeply as anything in her life.

"Will it address my suspicions that it's—"

"An artifact? No. I don't know whether it will work or not. That's the beauty of it. Like Einstein's prediction that stars observed close to the sun during a solar eclipse will be displaced because their light will be bent around the sun by its gravitational field."

He ignored her allusion to the history of physics. "However, it's still a single-subject experiment..."

"Yes, but I desperately want to get you on my side. I think this procedure, if it works the way I think it should—the way my theory says it should, will allay any remaining doubts you have."

He pushed away his uneasy feelings about where his consent might lead. "Okay."

After dinner, he dropped her off at an apartment in the U District. He decided not to ask why she wasn't living in Paul's condo in Wallingford. However, it gave him a depraved satisfaction knowing that she wasn't.

Jim Forrester had a problem—what grade to give Vanessa Trippett for his Neurosciences I seminar. Why did he hesitate to assign her an A? The questions she asked in class showed she knew the material better than the other students in the course, better even than his own advanced students in some cases.

She had chosen to make her hour-long presentation on neuroimaging research with the human face as a stimulus. It was so clear and thorough he could only conclude—reluctantly—that her command of this tangle of confusing experiments and explanations was better than his own. So, why not set aside this paper she'd just handed in? Because he couldn't understand it?

He didn't like the obvious implications of his answer. Because it seemed like a deliberate effort to humiliate him, disparage his expertise and his course? He couldn't find clear evidence of that. And surely not because she'd handed it in ten days before the deadline?

He couldn't give her less than an A just because he suspected she was a rebel who was disguising her contempt for what he and others in his field were doing. She seemed to have arrived in the department from an unmapped academic Shangri-la and was pursuing her own inscrutable agenda with questions nobody had thought to ask, not even the authors of the papers he had assigned to the class.

Her questions gnawed at internal inconsistencies in the studies and exposed the lack of direction in the field. He had come to dread her raised hand and the disarming innocence of her voice when she began, "I don't understand..." It was like she was turning on a meat-grinder. "I don't know," no matter how he phrased it, made him look incompetent, while the disappointment written on her face was like a fist in his gut. And now this paper. Wasn't it her parting kick in the balls?

He spent most of his time in his laboratories in the medical center, so his few hours a week in the psychology department were devoted exclusively to his teaching duties there. His office was a Spartan place—a few books and papers lying flat on the bookshelves, sometimes a stack of student papers, three straight-backed chairs plus a swivel chair at his desk, a monitor on its uncluttered surface often not even turned on. The walls were covered with enlarged illustrations from a textbook on brain anatomy.

He was grading exams from his undergraduate course in the psychology department when he heard her unlocking her office door across the hall from his. "Vanessa?" He tried to keep the frustration he felt when he thought of her out of his voice.

She turned. "Yes, Dr. Forrester?"

"I'm having a great deal of difficulty understanding your paper. Do you have a minute?"

"Yes, of course." She pulled the door to her office closed again and walked into his.

"Close the door, please."

She gave him a baffled look but turned around and carefully shut it, holding it tightly closed while releasing the doorknob so it didn't click. She faced him again across his desk still wearing a Chinese blue raincoat and her backpack on her back. She brought a faint smell of vanilla into his office.

He'd never understood why men found her so beautiful—voluptuous, yes. But that was because they'd seen her naked body. Her face had always struck him as bland. It would seem very ordinary, he thought, if it weren't for the exotic combination of pale skin, jet-black hair and Blu-ray laser eyes—especially the eyes. At close range they looked positively menacing.

With a massive mental heave, he got his thoughts back on track. "You'll be receiving an incomplete in my neuroscience course, Vanessa. I can't make head nor tail of your term paper."

"But—" Any other student would have looked shocked—even horrified. Her face expressed only puzzled curiosity.

He snatched up her paper, which he'd left on his worktable, folded open in anticipation of this meeting. He held it up and swatted it with the back of his hand. "You begin with five pages of equations and derivations, totally irrelevant as far as I can see."

"But that's my theory!" Suddenly her face was animated. "You said you wanted an *integrated* review. Theories are the way scientific knowledge is organized and integrated."

"Yeah? Did anybody ever tell you that science is also a collective activity? You're supposed to communicate your ideas to other scientists." He thumped his chest. "Well, here's one you didn't communicate with."

"Well, okay." Her shoulders slumped, the first sign of real emotion. "But a big part of the assignment was a literature review. Didn't I—?"

"Thirty-five pages of it. Divided into sections introduced by quantitative predictions—derived, so you *claim*, from your theory. But what you critique in every single paper you cite is the same. The psychological observations are too vague and intuitive, and there's no systematic motivation for tying them to activity in the brain."

"I'm baffled, Dr. Forrester." Blue sparks ignited her eyes. "Didn't you understand that's why my theory is so important? Neuroscience is full of exquisitely precise measurements of activity in the brain paired with blurry, ill-defined assessments of what's going on in the mind. We're never going to get anywhere until we bring measurements of brain activity together with exact, rigorous measurements of mental activity."

"Vanessa, you're too smart—you know too much—to take seriously a fairytale world like you just described. The experiments you propose to remedy the situation would require more money to run than a supercollider project."

"Not if they were guided by a theory like I'm trying to develop."

He carelessly tossed her paper on his desk. "So we're back to this theory of yours that requires Einstein to decode?"

"Yes! Except it isn't that difficult to grasp. Anyone who's had a course in differential geometry can—"

"Well, I don't have a PhD in math—or a master's, for that matter."

"I took the course as a sophomore."

He hit his desk with both fists. "For God's sake, Vanessa. Just because you're a math prodigy, you can't hold the rest of us to your standards."

"But we'll never make any progress in cognitive neuroscience, Dr. Forrester, if we don't—"

"Stop!" He threw up his hands as though he were blocking her from advancing on him physically. "Stop right there, okay?"

"Why?" She could carry on an argument with a kind of frigid self-possession that drove him straight up the nearest wall.

"I refuse to argue with you anymore." He plucked her paper from his desk and crushed it in his brawny fist. "You cannot expect me or anyone else in the field to evaluate this paper." He shook the mangled paper at her. "Why shouldn't I suspect this is a giant smokescreen for a completely naïve and superficial review of the brain imaging literature on faces?"

She gasped. "But I wouldn't—"

"How do I know you wouldn't?" At last he had gotten a rise of her. He waved his hand back and forth while shaking his head. "Enough. I know that's a devastating charge to make against a grad student. But by God, you asked for it. All quarter, you've taken advantage of everyone else in the class—including me. You've torn people's presentations apart, asking for precision that's not possible and analyses using statistics no one understands. And now this." He dropped the battered paper onto his desk again. "You've played unfair with me all quarter, so I'm going to turn the tables on you."

Her lower lip trembled. "So you're flunking me?"

"No, I'm going to find out whether all this math of yours is legit or just another one of your ploys to make someone look bad. I'm throwing you to the lions." He smiled unabashedly. "I've sent copies of your paper to three friends of mine, referees as it were. People who are specialists. And I've invited them to tear the hell out of your paper."

She straightened up. "I see," she said evenly.

"And just to be sure they treat you fairly?" He paused until she met his eyes. "I took your name off of it and told them it was a manuscript a colleague had asked me to comment on. One of these 'external reviewers' is a mathematician, another is a neurobiologist in the med school, and the third is a physicist, who, by the way, I asked to tell me whether your references to theories in physics are on the up-and-up."

She scowled. "Good! I hope you've chosen referees who are competent to review what I've done, since you claim not to be." She clenched her fists. "Although I think you're more qualified than you claim."

"And flattery will get you nowhere with me." *What a bitch she could be when she was angry!* "This may take some time, which is why I might have to give you an Incomplete." He smirked. "But I'll let you know when I've talked to all three of them. Under the circumstances and given the length and apparent complexity of your paper, I gave them at least a month."

"Okay." She straightened up again. "Did you ask them to put their evaluations in writing?"

And she could snarl like a cornered cougar when she was threatened. "You really are an obstreperous brat, aren't you?" He chuckled.

She held her breath and clenched her fists so tightly blotches of pink appeared on them.

"No," he continued, "I didn't say anything about writing something down. I told them to call me as soon as they decided whether I should take your paper seriously."

"Fine!" she said. "Is that all?"

"Yep! Have a nice day!"

He watched her unlock the door opposite his. There was a thud that sounded like she had dropped her books on her desk. A minute later she emerged without her raincoat, her pack over one shoulder. Her vanilla fragrance lingered in his office.

He was caught between laughing at her and throwing something himself. He had no satisfaction in knowing that he'd just made her as frustrated as he'd been the past ten weeks. Why did he always let her tie him in knots?

He'd been annoyed a year ago when he heard through the grapevine that she was interested in neuroimaging. It was his area, and he envied that lightweight Kovick when rumors of her stellar academic performance reached him.

When she signed up for his seminar, he thought at first about trying to lure her away from Kovick, especially when she asked for brain imaging research with faces as the topic of her class presentation. That was close to his own research, making her an especially good fit as his advisee. But after a week or two of her questions, he'd started to have doubts. Then Kovick keeled over, and he had his chance. When he hesitated to step forward, Michelle and Stan snatched her away. He was left with might-have-beens he wasn't sure he wanted anyway.

CHAPTER 10

For Stan's second session, he and Vanessa had agreed that he would meet her in her office after his last appointment. Both she and Brad Holmes were bent over their desks when he halted in the doorway for a moment.

"Vanessa? I'm ready to go to work."

"Oh, hi there, Stan," she said. "Give me a minute to finish up here."

He glanced around the room. Brad was eyeing him with insolent curiosity.

"Hello, Brad," Stan said to him. "How's it going?"

"So-so. End of the quarter runs, you know."

"Tell me about it."

"Ready!" Vanessa zipped up her backpack and slung it over one shoulder.

When the door clicked behind them on the stairway, he said, "Any more problems with Brad?"

"None of any importance. We exchange hellos. That's about it."

"He treats me with the same lukewarm courtesy."

She laughed. "He gets his strokes from his grad student friends. I gather they think he's a genius." She opened the door before he could reach for it. "He leaves me alone, though."

He grabbed the second door and held it for her. "Good."

Once they were alone in the lab, he said, "I hear you had a little run-in with our Viking warrior."

"What?" She broke into a broad smile. "Dr. Forrester, you mean?"

"Seems you've added him to your enemies list."

"He was already on it. Stan, I can't help myself. I see deficiencies in research reports, and they make me want to scream. How does anyone expect to understand the mind if we don't measure quantitative relationships?"

"Nobody can convince him to cool it," he said. "He treats us all like that at times, so don't feel like he singled you out."

"He was right, you know. I did devote too much space to mathematical exposition. And I knew perfectly well he wouldn't understand it. Why did I think he'd be impressed?" She turned her back on him and started the computer.

"Jim has a thing about people who challenge his authority," he said to her back. "He thought you were trying to hit him below the belt. Not a good strategy with any man, especially in his case."

"He accused me of playing dirty in my arguments. And he was right about that. But I was hoping he'd give me some feedback on my literature review. I desperately need that right now." She turned around again. "And you know what, Stan? I'm very grateful he's getting other people to read the paper for him. I couldn't get that kind of consulting on my own."

"That's an admirable way for you to see it. A bunch of us tried to convince him, however, that's it's not fair for him to put your grade at stake. He's taking advantage of you as a student."

She suddenly looked at her watch. "Oh! We're five minutes late. Sorry."

"It's okay. I don't have any commitments." And besides, the time he was spending with Vanessa recently had become the focal point of his life.

During the long break between sessions at the computer, they decided to take their walk outdoors since it was the first sunny day in two weeks. They used the nearly deserted outer stairway. Once out of the building, they turned right and started across the plaza between Guthrie and the Physics and Astronomy Building. He asked her what she'd done over the weekend.

"I made a lot of progress on my theory."

"Great! But I meant, what did you do for fun? For relaxation?"

"I didn't need to relax. I solved the problem of how to tie mental space to physical space without postulating three extra dimensions." She stopped and faced him excitedly. "And the key had been right under my nose for weeks. One dimension—another integrating dimension—to unify the three physical dimensions with a corresponding subjective three-space."

He shook his head. Her theoretical flights of fancy always left him mired in a painful awareness of his ignorance and a palpable sense of his inadequacy.

She began walking again, unconscious of her increasing tempo. "The answer's so simple. There has to be an axis from self to other, ego to alter, near to far, here to there. But it's both a mental *and* a physical axis. At one end there's the 'me' only I know about—no one else can ever experience it; at the other end is my knowledge of the far reaches of the universe and the unknown and unknowable." She was no longer talking to him. She was the lone pilot of an abstract vessel only she knew how to steer through a world no one had ever visited.

"In the physical world, the body, which the brain inhabits, is a point at the origin of the mental space that is identical to the four-dimensional manifold of the physical world. The body is frequently moving through time and physical space, equipped with senses to peer into the depths of the cosmos, listen to the heartbeat of unseen events, sniff the passing molecules from faraway—"

"Vanessa! Stop!"

She almost fell over trying to halt her headlong rush.

"You've lost your passenger. You dumped me in the ocean without a life raft."

"Where? When did I lose you?"

"Here? There?" He held up his hands, palms upward. "Who knows?"

"Okay, let me back up—"

"Enough. You've answered my question."

She gave him a blank stare. "What question?"

"What you did this weekend. You obviously were off in hyperspace on a journey more exciting than the best science fiction novel ever written. You—"

"It's not fiction, Stan."

"Better than the voyage of the *Beagle*, better than being on *Apollo 11*, better than—"

"Stan, it was better than being in Beethoven's head while he was writing the Arietta of his last piano sonata. Imagining that was the inspiration for my proximity dimension."

"How did…?"

"On Friday night, I started hearing the theme in my head. It's a simple, haunting melody I've probably heard a hundred times. But when I played my CD, I heard it differently. I realized it was a love song… because for the first time I was hearing it inside Beethoven's head.

"In the first variation, I slipped into his thoughts and memories… I felt his fingers on the keys—they were my fingers, too. In the second, he and I experienced the world in a universal way all human beings do. In the third, we inhabited the animals and plants and the earth itself. And in the fourth variation, we soared through the galaxies to the very limits of space, and we made love with the whole universe.

"I listened again and again until I finally understood that mental and physical space are one—a single coordinate system unified by an axis of proximity, which flows like time through both the brain and the mind."

"God, Vanessa, you make your theory sound better than sex."

The look that came over her face would have been inconceivable if Stan hadn't seen her *Playboy* photos. "No Stan… definitely not better than sex." She set off for the door leaving him gaping. Then she stopped, and eyed him lasciviously over her shoulder. "But it lasts a lot longer."

Fifteen minutes after that stupid thing with his screensaver, Brad Holmes knew he'd fucked up—completely fucked up. At first he just wanted to smash something. The whore had made him and Shawn look like sexist scuzzballs and then fooled that asshole Forrester into thinking she was the fucking victim. *Shit!* Then he discovered the slut had password-protected the folder on his hard drive where he had all her nude photos he'd downloaded from the Web. That was the last fucking straw!

Every time he thought of her—and it was practically the rest of the day—he wanted to slap her face. He couldn't get the goddamn image to fucking go away.

By that evening, however, his anger had cooled. As he was lying in bed waiting to go to sleep, he remembered how he'd dissed her to his friends when they were undergraduates. He also recalled that time she'd helped him with statistics. She wasn't really such a bitch after all. He'd heard she'd helped a lot of other people, too. And he and Shawn really had treated her like dirt.

I mean, maybe she had some reason for posing for those damn photos. Maybe the fucking Playboy guys put on makeup that made her look like a slut. Shit! Maybe it's time to start over.

The next morning he continued to turn over in his head what had happened between him and Vanessa. Hadn't he wanted to sleep with her when he first saw her in a perception class back at Wazzu?

Now that Kovick was out of the picture, maybe he could turn the screensaver business to his advantage. If he apologized and flattered her just the right way, persuaded her to spend an hour or two with him in a bar, asked her some questions about herself... And after all, wasn't that the only way he was going to get what he really wanted?

He spent all his free time the next day waiting for an opportunity to talk to her alone in their office. Of course, he'd have to leave the door open, but he sure didn't want an audience when he apologized to her. It was going to be tough enough just to say "I'm sorry." But that was the only way to begin.

Late in the afternoon, she came in and sat down without acknowledging that he was there. She opened her laptop, brought up what looked like a journal article and started reading. It was awesome how quickly she flipped through the pages. Was she actually reading that fast? Then she went back to the beginning, stopped to bring up a notepad window and moved it so she had the two windows tiled. She started through the pages slowly, pausing occasionally to type something on the notepad. She jumped around in the article a lot.

He watched, dithering. Suddenly, she paused, as though she were reading and re-reading a passage. Then she leaned back and stared at the wall. Was this the moment to interrupt her? He took a chance.

"Vanessa?"

There was no response. Abruptly, she sat forward. She typed briefly, then began jumping back and forth among the pages again. He coughed. Nothing. He stood up, making sure the chair scraped noisily as he did. She wasn't faking as far as he could tell. What the hell was going on? It was like she was fucking deaf.

"Vanessa, I… I mean… Can we talk for a minute?"

She flipped to the reference section at the end of the article, clicked on a citation, and began skimming another article. Damn! Her concentration was beyond awesome.

He took two hesitant steps toward her, making sure his shoes scuffed the floor. "Vanessa? I hate to interrupt you, but…" He touched her shoulder, feeling a jolt of electricity run up his arm. When she still didn't turn from the screen, he concluded his body was the source of the shock he'd felt. "Vanessa…" He shook her shoulder as gently as he could.

She jumped. "What?" She shot out of her chair and spun away from him all at once.

He put up his hands in a gesture of self-defense and backed away. "Sorry, sorry, sorry!" He crashed into his own chair and nearly fell over it.

"What are *you* doing here?" Her hands shook.

"I was just working here…" He pointed helplessly to his desk. "When you came in, I…"

"Oh… Okay." She seemed to relax.

"You didn't hear me or anything just now?"

She shook her head.

From what he'd just seen, he had to believe her. Still, there was something spooky about it. "I'm really sorry. I…"

"That's okay." She started to sit down.

Before she turned around fully, he cleared his throat. "As long as you're here, I've been meaning to apologize for what happened the other day. I mean…"

She turned back to face him. "So have I. I'm glad you brought it up."

A wave of relief gushed through him. "I mean, I really overreacted, and…"

"So did I. I'm very sorry." She seemed to think of something. "Do you have your laptop with you?"

"Yeah, why?" What was going on now?

"I shouldn't have locked you out of that folder. The password is the first seven digits of the Fibonacci sequence."

"Huh?"

She stared blankly at him for moment. "Oh. It's zero, one, one, two, three, five, eight. Each number is the sum of the previous two after zero and one."

"Wait! I want to write that—"

"Start with zero followed by one. They add up to one, right? One and one are two. One and two are three. Two and three are five—"

"Oh, I get it now. I should have guessed it would have something to do with math. Thanks!" He went through the sequence aloud once to be sure he had it.

She nodded.

"Anyway, it was a stupid thing for me to do, putting your photos on my screensaver." He lowered his eyes. "You had every right to—"

"But I could have asked you politely to take them off." She smiled at him for the first time since they started graduate school. "Let's agree to forget the whole thing." She held out her hand to him. "Okay? We have to live with each other in here, right?"

He took her hand, not quite sure what she had in mind until she began to shake it up and down. "Yeah, no kidding." He held her hand a fraction of a second longer than custom dictates for polite handshakes. "I'd rather be friends than… "

"Me too." She looked him in the eye.

That and her smile encouraged him. "I'd like to make it up to you. I really would."

"No need to. It was my fault, too. I think we're even."

"No, I mean, I'd like to get to know you better. We've hardly talked since we… well, since we became officemates."

"We grad students are pretty busy people." Her smile was gone.

"That's what I mean. I never see you except around the department."

"True enough."

"Look, there's a new Irish band at McCool's this weekend. Shawn's been playing their CD and they're fantastic. Why don't you come along with me to hear them Saturday night?"

"That's nice of you, Brad. Really nice, but—"

"No, no, no. This is on me."

"I'm really sorry to say no. But I don't like beer."

"They have cocktails—even wine." He hated how desperate he sounded.

"Besides, a noisy pub's not a place for a serious conversation."

"Okay. Then we can—"

"I'm not a fan of Irish music either, Brad. And I have too much to do. It's the end of the quarter, you know?" She smiled apologetically and turned to face her desk.

"What kind of music do you like?" he said to her back.

She looked at him over her shoulder. "Beethoven. And Bach. Classical music, almost exclusively. Sorry."

"All right." He should have known he'd be disappointed.

"Thanks again for offering, Brad. I appreciate your gesture. But I don't need any peace offerings. Let's leave it at being friends, okay?"

"Yeah, okay. Maybe some other time."

For Stan's third session in the lab, Vanessa came to his office to get him. She had her hair down again, but this time a generous lock fell across the right side of her forehead and swept just over the corner of her eye. No trace of makeup, though. She wore a pin stripe charcoal jacket over a fuchsia blouse with a V-neck. Her taupe miniskirt showed off her lissome legs without being risqué, and her two-inch heels matched the hue of her skirt. It was the first time he'd seen her wear anything but flat shoes around the department.

The work of judging the gender of given names was no different from before. He never saw any photos of faces, although he assumed they were there before each name appeared.

During one of the breaks, she turned to him. "Stan, I know almost nothing about you other than your research career."

"That's true. I've been so busy asking you about your life, I haven't given you the chance."

"You've been married, I guess?"

"Yes, and divorced…" He didn't turn his head to look at her, even briefly, as they walked. "Eight years ago—a very messy business."

"They seem to be more often messy than… what? Orderly? Especially if kids are involved."

"There are two of them, a boy and a girl. After the divorce, they lived with their mother in Massachusetts."

"That's a long way away. Do you get to see them very often?"

"One's a senior in high school, the other's a junior at Duke. They both love the Northwest—Matt, the older one, likes to climb, and Elise loves sailing. I see them—separately—every summer. First, I go sailing, then a week or two later, it's off to the mountains."

"Does Matt know what he wants to do?"

"He's a premed, majoring in chemistry. But last summer, he seemed to be losing interest in clinical medicine and drifting toward molecular biology. It's too early to tell, though."

"And Elise?"

He was surprised and pleased that she used their names. "She wants to be a writer. She's devoured fiction all her life. She's already written a novel."

"Wow! Have you read any of it?" Vanessa had her keys out to open the door to the lab corridor.

"Only parts of it. What I've seen, I think is good. But I'm her father." He held the door for Vanessa and followed her down the corridor.

Back in the lab she gave him a brief refresher on the recall and recognition procedures. "After you finish this, you'll have some new procedures." She closed the sliding door, and he began.

He was able to recall many more of the names than the first time. He had, of course, seen them repeatedly by now. Name recognition followed: pairs of names, one he'd judged previously and one he hadn't. After a short break, there was a round of face recognition: two faces, one that had been used throughout the preceding sessions and the other that hadn't although he hadn't seen either of them before.

The message signaling a two-minute break appeared. Vanessa returned through the sliding door. "We're finally ready for something new. You're going to see first names again, some you've been judging for gender and others you haven't. But now your task will be to indicate how much you like each one, using the numbered keys on this special keyboard.

She reached into the darkness behind the monitor and pulled out a small keyboard with a line of seven keys about an inch square along the upper half. Each key had a large numeral from one to seven on it. Below the numbered keys was a long key the size and shape of a space bar.

"Each trial will begin when you press the space bar. Go ahead and press it now."

When he did, HOWARD appeared on the screen.

"Look at the name and press one of the numbered keys to indicate how much you like or dislike it." She slid a card into a holder he hadn't seen until then. On it were printed brief phrases such as "like it very much" over the 7-key and "don't like it at all" over the 1-key.

After a total of six practice trials, he began working his way through the names again. He was tired of seeing them, and the novelty of the new task quickly wore off. He had trouble keeping focused after nearly two hours in the lab making such trivial judgments.

His mind kept wandering off to the same place. Vanessa had again agreed to join him for dinner afterward, and he wondered if it was too early to seduce her. Except "seduce" hardly seemed the right word. How do you seduce a woman so independent, so full of contradictions, and—most daunting of all—so much smarter than you are? He thought more in terms of "lighting a spark" between them.

He'd resigned himself to go with the flow, trying to be alert to signals from her. And hoping. He could not put out of his mind her remark five days ago: "Definitely not better than sex!"

The next task was rating faces the same way. It, too, quickly grew tiresome. He decided that he'd ask for a longer break when he finished this part of the session.

"One more task to go," she said brightly as she appeared silhouetted in the door frame. "There's something I haven't told you. The photos I've been flashing on the screen in random pixel samples have been full-length photos of the people whose faces you just judged. I need to run a detection procedure on them for comparison." She pushed the keyboard with seven numbered keys into the darkness and handed him the two clickers again.

"So… in this next series of trials you may or may not see a full-length photo of a person. Sometimes it will be very easy to see, sometimes it won't. Push the yes-clicker if you see it, the no-clicker if you don't. As always, there's a deadline for responding. By the way, there'll always be something there, but the deadline will be adjusted to keep your detection rate at about fifty percent."

He told her he understood the task.

"All right," she said. "I'm going to start you right off without practice, since this task is just like the one at the end of the first session." She pulled the door shut.

On the first trial he saw something. It was taller than it was wide and flesh colored. He pressed the *no*-clicker to beat the deadline, although he wasn't sure. On the second trial he saw nothing and clicked *no* again. On the third trial, he saw a full-length photo of a man in a business suit.

On the fourth trial, a photo of a nude woman appeared. It lasted only a fraction of a second, but there wasn't the slightest doubt what he had seen: a very attractive woman wearing nothing but high heels and a smile that could only be described as demure. With no pubic hair, she reminded him of a recent *Playboy* model he'd seen on the website.

He was so flabbergasted at what he had seen that he forgot to respond. The next trial had passed before he finally shouted, "Vanessa!"

As if she'd been waiting behind the door, she appeared framed in the dim light as the door rolled back.

"What is this?" he said not quite as loudly.

"I hope you aren't offended, Stan." Her voice was calm and completely serious. "You told me you've seen a lot of *Playboy* photos online."

In the shadows he couldn't see her face. "But this is deception, Vanessa. You didn't have an ethics review…" *But does she need one to test* me? "Okay, maybe you don't have to send this to the institutional review board. But…"

She said nothing, as though waiting for him to go on. The silence quickly became oppressive.

She had tricked him, sprung a trap. For at least an hour—maybe longer, depending on the design, he'd been exposed to concealed photos of naked women. That was the reason she'd had him rating names instead of judging their gender. The design of her study suddenly crystallized for him. And—

"You rascal." He jumped up and grabbed her arm.

She pulled back in surprise. "No!"

He seized her shoulders and was about to shake her like a naughty child, when the entire situation smacked him in the face. He burst out laughing. "Okay, okay. Score one for you. You owe me for this—big time."

That ironic smile of hers formed on her lips. "I owed you—big time—from the moment you agreed to let me test you."

She made no effort to escape from his grip, which he had relaxed the moment he began to laugh. But he continued to hold her lightly, unwilling to let go entirely.

"So you've had me looking at nudes the whole time."

"But you didn't see them, did you?" She suddenly looked very concerned.

"No, of course not. Otherwise, I certainly would have said something before this."

"I inserted them at the beginning of the second session." She brought her forearms up and grasped him awkwardly at the elbows. "But seriously, Stan. We need detection data to evaluate these full-length photos. You see why, don't you?"

They released each other at the same time. He went back to his place in front of the monitor. And indeed the task was a pleasant relief from the monotony of the past two hours.

CHAPTER 11

When the block of detection trials ended, she turned up the room lights and invited him into the lair where she'd been watching his results accumulate. As before the monitor in the corner displayed two nearly identical graphs side by side.

"These show our performance on the second session, yours on the right, and on the left, mine from last summer when I first began testing myself." She pointed. "I computed detection and learning parameters from our first sessions and adjusted the raw scores. What's interesting here is that I was presenting you full-length photos, whereas I continued to present myself faces."

"Fascinating!"

She clicked the mouse, and two tables appeared on the monitor. "Our name recall was similar, too." She pointed to the first line. "Again, adjusting the raw scores with a learning parameter computed from the first session, they're almost identical." She moved her forefinger across the second row of the table. "And on the second line are the comparable numbers for name recognition." The adjusted scores were indeed very close in both cases.

He nodded. "These adjustments you're making… How are you computing the parameters for each of us?"

She rooted through a stack of papers on the table near the book she'd been reading. Exhuming a thick paper, she folded back a dozen pages and flipped back and forth. "Here it is."

She laid the paper in front of him and pointed. "These are the parameters in the theory."

As she spoke, he glanced at the upper half of the sheet. One look at a formula with triple integral signs was enough.

"*Theta* sub-*i* is the fundamental learning parameter for individual *i*—"

"Hold it. I don't need details. You're deriving these values for each of us using your theory, right?"

"Yes, of course." She glanced at him, apparently puzzled. "That's the point. To test the theory."

"Okay. That answers my question." He pushed the hefty paper away. "I'm more interested in my rating data."

"So am I." She grinned at him and brought up a single table.

"So… These are your mean ratings broken down, first by gender, male versus female, and then, within the female names and faces, those paired with concealed faces only versus those paired with concealed full-length nudes."

"I'm not surprised, I guess, that I like female names better."

"And female faces."

"Okay, sure. But… this is certainly surprising." He pointed to the last column.

"You liked the names paired with the concealed nudes better? I guess some kind of information got through to your brain, even if you didn't notice, huh?"

He frowned. "Look at this." He pointed to the last number in the second line. "Does this mean…?"

"Yes, indeed! It means you liked the faces of the concealed nudes better. Even though the faces were only a small part of the concealed photos."

"Amazing!"

"And I'd like to point out that the photos of the faces you just rated? They were *exactly* the same photos as the concealed ones. Whereas—"

"Yes, of course. The faces of the other women were only part of the concealed bodies."

"No, they were *different*. Different expression and different camera angle, too."

"How bizarre!"

"And look at this." Another click of the mouse added two more rows to the table. "Turns out," she said, "you even recalled more of the names paired with the concealed nudes—and recognized more of them, too. The differences are small, but there they are."

"I'll be damned!"

"Why are you surprised Stan?" Her smile was full of mischief.

He was speechless. Was he really surprised? And if so, why?

"Seriously, Stan, when I thought of this design, I had no idea which way it would come out. You can't imagine how excited I am to see such clear results." She was in earnest now. "It gives me a whole new paradigm for testing the theory. Plus, it suggests another possible linking variable." She gave him a moment to reflect.

He hesitated, then gave in to an impulse. "But… but shouldn't I have, like, felt something?"

"I wondered about that."

"You understand what I mean?"

"Sure. And I even thought of trying to assess it."

He had primed himself to watch for any signs of attraction, but this was overload.

"But there are problems," she went on.

"Like you couldn't find a plethysmograph in my lab?"

"Or a DIR."

"A what?"

"Digital inflection rigidometer." She looked him in the eye. "Just what you think—well, maybe not quite. The *readout* is digital."

"You know about this stuff?"

"It's all on the Internet."

"Of course. There'd be a market among men with erectile dysfunction."

"The more serious problem should be obvious," she said, as if discussing the driest lab problem around. "If I hooked you up, you'd know something was going on."

He almost said something, but caught himself.

The corners of her lips turned up in a glimmer of a smile. "But we could do another session. The design shouldn't be that difficult to work out."

He clung to her use of *we*. "Then we're back to the equipment issue, aren't we?"

She cocked her head. "There are cruder ways to do it, I suppose."

He just about fell on the floor.

"But," she continued, "that would require—"

"I'd be willing—"

"You'd have to sign a consent form." She leaned forward.

"I'm okay with that. But wouldn't—under the circumstances, I mean—wouldn't you have to sign one, too?"

"We could mutually agree." Her face was now inches from his.

"It's…" He reached up with both hands and, taking her head in his hands, drew her lips toward his. Her body offered no resistance.

"Okay," she whispered just before their lips touched. She gripped his shoulders, holding their bodies firmly together.

The next thing he remembered was standing in an embrace, gazing at her face. Her lips were darker and looked swollen, the way his felt after their passionate kisses. He kissed her cheek, then moved downward in small steps following her neck until the collar of her jacket stopped him. He felt her lips lightly on his neck.

"This must be our consent form," she whispered close to his ear.

He chuckled as he leaned back to gaze again at her whole face. "Yes, but I hope you don't use this form for all your subjects."

She laid her cheek on his chest. "No. This is a one-of-a-kind contract. Just for the two of us, Stan."

He hugged her. "So what happens next? I mean, in this experiment of yours?"

"We can't use this lab."

"No. Nor mine. I have an—"

"There's a lab near here—on Twelfth Street."

"I think I know the address." He smirked. "Haven't I been there before?"

"The very same place."

They decided she should leave the lab first by herself. He waited fifteen minutes more in his office and then walked to her apartment. Passing through the busy U District in a light mist, he still could hardly believe what had just happened. How had his favorite daydream come to life?

The closer he came to this rendezvous with fantasy, however, the more difficult it became for him to ignore the ethical twilight at the verge of the erotic screenplay he'd conjured. He realized it was why he wasn't looking at people's faces as he usually did. He knew a tryst with Vanessa was risky for both of them, but it wasn't in him to turn back.

She'd given him explicit instructions for finding his way to her third-floor apartment in an old house. There was an outside door she'd left unlocked. He locked it behind him. As he started up the dark stairway to the lone attic apartment, she opened the door.

"I found the equipment we need." She held up a metric ruler and a protractor.

He guffawed as she closed the door behind him.

"Too crude?" She was frowning and her lips were a straight line, but the muscles twitched all over her face as she tried to keep the expression in place. "I'm sorry. It's the best I could do."

"I think they will be accurate enough, at least for a pilot study." He put his arms around her waist.

"Let's see how it goes." She broke free and went over to a desk where her laptop was set up. "I can test you on this, although I can't exactly match the refresh rate of the lab monitor."

His expression gave away his disappointment.

"What's wrong?" she asked.

"I guess I was hoping to see the real thing."

Her racy smile delighted him. "Actually, I was too." She shed her jacket and carefully hung it over the back of the chair in front of her desk.

He rushed forward. "May I?" He began unbuttoning her blouse from the top.

She grabbed his shoulders and planted a lingering kiss on his forehead. When he reached her skirt, he pulled the blouse up and undid the remaining button. He tugged at the fabric again, and it was loose. She had undone the button and opened the zipper on the side of her skirt.

With a shake of her hips, the skirt fell to the floor. While she was stepping out of it, he ran his fingers up her back, searching for the hook on her bra.

She wiggled out of his arms and spun around. "The bra will come off more easily without the blouse."

He politely held it for her, so she could slide out of the sleeves. By the time he had folded it over her jacket on the chair, she had unhooked her bra. He slid it off her shoulders but let her catch it so he could pull down her panties. But she evaded him.

Turning to face him while hitching them up again, she said, "My turn!"

A brief glimpse of her bare breasts momentarily blinded him to her sudden maneuver to push his sweater up under his arms before he could defend himself. He yielded to her hands on his arms and let her peel it off over his head. She pushed it up as far his elbows before stopping.

While he wrestled with the sweater, she swiftly unbuttoned his shirt. Her fingers danced up his torso pulling his T-shirt along under her wrists. She got the T-shirt to his shoulders, then grabbed the hem at the bottom and yanked it up.

"Hold it!" he said just as she covered his face with his T-shirt. "Let me get my—"

"Okay." She planted her lips on his left nipple and flicked it with her tongue for a second.

He was momentarily distracted from extracting his wrists from their shackles. As her lips landed on his right nipple, he could feel her hands at his waist. She deftly opened his belt, pulled down his zipper and started to fumble with the hook and button.

His clever little remark to Michelle, "I have a tigress by the tail," ran through his head. Suddenly his trousers enwreathed his feet. Then his penis sprang out of his jockey shorts as her hands ran down the outside of his legs.

"Wait, wait, wait," he gasped. "I didn't sign up for any bondage."

A finger hooked over the top of his T-shirt and her face appeared suddenly, an inch in front of him. "You didn't?" She stepped back and ran her eyes up and down his body. "Let me check the fine print." She went to her desk, where she kicked off her shoes.

She padded back in her bare feet, holding the ruler and protractor. "Sorry. It says very clearly that you agreed to being tied up during the measurements." She glanced at his quivering penis. "Darn! We waited too long to do the pretest assessment, but…" She shook her head. "I'm really sorry but we're going to have to wait until—"

"Vanessa!" He managed to lower his arms but felt just as silly with them handcuffed in front of him by his sweater.

She pulled off the sweater. "Turn around."

He thought she was going to hold his shirt, so he reached for a cuff to unbutton it.

"No, put your arms over your head again."

"What—?" But he automatically obeyed the urging of her hands under his arms. As the shirt fell over his face and slithered down his chest, it dawned on him what she was doing. He lowered his arms so he could see her.

She stepped back. "Yes, that's better." She inspected his shirt, which hung from still buttoned cuffs and covered him from the waist down. "You'll feel less self-conscious covered up like that." She maintained an absolute deadpan expression.

"Please, Vanessa."

"I know this will delay things a little, but make yourself comfortable and let me know when you're… um—"

"Flaccid, right? Look, we'll wait forever… I mean, if I look at you… at those lovely breasts—"

"Right. So, if you'll just look at the—no, wait. I'll bring my laptop over, and you can watch stock market quotations on CNBC while I work on my theory at my desk." She headed back with the ruler and protractor in hand.

He followed her this time, slowly because he could take only short shuffling steps with his pants around his ankles. "You realize you're running up an astronomical debt here?"

She stopped before picking up her laptop and turned. "You're absolutely right. This was supposed to be fun for you, too. I'm always getting carried away by my research."

After briskly unbuttoning the cuffs of his shirt, she grabbed the sleeves of both his shirt and sweater and freed his hands. Before he could reach out to touch her, she was on her knees untying his left shoe.

"I mean…" He bent and ran his fingertips down her back. "I didn't mean that we should discontinue—"

Her whole body quivered for a moment. Then he felt her hand on his calf urging his leg upward.

"Lift your foot."

He braced himself on the desk and raised his foot. "I just thought—"

"Yes, but you evidently don't like bondage—" She whisked off his shoe and pulled pants, shorts and sock over his foot in one quick move. She immediately went to work on the other shoelace. "Okay, the other foot."

He shifted his weight and let her hoist his other leg. "Well, to tell the truth… If it hadn't gone so fast… I was just beginning to, sort of, you know… enjoy it."

"Another time, okay…?"

"Thank you." When she stood, he put his hands on her hips. "You didn't need to—"

"I enjoyed it." She wrapped her arms around his chest and touched his lips with a fleeting kiss. "Now, relax. Let's both enjoy this, okay?"

"But I want to finish our experiment."

She gently pushed her stomach against his penis, pinning it up between them. "I just realized," she whispered in his ear, "I have a better instrument around here for measuring your, ah… level of arousal."

"Okay," he whispered back.

He moved his hands so he could fondle her breasts. As if reading his desires, she turned around and lifted his hands so his fingertips grazed her nipples. She stretched her arms over her head and with her hands stroked his hair. Her hips started swaying, moving his penis like a shift stick.

He began to worry about premature ejaculation. "We'd better do this assessment soon. You haven't told me what—"

She twisted out of his arms. Grabbing his hand, she pulled him to the edge of the bed. "Why don't you lie down and relax." She pointed.

"You're the experimenter." He stretched out on the narrow bed. "Whatever you say."

She pulled down her panties, but scurried back to the desk before he got a glimpse of what she'd unveiled. She pulled out a drawer and left it open when she returned to the side of the bed where he lolled on his side watching her.

For the first time since he'd begun to undress her, he was able to survey her butt and then her breasts and hips in motion, there in the same room with him. Every inflection of her skin scintillated like ripples on a lake reflecting the morning sun. When she was back at his side, he saw that she'd let her pubic hair grow back since her last *Playboy* photo shoot.

He was amazed when he reached out and she let him stroke it lightly, dragging his fingertips downward until they trailed between her legs. She stopped and closed her eyes, still clutching the object she'd retrieved from the drawer. He turned his hand over and moved upward so that his middle finger crept up between her legs and penetrated the wet furrow at the junction. At his touch she squeezed his finger between her legs and drew back in an involuntary spasm.

Then he heard the crinkle of stiff plastic and a moment later felt something on the head of his penis. "I have a condom, too," he said as she deftly rolled it down.

"Save it… for later. Just in case." She climbed on the bed and straddled him. As she lowered herself on his sheathed penis, she said, "Now hold very still while I insert the arousal indicator into this special cuff."

She caught her breath when he suddenly breached a stricture and penetrated her. "You may feel a little discomfort—" She clenched her jaw and her whole body shuddered. "—but once it's in place—" She gasped. "—it's the most sensitive plethysmo—"

He groaned when she leaned back and rocked her pelvis forward. Their bodies found a common rhythm.

"Are you getting good readings?" he asked between breaths.

"You're blowing out—uh—the fuses, but —uh—keep going. Please—keep going… please, please, please…"

It was dark when he awoke with his arm asleep under her head. He tried to extricate himself without disturbing her. But the limb was a dead weight—paralyzed.

She awoke with a start. "What's wrong?" In spite of the dim light filtering in from the street through curtains, he could see her distress.

She was at work massaging his arm before he finished telling her. As she worked, she showered him with kisses. The limb gradually came back to prickly life, and he winced in spite of his efforts to hide the pain. She cooed softly, sometimes articulating a word of comfort or solace.

As the needles relented, her ministrations changed. The complexion of her palpations shifted subtly and their scope expanded to his chest, then to his belly. With his good hand he stroked her body from her shoulder, over her sensuous rump, as far down the back of her leg as he could reach.

"I think the blood is coming back in your limbs, my dear." She wasn't looking at his arm any longer.

And indeed, to his surprise, he was as hard as before. "Would you mind doing it again?"

"We certainly can't waste this prize." She ran her fingertips up and down it like she was playing a clarinet.

"Could we—"

"Have some light?" She sprang from the bed.

"How'd you know?"

"Men are more visual than women. They like photos, movies, even paintings, right? And they like to see what they are touching." She turned on a light at the other end of the long narrow room.

"And women?"

"Most women? I'm not sure. But what lures this woman is authenticity and integrity."

He couldn't get enough of watching her perfect body move across the room.

"You wanted light. I want music." She pushed two buttons on a CD player and waited until a piano began a bouncy waltz resembling a European folk dance. Keeping time in a little jig, she crossed the room to the bed where she hopped into his arms.

This time they took things languidly, savoring each moment, punctuated only by monosyllables of pleasure building to ecstasy. She let him take charge, bending and turning to the slightest whim of his touch, anticipating the drift of his cravings and needs with uncanny awareness.

The tension built slowly, at first lighthearted and playful, then by fits and turns more rigorous and urgent. He had a peculiar sensation that their lovemaking was choreographed by the vagaries of the piano music that filled the room: Rippling arpeggios, leaping and diving runs, elegant dances, contemplative counterpoint, trills of exaltation, sad adagios, reflective largos—all variations on the pleasures and contradictions of this delightful woman.

At length, he was on top of her, plunging and pumping to the driving rhythm of pounding chords. And when they were spent in each other's arms, a triumphant minuet, recapitulating and ennobling the feast of love they had celebrated.

"What was that strange music, Vanessa?" he asked as they sat on the bed after it had ended.

"Beethoven."

"It didn't sound like… like anything I've heard before."

"It's the Diabelli Variations. My favorite piece of music—practically the only thing I listen to when I'm by myself these days."

They were able to make it in time for the last seating of the evening at Serafina. Over their split orders of Bigoli ai Pistachio and Ravioli di Bosco, he told her he wanted to become a subject for her long-term single subject experiment, if he could work out a testing schedule for himself with less hours per day over a longer period of time.

She seemed quite surprised. "Does this mean you've just had a conversion this evening?" Her impish eyes both taunted and tantalized him.

"Actually, no. There's a selfish reason."

"You mean I don't have to go more deeply in debt?"

"Consider yourself even. I want to ask for help with something I've been mulling over since my second session."

"Now you've got me really curious." She laced her fingers and rested her chin on them.

"Next year, my grant comes up for renewal. I'd like to build the renewal around your findings. And your theory, if I can ever understand it well enough to explain it on my own."

"Why wouldn't I want you to do that?"

"Because, Vanessa, it would mean writing you into the grant, as a co-principal investigator. You'd have commit yourself to staying on here after you finish your degree."

"Oh." Her face was suddenly solemn and her eyes no longer focused on the present.

"We're talking about your future. You and I need to talk about your hopes and aspirations. But think it over before we do. And take your time."

He hadn't planned to tell her, but it seemed like the right moment. There was no question; it would be a great collaboration for him. He knew she'd have many other options, and he wanted the advantage of his being her first offer.

CHAPTER 12

Stan saw Vanessa only once more during the busy ten days at the end of the quarter. He fixed dinner for her at his place in Green Lake on the last Friday of finals week, and she brought her suitcase so he could take her to the airport the next morning for a trip to Hawaii. Her mother was giving an invited paper at a mathematics conference in Honolulu. Vanessa was flying on her mother's frequent flier miles.

"I haven't been back to Orion Station for a couple of years now," she told him. "Mom still lives there, but she's constantly traveling, consulting and giving workshops and short courses. She did some fundamental work when I was a kid that turned out to be the key to a whole family of problems in cryptography."

"Your father?"

"He's out of the picture. I haven't seen him since I was seventeen. Talk about a messy divorce!"

He decided not to follow up her remark. "You don't seem like the type to lie in the sun all day. What are your plans?"

"Not the beach. With my skin? I'd look like a tomato after an hour or two." She took a sip of wine. "I'm heading for the volcanoes. And after the conference, Mom's joining me for a day. Then she's taking me along on a consulting job at Mauna Kea. I get to enjoy a couple of nights of recreational stargazing."

"Recreational? I thought you'd studied astrophysics."

One of her faraway looks came into her eyes. He was just beginning to distinguish her memory eyes from her problem-solving eyes. Maybe he picked up some cues from her face, too, but her eyes had more moods than he could count. He thought she'd stopped listening, but eventually she answered his question.

"The night skies are sublime to look at, but I'm happy I decided to study the mind. It's a more profound mystery, and probably more complex."

The next time Stan saw her was when she came to his office a half an hour before her master's defense started. She had been able to find a time all three of her committee members could meet on Friday morning of the first week of winter quarter, and the second-floor seminar room was available as well.

With most students he spent a great deal of time describing how oral exams usually proceed and what to expect the faculty dynamics to be, depending on who was on the committee. He even ran brief rehearsals for weaker students.

He'd decided Vanessa could handle herself without much help. So they chatted about her comfortable relationship with her mother and her vacation. She'd found the volcanoes as interesting as the stars.

Earlier he had warned her that she might be asked to begin the meeting with a brief summary of what she'd done, why it was worth doing, what she'd found, and what it meant.

"I'm ready," she said when he asked about the summary.

"Don't be surprised if one of them interrupts you before you finish."

She laughed softly. "If they let me go on more than three minutes, I have a couple of outrageous claims that will *make* them stop me."

"Good. I'm hoping for some fireworks. Let's go, shall we?"

She hitched her backpack over one shoulder and picked up her insulated coffee mug. She was wearing her usual work uniform, although the T-shirt had been replaced with a stretchy lemon yellow top with an embroidered image of Mauna Kea suspended between her two volcanoes of a different kind.

A long table made of what looked like oak dominated the center of the second-floor seminar room. Chairs of mixed styles and colors surrounded the table and lined the walls, restricting easy movement. Upholstery colors ranged from dull turquoise to the nondescript brown of the mottled carpeting. The chairs were the kind that look comfortable but aren't.

Stan pointed her to the second chair on the far side of the table facing the doors. "Roger and Michelle will sit across from you." He pulled back the chair at the end of the table. "I'll sit here and direct traffic." As she got out a stack of folders, he added, "By the way, expect me to call on Roger to start the questions, if no one interrupts your summary."

Michelle arrived with her inevitable mug of fresh coffee, jazzing up the dead air. Stan noticed for the first time that her insulated steel mug matched the one Vanessa usually brought to their meetings. Roger Zhrudsky arrived at exactly nine o'clock looking less tense than usual. He often said that he cherished the limited time he was able to spend on "…the real work of the faculty—teaching and research." He closed the door behind him.

"Well, then," Stan said. "Are we ready to begin?" When his colleagues both nodded, he asked, "Would you like Vanessa to start out with a summary of her thesis research?"

Michelle turned to Roger, who said, "That would be nice—if it's not too long."

"I have a two-minute and a five-minute version," Vanessa piped up.

Michelle grinned at her. "You couldn't stop talking about your thesis after just two minutes if your life depended on it." She reached for the watch on her wrist. It beeped several times. "Ready?"

"Tell me when."

"Go!" Michelle's watch beeped.

Vanessa had obviously practiced with a stopwatch. Stan tried to count the sentences, but her syntax was so complicated he lost track. When she stopped, there was a moment of silence.

Michelle jumped and reached for her watch. It beeped. "Two minutes, ten seconds."

"It was at least ten seconds before you stopped the clock," Roger observed. "You may be a great statistician, but as a time-keeper you stink."

Everyone laughed. Stan knew this kind of banter presaged a good meeting, especially when the student scored an early psychological success. "Roger, would you like to begin?" he said.

"Certainly." He took perhaps thirty seconds studying a yellow pad of notes before he addressed Vanessa. "I'm not going to ask you to defend single-subjects designs," he said dryly.

They all laughed again. Stan looked at Vanessa. Her smiling face told him she was as relaxed as she ever got during an intellectual exchange.

"Before I raise any questions, I'd like to praise your lucid writing…" He looked at her over the top of his glasses. "…in both the long and short versions."

Another round of laughter. Stan sat back to wait for the pyrotechnics. Roger then asked a long, rambling question, the essence of which was whether her work had any bearing on Hayes and Pellegrino's theory of controlled and automatic attention. She began to answer immediately, but Roger stopped her and asked her to describe their theory and research.

Vanessa launched into a detailed summary, which as always sounded like a carefully thought-out lecture, although Stan knew she'd never talked to a group about this important paper. She criticized several weak points in the theory and moved smoothly into a discussion of whether the theory could account for some of her results, and if so, how. After ten minutes, when she stopped momentarily to ask if anyone had "…any questions to this point," Roger had had enough.

"We're not here to listen to you lecture—quite articulately, I have to say—on the flaws and weakness of Hayes and Pellegrino." He glanced at his watch, consulted his notes, and without looking up said, "As we all know, you have *two* versions of this paper—"

"The geeky one for the math nerds—" Stan turned to Michelle with a smile. "—and the simple one for the rest of us."

Everyone laughed except Vanessa, who said, "Sorry, Dr. Zhrudsky." Her contrite smile was patently faked.

"Come, come folks." Michelle spoke sternly although she, too, was smiling. "This is a serious meeting, you know. You were saying, Roger?"

"Your second version, which we've also read—"

"*Tried* to read," Stan interjected.

Michelle frowned at Stan. "Please, I had a question about that one, too."

"Thank you," Roger said to Michelle. "Vanessa, the second version contained a very technical introduction with complex equations and a lengthy endnote containing mathematical vocabulary that I don't understand."

"Yes?" Vanessa seemed relaxed and inquisitive.

"Still, there's enough information that I feel I understand your approach. I'd like you to explain your theory to us in the simplest possible way you can. Can you do that without symbols?"

Vanessa nodded slowly. "Maybe with images?"

She held up her hands with her forefingers sticking up and the other fingers interlaced. "You know how people create a shadow show by hanging up a sheet with a bright light behind it, and then use their hands to create funny shadows?" She wiggled her thumbs and forefingers.

"My three-dimensional hands represent the reality that neuroscientists like Dr. Forrester and psychologists like the three of you have been trying to understand."

Stan chuckled. He understood enough about her theory that he saw where she was going. She could be a remarkable teacher once she understood what someone didn't know.

"It's obvious, isn't it," Vanessa continued, "that the shadows on the sheet don't contain all the information we need to reconstruct the shape and position of my hands, even when they move?" One of her pinkies suddenly stood up and waggled.

Only sage nods from the other three this time.

"For the sake of the explanation, I'm going to stipulate that the sheet is the brain and the shadows are the data collected by neuroscientists." She lowered her hands. "Now suppose we have two sheets at right angles to each other." With her palms, she mimed a corner.

"And aim the light at the corner?" Michelle asked.

"Right." Vanessa appeared pleased when both Roger and Stan nodded.

"The second sheet is what cognitive psychologists have been looking at. They see only the two dimensions of the mind. But again, the shadow projected on the second sheet is also incomplete information about the object of interest." She held up her folded hands again.

"So to get a complete picture of your hands…" Roger leaned forward. "…we'd need to get a third sheet at right angles to the other two?"

"It wouldn't be enough, Dr. Zhrudsky. Even if we could infer the surfaces of two hands, there are activities inside that we'd miss, if all we had were shadows."

"A*ha*."

"So, to review: We have the reality of the mind-brain continuum out here." She pulled her fingers apart and wiggled them vigorously. "The relevant information about the brain is over here on the first sheet." She jabbed one finger to the left. "And what we need to know about mind is over there on the second sheet." She jabbed the other finger to the right.

"What's missing is detailed quantitative information about mental activity—what's going on in the mind—collected at the same time as the kind of high-quality information we now can obtain about activity in the brain." She paused and looked at each of them in turn, as if expecting a question or comment.

"So a thought or a feeling?" Stan said. "It can be located with coordinates in both the brain space and the mind space?"

"In a single mind-brain continuum of six or possibly higher dimensionality, yes." She glanced at the three of them anxiously. "Could I be just a little more technical?" She didn't wait for permission.

"My geometry provides a framework for organizing all the information about the structure of the brain and how the components are connected, interact, and are affected by, for example, neurochemistry. But it also incorporates all the data psychology has accumulated about the mind—the way ideas, thoughts, and feelings are connected and interrelated. And like Einstein's space-time continuum, what happens in the mind and brain occurs over time.

"Assuming that at least two dimensions are required to represent uniquely mental events, the entire mind-brain-time continuum forms a manifold of at least six dimensions. And from my limited data, it appears that it's a non-Euclidean geometry."

The silence that followed made Stan anxious. Roger turned to Michelle with an expression of pained perplexity.

"Let me understand, Vanessa…" Michelle turned to Roger. "May I interrupt?"

Roger nodded, sat back, and exhaled deeply.

Michelle turned to Vanessa. "You've constructed your model—this mind-brain geometry—using published research on attention and consciousness from both neuroscience and psychology?"

"Well, I'm trying to." Vanessa frowned. "The parameters keep changing as I learn more." She looked Michelle in the eye. "But the real problem is that most research on the mind and brain simultaneously consists of two or three points here and there in the mind, or at best, a few points in rank order along a line.

"The data I collected for my thesis are quantitative information—not vague inequalities—about a mental activity that's critical to thought, namely, awareness. But to test my theory I need to do the same experiment with simultaneous neuroimaging."

"What about all the work on mapping the brain or simulating it with computers or neural networks? Are you trying to incorporate that, too?" Roger asked.

"It's all well and good to try to map the active brain, and there's nothing wrong with simulating the brain with computer programs or modeling it with neural nets. The problem is that the brain isn't just a collection of biochemical activities. It gives rise to cognition and emotions. Why isn't anyone worrying about precisely mapping the thinking and feeling going on at the same time?

"My research on the perception of faces shows that a map including thoughts and emotions requires a curved space of more than five dimensions. It's no more possible to draw a meaningful map of the active brain in three dimensions than it is to draw a map of the earth on a flat surface. I'm trying to work out the geometry of the brain *and* the mind—what I call the mind-brain continuum—so we'll have an accurate picture of both."

Roger leaned back shaking his head. "No wonder I've been having so much trouble figuring out what you're doing." He turned to Michelle. "I'd better give you a chance to ask a question or two."

Michelle asked Vanessa to justify the use of an unusual type of statistical analysis on the trends in her performance over time, in light of some shaky assumptions. Vanessa gave an intuitive summary of her approach, which Stan followed easily, and so apparently did Roger. Then she went to the whiteboard and began a derivation.

Michelle looked at the two men and then back to Vanessa. "Vanessa, I think your answer was enough for now. I've seen you derive statistics from scratch—several times."

"This one's pretty simple." Vanessa returned to her chair looking disappointed.

"That's okay. This is statisticians' shop talk," Michelle said. "You can explain it to me some other time. I have something more important to ask you."

"Yes?"

Stan was surprised to see Vanessa acting uneasy. He interpreted it as a measure of her respect for Michelle.

"Not a question about your thesis. You've done an excellent job on that."

"Yes, indeed," Roger added.

"Thank you both." Vanessa said.

"I was wondering if you've given any thought to where you'll go from here, what your PhD research program might be?"

Vanessa began fumbling with the stack of folders in front of her. She hadn't touched them until now. "Yes, I have," she said without looking up. She continued to turn up tabs on the folders, searching for something. "It won't be single-subject research."

At the sound of their chuckles, she looked up smiling. Then went back to her search.

"Ah, here it is! I thought I'd put it on top." She pulled out a folder near the bottom of the pile, opened it and gave each of them a copy of a three-page handout.

"You haven't seen this yet," she said to Stan as she handed him the last one. "I realized last night that it wouldn't be easy to describe orally what we talked about a while ago. So I made some notes." She smiled ruefully. "I got carried away—as usual—typed them up—and made copies." She leaned forward anxiously while the three of them examined what she'd handed out.

Her skill in committing her thoughts to written form always astounded Stan. He and Vanessa had discussed various directions for her PhD research in a general way back in December. She'd turned those conversations into clear, detailed research designs that mirrored the studies she'd done on herself.

Stan glanced around the room, meeting Vanessa's nervous smile with a reassuring nod of approval. Noting that the other two were still digesting the handout, he decided he might as well focus the questioning on the problem that was almost certain to come up anyway.

"I noticed that you haven't mentioned any alternative explanations that are simpler than yours. There isn't any effort to answer any criticisms along the lines that your priming and learning effects are artifacts, either."

"What explanations? What artifacts?" She gave Stan that innocent, what-are-you-talking-about smile of hers. "No one who's looked at my results so far has come up with any alternative explanations. Why give them any ideas?"

She was taking a new, more aggressive tack from the way she'd argued with Stan the last time.

Roger was looking at her with a mixture of confusion and disbelief. "Them?"

"Readers. Look, why should I waste my time pursuing explanations I don't believe in? *I* don't think my research is built on artifacts."

Vanessa looked paler than usual. And he'd never seen her shake like this before.

"Well, yes," Roger said. "But shouldn't you check to be sure you aren't pursuing a will-'o-the-wisp before setting out on an ambitious research program like this?" He held up the handout.

"Why?" Vanessa shot back. "There's only so much time in a year of research. I can either screw around trying to think of alternative hypotheses about my findings and testing them, or I can build up a body of data that fits a coherent theory of my own."

Stan was amazed at the change that had come over her. She was like a cornered tiger kitten surrounded by several much bigger predators. She was crouched to spring at the first attacker, no matter how outmatched she was. *Careful, my dear*, he warned her silently. *Roger hates being challenged in public as much or more than Jim Forrester.*

Her eyes bored in on Roger. "The fact that no one here seems to have found the alleged 'artifact' tells me there are no obvious ones floating around out there, waiting for some critic to harvest them."

"Yes, yes." Roger was using his calm-down-folks voice that made him such an effective chairperson when a bunch of unruly faculty started tearing into each other. "But see here. One simple experiment at this stage might show that your findings are phantoms that will disappear in the cold light of day."

"Fine. Let someone else try to explain the set of ten quantitative relationships my three experiments are designed to uncover. I expect to find the same pattern I found in my own data, even if the rest of you think they're 'will-'o-the-wisps.' It's a gamble, yes. But isn't any experiment a gamble? And if I'm right, all you skeptics are going to have ten quantitative relationships to account for, not one piddly little difference to explain as a so-called artifact."

Roger was uncharacteristically speechless. He'd actually tipped back in his chair as though dodging her punch.

"I think what she's saying, Roger," Michelle said, "is that it's up to this committee to think of alternative explanations between now and her PhD proposal meeting. I plan to set aside some time, off and on over the next month or two, trying to help her, if I can."

She had been looking back and forth between Roger and Stan as she spoke. Now she trained her demanding blue eyes on Roger. "I would hope the rest of you will do the same."

"Yes." Roger sounded contrite. "Yes, that's in the spirit of good science, isn't it?"

"Anything more, Roger?" Stan asked.

He shook his head.

"Michelle?"

She held up Vanessa's handout. "I have more than I expected to get."

"Okay." When Stan turned to Vanessa, she was already on her feet. "It's time for you to step outside."

"I know."

"Please don't go very far away."

She nodded, then looked at each of the others in turn. "Thank you." She grabbed her backpack and left, closing the door behind her.

When the door closed, Stan turned to Roger. "Well, what do you think?"

"I can't imagine any reason not to sign this thesis, Stan. Vanessa is a truly remarkable student. You know a student is good when you learn something worthwhile from her oral. When you're inundated with new information, caught off guard by new insights, and guided through it all with impeccable logic… I confess, I felt like I was in the presence of a genius."

"Wow!" Michelle shook her head. "What can I say to second Roger? It was pure Vanessa—at her very best. What could anyone say beyond that?"

"I thought you'd have some misgivings after the last few minutes," Stan said to Roger.

"That was pretty amazing, wasn't it?" he said.

"I've never seen her like that," Stan said.

"Nor have I," Michelle added.

"Seriously though, Stan," Roger said. "She's no different from the rest of us when our most cherished research is challenged."

Michelle laughed. "Except she's a good deal better at it than most of us."

Roger nodded grudgingly. "At least as good."

"So," Stan said to both of them, "we're agreed she's passed with flying colors?"

"Certainly."

"Of course." Michelle stood. "Shall I get her back in here, and set a new record for approving a thesis?"

Roger raised his hand. "If we could delay for just a moment. I'd like to discuss an issue of another kind."

Michelle returned to her seat. "Yes?"

Roger looked first at Stan, then at Michelle. The set of his jaw was grim. "I've been getting new complaints about Vanessa's nude photos."

"Oh for God's sake, Roger," Stan said. "Surely we're past that issue. Tell them it's none of their damn business."

"These are different photos, Stan. From much earlier in her life. Purportedly, she began modeling a long time before *Playboy*."

Stan's stomach clenched. "Good God! That's awful." What kind of bastard would make her pose naked when she was a vulnerable kid? Acid burned in his throat and he tasted vomit.

"How long, Roger?" Michelle demanded.

"Since she was sixteen, at least. Maybe fourteen. The reports I've been getting are based on…" He cleared his throat. "They came from people who haven't seen the photos. They're hearsay… So who knows?"

"Are they on the Internet?" Stan asked.

"Apparently they are."

"Shit!" A dizzying parade of images flashed before Stan's addled eyes. Involuntarily, he pictured her as a skinny preteen with budding breasts. Unbidden, he watched her grow up, her breasts taking shape, her figure filling out until, at sixteen, she became a youthful version of the woman in her first *Playboy* appearance. The spontaneous movement in his pants was disorienting.

"Do we know for sure she's the model?" Michelle asked.

"No, no. This kind of rumor is never based on such things as responsible fact-checking."

"Well, then," Stan said, "we come back to my original point. What business is this of ours? Of the department? Of the university's, for Christ's sake?" What business was this of his, for that matter? The most important question was what it had done to Vanessa? *Have I been blind to signs of damage left by abuse? And why do I feel guilty?*

"Stan, I understand where you're coming from," Roger said soberly. "My position in this is quite different from yours, however. I dismissed the complaints when they first came to me. I can't when they start coming down from above."

"Above?" Stan said. "Like from the Pope? The Lord God in Heaven?"

Michelle winced.

"Sorry," Stan said to her. He was usually able to restrain his language in her presence. But her expression was more bemused than accusatory.

"From the provost's office, Stan," Roger said. "I can't ignore it."

"Why did you bring this up, Roger?" Michelle said. "Is there something you think we—Stan and I—should do?"

"No, not at this point. If neither of you knows anything about this—I mean, about her being involved in child pornography—that's all I wanted to know for the moment. But if either of you find out anything…"

"Of course, we'll pass it on to you," Michelle said, "but surely you aren't asking us to… to bring it up with Vanessa?"

"No, not if it doesn't… come up. Just be aware than Vanessa may be confronted by this, more likely sooner than later, from what I've been told."

"Roger, I think we've spent too much time on this already." Stan got to his feet. "I'll go fetch her. It's time for congratulations." He was thinking about her waiting—wondering what had gone wrong. And he wanted to blot out the images that had turned his guts into a pit of snakes.

"Amen," Michelle said with finality.

CHAPTER 13

Out in the hallway, he looked both ways without seeing her at first. Then he recognized one of her running shoes bobbing up and down in an arc where there was a bench tucked away in an alcove. Volunteers usually waited for experiments there. As he approached, he saw that she was sitting with one leg crossed over the other and swinging the free one. When she heard him, she stood up and stuck a piece of notepaper in the book she was reading.

He held out his arms. "You wowed them both. We all thought you did an outstanding job." He gave her a hug, which she self-consciously returned.

Back in the conference room, Michelle met her with outstretched arms. "Good work, Vanessa." She patted her on the back with both hands as they embraced.

Vanessa murmured, "Thank you." As she and Roger shook hands, he said, "I told the others what a pleasure it is to come away from an oral feeling enlightened. In this instance, I profited more than from many of our visiting lecturers."

"Thank you, Dr. Zhrudsky. Maybe this sort of makes up for my behavior in your seminar last year."

"No apologies needed, Vanessa. I'd be honored if you decided to take another class from me." He gathered up his papers and nodded to Michelle and Stan. "You'll have to excuse me. I'm seeing our dean at noon about a funding issue."

After he left, Michelle handed Vanessa the document reporting that she had passed the oral exam and the title page for her thesis with the committee's signatures.

"Thanks, Michelle. You're the one who rescued me last fall. I wouldn't be here without you."

"You're welcome. But I think you'd have found some way to get here on your own." She patted Vanessa on the shoulder. "Anyway, good job."

After Michelle left, Vanessa put her arms around Stan and hastily kissed him. "Thanks, Stan. I couldn't have done this without you either."

He hugged her a bit nervously, aware that people passing in the hall could see them through the open door. She probably felt it, too, because she dropped her arms immediately and started putting her papers from the meeting in her backpack.

"We'll celebrate properly, tonight," he said.

"Amen!"

He did a double take, but she didn't notice.

He had had unqualified confidence that Vanessa would not only just "pass" her oral, but dazzle Roger and confirm Michelle's and his conviction that she was the best student in the history of the graduate program. That was why he felt there was little risk in making a reservation for them at the Herbfarm on Friday night after her exam. He decided to surprise her; he said only that they would go out for dinner if everything went well.

As they left the conference room together, he suggested they have lunch at Portage Bay Café. It was a twenty-minute walk away, and the clouds weren't threatening to rain for a while. When they reached Twelfth Avenue, she stopped and waved toward the north. "I just noticed that—conveniently—my apartment is less than a block away."

"Are you accusing me of devious planning?"

She tossed her head with a giggle. "Not at all. I'm impressed with your insight. How did you know that for a celebration, I like sex better than food or wine?"

He was completely at a loss for an answer, so he grabbed her hand and headed north toward her apartment. It wasn't exactly a quickie, but five minutes after he closed the door of her apartment behind him, they lay breathless and sweaty on her narrow bed, he on his back with one shoulder hanging off the edge, she beside him with her head cradled in his arm and her butt wedged against the wall.

He told her in a whisper about the dinner reservation he'd made. "It's a four-and-a-half-hour banquet of nine courses: Food unlike anything you've ever tasted with wines exquisitely calibrated to each tasty morsel."

"You mean big tables and people I'll have to make small talk with?" Her eyes could express so many emotions at once he couldn't sort them all out.

"No. A table for two."

"I was hoping we could make love again this evening." Her slack face told him she was truly disappointed. "I won't be up for much of anything after four hours of eating."

"You'll be pleasantly surprised. The portions are small, and it's amazing how spreading a meal out over the evening changes it."

"Hmm." She didn't look convinced.

He squeezed her shoulder. "From what I've seen of you, I'm sure we can—"

She raised her head abruptly. "You didn't know I had a raging libido, did you?" She didn't smile, and her eyes probed his like spotlights.

He hesitated. *Where was this going anyway?* "To be honest, no."

"You didn't wonder why I seduced you—in the lab?" The way she waited for his response made him squirm.

He felt himself flushing. Finally, he said slowly, "To be honest with you…"

She said nothing—only smiled and nodded.

"I did."

"Of course you did. Who wouldn't?" She propped her head so her face was a few inches from his. "So let me tell you why. First, as far as I can tell, I like sex as much as the average man does. Other women think I'm oversexed, and maybe they're right. But there's one big difference. I'm not promiscuous. I mean, I don't have one-night stands—or one-month stands. It doesn't have to be a long-term commitment—years. But I don't sleep with anyone else until it's clear my present relationship isn't working in some way."

"I see."

Her laugh sounded like a little hiccup. "If you do, you're way ahead of most people I try to explain this to."

"So… I mean, with Paul…?"

"That's the other thing. You should know that Paul and I had been fighting for a long time."

"Over your thesis, right?"

"Not only that." She brushed back the hair that was about to fall over her eye. "Before last summer, we could argue our heads off, especially about psychology, and not get angry. Excited, yes. But not angry. But when he came back at the end of August—and I'd been missing him a lot, it was clear he'd been with a woman in France. Maybe more than one. He likes sex, too, but he's promiscuous."

"He's a man." Stan couldn't help but laugh. "He's supposed to like it. More than like it; crave it."

Vanessa seemed more irritated with him than amused. "Just so you know, I hadn't slept with anybody while he was cavorting around Provence."

"Not even when he first got back?" He regretted saying it immediately.

"I could tell…" She looked away. Her lower lip trembled. "He wanted to…" She shook her head abruptly. "I don't want to talk about it."

"I'm sorry I asked."

"It's okay. The simple fact is, I asked him point blank."

Stan realized he had been holding his breath too long. "And…?" he said in a long exhalation.

"Give him this: He admitted it immediately."

Stan knew this conversation had moved beyond his emotional range. He was tongue-tied.

"I'll bet you're starving." She crawled over him and stood up. "Let's continue our walk, shall we, my dear?" She seemed to have snapped out of her somber mood.

He had some time to reflect on what she'd said. "Can I ask you one more question?" He was struggling with her revelations, even though she seemed to think she'd told him everything.

"Sure." She was already hooking her bra.

"You haven't really explained why I wasn't a one-night stand." He got to his feet to pull on his jockey shorts. "I mean, you just admitted that *you* seduced *me*."

Her head emerged from the neck of her T-shirt. "Good question." She looked around "How did my jeans and shoes end up by the door?" She padded over and stepped into her pants, managing to slip into her shoes at the same time.

"I learned something in college." She turned around, fully dressed, as she spoke. "I *was* promiscuous for a year or so. But after while I figured out that there are two kinds of men. A few of them think about what I'm saying and try to suppress their fantasies about getting into my pants. The other guys think first about what's under my clothes and how to get them off. It shows, Stan, in how they keep up their part of the conversation."

"I'm flattered." He was too busy trying to catch up with her dressing to say more.

"You were the first faculty member besides Michelle who treated me like my ideas were worth your thinking about. And I liked the way you were firm with me—telling me I had to jump through the hoops, you said. But you acted like maybe my research on myself had some merit."

He finally joined her by the door where she stood with her hand on the knob.

She stood on tiptoe to kiss him. "And I think you truly want to understand my theory—what I'm trying to do. That counted for everything with me, Stan."

On the way down the stairway, she stopped and looked up at him following her. "I may act like I think about sex all the time. But I don't. What I *do* think about every waking moment is how I'm going to really, deeply… fundamentally understand how the mind and the brain work."

She took two more steps and stopped again, smiling up at him in the dim light of the enclosed stairway. "Except when I'm actually making love. It's a perfect diversion for me. It takes one hundred percent of my mind, brain—and body."

On the street again, Stan discovered she was indeed a hundred percent back on her work. "I like the idea of your arranging a fête for me. Even though I didn't really do much this morning. I won't feel like I've accomplished anything until I get my first publication."

"All the more reason to get going on your PhD research." He took her hand.

She used it to tug them to a stop. "I read someplace that in the sciences the best single predictor of career productivity is the number of publications prior to the PhD."

"The correlation isn't that high." He drew her on with his hand.

A few minutes later in the restaurant, the first thing she said to him after they'd ordered was, "Did you notice?"

"What?" He glanced in the direction their waitress had gone, thinking Vanessa had recognized her from somewhere.

"My committee didn't make me promise to run the multi-subject design for my dissertation." Her eyes had as much challenge in them as her words.

"True enough," he said. "However, you promised *me*. That's enough. Or should be."

"What if I wrote a theoretical proposal?" She looked at him out of the corners of her eye. "That would fit better with the specialties you list on your website. One of them is theories of cognition, you know."

He sighed. "Vanessa, I hate to admit this to you unequivocally, but I can't understand the math in your theory. And—"

"But it's not that hard. I can teach—"

"Let me finish." He waited for her nod of deference. "Even if I could master the formal side of it—and I'm not sure I can, there's too much neuroscience for me. I'm not competent to evaluate that part of it either."

"Okay, forget the theoretical thesis." She continued as if she'd expected his answer. "You'll be happy to know that I have the program for my first experiment running in your lab. Kevin was very helpful, by the way."

Kevin Greenfield was Stan's graduate assistant and a genius with both hardware and software.

"Great! I'm happy to hear it. Remember though: You have to have a formal proposal approved by your doctoral committee before you start testing subjects."

"I'm going to write up the first experiment as a pilot study. There's all this crap about filing for 'candidacy'—whatever that is—and waiting for the graduate school to appoint a committee member from outside the department. And then I've got to pass out a proposal and schedule the meeting. By the time I'm *allowed* to hand out a proposal, I can be a third of the way through my research." She said the word *allowed* with a sarcastic inflection.

"But you don't even know how it's going to come out, Vanessa."

"I'll know plenty soon enough to write a different proposal if it doesn't come out the way my theory says it should. I learned from my master's thesis not to screw around waiting for the rules of the graduate program."

"I just hope that theory of yours is as powerful as you make it sound."

"The power of mathematics, my dear."

What a student! He'd learned by now that if he challenged her to write a proposal, he'd find the first draft in his inbox on Monday morning. He was also learning to get out of her way and let her run her education. And try to keep up with the pace. By now he'd also concluded that she was headed for something more momentous than collaborating with him on a grant to extend her master's thesis.

When she was half finished with her salad, she put down her fork. "Stan, would you disown me if I sent my thesis to *Science*?"

He looked up. "Disown you?"

"Yeah. So I have to find another sponsor? Or see if Paul—"

"Don't do that."

"There was a reason I wrote it up in that format first, you know."

"I've already told you why it would be a bad idea. The paper will be reviewed by a cognitive scientist, and Ebbinghaus-style studies simply aren't accepted as evidence today."

"I've revised it. There's a footnote describing the pilot experiment, and I added a paragraph explaining the rationale."

"That won't make any difference. I know, Vanessa."

She leaned back and crossed her arms just under her breasts. For a moment he flashed on one of her nude *Playboy* photos with much the same pose except in it her arms were obviously pushing up her breasts.

"Are you going to stop me?" she said.

"How could I? I'm trying to spare you the disappointment of—"

"Oh, I see. You're trying to protect me, are you?"

"I didn't mean to—" he stammered.

"Don't be condescending with me, Stan. I'm a big girl now."

"I'm not… Look, I can't prevent you from sending it, okay? But I don't want to be seen as condoning—"

"I get it now. This is about *you*, not me?"

"Vanessa, please be reasonable." He could see there was no point in arguing with her.

"You haven't convinced me it's unreasonable. Unless you can, I'm sending it… Monday morning."

"Then I'm encouraging you to try. And I promise not to say, 'I told you so.' I'll be very curious what kind of feedback you get."

"Thank you, Stan."

"And I want you to promise to come see me when you hear from the editor. Will you do that?"

"I promise." She held up her hand as though swearing an oath.

In spite of their little disagreement, they had a wonderful day. She wore a stunning little black cocktail dress—emphasis on "little." Courtesy of Paul Kovick, she told him. The meal lived up to all his expectations, including his prediction that she wouldn't feel too full to make love afterward. For her part, she talked about The Herbfarm for weeks.

Jim Forrester's strategy had backfired. His three consultants had all concluded that the parts of Vanessa's paper they understood were excellent, but none of them thought they were competent to judge the whole thing. That didn't stop them from raving about its originality. For example, Todd Marquart, his buddy in physics, told him he might very well be looking at the Einstein of cognitive neuroscience. But the part he understood best—the physics—was the least important part of the paper.

So now what was he going to do? She hardly deserved another put-down. But figuring out how to tell her the paper was extraordinary was beyond him. He still couldn't get past the suspicion that privately, Vanessa Trippett thought most of the research in cognitive neuroscience—and his in particular—was pretty shitty.

What was she really up to? He suspected she was a one-woman stealth campaign to reform the way his field approached the brain, that she saw him and his ilk as dust in the rearview mirror. And she was playacting the demur schoolgirl about to ask in a voice just loud enough for everybody to hear, "Why aren't these professors wearing any clothes?"

> 2009-01-13 07:36:44:
> Vanessa, Please see me about your paper. Forrester

He'd left his door wide open, so she rapped on the metal doorframe instead.

She met his eyes when he looked up.

"Is now a good time for you, Dr. Forrester?"

"It is." He thought she seemed less concerned than he'd expected. But then, it had been a brief exchange of words, and her emotions were hard enough to read with even bigger samples of her behavior.

She didn't close his door behind her. He decided not to say anything. It probably didn't matter who else heard him admit she had him buffaloed. He took his time pawing through the stack of papers on his desk. When he found hers, he tossed it on the uncluttered surface in front of her.

"So, the verdict is completely muddled." He decided to let her stand. "Everyone thinks your writing is beautiful. So do I, as a matter of fact—"

"Thank—"

"Too goddamn beautiful. It's like a siren song, lulling readers, even critical ones, into believing complete nonsense. My math consultant asked a colleague who's an expert in your kind of math for some help. They say your math's pretty good—a few nitpicks here and there, but otherwise brilliant... for someone in psychology. Hah! As for the rest of your paper, it might as well have been written in Aramaic. The mathematicians beg off, claiming they lack the expertise.

"My physicist friend duly notes the parallel to theories in his field. He infers you know as much physics as the majority of his graduate students. Oh, and by the way, he was dazzled by the way you use math as a tool. And he suggests, I hope not seriously, that you could just be that prophet of the Age of Aquarius in psychology—God help us! But, as for the neuroscience, well, it was all Aramaic to him, too.

"I was hoping my buddy in neurology would be more critical, but he claims to have understood all your theorizing and labels your achievement 'seminal.' I want to ask him about his ludicrous choice of adjective. He was so mesmerized he forwarded your paper to everyone in the neurology department." He leaned back in his chair and laced his fingers behind his head.

"I don't understand what you're driving at, Dr. Forrester."

"No? I think you do, actually, Vanessa. You're way too smart to have missed my point."

"I'm confused. There are too many contradictions in what you said."

"Exactly!"

"And too much irony."

She was getting feisty, but her level intonation belied the emotion conveyed by her words alone. "Contradictions" could be a cipher for burgeoning anger; "irony," for cryptic hostility. But she might as well have been the statue whose stony handclasp cast Don Giovanni into hell, for all her feelings showed on that face of Aegean marble.

"No, you're not confused, Vanessa. You know the field as well as my own students. You showed that in class."

"Thank you, Dr.—"

"Let me finish." He glared at her. "Your review of the literature was accurate, as far as it went. Under those circumstances, I couldn't possibly give you a B in the course, or even a C, just because your paper is a monumental insult to my expertise, and then turn around and give one of my own students an A, even though her paper is a fawning suck-up.

"On the other hand, the parts of your paper you knew I couldn't understand, the experts found competent. Since those parts also form the basis of your unconventional organization and vicious critique of everything that's being done in the field—"

"That's not what I—"

"No, no. It is. It is." He shrugged dramatically. "I'm admitting defeat, Vanessa. I hope you're satisfied and stay away from my courses in the future. I don't think I could take another quarter like the last one." He didn't smile. "I have some advice for you, if you're interested."

"Of course I am."

"I know you've made a career of ignoring advice around here, so I don't know why I'm wasting my breath."

"Please. I'm listening. I really am." Her rising voice signaled that he'd finally gotten a rise out of her.

"This work is way premature. Don't waste your time trying to get it published. Editors and reviewers will be a lot harsher on it than I have been, trust me."

"Thank you. I want to believe you're being honest with me. And I'm grateful."

"Okay," he said with a sigh, "I take you at your word."

"Is there any chance I could talk to your... your 'consultants.'? I mean, about my paper?"

"I'll tell them to contact *you*, okay?"

"Yes. Thank you again, Dr. Forrester."

He stared after her as she crossed the hall and disappeared into her office. Damn! He'd overdone it again. He just could not deal with that woman calmly.

He'd have given anything to have her as his student. Grant was probably right. She was the harbinger of a paradigm shift, and the math in her paper could very well be something he would need to master in the future to keep up with the field.

She could have taught him what he needed. He'd gone further in math than most of his colleagues in neuroscience, and his students claimed she could explain statistics better than Michelle. But he'd gotten off on the wrong foot with her, and now he couldn't possibly work with her. And she would want nothing to do with him.

CHAPTER 14

When Vanessa arrived at Stan's place that evening, her backpack was bulging. She lowered it to the couch and embraced him. After two spirited kisses, she pointed to the pack. "At least now I won't have to put on dirty underwear the next time I wind up spending the night here."

"The guest bedroom is ready for you."

"Great!" She hefted the pack again.

He followed her down the hallway and into the second bedroom, which he'd been using as a guest room. "I also cleaned out the closet for you."

She opened the door and glanced at the work shirt, T-shirt and jeans she'd left in his closet in the master bedroom the week before. "Thanks!"

He opened the top drawer of the dresser. "You said you only needed one drawer, but I went ahead and cleaned out the top two for you."

"A couple day's stuff is all I brought." She heaved her backpack on the bed.

He watched as she unzipped it. "You know, it would probably be simpler if you—"

"I decided three years ago that I prefer having my own place to retreat to. I moved in with Paul because it was better than sharing everything with Emily and Kayla. At least I had my own room and bath at Paul's."

She turned around and started neatly stacking her bras, panties and socks in the dresser drawer Stan had pulled open. "You have the same setup here, and a lot more space. But I really like my apartment, Stan. I like having my own schedule and setting my own agenda."

"I've spent enough time with you to accept your independence. I didn't mean to pressure you." But he sure wished he could somehow influence her more on this issue. Still, he felt he'd made a little progress.

Over the weekend, he'd persuaded her to bring enough of her personal things to his Green Lake house so she'd be comfortable spending a leisurely weekend morning with him after dinner the previous evening. She complained about not having extra shampoo and the like to keep in two places at once.

He insisted they go to a nearby Bartell drugstore and get what she needed. It amounted to surprisingly little: a bar of soap, a bottle of shampoo, another of skin lotion, a toothbrush and tube of toothpaste.

That morning she'd asked to borrow a nail scissors and nail file. Although she didn't complain at the time, she bought her own at the drugstore along with a comb and hairbrush. There were no cosmetics; he wasn't surprised. Except for a smidgen of lipstick when she dressed up, she never used anything else.

The trip to Bartell's solved one of the mysteries about her. She always smelled good—clean with a faint scent. When she selected shampoo and skin lotion, she quickly picked a bottle off the shelf as though she knew exactly what she wanted. He glanced in the cart: Orange blossom shampoo and "wild violet" skin lotion.

"Vanessa?"

She paused and turned from the toothpaste section. "Yes, Stan."

He held up the shampoo bottle. "Why did you pick wild violet? You smelled like cherry blossoms last night."

"I don't know. I just grabbed one." She braced herself on his shoulder and stretched to kiss his cheek. "Would you like me to smell like a cherry orchard?"

"No. I guess I like the variety."

"Sure? I can get a matching lotion, too."

"No, no. Let's see how violets and oranges get along."

While he was helping her stow the stuff they'd bought, he noticed a small bottle of prescription medicine. He almost reached for it out of curiosity.

She saw him looking. "Microgestin." She took the bottle off the shelf and handed it to him. "Even though you're more compulsive about condoms than any other man I've ever slept with, I don't intend to get pregnant in a moment of passion."

She put the bottle back on the shelf when he handed it to her. "I split my supply. It'll be a pain, keeping track of the regime. But at least I'll have some here."

While he made dinner, she sat at the table and told him about her meeting with Jim Forrester.

He had to laugh. "Just like Jim. Always a lot of bluster, but he appreciates a good piece of work when he sees it."

"I don't think so. He resents my use of mathematics that he doesn't understand."

"Comes to the same thing, Vanessa. He knows when he's out of his depth. He may not like it. He may feel threatened by it. In fact, now that I think about it, that's probably the best guess what's going on in his head. But he's honest enough to admit defeat."

"I just wish he'd help me a little more." She looked at him earnestly when he glanced around. "Stan, I need someone who knows the literature as well as Forrester does and knows as much math as the faculty member who read my paper for him."

"That reminds me. Jot down a note on my reminder pad. I'm going to talk to him." Stan kept pads of sticky notes everywhere in the house, including one on the dining room table. Every morning before breakfast, he collected them and pasted them into the master calendar he carried everywhere with him.

"I completely disagree with his not telling you who his referees were. One way or another, I'll pry the names out of him for you."

"Good luck! I hope you can. I'll be extremely grateful to you."

From the opening paragraph of Vanessa's paper describing her theory of the mind-brain continuum, Lin Xuan had been electrified. Here at last was someone who had a rigorous, empirically testable approach to the great mystery of the mind that had fascinated philosophers and scientists for centuries.

Lin was an odd bird in a medical school department. In addition to his MD, he had a PhD in a field outside the life sciences, and it was in physics, with all that implied about his mastery of mathematics. Thus, he was the first reader to grasp what Vanessa had accomplished.

He had received a copy of her paper from Grant Sayles, a fellow assistant professor in the neurology department of the medical school, who had been so impressed by Vanessa's theory that he had circulated the paper to everyone in their department.

There was every reason for Lin to believe that the paper was, as Sayles's covering email had implied, the work of a mature scientist at another university. Forrester, true to his word, had removed Vanessa's name and institutional affiliation. Sayles and Forrester were friends, who played racquetball at least once a week.

When Lin told Grant he wanted to communicate with the author, Grant checked with Forrester again and came away this time with the impression that Vanessa was a post-doctoral fellow in the UW psychology department. Consequently, Lin was even more amazed by the first email exchange he had with Vanessa.

2009-02-03 15:39:18:
Dr. Vanessa Trippett, A colleague of mine passed along to me your paper, "A Unified Theory of the Mind-Brain Continuum," thinking I might find it interesting, as indeed I did. Your approach is most original; however, there are several problems in your assumptions and derivations, which I believe can be repaired. I would like to discuss them with you, preferably in person. Please contact me at 221-0701. Lin Xuan, Department of Neurology, UW Medicine

2009-02-03 15:42:40:
Dr. Xuan, Yes, please! I have been desperately searching for someone who can help me with the details of my theory. I am also weak on the brain research I am trying to explain. And I haven't even tackled the pathology literature, which you have obviously mastered. I could meet with you tomorrow morning, Thursday afternoon, and anytime Friday. Please let me know if one of those times will work for you. And thank you for offering to meet with me. Vanessa Trippett [P.S. If it turns out you didn't stay online after you emailed me, I'll try calling you in half an hour. And, I'm a graduate student (just so you know).]

A graduate student? It hardly seemed possible! The paper was loaded with insights beyond any he'd thought possible—and phenomenally comprehensive in its coverage of research in both the neurosciences and cognitive psychology. The woman must be a genius—there was no other term for precocity of this degree. But what was going on? Why would Forrester have misled Grant—twice?

> 2009-02-03 15:46:57:
> Vanessa, Tomorrow morning at 9:00 would be excellent. I look forward to meeting you. And please call me Lin. Lin Xuan

He was in for still another shock when she stood in the doorway of his little office. She looked like one of the coeds he saw on his infrequent visits to upper campus. Looking at her initially, he was literally speechless for a moment.

It was her youthful face that immediately seized his attention. Such a curious concatenation of features: Dainty nose and lips looked as though they were shaped of pearly porcelain, like a China doll. Ultramarine eyes such a deep and saturated blue they could hold the secrets of the stars in their depths. And black satin hair—like his mother's long tresses, which he had loved to stroke when he was a boy.

"Hi!" She walked the two steps to his desk, extending a delicate hand. "I'm Vanessa."

"Lin Xu—Uh, nice to meet you."

Her hand felt warm and dry when they shook hands.

"Thank you for taking this time with me," she said.

"It's no trouble. In fact, it's my pleasure."

"Well, I hope this won't disappoint you." She laughed again and blushed. "Everyone else who's read it claimed it was very difficult to understand."

He shook his head. "No, no. I… Oh, please sit down." He waved her to the chair next to his desk and waited. Then he pulled a black rolling stool to his desk and sat on it.

Now that she was so close to him, he could think of nothing but her profound gaze. Neither of them spoke for a moment. Then they both began at once.

"I owe you an explanation—"

"You said in your email—"

They halted simultaneously. Both laughed nervously. He waited, letting her break the impasse.

"You were saying?" she said.

"Oh… I owe you an explanation of how I came to have a copy of your paper. Grant Sayles, a colleague of mine here in neurology, passed along your paper to me because it contains quite a lot of mathematics and references to physics, and I'm one of the few neurologists around who has a PhD in physics."

"Then I guess you weren't intimidated by the mathematics like everyone else who's looked at it?"

He ducked his head in acknowledgment. "You must have a thorough grounding in both math and physics to have written this paper." He held it up but kept it turned so she couldn't see the printed side.

"Just the undergraduate level. I majored in math with minors in physics and psychology."

"That accounts for the ingredients of your work without explaining the creative synthesis you've achieved."

"I… I was just calculating how long you've been in school and residency and the like. I've come up with sixteen, plus you must have been here at UW for at least a couple of years." She paused again. "If you don't mind… you look too young for that many years."

He laughed. "I had some educational advantages. I come from Singapore, where I attended a private school and was able to finish a bachelor's degree at the National University when I was eighteen. MIT let me start graduate school the following fall."

"In physics, you mean?"

"Yes, but it took me four years to finish because I began studying the nervous system. When I started med school at Columbia, I finally had classmates who were about my age."

"Sounds like my academic career so far, but writ large." Her smile lit up his small office like a bank of floodlights.

"However, you have the advantage of studying psychology. I know much less about the mind than I do the brain. Reading your paper whetted my appetite for more cognitive psychology."

She glanced up at the sparse collection of books he kept on one shelf attached to the wall behind him. "I'd be happy to suggest some papers and books you could read. But I hope you see that you're a perfect person to review my paper. I have two professors of cognitive science on my committee, but no mathematicians or neuroscientists." Her smile turned arch for a moment before she seemed to think better of it and made her smile less provocative. "Maybe you'd consider serving on my committee?"

"I'm not on the graduate faculty, unfortunately. However, I could suggest several neurologists in my department who are. Their backgrounds would make them more than qualified."

"But I'd still need a mathematician." She sounded a little plaintive.

"Yes. You seem to be working in the interstices of several disciplines."

"I've never thought of it that way. But you're more qualified than anyone I've met."

He laid the stapled sheaf of papers on his desk and pushed it toward her, turning it as he did so she could see that her name was missing from the first page. He'd handwritten her name in the upper right-hand corner with her email address below it.

"My colleague Grant didn't know who had written this paper. The author's name had been—what's the word?—'redacted.'" He chuckled.

"So how did you get my name?"

"Grant plays squash with your Professor Forrester, who asked him if he would help him evaluate your review of the neuroscience literature. Dr. Forrester told him that a colleague had been begging him to review the paper before she sent it to a journal. He claimed he was mystified by your approach and had already asked someone in the math department to read it."

"So were you involved in Dr. Sayles's evaluation? I don't understand."

"No, I got the paper later. After I'd read it the first time, I told Grant I wanted to talk to the author. Dr. Forrester hadn't told him your name. So the next time they played squash, Grant asked how I could contact you. He was surprised you were here at the UW; he got the impression you were a post-doc somewhere else."

"No. A second-year grad student in psychology here."

"Neither of us thought this was the work of a graduate student." He pointed to the paper on the desk in front of her. "It certainly doesn't read like a term paper, for instance."

"That's what it is. Or was." She started turning back the pages. "I'm thinking about making it my thesis, and in any case, I plan to submit it for publication."

"I think you should definitely try to publish it."

"I wouldn't have guessed that from all the comments you've written on it." She looked up at him.

He smiled. "But some of them are positive. Take a look at page two."

She folded the sheets back and began reading.

He waited until he saw her eyes shift lower on the sheet. "You see, I think your postulating an axis of consciousness with evolutionary implications is a stroke of genius."

"You don't think it's too ambitious?"

He shook his head slowly. "Not at all."

"It seemed fanciful at first. However, it's the mathematical key to integrating the two domains, mental and physical—psychological and physiological."

"That's only part of the brilliance of the idea. First, it gives your theory a phylogenetic logic, relating the development of the brain to the increasing intelligence of behavior from the simplest species to the most complex." He paused.

"You don't see any problem with ascribing conscious awareness to monkeys or dogs?"

"Nor to rats, or even octopi. But there's an even more important implication. The consciousness axis gives you a basis for incorporating genetic phenomena into your theory."

Vanessa stared at him, speechless.

He studied her face. "You mean, you hadn't thought of that?"

She shook her head. "Not at all. And I certainly should have. It's almost frightening to…"

"You absolutely must make that clear in your paper. I have a list of citations for you. I think you will find them helpful. They have quantitative results, as required to test your theory adequately."

"I'm anxious to look at them. I've been collecting some cognitive data on the consciousness dimension. They seem to be falling into line with my theory's predictions."

"You mean you're doing experiments, too?"

"For my thesis. I'll send you a copy of what I've done so far."

"I'm even more impressed. And I feel somewhat better about pointing out some problems I saw in what you've written here." He raised his eyebrows to stop her from interrupting. "I mean, your PhD program doesn't depend on completing a truly audacious theoretical project."

"So what are the big problems? Please don't keep me in suspense any longer." Her infectious smile rekindled her face—the same smile that had captivated him from the instant she appeared in his doorway.

"You wonder why I hesitate, don't you?" He waited for her to nod. "Well then, let's deal first with two large conceptual issues. Large, only because the sweep of your theory is so great."

He leaned toward her with both elbows on the table. "The major weakness in your theory, as I see it, is the virtual absence of the motor system. It is as though the only output of your hypothetical brain is thinking and feeling."

"I've tried to incorporate the motor system, but the equations were too unwieldy. And I guess I was discouraged by the fact that I'd have to account for the enormous literature on motor-skills."

"That would only widen the scope of your theory still further—a plus, I believe. Have you considered representing the brain as a barrier between the sensory and motor systems?"

He used his hands as though holding a volleyball, then squeezed and twisted them as though kneading it as it deflated. "Like an irregular asteroid with a crust, mantle and core—the brain is the mantle between the crust of the body that is in the world "out there" and the core, which is the mental world. Information flows from the outside, is transformed by the brain into—"

She took an abrupt breath. "—into mental representations?"

"Yes, yes. That's it exactly." He was getting excited, seeing how quickly she understood his line of thinking. He curled his fingers around an imaginary softball and pointed to the hollow space inside it. "Now, you need a way for the mind—the core, in your model—to send messages to the body—the crust, in other words—so it can do something in the world."

She nodded slowly. "Very early, I tried that approach. But I couldn't find a way to do it that gave me a solvable set of partial differential equations."

"Yes, that's the crux, isn't it? I've worked out a formalism embodying an idea that I think might be added seamlessly to your present formulation." He pulled a stapled set of yellow quadrille-ruled sheets off a pile and spun it around in front of her. "My gut feeling tells me that it satisfies integrability conditions. But of course, I didn't have time to work through it."

"I tried a ton of them that didn't." She paged slowly through the sheets as she spoke, then stopped suddenly and flipped back to the first page. "Wait a minute! If I partial out, for example, time…"

"A good choice. Isn't perception of time a marker of awareness?"

"Yes, of course. That's why I chose it. So partial out time in this equation…" She pointed, turning the sheet so he could read it. "…I think I see how to do it."

"But now, have you considered a patient who we know is at least partially conscious but can't speak and, therefore, can't tell us what's going on. If you flesh out your theory a little, we should be able to answer the question from a brain imaging study."

"That's the point of making this theory *quantitative.* The prediction is orders of magnitude more precise."

"Yes, and that's why anesthesiologists are going to be interested, too. They will be able to say from a real-time brain image whether the patient is aware of pain during a procedure, once they've mapped out pain perception using your geometry to precisely constrain locations in the brain."

She gaped at him. "I could never think of implications like that. It takes a physician to see the connections to specialties other than psychiatry and, of course, neurology."

"That's why you simply must pursue this line of thought." He shifted his weight uneasily. "Now the second major problem is that your handling of brain chemistry is woefully inadequate."

"I was afraid of that." She searched his face with a worried look. "Do you think it can be fixed?"

"Obviously I do, or I wouldn't be encouraging you. My suggestion would be to try introducing a parameter for each neuromodulator—"

"I thought of that, but there are hundreds, aren't there?"

"But they can be classified and ordered…" When she frowned skeptically, he went on, "…even scaled." He smiled.

"I know, but…" Her voice fell. "I wanted to derive them in a principled way."

"Of course. But that's too ambitious for now. Leave it for the future. To me, it belongs in your quantum neurology."

"Hmm." She stared at her paper again. "I'll have to look at the neurochemistry literature again with that in mind."

"I'll give you some references that I think will help."

"Okay." His remark seemed to have dampened her enthusiasm. "What else?"

"Let's look at two points in your derivations." He picked up the paper, flipped back two pages, and laid it in front of her. "This step here." He pointed to a section he had bracketed in the margin with a pencil. "I can't follow it."

She studied it for more than a minute. Then she dove for her backpack and pulled out a pad of yellow paper that was identical to what he had used. She copied an equation from the paper on to the first sheet with a pencil she'd pulled from her shirt pocket. "Okay."

She wrote another equation under the first, commenting as her pencil moved rapidly along the line. She turned the sheet so he could see. He nodded. She spun the pad back and wrote a third line, continuing to describe her logic. Again, she turned the pad for him. Using her hips, she nudged her chair closer to the corner of the desk so he see better as she added the next line. She smelled of sandalwood, but there was also a hint of the sea that reminded him of home.

He rolled his stool toward the corner and murmured "Uh-huh," as she completed the line.

She tore off the first page and wrote a new equation at the top of a clean sheet.

When she finished, he pointed to a symbol. "Hold on. Where does that come from?"

"It's my curvature metric." She stood as she grabbed her paper and folded back several sheets. "Here." She pointed and moved around the corner of the desk to show him.

He had gotten to his feet at the same moment and moved closer to look. Each of them sidled toward the other, absorbed in the contents of the paper she was holding.

"See," she said. "I've solved for *zeta* sub-*i*."

Still pointing, she thrust the paper at him. As he reached to take it, their shoulders and hips collided, and the paper crumpled between their outstretched hands and fell to the desk. They jumped away from each other as though the impact had detonated a percussion cap between them. Their startled eyes met.

"Oh! I didn't mean to—"

"Sorry, sorry! I—"

With a whispered rustle, the loose pages of the rumpled paper sprang loose and flipped over. The two of them simultaneously looked in the direction of the sound.

When her brilliant deep blue eyes met his, she began to snicker. It was infectious, and within seconds they were both laughing giddily.

Still chuckling, he picked up her paper and quickly found the page she had shown him. "So you substituted *zeta* sub-*i* into…"

"Don't you see, it follows—"

"Yes, of course." He smiled warmly at her. "So, the problem here is very simple to fix. All you need to do is add another line or two of explanation—and maybe this equation." He pointed.

"You think it's needed? Apparently, a mathematician didn't have a problem with this step."

"You aren't writing for mathematicians, Vanessa." He picked up her paper where she'd laid it on his desk. "Now, the other problem…" He flipped over the pages looking. "Here it is." Laying it in front of her, he pointed. "I don't think your conclusion follows."

When she glanced at her chair, he stepped deftly behind her and lifted it around the desk so she could sit on the same side as his stool. He held it for her and, when she sat, slid it forward under her.

While she studied the place he had marked, he pulled another sheaf of yellow paper off the only pile on his desk. "Maybe this will help." He laid his notes next to her paper.

He pulled up his stool and sat next to her. "Starting with your conclusion here, I worked backward. I believe I've demonstrated that it doesn't follow from your premises."

Again, she spent more than a minute examining his work. "Yes," she said finally, "I think you're right."

"However, take a look at the equation I came up with on the next page."

She turned the first page over. "This one?" She marked the top line with her thumb.

"Yes. I wonder if you reformulated the proximity metric that way, you could avoid the inconsistency. The metric's going to have to be different anyway, I think."

She smiled at him wanly. "That's a big restructuring."

They both turned to stare without speaking at the paper where it now lay, humped up because of its stapled corner.

She broke the silence. "I'm almost afraid to ask for more help. But I need all you can give me."

"This should also be useful." He retrieved another sheaf of paper from the other side of his desk, this one white. "These are papers I came up with that meet your criterion of quantitative rigor, including the ones I mentioned on neurochemistry."

She turned quickly through four pages of printed references. Her face was glum. "Thank you. These are journals I never even considered."

He glanced at his watch. "I'm sorry. I have a conference at eleven."

"Is it that late?" She stacked the papers he'd given her and slipped them into her backpack.

He stepped back when she stood.

She held out her hand to him. "Thank you, Lin. I really appreciate the time you've taken with me."

Her grip was strong, in spite of the delicate appearance of her hand. "It was a true pleasure, Vanessa." As she turned to go, he added, "Oh, and I want to know how you're coming with revising your paper."

"As soon as I make some progress."

"If I don't hear from you, I intend to email you for a progress report. In two weeks, I'll insist on another meeting."

"That's more than—"

"I want to see you publish that paper, Vanessa. It's too important to get buried."

"What can I say? I'll try."

CHAPTER 15

Brad had finally hit on a sure way to make some progress with Vanessa. Yeah, he knew she was probably sleeping with that asshole Harte. But she'd slept with Kovick earlier. And he knew *Playboy* models did their share of sleeping around. Besides, there was no way of knowing for sure that he didn't have a chance if he never took the first step, right?

He had the perfect first step, too. He'd scored two tickets to a classical music concert. And the band was going to play stuff by both Bach and Beethoven. How cool would she think that was? When he saw the ad for the show, he wasn't sure whether it was quite right. So he asked Carlie Winston—she was really into classical music. She told him, sure, there'd be lots of chances to talk, before the concert started and during the intermission. She also suggested a little wine bar in Wallingford—quiet, a good place to get acquainted.

"Romantic?" he'd asked.

"That too—but it'll cost you a shitload."

She even mentioned that she'd go with him if Vanessa turned him down. So at least the tickets weren't a complete gamble. Excellent! And Carlie would be okay company.

He had to laugh when Vanessa showed up in the office. She was so far out in her own world, she didn't look around—just walked over to her desk, flipped open her laptop as she sat down and started swiping at the track pad.

"Hey, Vanessa!"

She jumped. "Oh! Hi, Brad." She didn't turn around.

He stood. The door to Forrester's office across the hall was almost closed, and he could hear him talking with Hillary Freeburg inside. Brad hesitated. Forrester had said the door had to be open; he hadn't said how much. Brad carefully pushed the door until there was only an inch between it and the frame.

"Listen, I've got two tickets to a concert Friday night in the music school."

She turned around with a blank look on her face. "Friday night?"

"Yeah. Bach and Beethoven, your favorites, right?"

" Friday night?" she repeated. "I'm really sorry, Brad, but Stan and I already have tickets for it. The quartet is doing Opus 132, one of my all-time favorites. But thanks for thinking of me. Maybe Carlie would be interested."

Stan—the name was a dart hitting him in the gut. "You mean you're sleeping with your new advisor already?"

With a scrape she turned her chair so she wouldn't have to twist her neck to look at him. "What did you just say, Brad?"

"I said—" He sneered. "You're already fucking that dumbass Harte, and Kovick's not even back at work yet."

She stared at him for a moment like she couldn't believe what she'd heard. Then she rose deliberately from her chair and advanced on him, the top of her head barely reaching his nose. "That's completely out of line."

"Not if it's true—"

Her hand came up so fast he had no time to raise an arm in defense. The flat of her hand caught him on the cheek with such force that it knocked his head sideways.

Vanessa stepped back, looking stunned by what she had done. "The truth has nothing to do with it, and you know it," she blurted.

He grabbed her shoulders and shook her violently. "Whore!" he growled. He spun her around pinning her arms with his left arm and shoving his right hand into her pants in front.

Her body struggling against his aroused him in a way his anger hadn't. His middle finger, still outside her panties, groped its way toward the place his swelling dick wanted to go. They wheeled toward the door in slow motion.

"Let me go," she said, her voice rising. She kicked his shin with the heel of her shoe.

His grunt came out as a laugh. "I'll show you." His fingers fumbled with the elastic of her panties and probed down into her pubic hair.

"Brad!" Her shout was much louder than before but not yet a scream.

"Shut up, bitch!" he said under his breath. "You scream any louder and I'll shove something else up here." He wiggled his finger between her labia. She wasn't slippery yet, but just wait.

"Stop that, Brad!" It was her first full-throated scream. Another heel connected with a shin.

He snorted. His left hand, which bound her arm to her torso slipped so he had an unexpected handful of breast—but only for a moment.

One arm freed, she grabbed his scraggly beard and yanked it.

Neither of them heard the roar of Jim Forrester's voice. "What the fuck is going on in…?" He'd rammed the door so hard it slammed against the stopper on the floor, shuddered back and hit his arm. He swept it away impatiently.

Vanessa managed to put an elbow into Brad's ribs when he released her. "Whore!" *Shit!* Forrester had seen his hand in her jeans. He was fucked—doubly fucked. And now, he was face to face with a fucking alpha male gorilla.

Forrester advanced another step into the room. Vanessa had turned her back to the two men and was making a show of tucking her T-shirt back into her jeans, which she'd opened at the side.

"Vanessa?" Forrester's voice was only slightly less stentorian. "Are you all right?"

"Yeah. Let me put myself back together." She took her time hitching up her jeans, fastening the button and cinching the zipper. Finally, she turned to Forrester, and folded her arms over her chest. From her expression it was hard to tell whether she was incensed or disgusted, but she had herself remarkably well under control.

Brad had been sidling toward his desk during the exchange between Forrester and Vanessa. Forrester sidestepped now in front of Brad, blocking his way with his massive arm. "What happened to your fucking face?" Forrester's voice seemed to reverberate through the entire building.

"What's it look like? The bitch hit me."

Scowling, Forrester turned to Vanessa.

"I hit him." She glared back at him.

"Why?" He said it less loudly and with a hint of sarcasm.

"Ask him." She tilted her head in Brad's direction without looking at him.

Forrester looked at Brad, exasperated. "So?" His voice was louder again.

"It's none of your fucking business," Brad exploded.

"I'm making it my business." Forrester's face had turned a brilliant shade of vermillion. "I thought I told you to leave this door open when you're in here together."

"So?" Brad shouted back at him. "It was open, wasn't it? You walked right in."

Forrester advanced on Brad until his bared teeth were a foot away from his face. "Don't fuck with me, you little snot."

Brad fell back another step. Forrester followed him. Brad backed into his desk as he moved back again.

Forrester clamped Brad's arm with a hand the size of a bear paw. He was an inch shorter than Brad but outweighed him in muscle and bone by twenty pounds. With a brutal jerk he flung Brad toward the door. "I've had it with you, Holmes."

Brad staggered out into the hall, smashing his shoulder against the door. He would have fallen if three students hadn't been standing in the doorway. Forrester was right behind him and gave him another shove before he'd regained his balance. The crowd of students, who had gathered in the hallway, scattered in front of them.

When Brad tried to turn, Forrester jabbed him in the back. "Keep going," he snarled, "we're going to the chairman's office."

"Huh?" Brad appeared not to believe what he'd heard. "You mean, like the fucking principal's office?"

"If you don't shut the fuck up," Forrester growled at him, "I'm going to drag you by the balls to Zhrudsky's office."

Brad felt like a fool being marched through the hallways with people staring at him in every open doorway. It was like that guy in the movie being marched to a flogging: the curious stares were the sword-points in front of him; Forrester breathing down his neck, the drawn swords behind him.

"Dr. Zhrudsky?"

Roger Zhrudsky shook his head in apology to Hank Cavanaugh, who was sitting across his desk from him. "Excuse me, Hank." He swiveled around in his chair and pushed the intercom button on his phone. "Yes, Cathy?"

"Dr. Forrester is out here with a graduate student. He wants you to meet with them—now, if possible."

"What is it?" He spun himself back so he was facing Hank and raised his eyebrows.

"Tell him there's a sexual assault involved." The distorted voice on the intercom was Jim's in the background.

"Sexu—?" Roger's reaction was mirrored in the look of consternation on Hank's face. "Tell him to come in." Much as he enjoyed the chairman's position, at times like this he regretted agreeing to a second four-year term in the job.

Hank was already on his feet. "Good grief!" He laughed tensely. "Better you than me." He turned halfway around so he could watch them come in.

Brad entered first looking angry and defiant. There was a bright red splotch the width of tire skid on the left side of his face. Jim closed the door loudly behind him. Hank gaped at them for a moment more, then made for the door, nodding without speaking to Jim as he passed. He opened and closed the door quietly.

Roger made no gesture suggesting the two of them should sit down, even though he had three straight-backed chairs in front of his desk. "All right, Jim. Please explain what this is all about."

"I caught this slimeball with his hand in Vanessa Trippett's pants."

"Were they…?" Roger was incredulous. "Was she…"

"She was struggling to get away from him when I opened the door."

Brad brought both hands up like he couldn't believe Forrester was accusing him. "I didn't touch the slut until she swatted me in the face."

Roger ignored him. "You saw him with his hand—?" he asked Forrester.

"Yeah. And the other arm around her chest like he was trying to feel her up."

"The hell I did!" Brad shouted.

"That's what I saw, Roger." Forrester shrugged. "He let her go when he saw me."

Roger turned back to Brad. "Why'd she hit you?"

"'Cuz I asked her if she was sleeping with…" He caught himself. "I only asked her…"

Roger looked at Jim. "Anything else?"

Jim shook his head. "There was the earlier thing with the screensavers."

"Right. I'm aware of it." Roger pulled a pad of lined paper out of a desk drawer. "Jim, could you put your observations in writing for me, please?"

"Yeah, sure. I'll drop off the hard copy on my way out this afternoon. That will be soon enough, won't it?"

"Yes." Roger nodded. "And would you please sign and date it?"

"Do you need me for anything else, Roger?"

"No. Thank you."

"Sorry for dumping this shit on you." He spun around and wrenched open the door. It closed with a slam behind him.

Roger winced. "All right," he said to Brad. "Have a seat." He turned and pushed the intercom button. "Cathy? Could you please get in touch with Vanessa Trippett and have her come in to see me in about fifteen minutes?"

"I'll try, Dr. Zhrudsky."

"She might still be in the building. Maybe in her office. You could even try sending her an email; she could be on her computer."

"All right. I can send someone up to look for her, too."

"Thanks." Roger regarded Brad for a moment. Could he be trusted to leave campus immediately? He decided there was a good possibility he wouldn't. "Also Cathy?"

"Yes, Dr. Zhrudsky?"

"Would you please call the campus police? Tell them we need to have a law enforcement officer—"

"You're not calling the fucking police, are you?" Brad was on his feet, leaning across the desk. "Shit!"

"Excuse me a moment, Cathy." He released the intercom button. "Don't use that kind of language in this office under any circumstances, Mr. Holmes! Is that understood?"

Brad collapsed in his chair mumbling under his breath.

Back at the intercom, Roger told Cathy he wanted an officer to escort someone off campus in about fifteen minutes. Then he swiveled around to face Brad. "I believe Dr. Forrester's statement is sufficient to justify strong disciplinary action, Mr. Holmes."

"You're kidding? It's his word against mine."

"That will be for others to decide. I intend to recommend to the graduate committee that you be terminated from the program immediately."

"You can't fucking kick me out for—"

"I've warned you once about your language." He put on his sternest chairman's face. "The next time will be the last." He glowered at Brad before he continued. "Now then, my action here today is not final. The committee might not agree with me, and its action is subject to review by the graduate college and ultimately the provost. However, I do have the authority to suspend you here and now."

Brad leapt to his feet and began shouting. "You're fucking out of your mind, Zhrudsky!" He leaned over Roger's imposing walnut desk. "Do you have any fucking idea who my father is?"

"Now, Mr. Holmes. This action is clearly within the purview of my office and—"

"Fuckin' A, it's Mister Holmes! I'm the son of Frank Holmes, who's donated more fucking money to this university than you'll see in your shithole life." He slammed his fist on the desk. "You kick me out, we'll have you in court faster than you can say, 'the purview' of your fucking office."

Roger stood and pointed to the door. "I want you out of this building and off campus within half an hour." He realized his arm was shaking uncontrollably. Embarrassed, he lowered it. "Wait outside until the university police arrive."

"All right, motherfucker!" Brad spun on his heel and stalked across the room. He stood holding the door for a second after he had wrenched it open. "See you in court, asshole." As he stepped out, he yanked the door closed with a concussion like a six-inch howitzer.

Roger rushed to follow him into his outer office. "Mr. Holmes, come back!"

Brad turned before he reached the door to the hallway. "Make me, fuckface!" He strode recklessly into the hall. Outside, he collided with a police officer. "What the fuck?"

Roger hurried to join them. "Officer, remove this man from campus as soon as possible."

"Aw, hell," Brad groaned. "I'll leave, for God's sake."

""Do you want me to arrest him, sir?" The policeman looked at Roger.

"Christ, I'll go with him, Zhrudsky. He doesn't have to fucking handcuff me."

Roger and the policeman looked at each other. "You won't let him out of your sight, officer?"

"No sir, not if that's what you want."

"Then that will be sufficient, thank you."

"Yes, sir." The officer looked at Brad. "You ready?"

"Can I get my fucking raincoat and other shit out of my office?"

The officer nodded. "I'll come with you."

Roger whirled back into his outer office. "Is Vanessa…?"

Cathy pointed. "She's here."

Vanessa stood. "You wanted to see me, Dr. Zhrudsky?"

He let out a sigh of relief. "Thank God he didn't get a chance to act further on his anger. Come in please, Vanessa." He gestured to the open door to his office.

"Sit down, please," he said as he followed her and closed the door behind him. "How are you doing, Vanessa?"

"I'm fine now. Thank you for worrying about me."

He stared at her. *"Fine?" She's just been sexually assaulted—and she's "fine?"* It took him more than a second to regain his composure. "This entire incident is most regrettable, Vanessa. And disagreeable for everyone—especially, for you." He returned to his chair behind the desk. "I assume you plan to file a harassment complaint."

"No, definitely not."

Zhrudsky gaped at her. "No? But why not?"

"Several reasons. Slapping him was utterly out of proportion to what he said, and—"

"What did he say to you?"

"He asked if I was sleeping with Dr. Harte."

"That was inappropriate, I would think," Zhrudsky commented. *But I assume it's true.*

"He was merely repeating what everyone else in the department knows. Besides, it's true. I assume it isn't news to you, Dr. Zhrudsky."

That was remarkably forthright, he thought. Coming from anyone else, he would have been suspicious. From Vanessa, it was hard to tell what it meant. She was so mercurial.

"But see here, Vanessa. It was out of line for him to ask you. Most people would regard it as an insult."

"My second reason is more important, Dr. Zhrudsky."

"Yes?"

"My reputation in this department is bad enough already. Filing a sexual harassment complaint will just make it worse. Moreover, it will take a great deal of my time—time away from my work. It's not worth it to me. I don't want or need revenge."

Her speech was like a chill breeze blowing through the office. She was more coldly analytical than she had any right to be. He could still file an action against Holmes, but it was dicier without her complaint. He jotted down a summary of her two points.

"Filing a complaint or not is your prerogative, of course, Vanessa. Please do think it over, and if you change your mind before the end of next week, let me know. All right?"

"Thank you for your concern. But I've made up my mind."

"Very well. On a related matter, if Brad tries to contact you or worse, tries to follow you, I want you to call the police immediately. And report the incident to me as well."

"I don't think that will be a problem."

"Please. Let me be the judge of the situation. Take my advice. Especially in the building."

"Okay."

He could tell she wasn't convinced. He'd done the best he could. Now, he had to deliver an even more unpleasant message. His watch showed he had at least two more hours before he could go home and open a bottle of wine.

"Because this incident has put me in a position such that I might be the subject of a legal action, I must resign from your committee—reluctantly, I might add. Do you understand what I'm saying?"

"Yes," she said woodenly.

"I'm sorry this happened. I had been looking forward to reading your dissertation and participating in your defense."

"I'm sorry, too." She stood. "May I go now?"

When she was gone, he put his elbows on his desk and cradled his head in his hands. The last part had been the hardest.

She was a brilliant student, a joy to talk with about cognition. He would miss that intellectual stimulation, and he was still willing to give her the benefit of every doubt academically. But this was different. Continuing on her committee would make a tsunami in the department. He couldn't risk the peace of the department—and his job. Not with the administration looking over his shoulder, watching every move he made where Vanessa was concerned.

As for Holmes's threats, they probably weren't going to amount to anything. But you never knew with big donors. He wouldn't be able to sleep tonight. It was always that way, even when the chances were remote that an incident like this would blow up in his face. God, how he hated this job sometimes!

Stan turned on his cell phone after class that afternoon and checked his voice mail: "You have one new message… One new message sent at, three-thirty-seven today. Press—" "Hi, Stan. You've probably already heard what happened this afternoon. Take a look at the email I forwarded to you for more bad news. I'm taking the bus to your place; see you there. Bye-bye."

He had no idea what she was talking about. The email was a forwarded message from the editor of *Science*. There was a message from Vanessa at the top that was nearly identical to her phone message along with an attachment. The editor had declined to publish her paper. The attachments were the referees' comments.

Both made the same points: The evidence was extremely limited for a very improbable finding that cried out for an alternative explanation in terms of some artifact. Both expressed surprise at the use of the author herself as the only subject. One of the reviews was gentle—encouraging and diplomatic. The other was gratuitously harsh, claiming there were many possible alternative explanations, but stating none of them, and lampooning the use of one subject as, "…something out of the nineteenth century."

He rushed home as fast as the glacial traffic at that time of the afternoon allowed. When he opened the door, the sound of Beethoven's last piano sonata, the thirty-second, was coming from the living room. She'd played it so many times at his house that he recognized the exact point in the final movement, the Arietta.

He shut the front door quietly and went into the kitchen without looking into the living room, where he knew she would be sitting like a statue on the living room couch with her eyes closed. There was an open bottle of Chateau Ste. Michelle syrah on the counter with the cork still lodged in the corkscrew. He went to the cupboard for a glass. When he held up the bottle, he realized it was half empty. He poured himself a glass and recorked the bottle. Then he had a drink of the wine and sat down to listen.

András Schiff was starting the last sixteen-bar variation that began with the theme played along with a twelve-bar trill, then dissolved into a mad, two-handed chase of demi-semiquavers up and down the keyboard and at last sighed to a pianissimo conclusion. This long movement marked *Adagio molto, semplice e cantabile*—extremely slowly, simply and melodiously—is as graceful and serene as anything Beethoven ever wrote, yet at its conclusion, it intimates the calm, ultimate triumph of the human spirit.

He knew she would sit for several minutes staring off into space, so he rounded up some cheese and crackers in the kitchen, arranged them haphazardly on a platter and took them and his wine into the living room.

"How about putting something in your stomach to keep that wine company?"

Her glass was nearly full, so he judged she'd drunk no more than a glass so far.

She stretched. "Hey, thanks."

He set the platter on a coffee table, and she slid over on the couch next to him. They kissed with tender familiarity and restrained passion, then reached for their wine glasses in unison. After a perfunctory clink and sip, they set the glasses back on the coffee table. As they made up some cheese and cracker sandwiches, he marveled how they moved in tandem.

"You heard what happened this afternoon, didn't you?" she said.

"No, what was that all about?"

"No?" She eyed him with surprise.

"I came right home when I got your messages."

She sighed deeply. "I did something dumb. Now, Zhrudsky's resigned from my committee."

"What are you talking about?

"Brad tried to grope me after I slapped him."

"That son of a bitch again?" He jumped to his feet.

"No, wait!" She waved for him to sit down. "I'm not telling it fairly."

She began with Brad's invitation to the concert, which seemed like an insult, at least to Stan, even if she didn't think it was to her. Then she repeated his remark about their affair, word for word.

He was back on his feet again, fists clenched. "That goddamn motherfucker. He'd better not let me catch him alone. I'll bash that leering smirk of his into a bog of bloody lips and broken teeth."

When he stopped to look in Vanessa's direction, there was a hint of a smile playing on her face.

"What?" He realized he was still shouting.

She calmly reached for her wine. "Funny. Forrester said the same thing to Brad, with fewer ruffles and flourishes."

"Forrester? What the hell was he doing in… Wasn't this in your office?"

She sipped her wine deliberately. "You got so excited, my dear, I couldn't help getting ahead of the story." She smiled at him feebly. "If you'll sit down and promise not to interrupt me, I'll try to tell it in chronological order."

Chastened, he sat down facing her. He was amazed when she told him that she'd slapped Brad so hard, but his finger-fucking her enraged him even more. Stan leapt to his feet again without thinking and began pacing back and forth across the room. "Bastard!" he kept repeating under his breath.

Vanessa for all intents and purposes ignored him as she continued her account of Jim's intervention and the confrontation with Roger. She'd ended by telling how she'd shown up in Roger's office just before the campus police escorted Brad off campus.

"I hope he kicked the bastard out of the program as well as banishing him from campus." It seemed like too light a punishment for what he'd done.

She was shaking her head sadly. "Stupid, stupid, stupid! I could have ignored him, or told him to get lost. Or used his idea of creative language." A smile flickered momentarily on her lips. "'Fuck off?' Is that the correct syntax?"

When he rushed to her with open arms, she stood and wrapped her arms around him and laid her head on his chest. "Stan, why did I have to hit him? He didn't deserve it—"

"He absolutely did. You should have hit him harder."

She pushed away from him. "No. My hand still hurts." She started to rub her right hand.

He grabbed it and lifted to his lips, showering it with kisses. She tried to pull it back but he held on and began rubbing it gently. "You said Roger resigned from your committee? Just like that?"

She sighed again and reached for her glass with her free hand. "Yeah. He's worried about being sued, I guess. Serving on my committee would be a conflict of interest for him, right?"

"It means, my dear, that he's a diplomatic administrator, who doesn't want to look like he's playing favorites. He wants to keep his job."

"He said he was 'reluctant,' whatever that's supposed to mean."

"He's disingenuous. If he pretends he'd rather stay on your committee, he's less likely to piss you off—or me."

"He seemed sincere."

"That's his job, Vanessa. Who knows? Maybe he really is sad about it."

"So now I'm without a committee again. I was hoping I could add Paul as the *fourth* member. But who now?"

"We'll find someone." But Stan wasn't really sure who. They needed four members from psychology to which the graduate school would add a fifth from some other department. He joined her for another glass of wine. "This has been a tough day for you." He patted her on the shoulder.

"Did you look at the reviews?"

He nodded.

"I have to give you credit. They said exactly what you predicted they'd say: Ebbinghaus is dead, and anyway, my finding's just an artifact."

"Reviewer Number Two didn't have to be derisive. I despise people who write that kind of review."

"That's okay. He has a point. I should have listened to you." She took a long draft of wine.

He was amazed at her resilience. He was also left wondering if she had sent her paper to a journal to test his judgment. He had been so certain that she would be turned down, that he hadn't considered the consequences of *Science* accepting her paper. It felt a little creepy knowing that while she might be his lover, when it came to her research, she wouldn't hesitate to challenge his professional authority. The risk to her status as a student was minimal, but the threat to his, as her mentor, was potentially immense.

"I've been thinking of a place your paper might be accepted." He had been anticipating for several weeks the moment her paper was rejected, hoping it would occur before the deadline forced his hand. "Your first little between-groups experiment would make a good poster presentation, with the data on yourself presented as a kind of pilot study showing where the findings might lead. The deadline for submission for APS is next Friday."

"APS? Isn't that—?"

"Association for Psychological Science. The annual meeting in May will be in San Francisco. You know what a poster presentation is?"

"You mean like the Sigma Xi competition last spring? You put diagrams and graphs and short blocks of text on a bulletin board, right? Then you stand in front of it and answer questions for a hour or so, while people wander around a room full of other people doing the same thing?"

"Exactly. The instructions for submitting one are on the APS website. I'll email you the link. You'll see how well the figures you used in your *Science* manuscript fit the poster format."

"I only have a week?"

"You submit everything online. I've seen you write up much more ambitious papers over a weekend."

She wrapped her arms around his neck and kissed him. "That was before I started spending weekends in bed with you, my dear."

He idly fondled her butt. "Remind me to kick you out of bed at ten tomorrow and tie you to your desk with your computer."

CHAPTER 16

2009-02-13 08:39:20:
Michelle, I want to talk. It's going to take a while, too. I suppose you can guess why! Vanessa

Michelle didn't have to guess; she knew. It was hard not to hear some version of the story if one had talked to anyone in Guthrie Hall in the last twenty-four hours. Among the faculty women, Michelle found herself in the minority. Most were certain Vanessa was at least partly to blame, if for no other reason than her nude photos.

There was also universal agreement that Brad deserved to be kicked out of the graduate program. Michelle was withholding judgment, arguing that deciding on Vanessa's role should wait until the complaint was filed and Brad had a chance to defend himself.

Michelle couldn't help feeling sorry for Vanessa when she slumped into a chair in her office.

"I suppose you know?"

"What did Brad actually do to you?" Michelle's voice was uncommonly sharp.

"He stuck his finger up me," Vanessa shot back.

"Did you say that in your complaint?"

"I'm not filing a complaint, Michelle."

Michelle was taken aback. "Why not?"

"Because it'd be my word against his." Vanessa's eyes flashed. "And I don't want the hassle of a formal hearing."

"But that's not the point."

"The point is that I lost it and hit him."

"But—"

"Before he grabbed me. Don't you see, Michelle? He can argue it was my fault as much as his. A hearing would be contentious—and protracted. It's not worth it to me. I'm not looking for revenge."

"Okay." Michelle fell back in her chair. "I assume you did have some reason to hit him."

"It depends. He invited me to go to a concert with him. When I told him Stan and I already had tickets for it, he asked me if I was sleeping with Stan. I couldn't believe he'd said that. But then he went on to say he knew I was…" She stopped. "Okay. Quote." She raised her fingers in the quotation mark gesture. "'…fucking that dumbass, Harte.' End quote."

Michelle winced.

"You know it's true? Stan and I are lovers."

Michelle nodded. "I know. It's still an insult."

Vanessa slumped in her chair again. "Michelle, I'm tired of fighting my reputation around here. It's so unfair. Don't people have better things to do than gawk at other people's lives?"

Michelle licked her upper lip. "Can I be blunt with you, Vanessa?"

Vanessa frowned. "What? I sleep around?"

"It's in the eye of the beholder, to be sure. But for whatever reasons—and they're mostly deplorable—your affairs and your modeling make you the target of everyone's most malicious suspicions."

"Uh." Vanessa turned to stare out the window at the agitated clouds. After a moment, she started to speak again without looking back at Michelle. "If I were a faculty member… Let's just assume, okay?"

"If you'd been living with one of my colleagues, then—in a matter of weeks—were sleeping with another one, I'd consider it none of my business. And I'd say so—if asked what I thought. But I have colleagues who would blab about it—and hold it against you."

"And how would you feel about me?"

"Let's make a distinction, okay?" Michelle waited for a nod from Vanessa. "I don't approve of what you've done. But… I'm still your friend, Vanessa."

Vanessa turned and met Michelle's eyes. "Thank you for saying that, Michelle." A tear rolled down her cheek. "I'm glad what I've done hasn't cost me your friendship. That means a great deal to me."

Michelle pulled out a desk drawer and brought up a box of tissues. She held it out to Vanessa. She then set the box on the desk between them, took one herself and swiped at the lower eyelid on both sides.

Vanessa blotted her eyes with the tissue, then blew her nose in it.

"How about some coffee?" Michelle knew they were headed into a long talk.

"Yes, that always helps with difficult problems." Vanessa looked out the window again, a glum expression on her face. "It sure would be nice to be known for something other than my nude photos and my affairs with faculty members."

Michelle was busy with her coffee ritual and had her back turned. "I think everybody recognizes you as our brightest, most promising student." The coffee grinder growled, whined, and fell silent.

"Not everyone, Michelle. I believe you and Stan do. And Paul, too. But that's about it." She blew out a long sigh that seemed to deflate her whole body. "But to everybody else I'm the most exasperating student that anyone can remember. Not to mention that they think my photos are somehow ruining the department's reputation."

Michelle started the coffeemaker and turned back to Vanessa. "Maybe we're all jealous."

Vanessa looked back, her eyes wide. "We? You include yourself?"

Michelle leaned toward her. "Here's what I mean: I sympathize with the jealousy of those who wish they had your intelligence or your body—or both."

"And you agree with them that I'm using my body to get what I want? Even if I'm smart enough to get it without sleeping with my advisor?"

Michelle shook her head firmly. "I didn't say that, Vanessa. I said I can understand why the women envy both your brains and your beauty. And the men, I'm sure, would like to have your brains and are frustrated that you—"

"—won't have sex with them, right?"

"Yes, that's what I was going to say, if not in those words."

"I guess I understand the reasons they feel the way they do about me. That doesn't make it any easier to deal with the hostility. I mean, Brad's reaction to being turned down the other day was just the most extreme form of it." She gazed out the window again.

Michelle hesitated to continue. What was the most delicate way to get Vanessa to talk about her feelings and the possible reasons why she felt the way she did? Michelle sensed that there were deeper sources behind her rush into affairs with her mentors, men who were potential father figures. She didn't buy a lot of the theories her clinical colleagues subscribed to in their work, but she appreciated the dangers of unleashing the hidden demons of Vanessa's past.

Vanessa resolved Michelle's indecision by starting to speak again. "You know, I'm not as wanton as everybody seems to think. Unless you count liking sex as a form of depravity. But I learned pretty quickly that it's not any fun with someone you don't love and respect." A smile fluttered briefly on Vanessa's face like a butterfly drifting between them on a breeze.

"I'm not sleeping around, like everyone says. Yes, I'm having an affair with my major professor. It happens pretty easily when two people of the opposite sex are working together on the same difficult problem. Look at Marie Curie. She and her husband-to-be worked together on radioactivity when she was a student and he was her professor at the Sorbonne."

"As I recall the story, they didn't have an affair before they got married, but—"

"Or didn't get caught, which seems more likely."

"I agree that working together can lead to very close relationships." Michelle realized she'd never seen Vanessa pout, but her prolonged gaze out the window was a similar display of petulance. "Still," she continued cautiously, "there are so many ways in which your situation is different. For example—"

"—I didn't even wait until Paul was out of the hospital before jumping into bed with Stan? Is that what you're getting at?"

"Don't you think that's a very important reason why others see you they way they do?"

"Of course it is." Vanessa threw up her hands. "Did you know that Marie had an affair with a married man after Pierre was killed?"

"I read about it in Rosalynd Pflaum's book. But I wonder whether it's valid to compare yourself with a Parisian woman who lived in the early twentieth century?"

"No, but it's just as unfair as it was in 1911, Michelle."

"I think—and maybe this is just speculation on my part—but maybe almost everyone sees how smart you are—and maybe that's how you're similar to Marie Curie—and they think, 'Why can't she figure out that sleeping with her advisors could potentially get her into a lot of trouble?'"

"Why can't *they* figure it out?" Vanessa finally turned to face Michelle again. "They don't get it that the reason my two partners have been faculty members is because none of the students around here is as interested in research as Stan and Paul and I am."

"Or as smart."

Michelle's comment seemed to catch Vanessa off guard. "No. I don't think that's the…" Her head nodded ever so slightly. "Okay, maybe. But what's crucial—for me—is their interest in… maybe it's not too much of a stretch to say, their passion to understand the world, and not just so they can publish papers or earn recognition."

"That's a pretty rare quality, even among practicing scientists."

"It may be rare, but you have it, too." Vanessa raised a hand to keep Michelle from interrupting. "I've seen it in you. Don't try to deny it."

"Well, thank you. That's quite a compliment." Clearly, Vanessa was projecting her own zeal on those around her who shared even a spark of her own enthusiasm.

"I'm just stating the obvious, but as far as I can tell a thirst for knowledge is not what motivates the graduate students I know." Vanessa's gaze shifted to the Klee poster behind Michelle, but this time her eyes lingered only a moment. "You know, Michelle, if anyone here had known me at Wazzu, they'd have some basis for thinking I was a slut."

Vanessa's admission surprised Michelle, and she said so.

"You wouldn't have recognized me during my first two or three years." Vanessa blushed. "And you might not have liked me very much."

It was a good time to serve the coffee that had been ready for several minutes. Placing the mugs on the table and filling them, gave Michelle an opportunity to ask how Vanessa felt about her relationships with Stan and Paul. She tried not to show the trepidation she felt. "How were you different earlier—at WSU?"

Vanessa pulled her mug of coffee toward her and blew over it. "A good question." She looked up at Michelle, who was still standing. "One with a long answer."

"I have lots of time." Michelle sat down again and sipped cautiously at her steaming coffee.

"I was pretty wild—for a while at least. But I never did drugs. Except alcohol. And it took only once or twice for me to learn why getting drunk wasn't the way to enjoy that drug." She grinned at Michelle before drinking a little coffee.

"On the other hand, I went through quite a few guys trying to figure out what sex was really all about. It was a lot more fun than drugs. At least at first. But I eventually caught on that what happened after the fun was more important. That is, if you wanted to enjoy it as much or more the next time." Her constricted laugh sounded forced.

"You don't regret those relationships?"

"Not really. I finally settled down, so to speak, and lived with one guy my entire senior year. But he got a good fellowship in math at Michigan, and we parted friends." Her reverie seemed to shatter suddenly. "Were you asking whether I felt any guilt or shame about having lots of partners—for a while?"

"Yes, I suppose I was curious about your feelings about them now." Michelle was watching her closely.

"I'm not ashamed of what I did. I know why I'm sexually active—promiscuous, if you like. I enjoy sex. Okay? And it isn't because I have unresolved issues left over from my childhood."

Michelle shook her head. "I'm not doing a clinical assessment."

"Funny you should say that. I had a girlfriend at Wazzu who was convinced I was trying to get back at my father because he walked out on mom and me. We'd been friends since our sophomore year, and we both knew how many guys the other one had slept with. But for some reason she was really shocked when I told her I'd gone to the *Playboy* casting call and was going to pose nude for a website.

"She tried to talk me out of it. She admitted to me for the first time that she was seeing a counselor about her promiscuity. It had helped her get over being angry with her father for getting divorced."

Michelle was surprised by this new information. "Did she persuade you to see a counselor?"

"Sort of. I did a lot of reading before I went to the student counseling center. The first woman I saw gave me a bunch of crap about needing to recover memories of my father abusing me. I went over half a dozen papers I'd looked at showing recovered memories are bullshit and told her she was a charlatan for fooling people into thinking they remembered things that hadn't happened.

"The second one tried to convince me I felt guilty because I felt responsible for the divorce. Daddy's little girl fills out and grows tits—and scares him off? Give me a break!"

Michelle realized she'd reached a familiar spot in an argument with Vanessa. She intellectualized everything, and the more emotional the content, the more cunning the logic became. "So you quit going, I take it?"

"More like they showed me the door. The second woman referred me to the director, who asked, 'Is someone making you come here?' 'No,' I said. 'I'm trying to figure out if something's wrong with me.' 'Well', she said, 'we can't help you if you question everything we try to do.' I argued with her, but she wasn't having any of it. She said she was sorry but they couldn't help me."

"I'm not sure I can either, Vanessa." Michelle should have known what would happen. You had to have your facts and arguments lined up before you tried to help Vanessa.

"I'm used to solving problems on my own."

"I suspect you know better than I do the clinical literature on sexual promiscuity among girls whose fathers walked out on their mothers."

Vanessa's grim face gave way to a smile. "Don't be frustrated with me, Michelle. What I needed most was someone to listen while I vented my spleen over this."

"You're welcome. Anytime, Vanessa."

They sat for a minute in comfortable silence, each with her mug clasped in both hands, drinking thoughtfully.

Now, it was Michelle's turn to stare at the gray expanse of clouds outside her windows.

It had been vintage Vanessa: First, asking whether her reputation would suffer the same way if she were a faculty colleague instead of a student, then bringing up the striking parallels with the life and loves of Marie Curie, and finally the story of her confrontation with counseling.

In her imagination she could hear Vanessa telling a poor, outgunned counselor, "That isn't a good explanation of what I feel. Jarvis and Cline didn't demonstrate that anger at a father over a divorce was related to promiscuous *behavior*. They reported a correlation—and not a very high one, as I recall—between the anger and a positive *attitude* toward promiscuity." It made Michelle laugh. Vanessa was a counselor's client from hell.

The important question was how well Vanessa understood her own feelings and motives. Indeed, if she simply enjoyed sex a lot more than most women, and her choice of partners reflected a search for an intellectual equal—both premises that struck Michelle as healthy and plausible, then Vanessa's emotional life could be as well balanced as the psyche of any genius. To go any further would mean digging into her parents' divorce. Michelle knew she wasn't trained to do that.

Vanessa broke the silence. "I'm going to ask Paul to be on my committee."

"He's back to work, now. Part time, two or three hours in the mornings only."

"I know. I haven't had time to say hello even."

Michelle stretched. "He'll be able to stay over lunch next week."

"Do you think he'd do it?"

"I'd say the odds are high."

"I still need a fourth."

"Martha Yates might be willing. Let me feel her out."

"Another woman would be good." Vanessa drank most of her remaining coffee. "How's Caitlin doing with her swimming?"

Michelle's eldest daughter was swimming competitively for the first time this year. Her early successes had been a source of great pride to her mother. The two women finished their coffee talking about the two daughters' schooling and many extracurricular activities.

"Hey!" Vanessa pushed Paul's door open a few inches more than it had been and poked her head into his office. "You're back!"

"Hey, yourself. It's about time." He was sitting behind the old-fashioned wooden desk he had found in a university storeroom and restored himself. For a reason he couldn't quite explain to himself, since his heart attack he preferred the overhead fluorescent lights instead of working in a pool of light from an antique desk lamp on his desktop in an otherwise darkened room. He liked the dusty maroon curtains open rather than closed most of the time, as in the past.

He waved her toward one of the straight-backed chairs he'd bought to match the desk. "Come on in. I hope you have a little time to catch me up."

"Sorry I didn't stop in last week. Things have been a little crazy for me."

"So I hear."

She cocked her head. "You guys must have a faculty bulletin board with all the latest gossip posted on it."

"No, but there's a grapevine, and this was the first place it invaded when I came back." He laughed. "See, when you return to your job like this, everybody drops by to say hello the first week. And there isn't much to talk about except who's doing what to whom."

She colored slightly. "Well, it's been an eventful month since I saw you last."

"I guess! What's with this guy, Brad Holmes?"

"It goes way back, Paul. He was a psych major at Wazzu. I heard he was a pretty good student. He was very popular—at least with the women—and hung out with the best students in the program. I think he was even president of Psi Chi his senior year." She glanced over her shoulder at the open door.

"Go ahead and shut it," he said.

"No. Not a good idea for a woman with my reputation around here." She lowered her voice. "Look, you know I don't like to brag about my exams and papers or the grades I get."

"You don't have to tell me that, Vanessa. You make it seem so easy, there's no mystery why your peers are green with envy. I suppose it was the same when you were an undergrad?"

"Pretty much."

"In other words, your test scores stuck out at the top?"

She nodded.

"And Holmes was jealous?"

"I guess. I mean, the situation made it worse. It was the first psych course I took after Joel Greene's. It was small—twenty-five, thirty students—and a senior-level lab course. So here I come, a new face in this group of majors who all know each other."

"And a stunning-looking babe to boot."

She grimaced. "And on the first test, I get a 92. The distribution's on the screen at the front of the room: 92, 80, 75, 73… Something like that. After class he comes up to me—doesn't say hello or introduce himself—just starts right in: 'You a transfer student?' I said, 'Sort of,' and told him I was a math major taking psych as a minor."

"Zingo! Squashed his ego like it was a bug. Which is exactly how he felt. And don't shake your head and say you didn't mean to, Vanessa. I've been there. Smashed bugs don't care if it was an accident you stepped on them."

She bent forward earnestly. "He was even more ticked when he found out how few psych courses I'd taken, including the prerequisites for the course we were in. He didn't give me a chance to tell him that I got credit by examination for them. He just stalked away—didn't even ask me my name."

He'd seen this body language of hers dozens of times. She simply couldn't believe that anyone else was less intelligent than she was. "Why didn't you tell me this story before?"

"It never seemed worth telling anybody. He rarely spoke to me after that first time. We were in several more classes together…"

"And you always got better grades than everyone else." Paul was nodding his head.

"My test scores were the highest."

"What a strange bird." He spoke more to himself than to her. "And he kept up the cold shoulder even when you both came here?"

"I didn't know he'd applied to UW until I saw him at our orientation. Even then, he acted as if I wasn't there. He never acknowledged me when I said hello…" A frown of perplexity flooded her forehead. "Until a couple months ago. Then out of the blue, he asks me for a date."

"Hadn't he heard that you and Stan were together?"

Her eyes widened. "You know, then?"

"Remember, I predicted it. But yes, I'd heard. Why hadn't he? Or had he?"

"It's weird, Paul. Since this last thing with him, Emily told me that for the past year, he's been saying that I'm sleeping my way to a PhD."

"Hmm."

"Right. A plausible theory, huh?"

He waved his hand dismissively. "Is it true that Roger resigned from your committee because Holmes assaulted you?"

She flicked him a smile. "That wasn't quite the reason, but yes, I'm back to a committee of two."

"I stand ready to take his place, if you want me."

"Oh, thank you, Paul. I was hoping… I planned to ask you, so thank you for offering. I hope it won't be a disaster—like the last time we…"

"I've learned my lesson, Vanessa. I really want to see you get your degree."

She jumped to her feet but caught herself before she'd moved toward him. Now, it was his turn to glance at the open door. They both laughed.

"I understand, Vanessa. You're welcome."

"I'm profoundly grateful, Paul."

CHAPTER 17

Once Stan had committed himself to being Vanessa's second long-term subject, he decided to work out a formal rationale for supporting her research with his National Science Foundation grant. He found enough money to hire three or four part-time workers for two or three months. After clearing the change with his program officer in Washington, D.C., he waited until Vanessa came to his place on Friday night.

When he told her, she threw her arms around him and planted a juicy kiss on his lips. "That's the best gift you've given me all week."

He couldn't think of anything that would count as a "gift" since she spent the previous weekend with him.

Before he could tell her how she should handle the recruitment process, she had her fingers under his T-shirt, creeping quickly toward the secretly cultivated erotic power hidden in his nipples.

"I'm feeling a bit peckish. How about a snack?"

A "snack" had become their code for a quickie. When she said "peckish," she had her hand in his pants and her fingers wrapped around his very stiff penis.

Once they were naked on the bed, they slowed down and took their time making it to the summit. By now he'd learned that these long, slow climaxes were her special thank-you gifts to him. Hilarity, on the other hand, was her typical approach to a true quickie.

He left it up to her to advertise the "job" and choose the participants. She posted it on craigslist.com under the "part-time" and "ETC" categories. The listing mentioned "flexible hours." There was a deluge of applicants, evidently reflecting the nationwide unemployment rate.

Stan's wonder at Vanessa's energy level grew as the weeks passed. Not only did she continue to test subjects for her dissertation research—a time commitment of a dozen or more hours a week, she also insisted on being present in the lab every hour her long-term subjects were participating. He helped her set up his laboratory suite so she could test all four at once, reducing her time to four hours a day, five days a week.

She and the four participants quickly agreed that early evening was the best time, because it left them free to pursue their continuing job searches and Vanessa could keep her daytime schedule. She saw the extra twenty hours a week as time she could work in the control booth when the participants needed little of her attention.

When Stan expressed his concern that Vanessa would have to walk through the U District after ten at night, she told him she'd been doing it routinely since she moved to her apartment there. She often got so wrapped up in what she was doing in the late afternoon that she didn't notice until after dark—often long after dark.

By the end of winter quarter, they had fallen into a routine: On Friday evening, he'd drive back to Guthrie Hall, and she'd come to his office when she finished with her subjects. They walked to his car in the parking garage under Red Square, and he drove to her apartment to pick up the small, dark green duffel bag with a shoulder strap in which she'd packed her stuff for the weekend. Then they headed north to his house in Green Lake.

On a Tuesday evening as he was opening the door from the garage into the mud room, he thought about the collection of several thousand images of women in every stage of undress on his hard drive. He hadn't looked at it since he and Vanessa had made love the first time. That included more than a week of being alone during the Christmas break, although he had spent a lot of hours getting in shape for a 10K race on New Years Day.

While he sat in the kitchen nook and ate the take-out sushi he'd picked up, he turned over in his mind the possibility that his relationship with Vanessa had cured his addiction to pornography. As he stared at his empty plate and wineglass, he idly wondered whether it was time to delete all those images on his hard drive. He cleaned up the kitchen quickly and sat down at the computer in his study.

His first thought was simply to erase the huge folder on his computer that contained his collection. But instead, he opened the folder and then one inside it. At that point, he decided to archive the images on an external hard drive before erasing them—in case his relationship with Vanessa ended, as he had all along thought it would eventually.

Without thinking, he started the image manager program he used for slide shows. He navigated to the headshot folder inside his favorites folder and watched a parade of some twenty fully clothed *Playboy* models.

It was like walking into room full of old friends he hadn't seen for several months. With each new photo a string of his favorite nude shots flashed through his head. He paused the show on one incredible blonde that inundated his mind's eye with remembered pictures.

Carla had a lovely full figure with big unenhanced breasts, a perfectly proportioned waist, taut tummy, graceful ass, and unblemished skin. She'd been an early Cyber Girl of the Month, who had shown up a year and a half ago in a Cyber Girl Xtra. He had collected a hundred and forty JPEG files of her photos plus five videos. More even than he had of Vanessa.

He clicked on an early striptease series and sat back to watch as her fuchsia blouse, miniskirt of many colored squares of leather, flowery bra and matching bikini panties disappeared from her voluptuous body from one slide to the next. After the last slide, he pulled down his pants, so his penis was free to quiver in the air. For some *Playboy* photo shoots, both the stills and an on-the-set video were available. He found a video of another session in a separate folder and started it.

He stripped off his own clothes and began stroking his penis, as he watched Carla perform an undulating striptease in front of a bed, taking off everything but her nearly transparent turquoise panties. Then she stretched out on the bed and repeatedly stuck her hand in her panties, acting like she was playing with herself before finally taking off the panties, too.

With exquisite timing, just as she lay back on a pillow and slid both hands into her crotch, his erection shuddered into an explosive climax spewing semen into a handful of tissues he'd grabbed.

The video faded away to a white *Playboy* bunny symbol in the middle of a black screen while he snatched more tissues from the box to keep the come from slobbering out of his hands onto the carpet.

He went into the bathroom, his throbbing cock swaddled in tissues, and sat on the toilet to clean himself off. Meanwhile, his remorse mounted, and black billows of depression engulfed him, just like they used to before Vanessa. He was far from "cured." After he'd plucked the last shred of slimy tissue off his now flaccid penis, he stepped into a cold shower and tried without success to sluice off the sludge of funk he was sliding into.

It took him several days to recover. Over midmorning coffee Wednesday, he tried to share his distress with Vanessa, who picked up on his black mood right away. But he couldn't spill the secret burden dammed up inside him. Still, it was difficult to be depressed for long around Vanessa.

By the time she came to his office Friday evening, he'd recovered, more or less. And following a weekend unusually full of wine and lovemaking, he'd nearly forgotten what had happened on Tuesday. But two weeks later when he was alone at home on Tuesday working on his computer, the shadowy Gorgon of temptation crept into a brief daydream of Vanessa and bewitched him with his favorite *Playboy* image of Vanessa herself.

In a trance, he opened the image manager, and… As if watching an accident in slow motion, he slid back into the grooves of his old habit, spending hours with his sirens from the past and skidding into mini-breakdowns afterward.

Stan kept hearing in his head Vanessa describing to him how her theory explained addiction. "Experiences are scattered through mental space," she'd said, "like stars in physical space. They're connected by a network of relationships that operate like gravity in the space-time continuum.

"Experiences differ widely in mental mass—a passing whiff of sulfur is a bit of mind dust but a lover might be a galaxy—a trillion

trillion times more massive. Those associated with strong emotions—fear, anger, and great pleasure—form connections to many experiences. Addiction is a mental black hole; it pulls all a person's experiences into it. Everything in a person's mental life gets connected to it."

It didn't take much imagination for Stan to see that pornography was his black hole. Hardly any of his thoughts escaped the pull of sexual arousal. The life of his mind was a whirlpool of naked women, erections, and orgasms.

The more he stumbled, the harder it became to talk to Vanessa about it. He contemplated secretly seeing a counselor again, but each time he put off making the first appointment. And then after three weeks, for no apparent reason, the sickness passed. His roller-coaster moods evened out as though he had outgrown his need for video prostitutes again. Yet he never felt completely free of their allure.

To avoid reminders of his collection of pornography, he began working in his office on weekday evenings and taking Vanessa to her apartment when she finished up. Once in a long while they even made love at her place. Her narrow bed was fine for that, but not for him to stay over with her. She never asked why he'd started working in his office at night, and he didn't volunteer. They both enjoyed seeing each other more frequently.

> 2009-03-10 13:28:18:
> Stan, Look! They accepted my poster!! Vanessa

She had forwarded the message from the APS program committee to him.

> 2009-03-10 14:39:55:
> Vanessa, Congratulations!!! I'm making a reservation at Andaluca for Saturday so we can celebrate in Mediterranean splendor!!!! Stan

> 2009-03-10 14:41:06:
> Stan, I've got to meet our subjects at 6:00 this afternoon. Sigh... But hey, if you're not doing anything tonight, I'd be willing to make an exception (just for you!!!!!!!) and come over for a little preliminary celebration. That is, if you're not too busy. Vanessa

2009-03-10 14:42:32:
Vanessa, I think I can find a little time this evening. I'll put that bottle of Tattinger in the frig when I get home. Stan

2009-03-10 14:4:32:
Stan, What a deal!!!!!!!! See you at 10:30. Champagne in bed tonight...? ! !! ! ! !! Vanessa

They left a trail of clothes between the door and the bedroom. The next few minutes felt like an hour. He had noticed that time seemed to dilate when their lovemaking unfolded at a furious pace. Afterward, they lay flat on their backs panting between gales of laughter.

"Such a short celebration." Her head lay on his crooked arm.

"That was only the first act. Shall I go get the champagne?"

She rolled over and kissed him on the cheek. "Yes, please, my dear. Act Two comes after the champagne."

"As you like it. I was thinking of a five-act celebration." He extricated his arm and climbed out of bed. Grabbing his bathrobe, he asked, "You still want champagne in bed, don't you?"

She stretched out voluptuously on the bed. "Wasn't that the idea?"

"Just checking." He stepped into a pair of slippers and headed for the kitchen.

He decided to open the bottle in the bedroom. He put it and two tulips on a tray. At the last minute, he pulled out a clean white dishtowel and draped it over his forearm. He wasn't sure enough of himself to carry the tray balanced on one hand, the way he really wanted to.

"Your champagne, milady." He set the tray on the bedside stand and lifted the bottle to show her the label.

She was curled in the fetal position sound asleep.

He slipped out of his robe and crept across the bed. "Hey, lover." He kissed her on the cheek.

She stirred.

"I thought the point was to have champagne in bed, not fall asleep in it. At least not until later."

She unwound herself and wrapped her arms around him. They straightened out and clung to each other, their torsos fitting together like two pieces of a jigsaw puzzle.

"Let's do Act Three *before* Act Two," she whispered in his ear. In a split second she was on top of him, tickling places she had learned would arouse him. This time they nearly fell off the bed fighting to be on top. He ended up sitting on the edge of the bed with her on his lap.

"That was enough different to call it the second act." She pushed herself up and let herself drop onto the bed next to him, bouncing up and down like she'd landed on a trampoline.

He stood up. "All right! Let's get on with Act Three."

He opened the champagne with as much ceremony as his nakedness permitted. He handed her one of the tulips and raised the other in a salute. "I propose a toast. To Vanessa and her APS paper—with which, she bursts onto the cognitive neuroscience scene."

Their glasses chimed when they tapped them together lightly.

"Thank you," she said, tipping her head demurely.

Their eyes met as they lifted the glasses to their lips.

She had tucked her legs up, Buddha-like. "To the best advisor in the world." She held up her glass.

He clinked glasses with her. "That's much too flattering, especially in your case."

"For me, you are. You're exactly the person I need to guide me, and this APS paper has taught me a lesson." Like a spent breaker on a steep beach, her frothy declaration soughed away into tender adoration. "You knew exactly what to do with the work I'd done so far, and I promise you, Stan, I'll listen to your advice from now on."

He had been with her nearly three months, now, and he finally recognized some of the moods that lay hidden beneath her public face. This soft, feminine persona—with little sighs and a gaze of fondness—was the one he liked best.

"I think you're going to enjoy our three days in San Francisco," he said.

"Three whole days to spend with you. We'll be only a short elevator ride away from a snack whenever we feel like it—and all those great restaurants I've been hearing about in San Francisco."

He jabbed his finger at her champagne flute aiming for the top of the liquid inside. "I hate to burst your bubble, my dear, but you're going to be very busy."

"Not too busy for—?"

"Probably."

"No way. Why?" Her face had been a study in childlike curiosity and enthusiasm. But now there was a twinkle in her eyes that gave it all away as a pose.

"There'll be papers to go to and people you'll want to meet. We'll listen and talk, and talk and listen some more. By the end of these things, I'm usually so exhausted I sleep most of the way back on the plane."

"Will you introduce me to people like Hayes and Pellegrino?"

"Absolutely. I know them both."

"I have so many questions I'd like to ask them, I don't know where I'll start. But should I ask questions?"

He guffawed. "Just don't put them on the defensive with your very first one—unless they try to blow you off."

"Okay." She laid her head on his shoulder. "Just give me an elbow in the ribs if you think I should back off." She bumped him gently to demonstrate.

"We'll sit and listen to a lot of talks," he said, "and wander around poster sessions, but keep in mind that informal exchanges—in the hallways, in the coffee shop, in the bars—are often surprisingly important sources of information."

A quiver of excitement animated her whole body. "We'll get to spend the whole day talking about what's going on in the field?" The mask of pretense had vanished.

"And much of the evening."

"I saw in the program there were some big talks and symposia scheduled for the evenings."

"True. But sometimes what you learn over dinner is the most important. That and lunch." He stood up and refilled their glasses. "We'll also be going to some big parties—publishers' receptions and department parties."

"I hate that kind of thing. Who can have a sensible discussion of anything with everyone shouting at each other?"

"I know you don't like loud parties, which is exactly what they are. But here's the thing: The parties are where you meet a lot of people you'll want to know.

"In fact, you may get a chance to chat with them in a quieter place later in the meetings. They'll recognize you in the hall, or you can go up to them and ask them something about their talk or one of their recent papers. So try to go with the flow."

“Okay. You’re my guru.” An indulgent smile turned up the corners of her lips. “Or are you my coach?”

“Any other student, I’d say ‘mentor,’ meaning ‘model your behavior on mine.’ You? My advice is, first, be yourself. Watch how others handle things and follow your instincts.”

“You’re encouraging me to ask questions, then?”

“Of course.”

“Every time I do around here, I land in the doghouse.”

He patted her knee. “Don’t be shy. Ask. These are the smartest, most knowledgeable people in the world. They can handle challenges. Most of them enjoy dueling with people as quick as they are.”

“Now I’m intimidated.”

“Vanessa intimidated?” He laughed. “Give me a break.”

“Hmm,” she murmured skeptically.

“I’ve watched you in action long enough to know you’ll be more than a match for them. They’ll see you as the earnest student—the apprentice—and fancy themselves as the master craftsman.”

“A student—I’m good in that role.”

“You are, no doubt.”

“I want to start exploring new terrain.” She was getting a dreamy smile on her lips.

“That’s what you’re doing, my dear. Nobody’s ever tried to find out where your three experiments lead.”

“No, I used the wrong metaphor. I want to show the explorers—the experimenters—how to map the universe…” She tapped her temple. “…inside here.” Her voice drifted away along with her gaze.

“Can you construct a map without any surveys? A chart without at least a few soundings?”

“I’m embarked on a more fundamental expedition, Stan. One of my physics professors at Wazzu said in a lecture that mathematics is the language of science. That’s what’s been missing from cognitive neuroscience all along.

“The principles that govern our thoughts and feeling aren’t dictated by the activity in our brains but by the geometry of the mind-brain continuum. I want to devise that geometry so we can begin talking precisely about our thoughts and feelings.”

"One small step in thought, one giant leap in understanding thinking," Stan said. "But I doubt that NSF would have funded Euclid's work."

"Nor the work of Gauss or Riemann."

"They were mathematicians, weren't they?"

"In the early nineteenth century. They developed the mathematics needed for accurate maps of a curved earth. But I'll bet NSF wouldn't have given Einstein a grant either." Her gaze came back in focus as she rejoined the world he was in. "You know, Stan, he couldn't even get a PhD for his paper on the special theory of relativity. The faculty turned it down at the University of Zürich."

"I rest my case."

She shrugged. "His committee made the UZ look pretty bad, at least in retrospect. Aren't you worried about the UW's place in history?" There was the faintest of smiles on her lips.

CHAPTER 18

Vanessa half-rolled, half-somersaulted into a sitting position on the edge of the bed. "I'm hungry. Act Four is in the kitchen."

"I can offer you… fresh broccoli with hummus, honeydew melon wrapped in prosciutto, or…" Stan paused, as though trying to recollect what was in the refrigerator.

"Yummy. Melon with—"

"Or smoked salmon…?"

"Stan! You know what I want." She sprang out of bed and practically ran into the kitchen, completely naked.

When he came into the room, she was standing in front of the open refrigerator, pushing a dish aside so she could pull out a plate of salmon he'd made earlier and covered with plastic wrap. He closed the curtains on the breakfast nook, but there were several other windows facing the neighbors that had neither blinds nor curtains. He flipped on a light over the nook and crossed the room to turn off the overhead lights.

She stood up with the dish pulling the wrap off. "Thanks. Sorry about that. We don't want the neighbors calling the police."

He returned to the bedroom for the champagne tulips and picked up her bright turquoise bathrobe on the way back. She had already put the plate of salmon on the table in the nook and stood nibbling it with her fingers. She took the robe from him and tossed it on a bench in the nook. Then she slid in on it. He set the glasses on the table and stood indecisively, studying the parts of her body that were showing.

"Come on." She waved her hand at him impatiently. "Grab the champagne and get naked."

He followed her instructions in reverse order.

As he returned with the bottle, she said, "That's better. I may be the student around here, but when we make love, we're peers." She held out her glass for him to fill. "I get to look at your pecs if you can see my boobs hanging out."

He had just gotten himself comfortably seated, when she stuck her foot up between his legs.

He grabbed her ankle. "Stop that!" She offered a little resistance but let him push her foot away.

"Peers should have access to each other's private parts, don't you think?"

"I refuse to dignify that question with an answer."

She took a little sip of wine and held the glass up, watching the bubbles streaming to the surface. "I'm almost done collecting data for the second experiment, Stan. And I still don't have a committee."

"First, don't start the third one."

She shook head defiantly. "The data are falling into place too well to stop. Besides, it makes me nervous, showing people the data on myself and not having an answer to the question I know they're going to ask: 'Only one subject? Yourself?'"

"This is a convention paper, my dear, not a publication. You're trying to tantalize them, not convince them."

She scowled, a sure sign she wasn't going to settle for anything less than her own criterion. "It's not fair to tease, if you aren't sure you can deliver. And I'm very close to being able to."

"You always set your mark too high."

"That's me, Stan."

"Indeed."

He slid off the bench, pulling his robe after him. He ostentatiously put it on, hoping to set an example for Vanessa, in case she decided to leave the tenuous privacy of the booth. "I have a pot of coffee ready to start."

She didn't budge from the nook. "You know what I've been thinking about my committee, Stan?"

After he started the pot, he took off his robe again and slid back into his seat across from her. "Look, I'm really sorry I haven't come up with another committee member. But you have to keep in mind, Martha Yates is coming up for tenure. She can't afford to take chances, and…"

"And I'm toxic material, right?"

"I can't pretend that's not an issue."

"Of course it's an issue, Stan. I've burned too many bridges. That's also me."

He nodded his head in agreement. Michelle had privately approached Laura Montgomery and Sasha Rosenberg, both of whom had tenure. Laura flatly refused. "I don't want to get mixed up in that," she'd said. She listed as her reasons not only Vanessa's affairs with faculty—"…she's dangerously promiscuous"—but also brought up the numerous faculty Vanessa had irritated. "She's a troublemaker, Michelle. Whether she intends it or not, she just is." Sasha was a social psychologist and could dodge the problem by pleading that she had no expertise. Stan and Michelle had decided not to tell Vanessa.

"I told you I tried to convince Roger that he wasn't being fair to you if he went ahead and resigned."

"No," she said, before he could go on. "He has to maintain his distance. I understand that."

The coffee pot stopped gurgling. He got up again and crossed the kitchen, this time ignoring any neighbors who might be peering in. Placing two mugs of coffee on the table, he slid back into his seat across from her.

She brought her mug to her lips, blew over it, but decided the coffee was still too hot and set the mug down again. Suddenly, she looked up, straight into his eyes. "Stan, you simply have to let me do a theoretical thesis."

"Vanessa, please. We've been over that ground a dozen times already. I can't understand enough of your theory to be a credible sponsor, Paul sure as hell doesn't, and even Michelle claims most of it's beyond her."

"A friend of mine in the math—"

"And we also need a neuroscientist, don't forget. Because none of us feels strong enough there, either."

"Stan, listen. Last week a grad student I know in math helped me figure out which mathematician must have reviewed my paper. We ruled out everyone but Kashiba. It turns out he's on leave this quarter, but he'll be back in the fall."

"Okay, that might work. But we still need—"

"A neuroscientist, right?"

"And we've tried—"

"I have the perfect choice." She paused to test the coffee again. This time she took two cautious slurps, then looked up at him like a child with an innocent secret.

"Well? Does your sponsor get to learn the mystery guest's identity?"

"His name is Lin Xuan. He's in the neurology department."

He didn't recognize the name, but it would have been unusual if he had. "In the med school?"

"That's right. He has a PhD in physics as well as an MD. He's read the paper I wrote for Forrester…" She lifted her cup and paused just before it touched her lips.

"He understood it so well, he was able to do three things for me: Help me straighten out my derivations, give me two pages of references I hadn't even thought of looking for, and suggest a way to vastly broaden the scope of the theory."

She started to take a drink but stopped. "Oh, and he also encouraged me to keep on." She finally took a long draught of coffee.

She had been constantly throwing Stan off balance since that day she approached him after a talk. It was difficult for him not to feel superfluous. But she couldn't get a degree entirely on her own. Doctoral programs don't work that way. What was his role then? That was what he had to work out.

"Is he on the graduate faculty?"

"No, he's only an assistant professor, but I checked the graduate school policy statement on the so-called "doctoral supervisory committee"—Memorandum Number Thirteen, in case you're interested." An elfin smirk lit up her face. "Memo Twelve explains how assistant professors can be appointed to specific committees. Lin's working on it."

"We do it in psychology all the time. It's the usual first step to full membership."

"What do you think? Would you do it—chair my committee, I mean—if Lin supervised the writing?"

He frowned. Why did this feel like giving up his control? Was it admitting the truth, which was that he couldn't do it? That was silly. If he had any integrity, he'd be guided by what was in her interests, not his. This was, when you came right down to it, a test of how much he really loved her. So yes, he was ready to give up the sponsor's role as the control freak, no matter what his colleagues thought of him.

"Okay. Let's be practical." He wasn't quite ready to give up the mantle of mentorship. After all, he knew how Memos Twelve and Thirteen were applied in practice. "You have to face the fact that a theoretical thesis isn't going to fly until your mathematician comes back." He looked at her with what he hoped was a stern visage. "Don't—"

"He has to have an email address. I can get it from somebody. All I have to do is—"

"Don't interrupt, Vanessa. You're throwing away six months of research if you don't stop testing subjects and have a proposal meeting."

"Yes, you're absolutely right, oh Guru. And I have boundless confidence that you'll be able to conjure a committee for me out of the rapidly thinning air of the graduate faculty in the psychology department." She drank the rest of her coffee in one gulp. "Forgive me. I'm ruining an evening that should have been special."

She slid off the bench, stuck her arms out, and wiggled her pelvis. "Give me ten minutes to empty my bladder and get my brain back on the right hormones. And I'll be ready to rumble." She leaned across the table and kissed him on the temple. "Act Five. In bed." He couldn't take his eyes off her splendid breasts whose nipples pointed tantalizingly downward.

He watched her bare butt swaying in sensuous arcs as she walked out of the kitchen, a performance he knew was for his benefit. The sudden twists and turns of her comportment were vintage Vanessa, but that didn't change the fact that she had just insulted him and displayed her naked defiance in addition to her undraped body.

Vanessa had been spending most weekends with Stan, although she always brought along her laptop loaded with at least one project she worked on at his place. Her work habits astonished him. She'd jump out of bed in the morning before he woke up. When he staggered out of bed, often two or more hours later, she would be dressed and at work on her laptop in the study he'd set up for her.

Once she began working—on a paper she was writing or a collection of research papers she was reading, on an experiment she was planning or a thorny derivation she was struggling with, she was completely oblivious to the world around her. She literally did not hear phones ring. He discovered that he had to give her a gentle shake to get her to listen to something he needed to ask her. She always responded with a startled, "Oh! Sorry. What is it?"

He found Vanessa's sleep patterns were very peculiar. She fell into bed at night and was asleep an instant later. She usually awoke two or three hours later, jumped out of bed and dove into whatever she'd left off doing earlier. If her concentration began to wander while she was working, she'd pop back into bed or flop on the couch, only to emerge from sleep, whether a nap of fifteen minutes or a deep sleep of several hours, chomping at the bit to plunge back into her work.

She was the only woman he had ever slept with who fell asleep before he did after making love.

When spring break came, he persuaded her to stay with him during the day. To meet her subjects in the evening, she used his car with a faculty decal that allowed her to park close to the building, and he accompanied her Monday and Thursday.

He convinced her that they both needed a couple of days of vacation before spring quarter began. They took the *Clipper* to Victoria on Saturday morning and had two sunny days wandering the streets and stuffing themselves with good food. They had more sex than Stan had had in one weekend either before or since. They tried positions he'd only seen in books and movies.

At his request, she woke him up in the middle of the night—by the most erotic means imaginable—for a long slow session that felt like a dream the next morning. The only thing they didn't try was doing it beyond the confines of their luxury suite.

After a leisurely brunch Sunday morning, they went back to their room for what Vanessa suggested would be "…our last snack—one for the road." When the romp was over, she rolled out of bed, stood and stretched. "Time to get dressed, I suppose."

As she crossed the room, she caught sight of herself in a large full-length mirror. She stopped and gazed at the image. He sat up in bed, fascinated. He'd never seen her study her reflection in a mirror. She faced the mirror for a moment, then turned sideways, and finally another ninety degrees, looking over her shoulder into the mirror. Her eyes scanned her body languidly. Unexpectedly, they skidded off to meet his.

"Beautiful!" Her pose reminded him of a *Playboy* image of her. "Keep going."

"What do you mean?" She held the pose.

"Like your *Playboy* photo shoot."

She raised her arms over her head slowly, reminding him vividly of the video he'd watched the week before they came to Victoria. She rose on her tiptoes, making her legs more athletic—and erotic. "How's that?"

"Stupendous! Don't stop."

"I'm not in shape for this anymore." She lowered her heels to the floor again and rotated in excruciating slow motion. When she was facing him, she lifted herself on her toes again. "And you need heels for these kinds of poses."

"Give your head a shake." He focused on her breasts. They jiggled, hinting at their pliability under the fingertips. He was watching one of his videos of her, not only in 3D, but responsive to his commands.

"Would you play with your breasts?"

"You mean you don't want to do it?"

"No, there's something exquisitely arousing about imagining myself in your fingers while watching, like, over here."

When she brought her hands up her ribs toward her breasts, it was like he was the photographer coaching her poses, or the director of one of her videos. "Why don't we pretend I'm a film director for one of your *Playboy* videos—calling out stage directions, you know?"

She gave him a quizzical look. "If it gives you pleasure, sure." She cupped her breasts and leisurely grazed the nipples with her fingers, letting them pop up as they slipped free. Her hands moved on, unhurriedly releasing each breast individually.

"Again?" How he loved that delightful reconfiguration. He'd watched it repeatedly on a video, looping it at quarter-speed on his computer—over and over until he couldn't stand it any longer.

She complied, but looking at her smile made him wonder if it was forced.

After hesitating only a moment, he went on. "Okay. Now, could you slide your hands down across your tummy…? Yes…"

Slowly, slowly, slowly, her hands started downward, curving out around her breasts, with only her fingers tracking straight to flick her nipples.

"Yes! Keep on, keep on. Like that. Yes." His prick was throbbing with anticipation.

Suddenly, her fingers splayed out and her hands swerved out onto her hips, the right more than the left in concert with a thrust of her hips in the same direction. "Like right here?"

"No, no. You know the place I mean."

"Here?" She slid her hands back on her buttocks.

It was such a fetching pose with her breasts thrust forward that he hesitated for a moment before making the next request. "Come on, Vanessa. Your… you know." He pointed to his pulsing, cerise cock.

"I don't have one of those, Stan." Her tone of voice struck him as feigned irritation, as though it wasn't the joke it seemed. "You mean my cunt?"

"Yeah. Yeah. Pretend you can't resist playing with yourself."

"Wouldn't you rather 'play' with me?" The word was coated in sarcasm.

"Later, later. I'm really getting into your pleasuring yourself."

"Even if there isn't any pleasure? I think you need an actress rather than a lover." Her hands went to her pussy with clumsy urgency. "Oh!" She jerked suddenly, as though someone else had stuck her finger into her. "Uh! Uh!"

"That's right! You're doing fine now."

"Oh… Oh… Ah!" She began writhing, her legs squeezed together. With one hand she covered her cunt and with the other she massaged her breast.

"Hah—Hah—" Her breath came in gasps. She took one sidestep and began thrusting her hips against the hand in her pussy. "Uh… uh… UH—" Her eyes fluttered shut. "UHHH!"

He leapt off the bed and pointed to it. "Now, over here… on your back."

Her orgasm ended abruptly—obviously, she'd faked it, but well enough to fool an aroused man. She marched flatfooted around the bed and lay down with her legs away from him. She'd stopped looking at him. He was so busy watching her boobs bobble, he only vaguely sensed the growing anger she was exuding. Okay, he thought, she doesn't like this, so I'll ask for just one more favor, and then…

She put her knees up and raised her hips so her breasts flattened out, their graceful curves reversed. Her middle finger went back inside her like a jackhammer. When she started to moan again, he failed to notice the false note. He only needed a minute more. He'd always wanted to circle the model in this pose, caress her inner thighs, kiss her pink insides and then take her. He rushed to act out his fantasy.

Just as his fingertips had reached the fork of her legs and begun to tiptoe under her buttocks so he could support her for his first kiss, she jerked away.

"Stop it!"

Her scream froze his body. "What?" he croaked.

"I'm not your slave."

"I didn't say you were." He still had her buttocks firmly in his hands.

She began violently twisting and turning her body, trying to wrest herself from his grip. "Let go of me."

Primal desire, the strongest he had ever felt, surged through his body like lightning and collected in his quivering penis. "Not until I give you—" With a vicious jerk, he hauled her pelvis toward the magenta head of his penis. When he slid it into her gaping vulva, it felt like it spewed a ball of static electricity.

He folded her legs under his weight as he slid as far as he could go into her. When he lifted himself for a second stroke, she wedged her knees under his arms. All his conscious energy had pooled in one small cylinder of flesh and blood. He felt only what it felt, aware of nothing else, as he plunged into her slippery folds again.

At the bottom of his descent, she uncoiled the full power of her legs, sending him stumbling backward across the room and into an overstuffed chair. She rolled back and launched herself to her feet. Without pausing to look at him, she padded around the bed.

"Vanessa!" he bleated.

"What?"

He'd never heard so much suppressed rage in her voice. "I… I…"

When she rounded the bed, she finally stopped and glowered at him. "Are you hurt?"

"I don't think so." He pushed himself out of the chair, checking to see if there was any damage.

Vanessa, hands on her hips, watched impassively.

Finally, he asked, "What happened?"

"You were treating me like a piece of meat."

"What?"

"How else can you describe it, for God's sake?"

"I was trying to live out a fantasy I've had for years." He took a step toward her and spread his arms to hug her.

"You fantasized raping me!"

He froze. "Rape you?"

"What do *you* call what you were doing to me then?"

"I thought we'd… you'd agreed to pretend you were a model, and I was directing you… you know?… telling you how to pose."

She looked at him with evident disgust. "No photographer ever tried to rape me."

"No, no. You don't understand. I meant—"

"I understand, better than you do, and I think it's a pretty Goddamned sick fantasy, Stan."

"Please, Vanessa. Let me explain. I—"

"Let *me* explain: I'm not a *Playboy* model. Damn it, Stan, you're as bad as Brad Holmes."

He started to protest but a sound like the caw of a crow came out of his mouth instead.

"And, Dr. Stanley Harte, I'm your graduate student. Remember? It's me right here." She pointed to her heart, making it impossible not to look at her breasts.

"Shit! Don't look at my boobs. Look at *me*, just once. See, I'm standing here in front of you. The woman who's trying to be your protégé. I thought you were supposed to be my teacher. My mentor, someone I could look up to—a scientist and professor I could aspire to become."

He had half-turned away from her, wishing at that moment he could escape her indictment by dashing for a window, diving through it and falling to his death on the sidewalk below.

She took a step and with both hands, roughly twisted his head, forcing him to look directly into her eyes, whose depths contained a chamber of justice more forbidding than the throne of Solomon. "I thought you were my lover—"

"I am, Vanessa." He tried to look away, but those eyes pursued him like the Furies. "I love you with—"

"That's not true. I'm just a sex toy of yours. All this time, you've been acting like you care only about my best interests, my future, while you've been imagining me like I am in those damn photos—and drooling over my boobs and my cunt…" She pointed to each as she spoke. "You've been 'mentoring' me—" She hurled the word at him like a sack of wet garbage. "—to keep a good piece of ass around."

"You're absolutely right… And… and I deserve your scorn, but…" He sobbed uncontrollably when he tried to take a breath. "But I also believe in you and what you are doing."

"Yes… Yes, you did. But—"

"Listen, let me explain about the photos and fantasies and…"

"Wait. Stop, Stan." Her voice wasn't as harsh.

"Yes?"

"We need to talk. There are apparently some things I don't know about you—"

"And I want to tell you why—"

"Okay!" She cut him off unceremoniously. "But there is also something you don't know about me." She started for the bathroom. "I'm going to take a shower and get packed up. We should have an hour or so for me to tell you the whole story of my nude modeling career." She turned in the bathroom doorway. "Okay?" She closed the door without waiting for an answer.

CHAPTER 19

Stan sat on the edge of the bed with the same hopeless feeling he'd had when his family went to an emergency shelter set up in the high school after the 1972 Rapid City flood. They had spent three dazed nights and days there, not knowing how much damage the murky, fetid water had done and whether they would ever return to live in their home.

Wave after wave of memories from his eleven years had washed over him as he remembered precious possessions he might never see again—his model railroad with its steam engines and rolling stock, his collection of books and comics, his baseball glove, even his favorite T-shirts and shoes. A few of them haunted his dreams for years afterward.

After what had happened, he couldn't tell whether he and Vanessa were through, whether she'd even want him to continue as her sponsor. Like his childhood flood experience, one cherished moment with Vanessa after another paraded through his head, each bringing another wave of grief for what he might have lost.

His stomach felt like he was falling in empty space, not knowing whether his landing would leave him impaled on the spire of a ragged mountain ridge or treading water in a murky swamp with Vanessa as a spectral companion, just beyond his reach. Only once did he let himself hope for a second that he'd begin flapping newfound wings as he mounted into the skies of a new, richer and more honest relationship with her.

He was vaguely aware of the shower running briefly. Vanessa rarely ran the shower until it warmed up. She simply stepped in and began soaping up. She took half the time Stan did, or less. He jumped when she opened the bathroom door.

"Want to come in and get started while I finish blow-drying my hair?"

"No… no thanks."

She noticed that he was still naked. "Hey! Aren't you going to get dressed? And packed up?"

"Yeah." He stood and started around the bed.

She disappeared behind the open door. "I don't want to talk about this in public under any condition. I'm guessing it will take me at least half an hour. I've only told two or three people who didn't already know about it." Her voice echoed against the tile walls and floors of the bathroom.

He pulled on the sweater and jeans he'd laid out for the trip home and threw his remaining stuff into the small duffel bag they had shared for the overnight stay in Victoria. He sat down in one of the straight-backed chairs at a small table and waited gloomily. It was hard to believe that they had been so lighthearted for the past thirty-six hours.

He made up his mind that before they went to bed—or split up—tonight, he was going to tell Vanessa everything. And apologize for the way he'd treated her. Because she was absolutely right. Thinking of her as an object to play with whenever they were together—imagining her nude photos when he looked at her—demeaned her and diminished him.

He thought he'd gotten beyond his obsession with her *Playboy* photos. But he realized how helpless he was. Even the rich and varied sex life he'd been living with the most beautiful woman he'd ever known hadn't changed his degrading habit of looking at naked women, his insatiable appetite for watching them take off their clothes—in photos, movies, videos—in magazines, on the Internet, in live strip clubs. He'd been jerking off to images of women in the buff since high school.

When she emerged from the bathroom still naked, he was erect in a flash. In spite of what had happened. By the time she'd dressed and added her things to their bag, it had subsided, but what had happened was one more dismal reminder of his miserable state of enslavement to a revolting habit.

She appeared not to have noticed the boner straining at his pants. She briskly pulled out the other chair and sat down facing him. "So. When I went to that casting call in Pullman, it wasn't the first time I'd posed with no clothes on. I was by then an old hand at it."

"You said you posed for art classes."

"I lied. I'd been posing naked for a photographer for years by then."

"Years? You mean before you were legally…? Before you were eighteen?"

"Before I was born."

"Say what?" Had he heard her right?

"And the photographer was my father."

"What?" He could not take in what she had just said. That her own father had asked her, had used her, treated her as an object, a prop—and to further his career apparently. He tried to imagine photographing his daughter, Elise, naked, and it was inconceivable. His mind's eye closed involuntarily and his mental body looked away.

She was nodding. Her face was completely inscrutable—not a clue as to how she felt about such an appalling experience. "I told you he was a professional, didn't I?"

"Yes, but you said he was a *landscape* photographer—wilderness landscapes…"

"He is." She grimaced. "Or was."

"You mean he sold nude photos of you on the side?"

"No," she said flatly. "His best work—the work he is still famous for—combines landscapes and figure photography. He's sold his best stuff to both *Playboy* and to museums of photography, like the International in New York, the Getty in LA, and the Griffin in Boston."

Vanessa had grown animated as she spoke. "Picture a remote mountain lake with a reflection of Mount Rainier, except close to shore a beautiful naked woman stands ankle deep, arms raised—full frontal—scooping up a plume of water arching toward the camera."

"It sounds exquisite."

"Perfectly composed. That's my dad's signature work." Vanessa leapt to her feet and began pacing the room, full of nervous energy. "That's how my parents met. They were at a party.

He asked her to pose for him. They drove out into the desert east of LA—in the dark, so he could shoot at dawn."

She stopped and faced him. "That one, with the arc of my mom's body completing the arc of a Joshua tree—" She drew a circle in the air with her forefinger. "It won a prize."

"How extraordinary." The image he conjured in his mind was sensational—and singularly erotic. "I've seen very few photos of nude women in wild settings."

She smiled—the first time since this awful incident began. "*Playboy* did a whole pictorial feature of his photos," she said. "It was called 'National Park Girl.' It had some of his best work before I came along."

"You know, I think I remember that feature." It was a long time ago, but he recalled that years after it had appeared, he went back and fantasized that he was in those spectacular settings with a woman as captivating as Vanessa. "I loved one of those photos—the one of the model running on a beach—"

"My mother." Her smile blossomed into a wide grin.

"She was a real beauty." He tried to put a face to the image in his memory but couldn't. What a revelation that was! All he could see was a model with arms spread wide and her pubic hair blurred by the motion. His aroused mind had saved *only* the sexual aspect of the scene, with the exception of the spectacular background. "It had unforgettable seastacks in the—."

"That was Shi Shi Beach, I think—on the wilderness strip of the Olympic Park."

"I remember thinking at the time, why aren't there more photos and paintings like this? They are works of art as much as Goya's *Naked Maja*."

"Well, Dad *was* an artist. And when Mom got pregnant, Dad kept on shooting the same kind of photos. My mom's bulging body—naked, of course —mirroring the fan of water of the Bridal Falls in Yosemite, the hillock of her belly sticking up on a sandy beach—" She traced the line with the flat of her hand, making it clear that the woman lay on her back. "—mimicking a domelike island in the background."

Vanessa paused. The only sounds were the muffled conversations of the housekeeping staff in the hallways and an occasional door closing.

"So I posed for photos even before I was born—naked, obviously." She laughed spontaneously. "He didn't stop when I was born. All my baby pictures are nudes, Stan. All of them. Including hundreds of me with Mom—also nude. There's one of me nursing in the Olympics that's a masterpiece."

"Like a Madonna with Child?"

"A lot of them had historical allusions to famous paintings. Knowledgeable people recognized their aesthetic value."

"What else was your father doing? I mean, he wasn't just taking pictures of you and your mother?"

"Believe it or not, that's all he was doing. He was obsessed. There was still a market for his work. More private collectors than before, but a couple of the big galleries continued to show them. He kept a complete photographic record of me growing up. There are all these photos hanging on people's walls—all over the world. Baby Vanessa crawling around in a meadow of wildflowers in the Cascades, toddler Vanessa looking goggle-eyed at Crater Lake, preschooler Vanessa playing in the surf near Point of the Arches, fifth-grader Vanessa posed just like her mother, completing the circle of a Joshua tree—at dawn, no less."

She laughed again. "No photos of Vanessa—naked, as always—running from the rattlesnake a few minutes later, however."

"Jesus! That sounds dangerous."

"No kidding. It seems funny now. But it scared the sh—" She smirked. "I peed my pants—except I didn't have any on."

They both broke up with laughter.

"Did that sort of thing happen often?" He realized as soon as he said it that they might be coming to an opening where he could ask his touchiest question.

"Plenty of times. But you know, I was probably in more danger crossing the Sol Duc River on a log or coming down the back side of Table Mountain on the snow."

"Was your mother along on these trips?" He held his breath.

"Early on she was. But later, it was just Dad and me." She stopped abruptly, squinting at his sudden change of expression. "Nothing happened, if that's what you're thinking. I'm not the victim of sexual abuse, Stan."

"I was hoping that you weren't." He let out his breath feeling very relieved.

"Oh, I forgot the best. It was the summer between seventh and eighth grade. We'd been climbing on Mount Baker, not trying to summit, just looking for a good shot—and privacy."

"But real mountain climbing, you mean?"

"Crampons, ice axes, ropes—the whole thing. When we stopped for lunch—"

"Your dad and…"

"Just the two of us." She gave him another warning look. "So there I am throwing snowballs in June on Squak Glacier. Naked? What else? My feet were freezing. But the best shot turned out to be where I'm stretching to catch one he lobbed back at me."

"So you were, what? Fourteen?"

"Thirteen."

"I thought there were laws about selling photographs of young children. Nude, that is."

"There are." Vanessa said nonchalantly. "But the line between art and pornography is hazy. That last one was part of Dad's big show at the San Francisco MOMA." She frowned at him. "Where do you stand on those legal issues, Stan?"

"Well, I…" This was potentially a trick question, but since he was going to confess his addiction to pornography anyway, he decided to go the route of honesty. "You know, of course, that I used to look at *Playboy* photos a lot. Just looking at them is enough to—"

"To get a hard-on?"

"An erection, yes." He was blushing, but she showed no particular emotion. "To be perfectly blunt, I masturbated while looking at them."

"Isn't that the point?" She shrugged. "Look, I knew when I went to that casting call that I could make more money from men jerking off to my boobs and twat than I could any other way in Pullman. It's not that big a deal to me, Stan."

"Well, I'm very ashamed of myself for doing it. I'm appalled that all I can think about is your breasts and labia when I look at you. It's unforgivable, Vanessa."

"No, it isn't. I think I understand a little bit about addiction. If you try to change, that's all I ask. But you don't understand the real reason why it bothers me so much. You've only heard the first part of the story." She stood. "Excuse me a minute. I need a drink of water."

She went into the bathroom and returned with a half-empty glass. She began talking again before she'd reached the chair. "So far I've only explained why cavorting naked in front of a camera and later having every man and his brother gaping at my private parts didn't bother me much a few years later. The second part of the story concerns how Dad's photos got him into a lot of trouble."

"Before you go on, Vanessa. What kind of poses did he…? You know, uh, like the *Playboy* ones showing… uh… everything?"

"Pretty much." She scowled. "He taught me a lot about how to pose provocatively, as opposed to artistically. Like looking into the lens with your head tilted." She demonstrated. "That sort of thing. And he showed me lots of examples, so I knew the difference between art and porn, and between soft and hard porn."

"There's something really sinister about that." He was thinking about how shocked he was the first time Elise pouted in a provocative way she certainly hadn't learned from Heidi. She was so young to have picked that up, and so naïve, trying to use it on him.

"Some people would be bothered by it. But they're the ones who get all bent out of shape by seeing women's boobs in public. And I was becoming sexually active by this time. I could see the effect certain poses and gestures had on my boyfriends. I'm not proud of using what I learned to get what I wanted sometimes."

"I think your father was treading a very thin line."

"I suppose. But galleries were still selling his work. At least the better ones." She paused to gulp some of her water. "Unfortunately, a photographer can make a lot more money from pornography than from art."

They both jumped when someone tapped on the door to their room with something more solid than knuckles. "Housekeeping."

He was on his feet instantly. "Just a minute," he shouted.

"Oh, excuse me. I come—"

He opened the door on an overweight woman with a dark skin wearing a peach-colored dress and apron with the hotel logo embroidered on it.

"Oh, sorry, sir." Her accent sounded African to him. "I come back later."

"Could you please? They told me at the desk we could stay in the room until three-thirty or so."

"Yes. It okay. I come back. Four o'clock."

"Thank you." He closed the door.

Vanessa resumed talking before he reached his chair. "I don't know when my dad started selling my photos to people who weren't part of the art world. Dad suddenly seemed to have a lot more money. On his own, he started an investment account to pay for me to go to graduate school. Around this time, he and Mom had several really vicious fights. I gather he must have told her about the photos, because I certainly didn't. Then Dad moved out and ended up in LA—eventually."

"You mean your mother didn't know what he'd been doing?"

"She was doing a lot of consulting then. It seemed like she was traveling more than she was working at home."

"What did your parents tell you was going on? Or is that a rude question? Don't answer, if it is."

"No. It's a good one. My dad didn't say very much to me. My mom—she claimed it was all Dad's fault. She refused to listen to me, even when I told her Dad had never, ever touched me or said anything sexually suggestive to me.

"She never said it, but I think she was more incensed that he hadn't told her earlier what he was doing than what he actually did. If he had, she could have set some limits. She seemed especially upset by my suggestive poses and facial expressions."

"You don't know when he sold the first one to someone interested in pornography?"

She shook her head. "It may have been going on for a long time. I think it happened when he started having trouble selling the ones of me in my teens."

She looked up abruptly. "What time is it?"

"It's only two-thirty. We have lots more time. Especially if… talking about this is helpful."

"It is, Stan. I haven't told anyone for a couple of years." She reached out and twirled the rod that opened the Venetian blinds. A moment passed while she looked out.

"After Dad moved out, he didn't let us know where he was for more than three months. Then he sent us a picture postcard with no address. The postmark was from LA. That was it.

"I don't know what happened in LA, but the next thing we knew, the FBI was knocking at our door to question us. That was when the real nightmare began. But the worst part was that we found out where Dad was—he was in prison briefly and then out on bail—we had his lawyer's name and address, but when I wrote to him—letter after letter—he never answered me." She whimpered. "Never."

He'd never seen her cry. It brought tears to his eyes as well. He hid them from her by turning to look out the window. She continued to sob quietly for a minute or two.

He finally stood, went over to her, and put a hand on her shoulder. "Are you sure you want to go on? This obviously hurts."

She shook her head weakly. "Thank you for listening." Her eyes glistened, when she looked up at him, and tears dribbled down her cheeks.

She got up and went to the tissue box in the bathroom and came back blotting her cheeks and blowing her nose.

"The FBI questioned a bunch of people who'd bought the legitimate photos, the ones the critics would say had so-called artistic merit. They found two or three men who'd bought directly from Dad instead of from a gallery and threatened them with prosecution, even though they couldn't have made it stick. One way or another, none of these buyers could afford the publicity of a trial.

"Eventually, the FBI agents also found some dealers who were selling the so-called obscene ones. They and the galleries caved in, too. A criminal charge would have cost them a fortune, even if they won it eventually. If the case had gone public, it would have killed their business.

"Dad decided to fight the charges in court. He had some good ACLU lawyers, but..."

"You mean, he lost?"

"He got a short prison term, they said. Four years? Short—shit!" She started to cry again, but instead of sobs, she kept talking with stubborn ferocity.

"From the very beginning, I refused to answer any questions beyond acknowledging he was my father. I claimed I was afraid I'd be charged with a crime for posing. As a witness I couldn't have gotten away with a Fifth Amendment plea, except that I was a minor. The judge interviewed me and decided the prosecution didn't need my testimony. There were plenty of other photos of me around, and anyone could see I was the person in Dad's photos.

"I thought about going to see Dad in prison, but he didn't answer any of my letters, even when I begged him, told him I was to blame for not refusing… I mean, I could have said I was a little uncomfortable because I wasn't sure if it was legal. Yet not one letter. Not one."

She stood suddenly. "Excuse me."

She spent several minutes in the bathroom with the water running almost continuously. He began to worry about her and almost went to knock on the door. But then it opened and she returned, dry-eyed but her face still eroded by her weeping.

"Feeling better?" He hesitated to embrace her.

"Somewhat. Thanks again for listening." She squeezed his shoulder as she walked to the window. "It's nice out. Lets stop at that cute coffee house on our way to the boat."

"Great idea." He stood. As he hoisted their duffel bag onto his shoulder, he caught her eyes. "I'm really glad you shared that story with me, Vanessa dear. I can see how much you were offended by what I—"

She stepped up and kissed him lightly on the cheek. "I'm glad, too."

"But, see, knowing how you feel—what posing nude reminds you of and all… It makes me feel even guiltier about how I look at you sometimes and see only… like you say, 'tits and twat.'"

She laughed. "You mean, mentally undressing me? I'd expect that of you. You wouldn't be normal if you didn't—sometimes. Not all the time, of course."

"No, I meant flashing on the *Playboy* photos I own. I hadn't looked at them since we—"

"—did our little experiment last fall?"

"Right. But a few weeks ago I…"

"Fell off the wagon?" She slid an arm under the strap of their bag and hugged him. "Maybe I can help."

He hugged her awkwardly around the bag. "I don't know. Counseling didn't help and…"

"I was thinking of something else." Her pixie look replaced the dispirited one. "The next time you have a hot flash, tell me. We can quick run over to my place for a snack."

They kissed briefly.

"God, if that doesn't cure me, nothing will."

On their way out of the hotel lobby, the anticipation of their first midday rendezvous remodeled his future with warm sunshine. As they stepped out into a sunny Victoria afternoon, he took flight with Vanessa at his side, and they soared over the city before wheeling south to return to their nest in Seattle.

With the start of spring quarter, Stan and Vanessa resumed their previous routine. They saw each other nearly every day—shared coffee breaks, went out to lunch together and met in his office as their schedules allowed or required. She spent the weekends with him, and they slept together Friday and Saturday evenings.

For the first three weeks of spring quarter, they managed to have at least one "snack" between Sunday night and Friday afternoon. But both of them were too busy during the fourth week and by Wednesday of the fifth, ten days of Stan's "hot flashes" had gone unrequited. Around ten o'clock that evening, the mere thought of Vanessa—and she was always on his mind—the tiniest of reminders provoked a string of *Playboy* images intercut with memories of notable love-making episodes.

As he sat staring at the unread page of an online journal article, he idly clicked on his photo manager. The furrows of habit were so deeply plowed that the cursor seemed to move on its own, clicking its way to the *Playboy* folder and starting a slide show of Vanessa as she stripped from skimpy workout clothes to pose nude on treadmills and weight-training machines in a gym.

The last frame stayed on the screen waiting for him to press the escape key. It was an image of Vanessa sitting on an exercise ball with legs spread and her middle finger just touching the top of her labia. She was smiling seductively, as though she'd enjoyed the striptease and was ready for a hand-to-hand romp on the mat under her feet.

As the screensaver wiped out the image he found himself with a charged up power drill and nothing to ream with it. What happened next was so physically compelling that he thought afterward that an alien had taken over his body. Grabbing his mouse, he began a calculated search of the Web for the photos Vanessa's father had taken before she was eighteen.

Searches with "trippett photo moma" and similar search terms went nowhere. Then it occurred to him that Vanessa had used only her first and middle names as a Cyber Girl. "vanessa marie nude" turned up over a quarter of a million hits, but at the top of the third page was a Bulgarian website.

With serious misgivings he entered the credit card number for his account with the lowest credit limit and paid to download all forty images. When he had the files in his image manager, there was no question that the last fifteen had been taken when she was between sixteen and eighteen.

The first twenty-five were surely the ones Russell Trippett had shown at the MOMA. They were very discreet nudes that displayed the anatomical aspects of Vanessa's maturing body without breaking through the very thin line that separated art and obscenity.

The settings were spectacular—recognizable glimpses of the Pacific Northwest's pristine wilderness, in which an Acadian sylph cavorted with uninhibited youthful abandon. Trippett was a consummate artist. That seemed to be beyond question. The sequence followed the chronology Vanessa had described, beginning with her pregnant mother and recording her childhood.

The last fifteen photos were different from the ones that preceded them. The facial expressions were seductive, the poses deliberate—and unmistakably provocative: her hips canted, her back arched, her head aslant, her startling blue eyes looking sideways directly at the viewer, both inviting and challenging. Her face alone could stir a man's penis, as could the shape of her body seen from a distance.

He selected the last five—sixteen and seventeen she must have been at the time—and cycled them twice at the rate of two per minute. His prick strained against the fabric of his pants, quivering with excitement. The faintest stroke of his fingers was all that was require to detonate a jet of semen. He threw his head back, moaning. His whole body shuddered with the utter joy of the moment.

And then the moment passed and with it, all remnants of pleasure were swept away in a Santa Ana wind that scoured his spirit with shame, guilt, remorse, and recrimination—enough to strip any enjoyment from an entire week. He staggered into a pit of depression from which even Vanessa herself could not wrest him during the weekend that followed.

He tried several times to tell her, to answer her anxious questions with a complete confession. But he could not. He could not face the reality of his flaccid will power, so puny that he had gratified his sexual urges with shadowy electronic apparitions when the warm flesh and affection of the most perfect lover he would ever find awaited him less than forty-eight hours later. He could delay gratification no better than a four-year-old boy.

He had barely regained a few shreds of self-respect a week later before he went back to his computer and discredited himself yet again. This time he managed to hide his shame and despair from Vanessa. But now their relationship seemed doomed. He was rarely without a demon on his back, whispering scorn on every word he uttered, mockery of every act. Only as the date approached for them to depart for the APS meetings in San Francisco, did he recover a little confidence in his future.

CHAPTER 20

Anticipating the trip to San Francisco, Vanessa asked Michelle for advice about a professional wardrobe. Michelle offered to spend a Saturday helping her select some clothes for the meetings. Vanessa seemed excited about the jackets, pants, and blouses she modeled for Stan that evening.

They struck Stan as exactly the kind of versatile, sensible things Michelle herself wore much of the time. The difference was that on Vanessa, the fit suggested the perfectly proportioned body underneath. The colors were also quite different, being similar to the icy, vivid hues of her dressiest blouses and accessories and the severe black and navy blue of her two cocktail dresses.

The two of them flew to San Francisco together and took the shuttle bus to the Hyatt Regency. As they entered the lobby, he paused to look for the hotel registration line. Vanessa glanced up for a moment. The huge central courtyard was designed to appear open to the outdoors. It stretched all the way to skylights many floors above, and deep balconies on every floor served as the hallways. An exotic fragrance of flowering plants mingled with a buzz of social activity. He found the line, which snaked up three shallow steps and under a low-ceilinged alcove off the lobby.

Once in line, they gazed out at the chaotic, constantly changing groups of two to eight that swirled over the main floor like a slow-motion video of a suddenly exposed ant colony. Except for those who hadn't yet checked in, everyone had a nametag in a clear plastic sleeve with a name and an institutional affiliation printed in block capital letters. Bits and pieces of conversation drifted over them as they waited. "The food was lousy…" "…for sixty-four trials, and then we shifted them to the two hundred fifty millisecond condition."

They had been in line less than two minutes when Stan spotted Don Latourette, emerging from the crowd and headed their way. Stan indicated him with a nod of his head. "Don Latourette. Just moved to Indiana."

He was a jaunty man in his early thirties with a crown of dark curly hair, and he was smiling at Vanessa as though he recognized her. Only when he was two paces from them did he shift his eyes away from her.

"Stan!" His deep voice was sweet with the speech of the South. "Good to see you." He stuck out a brawny hand. He wore a short-sleeved shirt the color of pineapples.

"Well, well! The devil himself!" Stan took the hand Latourette held out.

Muscles rippled under the dark hair of Latourette's forearm as he gripped Stan's hand. "Up to no good as usual, I see." Even as he shook hands, he was turning to Vanessa. He pulled his hand away the moment their grip loosened. "And you must be Vanessa Trippett. Hi. Don Latourette." He offered his hand to her.

She looked surprised. "Oh!" She looked at his hand a second, then blushed and took it. "Sorry, yes. I'm Vanessa."

"Vanessa is my student, Don," Stan said quickly.

Latourette pointedly gazed into Vanessa's eyes. "I suspected as much, Stan." He didn't take his eyes off her. "Vanessa Trippett of random pixel samples?"

"Yes?" She frowned.

"A fantastic finding!" Dimples like double parentheses formed around Latourette's mouth when he smiled. His white teeth sparkled against his tanned skin.

"How did you…?"

"I saw your abstract in the program. I'm looking forward to seeing your poster tomorrow."

Vanessa nodded, apparently not quite sure what to make of Latourette's praise. "Uh, thank you."

Stan intervened. "Vanessa's collecting data for her thesis with me."

Latourette finally acknowledged Stan's presence. "But subliminal perception is hardly your field, Stan."

"True," Stan said, "but Vanessa's approach—to data analysis and interpretation, I mean—doesn't fit neatly into anybody's specialty."

"Now that's a teaser." Latourette turned his full attention back to Vanessa. "You know, Vanessa, I think your advisor is being a bit coy here. I hope you're not."

Vanessa didn't smile as Latourette was apparently hoping she would. "I'd be happy to explain it, uh, Don. However, I can't do justice to it in less than—"

Stan guessed Latourette was getting ready to suggest that she'd have his undivided attention all evening if she'd join him for dinner tonight. "And *you* won't be able to do justice to understanding her approach, Don, unless you've mastered differential geometry and are facile with tensor calculus in seven-dimensional manifolds."

The other two gawked at him.

"Stan! Don't scare him off." She turned back to Latourette. "The intuitions aren't that hard to grasp; the derivations do get a little complex."

The three of them had been moving toward the front of the line in increments of a yard or two at a time. All at once, three clerks at the registration desk finished at once. Stan turned to see that the two people in front of them were gone. A clerk repeated her call, "May I help the next person, please?"

"Excuse us, Don." Stan picked up his bag. "Are you ready, Vanessa?"

"I'll catch you later," Latourette said as they headed for the registration desk.

A few minutes later in their room, Vanessa said, "You know, Stan, I appreciate your fending off pests like Don Latourette. But that bit about tensor calculus was uncalled for."

"Pest is right! I assume you could see he isn't interested in your research."

"Hmm." She hung up her slacks in the closet. "So that's the pickup line at scientific meetings—'Come up to my room and tell me about your research.'"

"You've got it. Or, 'It's too noisy here. Let's go up to my room and I'll explain it to you.' That's the one you might fall for—given your distaste for loud parties."

"Thanks for the warning, pal."

"You're welcome, my dear. You'll encounter a whole zoo full of pests here. Keep an eye out for the wolves. Some of the biggest names in the field are notorious Lotharios. Don't let yourself be hoodwinked."

They registered for the meetings, collected their nametags and headed for the "no-host" reception in the Seacliff Room. Vanessa visibly winced at the noise as they walked in.

Stan consulted his watch; it was only four, a little early for dinner. "We'll be here for a while. The bar's over there." He pointed to the most packed part of the room. "Do you want to wait here for me to get drinks?"

She grabbed his hand and gripped it tightly. "No, don't abandon me to the pests." She spoke much louder than usual and glanced around as though embarrassed by what she'd said.

He squeezed her hand to reassure her. "Let's go."

Even before they reached the bar it began—the gathering of the wolf pack. They were only halfway across the room, when a gruff bass voice called out Stan's name.

It was Charlie Templin of Columbia. He stuck out his hand. "How's it going?" He was a burly man whose mischievous blue eyes peeked out of a ruddy face.

"Fine, Charlie. I see you and Jones have another big paper in *Perspectives*."

"Yeah. We finally got around to integrating all our data with the theory." Charlie glanced in Vanessa's direction.

"Oh… Charlie, I'd like to introduce Vanessa Trippett. Vanessa, Charlie Templin."

"Nice to meet you, Vanessa." His oversized mitt completely swallowed up Vanessa's dainty hand.

"Vanessa's working with me on—"

"Yes," Charlie said, nodding to Stan and quickly turning back to Vanessa. "I saw your abstract." He examined her face thoroughly, beginning and ending with her lips. "I'd planned to stop by tomorrow afternoon, but something's come up."

He paused thoughtfully before turning back to Stan. "I have an idea. A couple of us are going to Acquerello for dinner tonight. Would you and Vanessa…" Here he turned and focused the full spotlight of his smile on her. "…be able to join us?"

"Yes, certainly," Stan said. "Knowing your discerning taste in food and wine, we'd absolutely like to. What time?"

"We're meeting in the lobby at seven." Charlie finally gave his attention to Stan. "You know Neil Sussex and Rámon Garcia, don't you?"

"Neil and I go way back, and I've met Rámon. We'll see you there."

"Good. " His eyes were back on Vanessa, this time glued to her eyes. "Nice meeting you, Vanessa. See you this evening." He glanced down at her hand, still tightly gripping Stan's. Turning, he shouldered his way across the room toward the door.

Just then the crowd jostled them together.

"Wow!" Vanessa said in a loud whisper, "A leading name in the neural mechanisms of perception and the director of the largest functional MRI lab in the country. What a treat to learn something from them. Plus Sussex is the editor of *Neuropsychology*, right?"

"Yeah. I have almost no overlapping interests with that trio."

"What do you mean?"

They were facing each other, so when the person standing behind Vanessa bumped into her, she was thrown against Stan's chest.

"Oh, terribly sorry!" The accent sounded French with a hint that the man had learned English in a British school.

Stan didn't recognize him, but when Vanessa turned around, it was clear the guy was going to introduce himself to her. Stan tugged on Vanessa's hand. "Come on. Only three more layers of people between us and the bar."

In another five minutes they had glasses of second-rate wine and began pushing their way toward the less-packed periphery. Stan introduced Vanessa to Vicki Townsend, who had been a fellow graduate student at Wisconsin. It turned out that Vanessa had used her developmental textbook in an undergraduate course, and they immediately hit it off.

He also managed to introduce Vanessa to Gary Hayes and Maria Pellegrino. The husband and wife team drifted by separately at different times.

Stan veered between amusement and annoyance as his male colleagues caught sight of him, took one look at Vanessa, and headed their way. He was reasonably well-known for his published work—a yeoman recognized for his craftsmanship. But never before had he been able to chat with as many acquaintances—all of them men—without moving an inch during the first reception of a three-day meeting. To a man, they spent more time looking at Vanessa than at him.

He did take some satisfaction in turning down two more dinner invitations with an airy, "We'd love to join you, but we've already promised some friends."

On the way down the escalators to the lobby, Vanessa, still holding his hand, said, "Will you be able to introduce me to a few more women?"

He nodded. "Tomorrow, I'll make sure you meet a bunch of them. It should be easier when the crowds are a little thinner."

At dinner, Charlie saw to it that Vanessa was seated in the middle chair directly across from him. Stan was curious how much Vanessa would participate, but if she was awed by the scientific brainpower, it was well disguised. She jumped in uninvited with questions and an occasional observation.

Only once did she try to pin Rámon down on his interpretation of some recently published brain imaging experiments. She did it gingerly, and when it was evident to everyone that she'd found a hole in his logic, she graciously backed off.

"I'm sure we could reformulate the hypothesis," she said with a self-effacing grin. "I really don't understand the constraints."

Stan was pretty sure she did and probably had a more consistent hypothesis ready to describe, but Rámon decided not to pursue the matter. Watching Vanessa, Stan felt an undeserved pride. Any other student, he could have taken some credit for what she had learned and the style of thinking she'd absorbed from him. But in Vanessa's case, he knew that wouldn't be true. What she did at dinner that first night in San Francisco, he couldn't have done himself and never would.

As if in confirmation of his thoughts, Neil Sussex pulled Stan aside as they waited near the door while a cab was being called. "I had a chance to look at Vanessa's handout this afternoon. Do you have any idea how big an advance she might be making?"

Stan shook his head. "Do you understand the math?"

"Enough to know that it's an astonishing piece of work. It looks to me like the double helix of consciousness—with Rosalind Franklin's crystallography of the brain into the bargain."

"Well, I can't follow her derivations," Stan said. "But I know her work is important."

"Important? Stan, that's like saying Einstein's work was 'important.' You'd better see to it that the paper she was passing out today gets into print immediately."

"Can she send it to you?"

"Why am I telling you this?" Neil turned to watch Vanessa coming toward them. "And why did the Good Lord pour so much brainpower into a body like that?" he whispered just loud enough for Stan to hear.

The next day Stan helped Vanessa set up her booth for the one o'clock poster session. She was better organized than anyone he'd ever seen. During an earlier session in the same room, she'd checked out the exact booth she'd been assigned. The sketch she then made along with the numbered panels made it easy for him to start putting up her laminated sheets with pushpins while she readied her laptop on the table.

Her knack for finding exactly the right words and arranging graphs and text in a unified visual display was the equal of her skill in writing clear, concise, and logical papers.

When the crowds of hunters and grazers flooded the aisles, they divided up the work of dealing with those who stopped by. The table and partitions around the booth formed a well. Stan took up a position at the entrance to it, where he served as an informal gatekeeper, letting in the serious searchers and fending off the curious skimmers.

Inside the well, Vanessa spent much of her time describing the two lines she'd drawn through the clusters of dots on the graphs. The black line in all four graphs was a simple statistical summary of her data; the red one in three of them was derived from her theory—not the full unified theory but a five-dimensional model of the role of consciousness in the perception of faces. She gave out lots of handouts from the pile on the table to people who went off flipping through the pages and shaking their heads at the daunting thicket of mathematical symbols.

Halfway through the hour, there was a lull. Vanessa looked a little droopy.

"What's wrong?" Stan asked.

"I don't think a single person yet has gotten it."

He laughed. "Remember, my dear. Few of these souls have ventured much beyond the first year of undergraduate math. They don't speak intergalactic Lobatchevskian."

"Yeah." She sighed. "I guess I was hoping for at least one fellow speaker of my native tongue."

Moments later, Susan Hurst—a friend Stan had made several years ago while working on the APS program committee—stopped by the booth. She was a little overweight now, but her flaming red hair and pink, freckled face were still sensational. Her appearance belied the fact that she was the world's leading authority on motion perception.

Stan interrupted an earnest grad student who was frowning with concentration trying to follow Vanessa's detailed explanation of how she'd derived the parameters for the three red lines. Stan figured the student, a bright-eyed woman in jeans and a checked tailored blouse, would feel compensated being included in a conversation with a luminary like Susan.

Susan stood a fighting chance of following Vanessa's derivations, and her first request for clarification was clue enough for Vanessa to delve into differentiable manifolds and Gaussian curvatures.

While the three women were chatting away in their own impenetrable dialect, Ben Steinberg wandered up. He was a stout phlegmatic man whose graying hair and beard turned his round head into a sphere. "What's with this, Stan? Isn't it a new departure for you?" The intensity of his grey eyes was riveting, even through the distortion of the thick lenses of his black-framed glasses.

"No. I had very little to do with this particular enterprise, Ben. Vanessa's a student who's doing her own thing while I scurry around trying to make sure she doesn't jump over tall buildings without first stepping over graduate program hurdles."

"This I've got to see."

Stan waved in Vanessa's direction. "She's explaining her theory to Susan Hurst at the moment."

Ben raised the gray caterpillars of his eyebrows. "Really? May I eavesdrop?"

"Sure." Stan stepped aside so Ben could move closer to the trio of women.

Stan enjoyed watching his reaction. There was just enough context in fragments of their technical language and their gestures that someone like Ben could get the drift of what Vanessa was saying. He was immediately mesmerized.

During a pause in the conversation, he broke in. "Susan, mind if I ask a question?"

She looked around recognizing the voice. "Oh hi, Ben! Meet Vanessa Trippett." She turned to Vanessa. "Vanessa, Ben Steinberg of Princeton."

"Hi, Ben. It's a bit intimidating meeting the editor of *Psychological Science*."

Susan chuckled. "Don't worry. He doesn't bite. Just writes rejection letters."

"Now, now. I've never sent one to you, have I?"

"One manuscript in… What's the acceptance rate now? Two percent?"

He held his forefinger to his lips. "Shhh." He turned to Vanessa. "What do the dots represent?"

"They're means of between twelve and forty-eight *d*-primes," Vanessa answered.

"*d*-primes on that many subjects? That's a lot of lab time."

"Yes. But it's data from only one subject." Vanessa caught Stan's eye, then raised her eyebrows.

"That sounds like a full-time employee."

"I am." Vanessa could turn her captivating features into a cute little schoolgirl's innocent face.

"You?" Ben was stunned.

Vanessa nodded her head. "I know the objection, Ben. I'm currently trying to remedy that with my thesis. I've already run two experiments with twenty-four subjects each, and I'm nearly done collecting data for a third with another two dozen undergrads. The results look pretty much the same as mine so far." She pointed to the graph.

"She was just telling me," Susan broke in. "The group data not only replicate her individual data. They also fit her theory."

Ben looked mystified.

Susan had been studying Vanessa's handout. Folding it to form a pointer she swept it along one of the red lines while she explained. "The red lines are predictions derived from Vanessa's theory using parameter estimates from this experiment." She pointed to the graph without a red line.

"Tell me about the theory," he said to Vanessa.

Susan wheeled around, picked up another handout from the pile and thrust it into Ben's hands. "Here. It takes more than five minutes to explain."

Ben was already on page three. "I see that."

Susan consulted her watch. She excused herself after telling Vanessa to stay in touch.

Ben also apologized for having to leave, but he asked if he could take the handout. Before he turned to leave, he said to Vanessa, "When you finish your thesis, I hope you'll give me a chance to consider it for *Psychological Science*."

Vanessa was uncharacteristically flustered. "If you think…"

"I'm sure *PS*'s readers would be interested." He slipped by Stan on his way out of the booth. "Remember, Stan," he said as he walked away, "Einstein wrote his first relativity paper as a grad student. Don't let that woman stumble over any petty hurdles."

"Huh?" Stan spun around, but Ben had already disappeared into the crowds.

On the flight back to Seattle, Stan and Vanessa rehashed the meetings. They started by talking over the invited address they had heard by Andy Dhang, the winner of the young investigator's award. As they continued, he realized that with the exception of the roughly ten minutes he was away from the poster, looking at a couple others in the session, they had spent virtually the entire convention together.

"On another topic," he said, when the conversation petered out well into the two-hour flight, "Anything interesting happen while I was gone from the poster?"

"Hey, I was going to ask you about that. Do you know a guy named Søren Vestergaard? Big blond hunk, who thinks he's God's gift to women?"

He couldn't help but wince. "He's at the University of Copenhagen, right?"

"Uh-huh. But he's spending the year at Stanford on sabbatical."

"Yeah. I was introduced to him at the International Congress in Beijing a few years ago. What happened?"

"He was the only other person besides Susan Hurst who I think understood my theory."

"I think he minored in math at... Where did he get his degree? Chicago? I'm not sure." He tried to hide his concern. *The guy* would *pick the only time I was gone to show up.* "What did he want to know?"

"Everything!" She threw up her hands. "He spent five minutes looking at my preprint and then asked very detailed questions about my derivations—and wrote extensive notes in the margins. He wanted to know about the rest of my theory. And he questioned me on the minutiae of my experiments." She scowled. "He also came on to me. As if his charm and virility would dupe me into revealing some secret I had."

Stan shook his head. "He's probably up to no good."

"Should I have told him about the unified theory paper I'm working on?"

"I'd have said no." He scratched his head. "Guess you did, though?"

"Yeah. He asked me to send him a copy."

"Don't. You're going to be very busy and forget all about it, okay?"

She knitted her brows. "What? I thought science was—"

"The guy has a reputation, Vanessa. About six years ago, he talked to one of Neil's students at a conference in Berlin."

"And…?"

"Eight months later, he published a paper using virtually the same designs. He didn't even acknowledge talking to the student."

"Good Lord, Stan! Are you saying…?"

"I don't think so. Your theory is an order of magnitude more ambitious. Still, I certainly wouldn't give him any more help."

"I kind of promised I'd send—"

"Don't even answer his emails. You're just too busy."

There was only the rumble of the plane's engines for a long interval before she spoke. "I thought science was an open, cooperative enterprise."

"Welcome to the real world, Vanessa. There are crooks and scoundrels in science, too. Fewer than in many professions, but they exist."

"Hmm." She gazed out the window at the plane's wing glistening in the sun.

CHAPTER 21

2009-06-21 04:37:19:
Vanessa, I've just finished reviewing the revised manuscript you sent me. I'm even more impressed than I was the first time around. I'm attaching a markup copy with minor corrections and comments. However, there are several more global issues that would be easier to discuss in person. I won't be on call next week. Name a time starting Tuesday afternoon at 1:00. Lin

2009-06-23 05:47:13:
Lin, Thank you so much for all the corrections. I'm attaching another revision. Would you have time to look at it and see if I've responded to your comments? The studies cited on p. 12 still baffle me. & yes—let's talk! How's Wed at 2:15? Vanessa

2009-06-22 23:42:39:
Vanessa, Remarkable! That was fast! And another big improvement. Those studies of EEG phase in visual perception are indeed puzzling. They are another thing we need to talk about on Wednesday (at 2:15). Lin

Lin had left his office door open, so after knocking Vanessa came in and went straight to the chair by his desk. "I have something else I'd like you to look at." She held out a paper. "I mean, only if you have the time… But…"

"Yes, certainly." He raised his eyebrows as soon as he began skimming it. "You've been working on this, too? When do you sleep?"

She looked at him with wide eyes of honest puzzlement. "At night… mostly… Why?"

He laughed. "Then you must have very little social life."

She blushed. "Maybe so." She pointed to the paper he was holding. "I told you I presented a poster at APS?"

"You mentioned it."

"Well, Ben Steinberg, the editor of *Psychological Science*, looked at it. When he acted surprised that I'd only tested myself, I told him about the experiments I was almost finished running. He said that when I had them written up, he'd like me to send them to him.

"I just finished collecting the data, and I was wondering whether you had time to help me improve the write-up." She looked at him earnestly. "You've already improved my theory paper immensely."

"You did all the work."

"Only because you told me where it was needed. Anyway, assuming you're not too busy—and I'm in no hurry, really—I'd be really grateful."

He was developing a real appreciation for this woman who looked so much like an air-headed undergraduate and acted like a senior professor—most of the time. Here she was disarmingly asking him to critique her writing, and a moment later she'd probably be spewing out wildly inventive ideas like an exuberant fountain. It made him feel even more apprehensive about what he planned to ask her today.

When he was nearly finished running his eyes over the pages of her manuscript, he realized she'd told him earlier she was going to do an empirical dissertation. "Is this your thesis?"

"Yes… no… well, it was going to be." She lowered her eyes. "I'm not so sure anymore." She took a deep breath. "Here's the dilemma. Remember that manuscript I sent to *Science*? I showed you that, didn't I?"

"Yes, the one that was rejected, right?"

"For good reason. But my committee gave me a master's degree for it as a pilot study. At the meeting I proposed this series of experiments as a way to demonstrate that my own data could be replicated in the standard way—on groups of undergraduates in relatively short sessions."

"Then, why not schedule your final oral?"

“Because I don’t have a committee yet, and when I do, I can’t—in good faith—‘propose’ to run experiments I’ve already completed.”

“That seems like a technicality.”

“I just don’t know.” She drew up one corner of her mouth in exasperation. “Stan Harte, my advisor, warned me there is a rule against it.” A naïve smile broke out on her face. “So I think maybe I’ll do a theoretical thesis… if you’ll sponsor me.”

“But I can’t—”

“Sure you can. All we have to do is throw away the graduate handbook—burn the damn thing, and…” She heaved a sigh. “Just ignore me, Lin.” The smile she gave him might have induced wise old professors to burn their rulebooks. “Seriously, I need you to serve on my committee.”

“But—”

“I already know you’re not on the graduate faculty.” She laid her hand on his arm and shook her head. “But Stan tells me there’s something called ad hoc status. I can request that you serve on my committee with Stan’s approval—and the graduate dean’s signature. You can even be a co-chair. And Lin, you seem to be the only person in the university who can understand everything I’m trying to do. I really need your help.”

Her hand on his arm triggered a distracting sensation that ran through his whole body. “I can try. Doesn’t Larry have to sign off on it, too?”

She gave his arm a little squeeze before she took her hand away. “Then I’ll put your name down. That will make four, and that will meet the requirements.”

“Vanessa, my only real reservation is that I want to see your paper get published—your theory paper that is.” Should he tell her now what he had in mind? It seemed selfish to bring it up now, when the issue was her progress toward a degree.

“It still seems a long way from publishable—to me.”

“No, look. I just realized something.” He snatched her paper off his desk. “You need to say in your very first paragraph what you put at the end.” He opened the paper. “Here.”

He pointed and read it aloud to her. “‘The geometry explicated here represents a radical departure from previous attempts to integrate large bodies of data from neurophysiology and cognitive psychology. By formally synthesizing the heretofore independent structures of the brain and the mind, the present mathematical structure brings the mental world into the natural world of biological and physical phenomena.' It's that last clause, Vanessa, that crystallized for me what you've done. It makes everything else you write fall into place. And it's eminently quotable."

"I don't know, Lin. I was afraid it was too imperious. I mean, why should a reader take me seriously until they've been through my complete argument?"

"No, no. In the beginning, you tell the reader, 'I'm going to bring "...the mental world into the natural world of biological and physical phenomena."' That's *exactly* what you proceed to do, Vanessa. What follows delivers on the promise in that assertion."

"Then why not go ahead and schedule my oral defense?" There was a edge of mockery in her voice.

"Because..." He stared at the meager library on the wall behind her. "Yes, perhaps you're right. Why not? You're not proposing to do something you've already done, are you? But how is it different?" His eyes moved as though they were reading a text on the wall behind her.

"It doesn't depend on an empirical outcome. Is that it?"

"Yes, but what does it—? No! That's it, Vanessa. With a theoretical paper, the test lies entirely in the judgment of the committee. They must evaluate the logic. Is it internally consistent? Does it explain the existing data? Or how well does it explain them? And finally, is it more than just a description of what's known? Does it make fruitful predictions?"

"So, does that mean I can hand out the finished dissertation and schedule a defense without passing a general exam and collecting a hundred different signatures?"

She had her arm on his desk in the same position as his. Without thinking, he reached out and patted it just once. "I think it does."

"Then, I'm ready to form a committee."

He pushed her theory paper across his desk toward her. "Is it still sunny outside?"

Wide-eyed, she studied his face. "It was when I walked down here. Why?"

"I was wondering if you'd join me on a short walk through the Arboretum."

"I've never been there. But, why not? Sounds like fun."

They took his car to a parking lot at the far end of the winding road that meandered through the city on the south side of the Montlake Cut. He led her over a footbridge and up a wide green swath lined with trees and shrubs. It was a mild June day with a light breeze rustling through the trees and many flowers in bloom.

For the first time since they met, they talked about something other than cognitive neuroscience. She told him about Orion Station, its history and her family's role in it. He was especially fascinated by her mother, whose work he'd heard of.

"She sounds like both my parents rolled into one," he said. After half an hour, they turned and began retracing their steps. She had fallen silent, and his heart began to race. The moment to ask her had come.

"Vanessa?"

She glanced up at him with an encouraging smile. "What is it?"

"I need your help." He'd thought of so many ways to begin. This one seemed lame when he spoke it aloud, but he couldn't figure out how to express the whole idea in a single short sentence.

Her smile was inviting, "If there's anything I can do to repay you—anything—just tell me, Lin."

His heart fluttered. "Would you join me…?"

"What?" She stopped and looked at him, her face full of uncertainty.

"I'm writing a proposal. It's for a faculty development grant—seed money, for some modest resources to develop an NIH proposal."

"Yes, please. If you want me to read it, just send it to me. I'll try to give you as much feedback as I can."

"It's more than that. I need you to be my co-investigator."

Her smile faded leaving behind a solemn countenance. "Can I be that? I don't understand."

He raised both hands as though in defense. "Please. I hope you won't feel I'm somehow using you—"

"Using me? I don't follow you, Lin."

"I want to use your theory as a basis for ultimately funding a neuroimaging lab in the med school. But it would be your theory, not mine, you see. That's the issue. A funding agency won't consider it unless you're part of the project. This in-house grant will fund some exploratory brain imaging experiments, but to carry out the research I want to do, we need to have our own machine. And there's new German technology we could use here to do—"

"Wait, wait. I get it now. You have a way to fund an *f*MRI experiment?"

"A modest one. I have a design, but I need your input to—"

"Why would I ever turn down an offer like yours?" She sounded almost insulted.

"No, I'm sorry. Let me explain, please."

They were standing under a huge magnolia tree several times their height. He heard a bird call and the sound of wings fluttering against leaves somewhere in the leafy interior.

"I've already discussed this idea with Larry. The thing is, I've been here long enough that I should be working on getting my own research funding. He'll support a proposal, but since it'll be housed in the neurology department, you can't be the principal investigator."

"I'm not even a student in neurology. How could I be principal investigator?"

"Because it's your theory." He meant it as a statement of fact but it came out as a plea.

"That doesn't mean you can't use it in the neurology department."

"It doesn't seem right. This should be your project, first and foremost."

She shook her head emphatically. "I don't see that. But I'd give anything to help run a functional neuroimaging experiment with random pixel samples."

"Yes, that's the first experiment in the proposal." He sighed with relief. "It's just that it doesn't seem fair to you."

"Why? You're the one with the degree. You're on the faculty. I'm just a student. And not even a student in neurology. Dr. Nietz is right."

"But you'd agree to having your name on the proposal?"

She nodded enthusiastically. "How much have you written?"

"Just a draft. I was waiting for your approval." He smiled broadly. "I'll email it to you when I get back to the office."

Suddenly, the color left her face completely. "Lin, what time is it?"

"A little after five." He glanced at his watch. "Well, five-thirty-three, to be exact."

"Oh my God! I forgot about the party." She turned and began striding back toward the car. "Can you take me…?" She stopped so abruptly he almost ran into her. "Wait." She pulled her cell phone out of her pants pocket and opened it. Gazing at the display, she thumbed the keyboard. "Damn! The battery's dead. Can I use yours?"

"Sure." He pulled it deftly out of a holster on his belt.

After a second's hesitation, she dialed a number from memory.

When Stan's phone rang, he didn't recognize the name in the display for a moment—Lin Xuan. He caught his breath.

"Yes?" he answered noncommittally.

"Stan, this is Vanessa. I'm sorry I screwed up and forgot about the party."

"Where are you?"

"I'm with Lin in the Arboretum. We went for a little walk and started talking about… about doing some research together and applying for a grant and—"

"But what about our party? You forgot?" They had talked about it off and on for the past week.

"What can I say? I'm ashamed of myself. I'll try to get home as soon as I can."

"I'll give you a lift." There was a male voice in the background. "We can go straight from here."

"Okay. Listen, Stan. Lin can bring me home." He could hear that she was walking rapidly as she talked. "I don't know how long it will take." Her voice dropped a register. "Stan, how can I apologize for this? All I can do is try to get there as soon as possible, okay?"

"Hell, don't worry. I'll just keep pouring more wine while we all wait for you. Everyone's already here, you know."

He heard car doors closing, then the sound of an engine starting.

"We're back in the car, now. I don't know how long this—"

"Take your time. Don't make your friend get a speeding ticket."

"Okay, I'll—"

"But just as sort of a little favor—to me and *our* guests?"

"Yes, if I can—"

"Give me a call again when you're a few blocks away so I'll know when to put the salmon on."

"Okay."

"Enjoy your trip." He paused dramatically. "Oh, yes, and give your friend my very best greetings." He hung up quickly, but he was almost certain he heard her whimper, "Stan."

Stan was on the deck when he glimpsed Vanessa through a living room window, making her way from one knot of people to the next in the crowd of noisy people. There was a clear system to the course she took that guaranteed she eventually greeted everyone who'd come. They had invited all the neighbors who lived within two houses, only a few of whom either of them knew well. There were also several acquaintances from the university who lived in the Green Lake neighborhood.

Stan guessed she had gone through the kitchen where he had laid out the food, because she was carrying a plate with meager servings of salad and marinated asparagus. Most of the plate was taken up with an open baguette. She mingled briefly with several of the people on the deck that she hadn't yet talked to. Finally, she approached him at the grill.

"We're nearly out of lettuce and tomatoes." Her demeanor suggested she was responsible.

"Is that the reason for the naked bun?" He pointed to her plate with his spatula.

"Uh-huh. If there's not much salmon left, you can give me one of those sausages we bought."

"The salmon's holding out fine." He opened the grill and shoveled a chunk of the bright orange meat with black grill marks on to her bread. "We're not out of mayonnaise, are we?"

"No, I'm fine."

"Don't tell me we're out of wine. There's a case in the basement."

She shook her head. "I brought up three more bottles of merlot. And put another viognier on the table."

"Thanks!"

She scanned the crowd on the deck. "People will probably come out here before they leave. I'll hang around until they do."

She walked over to where Terry Richardson and his wife, Katie, were sitting watching the action but not talking. The Richardsons were in the anthropology department, and since they were next-door neighbors, both Stan and Vanessa knew them fairly well. Vanessa sat down next to Katie on a bench and spent the next half hour talking to them. Their conversation was subdued and serious.

When the guests began to leave, Vanessa excused herself and joined Stan at the grill. Remarkably, she remembered everyone's name. So despite her belated arrival, she played the role of hostess pretty well.

When the last people were gone, Vanessa collected a stack of plates from around the deck and took them to the kitchen. She poured herself a tumbler of red wine and took a long gulp. Setting the glass on the counter, she began loading the dishwasher following her rigid system of placement. Stan brought in another load of plates and glasses and set them on the counter for her. She put in as many dishes as she could, closed the door, and started it.

He returned with the remaining plates and glasses from the living room and set them on the counter. She was sitting at the table sipping her wine. She lowered her eyes when he looked at her. "That was unforgivable, Stan."

"You acquitted yourself well, once you got here."

"Hmm."

"So. I've seen you get so involved in something the outside world disappears. Tell me. What did you and this guy Lin find so intriguing in the Arboretum?" She didn't answer his taunt. "He's a neurologist, right?"

She nodded without looking up.

"What? The neurology of azaleas?"

Her body sagged visibly.

"The anatomical secrets…? Of the rhododendron brain, no doubt?"

"He wants me to help him write a grant proposal," she said in a wooden voice.

"Ah." He was losing patience. "Vanessa, look at me and tell me what you were talking about. I accept your explanation, okay? I know what happens to you when you get wrapped up in something."

She raised her eyes and wiped a tear from her cheek. "The med school has a seed-grant program. Lin wants to apply for time in the *f*MRI lab to test my theory. He—"

"Okay, that explains it."

"It's no excuse. I forgot an important commitment to you."

They sat listening to the swish of water in the dishwasher. What Stan found most attractive about her—the intensity of her intellectual pursuits—was also the most exasperating. Living with her—even part time as he was—was like living in a cognitive dishwasher. Wave after wave of scalding analysis, punctuated by brief moments of sexual ecstasy. But this machine never let up. Just when he thought it was finished, fresh ideas came surging in, and her indefatigable impeller started up again.

He suddenly felt exhausted—and very old. "These can wait until morning." He pointed to the dishes she'd neatly stacked on the counter in the order she planned to load them. "I'm bagging it." He stood, assuming she would follow his lead.

"I'll take care of them."

"As penance?"

She barely moved.

"Forget about them." He started out of the room. "C'mon."

She followed him into the bedroom but went straight to her backpack. She pulled out her laptop.

"Jesus, Vanessa. Aren't you tired?"

She looked at him vacantly. "No…" She seemed to be running a test of her brain circuits. "No, I want to take a look at Lin's draft." Without further comment she went down the hall to her study and shut the door all but a crack.

CHAPTER 22

2009-06-30 10:12:23:
Stan, I've decided to send the three group experiments to Steinberg. Could you please help me improve the attached manuscript? Vanessa

2009-06-30 13:48:16:
Vanessa, It reads especially well (except for the math at the end of your introduction—I think you should consider putting the detailed derivations in an appendix). I spotted a few minor points you might want to consider. Stan

2009-06-30 13:57:45:
Thanks! I would have missed that point on the arbitrariness of the ψ axis. Should I put in a note that in a large theory "under development," the orientation is constrained by two additional axes, φ and χ? Also, how much more should I tell about my APS paper, since the results replicate the group data, and I hope to have a manuscript ready soon on the single-subject study? V

2009-06-30 14:06:21:
You can never have too many self-citations, even convention papers and papers "under development" (or "in preparation," which implies you hope to have another publication coming soon). S

2009-06-30 14:09:02:
Thanks for the advice. Sounds like bragging to me, but I'm taking your word for it. V

2009-06-30 14:11:37:
I'm tired of telling you this is a bad idea. Can't you wait until fall when you can have an oral? S

2009-06-30 14:17:51:
I've given this a lot of thought, Stan. Two arguments for trying to get this in print NOW. (1) I talked to several people at APS who as much as said, "I'm going to try this in my lab when I get back." It's too easy to run my random pixel presentation at home. I HAVE to beat these folks into print. (2) After what you told me about Vestergaard, I also want to be in the literature with something that hopefully shows I was the first to think of a geometrical approach to integrating the mind and brain. My "special theory of consciousness" (Forgive me, Herr Doktor Einstein) demonstrates that both the math and the empirical predictions work. Vestergaard will have, at most, my APS paper. I have more than a hundred thousand data points he doesn't. V

2009-06-30 14:20:03:
Okay. It's your PhD you're betting here. I'll try to persuade your committee to approve in-press work for a degree, but it's, as they say, highly irregular to do so. S

2009-06-30 14:22:09:
It won't be necessary. I've decided on a theoretical thesis. With Lin on board—and possibly Kashiba—you can't argue we don't have the expertise. AND we shouldn't need a proposal meeting. The issue is whether I pulled it off, not whether some future data will support it. V

2009-06-30 14:26:33:
The issue will be whether they'll allow such a highly irregular modus operandi! S

Stan saw less of Vanessa during the week after the party. They stopped by each other's offices three times to chat over coffee and had lunch together in the U District on Thursday. Afterward, she drove him home so he could mow the neglected lawn and clean up his weed-infested flowerbeds. She took his car back to campus so she'd have it to drive out to his place when she finished testing subjects.

He gave up fighting the weeds around seven and took a shower. When he started soaping up his penis, it hardened a little. The slippery lather was erotic and he soon had a full-blown erection and a visual fantasy that began with a *Playboy* picture of Vanessa soaping her crotch in a shower and led to one of her pre-*Playboy* photos. He stepped out of the shower and kept the engorgement at ninety degrees with occasional strokes with his fingertips and towel.

Throwing on a terrycloth bathrobe, he went to the living room turned on his home theater system. He'd put together his stereo, which was wired to speakers throughout the house, with a wall-mounted sixty-inch flat-screen monitor. It was fully integrated with a wi-fi network so he could display downloaded photos on it from his laptop. He'd barely turned the monitor on since he and Vanessa first made love.

From the image manager on his laptop, he began playing the five photos Vanessa's father had taken most recently. He set the program to play a loop of the five photos over and over for a minute each. With the lights dimmed, he stretched out in his zero-gravity home theater recliner and began little by little exciting himself almost to the tipping point and keeping himself there as long as possible.

The lithe figure on the screen nourished an elaborate fantasy of foreplay in mountain meadows, beside backcountry waterfalls, and on solitary ocean beaches. Vanessa had more than once refused to consider, "even for a minute," making love outdoors. Finally, the moment of release came, and he pumped his prick while imagining humping a seventeen-year-old Vanessa.

His body was in the shuddering throes of ejaculation when the garage door opener came on. He shot out of the recliner, flinging gobs of come in all directions. He snatched his robe and headed for the bathroom. Inside, he locked the door and stood trembling, unable to move his shivering limbs. He held his breath in an effort to hear every nuance of sound in the house.

He felt like a gopher trapped in the only cul-de-sac in his burrow while a grizzly bear tore off the ground above with its claws, its snorts echoing through the walls and making the ground shake. He nearly fainted when his first well-formed thought took shape. Are there any razors or a knife in the medicine cabinet?

"Hi!" Vanessa called cheerily. "I'm home. What's for dinner?"

He imagined her stepping into the darkened living room. He gasped: he'd left the slideshow running. He heard a faint click—the overhead lights coming on. A laggard glob of semen dripping onto his big toe brought vividly to mind the slimy gobs his waggling dick had spewed around the living room.

"Stan?"

Before he could grab a towel, his arm froze. He opened his mouth to answer but nothing came out of his constricted throat.

"Stan! Where are you?"

He heard her bare feet on the hallway floor. She was right outside the door.

"Stan, what is going on?" She rattled the doorknob. "What the hell?" A moment's pause. "This is ridiculous, Stan. Unlock this door." The doorknob clattered spastically. "Come out of there and explain what you've been doing."

"I can't," he whimpered.

"What? I can't hear you."

"I…" He tried to shout. "I…"

"Stan, are you all right?" There was suddenly anxiety in her voice. "Stan!" Again, she shook the knob back and forth. "Oh, for God's sake."

There was a thud that made the panels in the door crackle. It took him a second to grasp what was happening. With the second thud, he realized she was throwing her weight against the door to batter it open.

Something inside him gave way. His whole body turned to mush. He flipped the lock tab and stepped back. This time the knob turned decisively and the door slammed open.

"Thank God!" Then she froze, transformed into a statue that gaped at him.

"I'm sorry," he whispered hoarsely.

When he raised his head to look at her, the bafflement in her face gave way to clarity, and clarity turned to rage.

"Where did you get those photos?" She pointed to the living room.

"The Internet… a website in Bulgaria."

"Bulgaria?" She frowned. "Jesus. The FBI confiscated everything." She shook her head. "Those sons of bitches must have sold them into the black market."

"I don't know. There were others that looked like your father's MOMA show—I mean, the photos."

"Goddamned copyrights don't mean shit when people think it's porn."

"Look, I—"

"I've seen enough to—"

"Please give me a chance to explain. Please!" He raised his hands.

"You don't have to explain anything, Stan." She turned and took a step toward her study at the other end of the hall. "I get the picture."

"Wait. No. Can't we talk?"

"What is there to say? You were using photos of me as a teenager to masturbate. I assume you were imagining screwing me when I was a kid."

He hung his head, unable to meet her gaze.

"What does this say about you? Your daughter's sixteen, isn't she?"

"She'll be eighteen in October."

"So how would you feel about some forty-year-old high school teacher fucking Elise? Would you fuck her yourself?" She walked away.

He followed her down the hall and into her study. She made no effort to stop him, didn't even look back. Opening her closet, she pulled out her small duffle bag and flung it on the futon behind him. It grazed his arm as it sailed past.

"Listen, Vanessa. I've had this problem since I was—"

"You certainly do."

"Please listen to me," he said to her back. "I need help because I—"

"You mean having sex with me five times a week isn't enough help?"

"It's not that. It's—"

"You need more variety. Is that it?"

"No. I know this sounds lame, but—"

"I'm not good enough to satisfy your lust?" She spun around, facing him. "Shit!" She yanked her T-shirt over her head and hurled it at him. "These tits aren't big enough for you?" She unhooked her bra, caught it as it slid down her arms, and threw it at him, grazing his head.

"No, Vanessa!" He raised his hands in defense. "Please don't do this."

She cupped her breasts and began jiggling them. "They're too flabby, aren't they, Stan? You want firmer boobs, don't you?"

"No, please! That isn't—"

"Yes, it is. You craved an empty-headed teenager, didn't you?" She peeled her jeans and panties down her legs together and stepped out of them. "I guess this doesn't measure up to the *Playboy* standard anymore, huh?" She gyrated her hips provocatively.

He shook his head helplessly.

"Admit it, Stan. You don't give a shit what's in my head. All you wanted—from the very beginning—was to get your goddamn penis in here." She stuck her middle finger between her legs.

"No!" he wailed. "That wasn't—"

She suddenly averted her eyes. In the same instant he saw himself as he must look to her. He involuntarily covered his genitals with both hands.

She wagged her head and turned away. "Go get dressed. I want you to help me haul my stuff back to my apartment."

Caught in a wave of self-loathing, he stumbled out the door, his hands still clutching his crotch.

Back in his bedroom, he sat down on the bed and stared at a blank wall. He couldn't get his mind around the events of the last half hour. All he knew was that he faced a future so bleak he could barely contemplate it. These past eighteen months seemed like a dream from which he had emerged to face a waking nightmare of loneliness unlike any in his life.

A sense of inevitability hung over what had happened. Was there really any other way it could have ended? From the beginning he had treated her as the embodiment of his fantasy lover. He'd thought of his role in her education as a means of beginning a carefully contrived courtship dance, the price of an escort service for a night or the cost of a life-sized silicon love doll.

His motives were loathsome, and whatever she did to him, short of killing him, would be morally justified. Yet whatever the punishment, what he dreaded most was his empty future.

"Are you dressed yet?" asked Vanessa from the hallway.

"No." He picked up his socks and started dressing hurriedly.

"I'm loading up the car." She stood in the doorway with her duffel bag over her shoulder and her large, wheeled suitcase in tow. "I can drive over there if you want me to, but I'm not coming back."

By the time he was dressed, she had everything stowed in the trunk except her backpack.

"I'll drive," he said as he followed her to the garage.

She held the backpack on her lap, saying nothing until they pulled away from the house. "You know, it's odd. You never told me how big your problem with pornography was. I mean, you dropped a hint the first time we had dinner together. I remember you told me you'd followed my career as a nude model from the very beginning. Later, when we knew each other a little better, you should have told me more."

"The time never seemed right."

"What was wrong with elaborating some evening when I started spending the night at your house? That's certainly private enough, isn't it?"

"I was afraid you'd dump me."

"Of course. That was a risk you had to take, sooner or later. Maybe at first you thought you were cured, so to speak. But at some point between then and now, you must have fallen off the wagon? It must have happened sometime when we were making love regularly."

He nodded. "When I missed you during the week."

"That ought to have been a warning sign. Because that says you're really hooked and can't help yourself."

"Hopelessly hooked. It's worse than cocaine. And it's been going on since I was in high school."

"Have you ever looked for help? A support group? Counseling?"

"I did when my marriage was breaking up."

"It obviously didn't help."

"It was one of the reasons our marriage fell apart. I couldn't make myself stop for the kids' sake. Not even when Heidi and I tried making romantic time for ourselves and were having sex once or twice a week again. I was incorrigible."

"I don't know the research, Stan, but I'm pretty sure it's not genetic."

"I've been at it twenty-five years now. You know the data on long-term repetition. Incredibly powerful habits form when you do anything over and over again for a decade or more. Practice really does make perfect."

"What happened in high school, by the way?'

"A friend and I got our hands on some nude photos of a cheerleader, and I jerked off with them. Then he bet me I wouldn't ask her for a date, so I did. And she accepted."

"Sounds like you also have a history of self-doubt."

"Justified self-doubt. She dumped all over me when—"

"When she found out about the photos?"

"No, no. She never found out about them. Because I made a complete fool of myself on the date. And she told our whole school afterward." He shuddered when he remembered the humiliation. "I was lonely as hell after that. And godawful horny, too. At that age, it's all a guy thinks about until he shoots his wad."

"And college, too?"

"With the exception of one little interlude."

"You aren't physically ugly, Stan. You don't act offensively. And you're bright. Surely you had chances with other women you knew."

"I suppose. Things weren't as relaxed as they are now."

"I wouldn't know."

"I've never been any good at making friends with women. And I was so lonely after Heidi and I split, no amount of counseling could change me."

"I'm surprised. You're one of the smartest men I know. How can smart women not find you attractive, the way I did?"

"Thanks for saying that, but… well, I can't seem to make it with most women."

"Maybe I have a similar problem."

He laughed. "You, of all women? Trust me. You do not have a problem attracting men."

"I attract the wrong kind of men. And at the same time, I'm a sucker when it comes to brainy men. I'm perfectly competent to judge how bright a man is, but I can never see behind a sincere façade. So round heeled Vanessa falls into bed with the cleverest Casanovas, legs spread wide."

He braked suddenly for a pedestrian who couldn't seem to decide whether or not to step into the street. They were thrown forward against the seat belts.

"Sorry!"

When they started up again, he said, "I want to apologize for not confessing to such a serious addiction problem. I admit that I first agreed to sponsor you in large part because I wanted to get better acquainted with a woman who'd posed for *Playboy*. I even had the fantasy that I might get to sleep with you—although it seemed beyond the realm of possibility until it happened. But helping you was really a quid pro quo."

"For sex?"

"Yeah. Like you were some call girl, instead of the wonderful person you really are. And without qualification, the smartest person I've ever met."

"Thank you. But I probably deserve some of the blame."

It seemed unlikely to him, but he decided not to comment.

"All three of us probably have problems with sex," she continued.

"Three?"

"You, with your pornography."

"And?"

"And Paul. I told you about last summer, didn't I?"

"Yeah, but he has no problem—"

"Seducing women?"

He nodded, but couldn't envision it as a problem.

"That's just his problem, Stan. A woman catches his fancy—"

"A desirable woman."

"A woman. He's immediately consumed with how to get between her legs."

"Well, sure, but…"

"It's just as big a problem for him as jerking off to pictures is for you, Stan. Believe me. I personally saw it take over his life. From what he told me, it had happened many times before."

"I'm amazed."

She laughed. "Amazed, and maybe not so envious?"

"Maybe." He'd have to think it over—such a radical idea. "But wait! You said three of us, didn't you?"

"I did. I think I like sex too much for my own good. That's why Paul and I got along so well… for a while. Why you and I were so happy together… for a while."

"I should have told you sooner—right away. You might have made it easier for me to look for help."

"I don't know. A girlfriend of mine at Wazzu claimed I was addicted to sex. She talked me into seeing a counselor, who told me the same thing. But I think they're wrong. I like lots and lots of sex but only with the same man—a smart man whom I respect and love."

He turned to see if that was all she was going to say.

She saw him looking at her. "I guess I'm old-fashioned, Stan. I insist on fidelity in my partner and in myself."

"I didn't ever cheat on you, Vanessa."

"I consider masturbating to pornography infidelity. It's also an insult—to me."

"I agree. But like you, talking to professionals never helped me much." His dejection was evident in his voice.

"That's what Paul said, too. You see, we three are all oversexed *and* overrational."

They both chuckled.

"Paul told me he found a support group after his heart attack," she said. "Other men he could respect, who are helping each other. Maybe you should talk to him about it."

"Maybe I should." But could he confess to Paul that he had been squirting his semen at pictures all these years?

He pulled into the driveway in front of her apartment house, and turned off the car as he'd done every Friday afternoon. "Do you want me to resign from your committee, Vanessa?" He stared straight ahead, not able to face her for fear she'd see how much he dreaded her answer.

"No, probably not. I need time to think about you and Paul. I need to talk to Lin and Michelle about finding another faculty member to replace you. But I doubt I will. Whatever your motives, you've been a wonderful and understanding advisor, and I'm grateful for all you've done for me. And you were good at it."

He turned back to her. "Anyone could have done what I did. You've never needed more than a figurehead committee chairman for your sponsor. Except for the formalities, you could have done it on your own."

“I don’t believe that, you know—in spite of the number of times you’ve said it to me. I was lucky you were there when Paul couldn’t be.” She put a hand on his shoulder. “I want you to know that I don’t hate you. I am profoundly disappointed in you. And fervently hope you’ll look for help again—and I wish you the very best.”

“I’ll do everything in my power to help you, as long as I can, Vanessa.”

“Thanks, Stan.” She got out of the car.

He popped the trunk for her. He tried not to cry as he watched her unlock the door to the enclosed stairway with her backpack on her back and her duffel bay slung over her shoulder. She returned to get her suitcase and close the trunk. When she set the bag down to open the door again, she turned and waved. He thought he saw a faint smile through his tears..

CHAPTER 23

Hank Cavanaugh eventually got to know every graduate student who made it to the third year of the program because he was in charge of their required year of supervised teaching. Thus, Vanessa Trippett appeared in the group of twenty-four students in his seminar in the fall.

Even if she hadn't been a stunning beauty, she would have attracted his attention almost from the beginning. The graduate teaching assistants were required to attend his weekly lectures, and they always sat together in the back row of the lecture hall. She sat in the first row. They yawned and poorly concealed their electronic entertainment; she took notes. They participated in vigorous seminar discussions, while she sat placidly, taking it all in and saying nothing.

Her reputation as a troublemaker preceded her. But except for her classic features and seductive figure, she was an unremarkable student. Until, that is, he began collecting a thick folder of complaints about her section over the first month of the quarter. He routinely met with each assistant after his classroom visitation, and he was feeling ambivalent about her conference.

He saw her in his doorway before she greeted him with a cheerful, "Hi, Dr. Cavanaugh. Are you ready?"

He tried not to be too obvious when he looked at her. Happily married with two preteen children, he had no desire to see more than was actually revealed by the clothing of the many attractive young women he saw every day in his lecture hall.

Vanessa's garb should have insinuated very little, but for reasons he didn't like to admit to himself, hinted at a great deal.

He began with a positive comment, planning to alternate between the pluses and minuses. "Your section yesterday was a pleasant exception to most I visit, Vanessa. Your students pay close attention to what you say, and they ask a lot of questions."

He didn't expect to see her grimace.

"It helps that I wound up with a classroom full of men, Dr. Cavanaugh. They're more interested in me than in psychology, by and large."

"I wouldn't give that much weight." Her section had seen a huge turnover during the first two weeks of the quarter, when students could drop courses without prejudice. When the dust settled, her section was eighty percent men. "But they must be learning something. On the first two tests, your section has the highest average grades so far."

"Perhaps that's a matter of self-selection, Dr. Cavanaugh. Maybe all the weaker students, men and women, dropped my section, and smart, motivated men took their places."

There was that, too. She was raising all his negative points for him, although not quite in the order he'd laid out. "But give yourself part of the credit, Vanessa," he responded. "Your teaching by testing method appears to be quite effective."

She spent her two-hour recitation section giving a series of multiple choice questions. The students used their laptops or cellphones to respond, and she kept a record of each student's answers. The percent correct became the student's grade for five percent of the course. The rest was based on tests given to all sections attending the same lectures.

Her questions were constructed and graded in a unique way. The four alternative answers were ranked from best to worst and assigned number scores from three to zero. She generated a lot of class discussion and often provoked heated arguments.

"I was going to ask you," he said. "Would you be willing to give a presentation about your method to the seminar?"

"If you like. I've gotten lots of complaints about it from the students, though."

"I've heard those complaints, too, Vanessa. Also some bellyaching about the fact that they have to read the text before coming to class in order to have a chance with your questions."

"Should students expect me to cover the answers before testing them on the information they can find in the reading assignments?"

He sighed. "Unfortunately, our young people would prefer we gave them music videos to watch, from which they expect to absorb the material subliminally and painlessly."

"I don't like the music they listen to, Dr. Cavanaugh. And from what they tell me about the TV shows and movies they watch, their lives seem intellectually vacuous."

"Yeah." He blew out his breath between his teeth. "Their music amuses me, but I can't stand a lot of what they watch. It helps, though, to keep up with their culture. Makes you seem more down to earth to them. Not to say down to their level."

"I'm not a popular instructor, am I? I won't do well in the *Daily* survey, that's for sure."

Ah yes! The infamous Daily *survey.* The university's student-run daily newspaper had been a national leader in using student evaluations of courses and instructors. Their published results during the registration period could decimate a course and destroy a faculty member overnight, notwithstanding the blistering critiques Hank's psychometric colleagues had written to the editor of the paper.

He, on the other hand, considered himself a beneficiary of the survey. In large part because of his stellar ratings more than a decade ago, he had won a university-wide master teacher award for his undergraduate teaching. Winning the award had established his niche in the psychology department as the expert on teaching freshmen and sophomores, and especially the introductory course. He had been happy to abandon his modest research activities and devote the remainder of his career to teaching lower-division students.

He liked undergraduates, enjoyed the music they did, shared their addiction to video games, and text-messaged compulsively. For more than a decade his course-load had included two weekly lectures to an introductory psychology course of over two hundred students and a graduate seminar in teaching.

"There are serious questions about both the reliability and the validity of those evaluations, Vanessa."

"I know that. But that won't prevent them from ruining my ratings as a teacher." She lowered her eyes. "I'm worried about what they could do to me."

"They play a very minor role in my evaluation, I assure you."

"That doesn't help my reputation," she said in a toneless voice.

He decided to let the remark pass without comment. Ditto the complaints Roger had passed along to him: There were students from other sections who were unhappy that they weren't getting the benefit of Vanessa's teaching methods; the multiple choice questions were seen as unfair preparation for the biweekly test on which the majority of their grades depended.

There were also women who thought Vanessa was giving men preferential treatment. And then there were the largely unjustified claims that her grading policies virtually forced them to attend her class every week. He'd taught enough undergrads to find this last collection of Roger's notes hilarious.

"Would you be willing to share your multiple choice items with the other teaching assistants?"

"I already have. Zack and Ashley asked me for them. I've been having them ready at the beginning of the week for them."

"Don't be surprised if I ask you to share them with everyone. I have a feeling they think your section has an edge over theirs."

"I'd be happy to, Dr. Cavanaugh."

"Good. Thank you. I'd like to summarize my feedback: As far as I'm concerned, you're doing quite well at teaching. Your unconventional methods are creating some problems, but on the whole, I think your innovations are aimed in the right direction.

"I encourage you to keep on trying. You might be surprised that the grades your students are getting will tip the balance in the *Daily* survey, Vanessa." He didn't add that the halo effect of her attractive appearance, especially among the men, would probably boost the ratings, too.

"Thank you." She stood and was gone too soon. Her lingering fragrance called to mind his response when his wife chided him for watching some passing miniskirted teenagers a little too obviously: "I'm not dead yet. And I can't control what dreams I have. But not to worry; they aren't the wet kind anymore."

2009-11-12 16:29:03:
Stan, Steinberg has accepted my manuscript contingent on my adequately responding to the referees' "important" comments (see attachment). Can you help again? Thanks! Vanessa [P.S. I'm not mad at you, just too busy to stop by for a chat.]

2009-11-13 19:58:46:
Vanessa, See markups attached. (Note also my comments on the referees' evaluations.) Good job! Reading between the lines, "...contingent on your adequately responding to the referees' comments" = Their comments are advisory. He'll take your paper if you can deal with the points he's listed as "important." Notice, too, he's giving you a deadline—important because you won't lose your place in line for publication if you meet it. See me if you want to discuss anything. And congratulations! Stan

Since Stan had helped Vanessa move her stuff back to her apartment, he'd only seen her in the halls. She was unfailingly friendly, but she gave no indication she wanted to talk to him. Hank had passed along to him a summary of her performance as a teaching assistant—pure Vanessa, always full of contradictions. But the fact that Hank sent the memo to him meant that she hadn't formally asked to have him removed as her official sponsor, yet.

She stopped by his office the following Monday.

"I want you to resolve a disagreement." She slung her pack on a chair and dug out a manuscript already folded back to a page. She came around the worktable and laid the paper in front of him. "You remember I had the complete derivation of my consciousness equations—the ones that predict the results—in the introduction?"

He stared at the first page for a moment. "I recall giving up after about the second equation." He looked up at her leaning over his shoulder, her open shirt lightly brushing the skin of his neck. He could almost feel her breast less than a inch above him, her orange blossom skin lotion filling his nostrils. For a second it felt like before.

"Exactly. And you, like everyone else—except Lin—said, 'Put it in an appendix.'"

"For those who have enough background to understand it..." He smiled at her. "And evaluate it."

"So that's what I did before I sent it to Steinberg."

"So what did Ben say?"

"He said I should consider Referee Two's suggestion about the appendix but that the decision was mine." She handed him another set of stapled sheets of paper. It was also folded back, and a paragraph near the middle of the page was surrounded by a box drawn with a pink highlighter. "This is what Referee Two said." She waited for him to read it.

When he scanned it, he remembered the insistent wording. "The appendix contains the core of the author's scientific contribution—and the most exciting."

He glanced at the first paragraph of the referee's comments and after a moment, he began to read aloud. "Ben, this is the most significant contribution to cognitive science you're likely to publish in your tenure as editor. It is to our field what Watson and Crick's paper describing the double helix would have been to molecular biology if it had also contained Rosalind Franklin's crystallography as supporting empirical evidence."

He smiled up at her. "Now, that is what I call *extravagant* praise."

"It's *too* extravagant."

"No, it isn't, Vanessa. Here's the answer to your appendix question." He read aloud from the manuscript again. "'As it stands, it is as if Franklin had published her results and put the Nobel Prize in an appendix.'"

"Well it isn't a *double* helix yet, but maybe… I don't know, like the special theory of relativity?" She paused for a moment and lifted her head to window. "Maybe I should change the title to, 'A Special Theory of Consciousness.'" She laughed—a girlish giggle that reminded him of a hallway conversation in Spanish.

"Just kidding." She smiled for the first time.

Her pixie face unleashed too many happy memories of moments he'd spent with her. "You should think about it. Ben could hardly say no after getting a review like this." He picked up the comments again.

"I'm still not sure all the logic needs to be so prominent." She grabbed her manuscript and flipped to the appendix.

Stan had a sudden flash of insight. "How about…" He held out his hand. "Can I take a look?"

She handed the stapled manuscript to him. "What?"

He studied the appendix briefly. "Okay. Suppose you move it to… Put it back at the beginning…?"

"Yes. And…"

"Keep the first paragraph in regular type, but put the rest of the derivation in smaller type."

"Except the last paragraph… which can replace the shorter one I now have in the introduction? The one that contains the equations predicting my results?"

He flipped to the last page of the appendix and after a pause said, "Perfect. That's your answer."

"Can I get Ben to do that?"

"I think he'll do anything you ask. You might even move in the margins of the section you want in smaller type a couple of spaces. But let him change the font size."

"That's how it's done?"

"Just be sure you're clear and forceful in your letter."

"Thanks!" She returned to the chair and stuffed the manuscript into her backpack. "I have a manuscript reporting on the individual data ready to send to *Nature*. Since your grant supported the data collection, you have to approve it. What do you think?"

"I'd like to look at it. But I assume it's pretty much the same as the one *Science* turned down."

"With more data, and a more complete and concise statement of the theory."

"Uh-huh." He tented his fingers. "I'd like to take a look. And I'll offer you whatever advice I can. But you're on your own. You have my permission to submit it."

"You should be second author, Stan."

He'd gradually slouched into his chair. Now, he sat up. "No. You're taking full responsibility for it. Just acknowledge the grant in the footnote."

"I want you to approve the wording, as well as a personal acknowledgment. Okay?"

"Email it to me, and keep a copy of my reply."

She started to lift her backpack. "Just how 'full' a responsibility did you mean I was taking?" She dropped the pack back in the chair.

"For the full thing." He gave the baseball umpire's "safe" signal with his hands. "Everything. It's yours, from beginning to end." *It was never mine anyway, was it?*

"There's a subtext here. Want to share it?"

He let out his breath. "It was another project you could have used for a dissertation."

She started to sit down but then seemed to change her mind. "As I see it, I need a wider audience for my results and for the special theory."

He shrugged his shoulders. "It's just one more bridge you're burning, Vanessa."

"Are you saying that if I torch another completed project—assuming this paper is accepted, you can't sponsor me?"

"No, I'll shuffle and sign the paperwork and chair a meeting. But I wash my hands of all the rest of the responsibilities of a sponsor. That's what I meant. You're on your own."

She smiled broadly. "Good! Thank you." She had the pack over her shoulder again but hesitated. "I'll be sure you're kept in the loop. For your information, Kashiba's on board and Larry Nietz—do you know him…?"

"I've never met him. He's chair of neurology, in the med school, right?"

"Right. He's happy to sign off on Lin as ad hoc member. He even told me he's comfortable with Lin serving as de facto chair. Do you have any problem with that?"

"I can think of one instance where that happened in this department. It certainly doesn't bother me." It was another demotion for him, but he didn't care any longer. It was a pleasure to be part of this woman's success.

The route she was taking to reach the heights of the field was steeper and more treacherous than anyone else he knew would dare to choose. But there was no point in his telling her she couldn't do it. He was more than ready to make sure she did.

"Thanks, Stan!" She left his office as briskly as she had the first time. Remembering made him feel like an old man looking back on a career and forward into a future without a soul mate.

For more than three months since his breakup with Vanessa, Stan had been mulling over whether to do something about his pornography problem. It had begun taking up an increasing amount of his time, and it certainly wasn't making him any happier. He kept coming back to what Vanessa had said—that he should talk to Paul, that he and Paul had similar problems.

What had stopped Stan was the prospect of confessing to Paul the secret he had kept from all his colleagues until now. But for the first time since adolescence, he wanted to quit. If he still could. He wasn't so sure he could.

Vanessa's visit to his office stirred enough resolution in him to make the move. That and the opening presented by his conversation with her. He hadn't talked to Paul since she had left him at the beginning of fall quarter, and he wanted to bring Paul up to date on the latest developments in her career.

The final straw was an entire Thursday evening Stan had killed wallowing in his *Playboy* photo collection. He caught Paul in the hall with some free time late on the Friday before Thanksgiving. They went to Paul's office, which was the closer of their two. Stan closed the door and took the place on the couch next to Paul.

"Sorry to hear about you and Vanessa," Paul began. "How are you doing?"

Stan was caught off guard. "O-okay… thanks… But how did you know?"

"Vanessa told me."

"Oh."

"She came to talk to me about her committee."

Stan wasn't surprised by this information, but it still pricked his unhealed wound. "Did she approach you about chairing her committee again?"

"She sure did! I told her nothing doing." His face lit up with amusement. "I don't want another heart attack—even if she could save me again."

"I guess she asked Michelle, too?"

"She went to her first. We both told her she'd be an idiot to switch now." He laughed gently. "She said she thought the same thing but wanted my view."

"Did she… um… say anything about why we broke up?"

"No, actually not. She prefaced her question about me chairing her committee by saying you two are still on civil speaking terms, and she wanted you to continue on her committee in any case."

Stan couldn't help smiling. *On civil terms, huh? True enough, the one time they had spoken this quarter.*

"Paul, Vanessa said something the night we broke up about you and me having the same problem."

"You were cheating on her, too, Stan? You don't seem like the type."

"Not cheating on her the way she said you were—" He hadn't meant to bring it up. It just slipped out.

Paul interrupted with braying laughter. "You mean my peccadilloes in Aix-en-Provence last summer?"

Stan nodded. Even with Paul's admission, he felt uncomfortable. He pushed himself on. "My problem is pornography, Paul." There. It was out. He'd finally told a colleague.

"Don't imagine you're the only one. It's incredibly common. Always has been, of course. But today, in America, with our super-relaxed morality and the privacy of the Internet, it's hard to find a man who hasn't at least indulged. And very easy to find one who's addicted."

"Thanks. I didn't know—"

"Most of the guys in my support group have a porn problem." He looked Stan in the eye. "She told you about that, didn't she?"

"Not exactly, but—"

He smiled. "I don't advertise it, but I don't hide it if someone asks. My problem is just plain old sex. I see sexual opportunity in every woman I lay eyes on. Can't break the habit, but I've managed to disconnect the desire to act on it.

"I used to go ahead and follow my impulses, and I rarely failed to get what I wanted." His smile suddenly vanished. "I'm not bragging about it. I'm here to tell you it meant trouble for both me and my quarry."

"I've never been any good at meeting women, Paul. I confess to being… well, envious."

"Stop right there. What you really mean is that you aren't good at seducing women. Right?"

Stan didn't know quite how to say Paul had his number. After enduring Paul's silence for the better part of a minute, he said, "I have to admit, you're pretty much on target. I used to think I should ask you for some advice on getting women into bed."

"Funny thing is, if you'd asked me three years ago—before Vanessa showed up—I'd have gladly taken you under my wing and taught you a few tricks."

"Did you get counseling?"

"Are you kidding? With my contempt for those charlatans?"

"I spent three or four years and I hate to admit how much money it cost finding out they couldn't help me."

"I found a better approach. One that seems to work for some of us anyway. I located a support group on the Internet, one made up of a bunch of intellectuals like you and me, who don't suffer therapists willingly. We talk about our problems and help each other figure out what's going on and what to do about it."

"It's sounds interesting. Could I…?"

"I'm hosting our meeting at my place on Tuesday. Want to come as my guest? We follow the AA's twelve step program—with none of the bullshit. And to prove the latter, we drink lots of wine and beer while we talk."

"Will I be expected to tell about my… ah, problem?"

"Not at all. It's up to you. It's the usual way a new guy joins the group. Some tell their story the first time; others hang back and eventually do, or they stop coming. Come find out some of the other guys' stories. You'll be intrigued."

"I'll come," Stan said. "Thanks."

He'd done it—and it had been easier than he thought.

CHAPTER 24

2009-11-18 16:26:38:
Ms. Vanessa Trippett [cc. Stanley Harte, Sponsor]: At a recent meeting of the graduate committee we noted that you have not yet filed an application for candidacy to the graduate school. It is expected that students will form a committee to oversee their dissertation research, and this requires that you file a formal application, so that the graduate dean can appoint a representative to join your committee and proceed to a proposal meeting. Please see Lisa at your earliest convenience to make an appointment, so we can discuss your progress and any extenuating circumstances the committee should be apprised of. Floyd Brooks, Vice Chair and Graduate Advisor

Floyd Brooks had a suite of offices on the third floor. There was an outer office occupied by his secretary, Lisa Furman. His corner office was larger and more airy than those of other faculty because it had windows on two sides. It also commanded a spectacular view of the city and Lake Union. From Vanessa's quick, purposeful entrance, she didn't seem to notice her surroundings when she took her seat opposite him at his desk in the middle of the room.

Brooks had been looking forward to this meeting. He'd admired Vanessa from afar for two years, reviewed her steady accumulation of good grades, and listened with increasing curiosity as the stories and rumors built up around her like the clouds he remembered gathering around the Rockies for a late afternoon thunderstorm when he was at the University of Denver. In person, it was difficult to ignore the exquisite lines of her face or to put entirely out of mind the photos everyone in the department had seen by now.

He began with some formalities. "As you probably know, Vanessa, at the time I emailed you, a formal letter of concern was placed in your file."

"I received a copy of it, Dr. Brooks."

"A letter of concern is just what it says: a notification that the department may be missing some information or that you may be having academic problems of which we are unaware. Is that clear?"

She nodded. He was struck by her rigid posture and grave demeanor.

"Let me review your status as shown in our records. Your master's committee consisted of Dr. Harte, as sponsor, and Drs. Zhrudsky and Davidson. Since then we have received a letter of resignation from Dr. Zhrudsky. I understand from Dr. Kovick that he has agreed to serve in Dr. Zhrudsky's place. However, you understand that four committee members are required, and that the graduate school then appoints the fifth. A committee of at least five graduate faculty members is, of course, required."

"I'm aware of that, Dr. Brooks."

"And have you talked to another member of the department about serving on your committee?"

"No, but Dr. Misao Kashiba of the math department has agreed to be on my committee."

"Could you spell that for me, please?" He took out a pen and wrote down the name. "That will be fine. The four members don't all have to be from psychology, of course."

"I also want Dr. Lin Xuan of neurology to be on the committee."

He raised his eyebrows. "Neurology? You mean in the medical school?"

"Yes." She spelled the name without being asked. "Dr. Nietz has agreed to support his application for ad hoc status on the graduate faculty."

"I see." He laid down his pen and frowned. "Well then. You can proceed to apply for candidacy. Do you have a copy of the form?"

"Yes."

"Then?" He was growing more puzzled. What exactly was her problem? He'd heard glowing reports about how much research she had been turning out and how well she could write. Stan had come back from APS bragging about how poised and articulate she had been there.

"I don't have a proposal yet."

Not an uncommon problem. But it didn't fit with the rest of his information about her. "Vanessa, I think you need to be more forthcoming. Is there some problem you…" He was about to say "…aren't telling me." At the last minute he chose "…haven't mentioned or feel you can't discuss? Because the committee's purpose is to see that—"

"I gave my master's committee a sketchy proposal—"

"But a full, official committee of five must—"

"It's moot, Dr. Brooks. The research will be published in *Psychological Science*."

"Really?" He raised his eyebrows. "Did Dr. Harte authorize…"

"I'm taking full responsibility for what I've done. I want my work in print as soon as possible."

"And you don't have any other research in mind?"

"I'm submitting it to *Nature* as soon as Stan has a chance to look over the manuscript."

He was incredulous. "You should withdraw—"

"I'm doing a theoretical dissertation, Dr. Brooks. Besides, the research on which both papers were based is finished. I can't very well propose to do research I've already completed, can I?"

"Well, technically no. But…" This was astounding. Did the woman have a self-destructive urge?

"I believe I have a committee lined up, Dr. Brooks. I'll be submitting the form within the week. I'm nearly done rewriting a manuscript in dissertation format and plan to hand it out when I schedule a meeting with my full committee."

"But you can't do that. You have to have a general exam and—"

"The work is done. But it's not empirical research. The committee's only conceivable function will be to evaluate the validity of my work. There's no need for a general exam and proposal meeting, where the issue would be whether I can reach a specified goal. I believe I've already achieved that —"

"Now wait a minute."

"I don't want to waste faculty members' valuable time screwing around with administrative niceties, Dr. Brooks. I want them to devote their time and energy to picking my work apart and improving it—if possible."

He was speechless. He hadn't the faintest idea how to deal with a situation like this. There were no precedents. And she had recruited a mathematician and neurologist for her committee. If that kind of expertise was needed, what was she trying to do?

For the first time he understood why her academic reputation was so explosive. And he realized he'd joined the ranks of his colleagues whom she had blasted out of her way to get whatever it was she wanted.

"Well, Vanessa, when you submit your 'Request for General Exam,' I'll tell the graduate committee what you've just told me. I can't say what they'll recommend to the graduate dean, but, of course, it will go forward as soon as you do."

She grabbed her backpack. "Thank you, Dr. Brooks." She left quickly, giving no sign of any emotion—somewhat surprising, given the precarious course she planned to follow.

Stan had been appointed by the graduate dean to serve on a doctoral committee in the philosophy department, and after a late afternoon proposal meeting on Monday, he was returning to the building from Condon Hall in a light mist. It was typical Seattle weather for November: just enough mist in the air to dampen every exposed surface and leave a blanket of water beadlets clinging to the fabric of one's clothes.

Ahead of him on Campus Parkway, he saw a figure in a pink rain parka, with a royal blue backpack slung over her shoulder. A black ponytail bobbed from the back of her head as she walked and turned her head. She had one arm looped through her companion's, and she turned frequently to speak to him.

The couple stopped at Brooklyn Avenue to wait for a light to cross the parkway. He slowed his pace so he wouldn't catch up with them. Suddenly, she stood on tiptoes to kiss her companion on the cheek. They kissed twice in quick succession, then broke into laughter.

When Stan saw the man's face in profile, he came to a halt. The black hair and pale complexion were strikingly similar to

Vanessa's. His face was a masculine version of hers. Vanessa's companion could have been her twin brother.

The traffic light changed, and they crossed the street where they had to wait in the center parkway for another light. Stan continued across Brooklyn the way he had been going, took several hurried steps, and turned to stare at the couple unabashedly. They seemed to have their hands inside each other's jackets and were wiggling as though they were tickling each other. Then they embraced in a prolonged kiss.

The light changed but they were oblivious. It had a short cycle, so it was yellow when they noticed. They stood laughing in each other's arms.

Stan finally turned and trudged on toward Guthrie Hall. His nose twitched with incipient tears. On weekends like this, he and Vanessa had taken long walks together in the Green Lake neighborhood, heedless of everything in the world except each other. The image of the intertwined figures alone on the grassy divider between two one-way streets would frequently return to torment him in the months ahead.

A week later as Stan was scanning the gallery announcements at thestranger.com, his eyes froze on "Vanessa at the Beach," which was opening on Friday at the Underground Photo Gallery in the Pioneer Square area. The photographer was Jon Langley. Feeling at loose ends, as he often did on weekends since Vanessa moved out, he drove downtown for the opening.

The moment he entered the gallery, he knew. The first photo when he entered the show almost stopped his heart. In a four- by six-foot black-and-white photo, a naked Vanessa ran toward the camera, arms spread wide, head thrown back and mouth open in ecstatic laughter. Her stark white body was etched against the brooding sky, sullen seastacks, and raging surf of a stormy autumn afternoon.

It took him a moment before he recognized the place as Shi Shi Beach. The photo was exquisitely composed and almost leapt, like the model, from the frame and engulfed the viewer like the incoming comber in its background.

He moved with the other people along the wall in a fugue state, spellbound by the beauty of one magical moment after another frozen in time. At the corner of the narrow exhibition room, he paused to look back. In every one of the photos he'd seen so far, Vanessa was either smiling or laughing.

When he surveyed the wall at the far end of the room, however, he was transfixed by two enormous enlargements. In the first, Vanessa was on her knees, her body palpably vibrating with tension, her face, a mask of sexual rapture. In the other, she lay on her back facing away from the camera, knees up, legs apart, her pelvis aslant, as though the photographer had captured the act of love with an invisible lover on top of her.

As he turned to look at the next photo along the adjacent wall, he realized his penis was pressing visibly against his trouser leg. He moved into the corner and bent over, pretending to study the title card until the moment of arousal passed. Stepping back, he was struck by the contrasting mood of the next photo: A naked Vanessa gazed in contemplation toward the sea against the background of a bare ribbed cliff topped by vegetation contorted by the buffeting coastal wind.

As he continued along the third wall, the poses became more contorted, and Vanessa's expressions, more tormented until the last one was so poignant, it seemed to capture the very instant before an overwhelming grief breaks the surface of time.

He could barely breathe. When he turned away and swept his eyes around the room, surveying the entire series again through the restless motion of the crowd, it was like another journey through the wringer of his affair with Vanessa. He relived the emotional arc of their time together—not Vanessa's emotions, which he would not dare to guess, but his own.

At length he began to look at the faces in the room, looking for Vanessa. It was easy to identify the photographer by the cluster of people surrounding him. Jon Langley was the dark-haired man he'd seen with Vanessa on Campus Parkway two days earlier. When Langley suddenly turned in Stan's direction, Stan lurched backward, bumping a woman behind. After apologizing to her, he saw that Langley was no longer looking in is direction..

Stan edged closer until he was within range of Langley's voice over the din of conversation in the room. A middle-aged woman was asking him about the location. Were his photos all taken on the same beach? No, was his answer, it took several trips to the Olympic beaches. As the exchange of questions and answers continued, it became clear he and Vanessa had stayed together, either at Kalaloch Lodge or in a tent on wilderness beaches.

"Are you married, then?" the woman asked.

"No, we've only been together for a couple months," he replied. "But Vanessa's been running around naked in wild places since she was a kid."

"Oh, I see," the woman exclaimed in a stilted voice.

"And she's a good sport about sleeping in a tent," he added with a laugh.

Stan surveyed the exhibit one more time in an attempt to sear the images on his memory like a flashbulb in a dark room imprints an image on the mind's eye for several minutes afterward. Moving quickly from photo to photo, he paused just long enough for one full glimpse.

It struck him as he finished that there was little explicit eroticism—no low-angle shots, and only the one spread-leg pose, like those *Playboy* uses so often and so artfully. And throughout the series, those precious lips and tender tongue were concealed beneath nature's own clothing.

He'd had enough. Leaving the gallery emotionally drained, he wandered the streets around the square for half an hour, mingling with the Friday night crowds. He was sure that Vanessa hadn't been there, and he was glad.

Roger Zhrudsky was definitely not looking forward to his meeting with Vanessa Trippett this time. He hated formal complaints, especially those involving sexual issues. Invariably, they were particularly contentious and charged with emotion. And this one was a doozy.

Usually, if he studied the written statement long enough, he saw a way out—a compromise that left both parties sufficiently satisfied that they agreed that a public hearing wasn't needed. This one seemed to offer nothing but an action on his part that was both distasteful to him personally and potentially embarrassing to his department.

She entered his office with a deferential greeting. As always, she was a model of courtesy. On the surface her delicate features and demure expression gave no hint of the lust she stirred in men smart enough to capture her attention. She was so poised, sitting across from him, that he hated to begin something that he was sure would unhinge her. He saw no other way than to be as concise as possible and get it over with.

"Ms. Tra— sorry, Vanessa, there's been a formal complaint against you. It is—"

"I know about the complaints, Dr. Zhrudsky. Dr. Cavanaugh went over—"

"This is more serious, unfortunately. Although it does concern your teaching."

She frowned but said nothing.

"A group of your students," he continued, "have filed a formal statement alleging favoritism. There are fourteen signatures." He carefully avoided the obvious point that the number was almost half of the class.

She lowered her eyes. Her expression gave no hint of her reaction.

"They allege—and mind you, it is exactly that, an allegation—that you have given one particular student—a male student—higher grades and preferential tutoring outside class because you and he are, for lack of a better term, romantically involved."

He had expected the protestations and denials to begin here. He was preparing himself for the worst. And he had girded his intellectual loins for a frontal assault of the reasoning power he knew she was capable of marshalling.

"He's very intelligent." Her tone was almost matter of fact. "He earned the grades himself. But the tutoring part is true, for all intents and purposes."

A moment of panic swept over him. He had no idea what to say. It was a response so far from his imagined scenarios for this meeting that he had not the slightest notion how he was going to proceed. She resolved his dilemma by filling the gap in the conversation.

"I'm afraid I was caught off guard. I'd never imagined it would be so easy, so natural to strike up a friendship with a student. And so difficult to maintain a distance, not so much in the classroom, but outside it."

"Well, then, there may not be as big a problem as I thought." He had a glimmer of a resolution, and he snatched at it from the current of thought swirling around him. "If no more than a friendship—"

"Unfortunately, it isn't."

His heart sank. Was she simply admitting it? Without protest? It was too bizarre to take in. "You mean, then, that your friendship has gone beyond—?"

"What happened between us is nobody else's business. But we have not been very discreet—not that that changes the ethical issue. Some of my students have undoubtedly seen us kissing on campus. And we both live near campus. Someone could have easily followed us home after class recently." Incredibly, she smiled. It was no more than a flicker on her lips but an unmistakable sign of amusement. "An apartment's not a suitable place for a student conference, is it, Dr. Zhrudsky? Nor for tutoring, huh?"

He was dumbfounded. "Then you…"

"I admit that I'm having an affair with Jon Langley. Isn't he the student they say I'm giving preferential treatment?"

He searched the two-page document to see if a name was mentioned.

"It doesn't matter." She sat back in her chair. "It was a foolish thing for me to do. I know that. I knew it, even as I was letting myself slide into it. But I discovered something I hadn't realized before I started teaching undergraduates.

"Ninety-five percent of them didn't come to school with the intellectual curiosity I did. They have no intrinsic interest in learning. Yes, they can be stirred—motivated—to pursue a subject, but they expect their instructors to generate that interest by entertaining them.

"Moreover, they have neither training in elementary logic nor an understanding of the significance of facts, and they are not persuaded by arguments predicated on logic and facts. And they turn off their brains at the mention of numbers and completely freak out when they encounter the simplest kind of algebra."

"Sadly, I have to agree," he interjected, "but—"

"So when an exception steps forward and displays real, self-starting interest in a subject I love deeply, I… What's the best way to put it? I'm like a hyperactive trout leaping out of a lake to gulp down the fly that turns out to be a fisherman's lure."

The woman's metaphor was breathtaking—and distracting. He almost complimented her on it. Instead, he simply gazed at her and said, "So…"

"Would it help if I wrote out a statement and signed it, Dr. Zhrudsky?"

His mouth fell open.

She hoisted her backpack on to her lap and pulled out a pad of yellow paper ruled with squares instead of lines. "What are the important points I need to cover?"

With an unpleasant feeling he'd lost control of the situation, he sat up very straight and squared his shoulders. "That would be up to you, of course. However, you shouldn't be hasty. You need to consider the implications of what you do."

"I don't want to create any more problems for the department, or for you, than I already have. I certainly wouldn't want a formal hearing. That wouldn't help me, or the department."

"You should be aware of the fact that it will be necessary to remove you from the classroom—"

"Because of the formal complaint, especially if I don't contest it?"

"Yes, the department would have no other alternative. And I must tell you that I've already discussed with Dr. Cavanaugh and Dr. Brooks how we would arrange for a replacement for your section of 201."

"I'll never be a good classroom teacher, Dr. Zhrudsky, especially with undergraduates. There's no point trying to teach me how to entertain twenty-year-olds and get them interested in scientific questions—" Again, there was a glint of mirth in her eyes. "—instead of what's under my clothes and why I'd take them off for a photographer."

"I'm sure you know that not all PhDs work in the classroom. Outside of your grade in the teaching seminar, the program doesn't require you to have teaching experience."

"It's difficult finding out there's something you can't do well, Dr. Zhrudsky. Something in which you really want very much to excel."

She kept jerking the rug out from under him by twisting the conversation away from her perilous status to other people's inconveniences. How was he going to deliver the worst part of his message?

He cleared his throat. "It would be one of the few skills you couldn't master, Vanessa."

"Thank you, Dr. Zhrudsky." Her voice was almost inaudible.

"Sadly, we have to terminate your teaching assistantship—"

"That's understandable."

"And after this last truly brutal round of budget cuts, we won't be able to fund a research assistantship for you out of department funds." He couldn't discern any emotion in her face, which now reminded him of a Grecian statue.

"Now, that doesn't mean you won't get your last paycheck for this quarter, even though you'll be relieved of all teaching responsibilities immediately. It does mean that you may not have a contract for winter and spring quarters. I'm still trying to find an assistantship slot for you. I hope this doesn't mean you'd have to…"

"Will I also be suspended—academically?"

"No, no. That definitely won't happen. Absolutely not." Her voluntary written statement would certainly obviate any academic action.

"Then I'll find some way to make ends meet. I have a little money in a savings account… and it helps that I have one more paycheck coming."

"Please don't forget, Vanessa. I've told you all this because I don't want you to feel pressured to sign a formal statement. Please give it careful thought before you—"

"I will." She adjusted the pad on her lap, pen poised. "But we might as well go over the points in my statement. So we won't have meet again."

He heaved a sigh, whether of relief or frustration, he didn't know. "Very well. Perhaps a simple resignation would be the… most straightforward and uncomplicated."

"Fine." She slipped the pad back into her backpack without looking down. "Is there anything else, Dr. Zhrudsky?" She pulled the zipper closed on the pack as she spoke.

"I'm sorry this meeting was necessary. You've handled the bad news better than I expected."

She was on her feet. "You've been very kind, Dr. Zhrudsky. Thank you."

She hurried out, leaving him mulling over what had happened. Glancing down, he realized he'd barely written on his pad of notepaper. Would he be able to say for sure what had been said?

CHAPTER 25

Zhrudsky had already scheduled a conference with Michelle, Paul, and Stan soon after his meeting with Vanessa. "I'm hoping," he began, "that if the departmental rumor mill starts with unadulterated grain from three different sources, the information that will reach everyone in a day or two will be closer to the truth."

A moment of startled silence followed Roger's brief recital of what had transpired. "It's just like Vanessa," Stan said, breaking into the quiet.

"The affair or her reaction to the complaint?" Paul asked.

"Her honesty," Michelle said before the others could respond. "I don't understand how she could let herself get into this kind of mess." She looked first at Stan and then at Paul. "Do you?"

Paul shrugged. She looked back at Stan. He shook his head without conviction. They finally settled down to a serious discussion of the options Roger had for possible assistantships. The prospects were bleak.

Just before they broke up, Michelle said, "Let me talk to her first, Stan, if you don't mind."

"Good idea." Stan was glad he wouldn't have to be the first. "Try to persuade her she needs to see me right away. She may not want to… under the circumstances."

The three of them trooped silently out of Zhrudsky's office and returned to their own offices not yet quite believing what they'd just heard.

Michelle went straight from the conference to Vanessa's office. Only Vanessa's officemate Christy Thomas was there, but she knew that Vanessa was in a seminar that afternoon. Michelle waited until the class was almost over and then staked out the conference room until she caught Vanessa before she left the building.

"Michelle! What are you—?"

"I want to talk to you."

Vanessa studied her a moment, searching her eyes. "You must know, then?"

"Yes." She impulsively grabbed Vanessa by the arm. "You and I need to talk."

"What is there to talk about?"

"Vanessa. You owe me this one." She regretted it the moment she said it. "Owe me" was too close to "an explanation."

"You're right. I do." Vanessa's face showed no offense that Michelle could detect.

They said nothing more until Michelle had her coffeepot going. When she sat down opposite her, Vanessa began without preamble.

"Okay. So I did something really idiotic this time. I'm sleeping with one of my students."

"Then it's true?"

"Jon Langley's one of the smartest people I've ever known. He caught me off balance the first day of class by coming up and asking me—you're not going to believe this either, Michelle. He asked how much of psychology I thought could be explained by brain mechanisms. '…by brain mechanisms…!' I swear, those were the exact words he used. And before we were done, he was asking me to recommend a book he could read to learn—and I quote—'…enough about neurology so I can fill in the blank spaces you'll be leaving.' Are you getting the idea?"

Michelle shook her head.

"You don't? You don't know me well enough by now to—?"

"I do. That's the thing, Vanessa. I'm deeply worried about what's—"

"What's going to happen to me? Well, I hardly care—"

"No! What can possibly be going on inside that Gordian brain of yours."

"What's going on is that I've fallen in love with a strange and wonderful guy who's not mixed up in my future as an independent scientist."

Michelle stared at her. "Not mixed up in your future? Vanessa, was this Jon person some kind of lightning bolt that fried the circuitry connecting your logic to the rest of your knowledge? You're telling me getting fired as a teaching assistant doesn't affect your future as an independent researcher?"

Michelle realized she was shouting. And every time she shouted at her daughters, she was sorry afterward. Why did she think it would help with Vanessa?

"Maybe." Vanessa paused, not the way people pause to reflect on what they are saying but with cold, purposeful drama. "Maybe not. I'm a lousy teacher. I want to do research full time, anyway."

Michelle could see that Vanessa's reasoning hadn't failed her. Something deep and hidden was driving her rational faculties. She wasn't going to discover what it was by screaming at her, she told herself. She noticed the sweat in her armpits for the first time.

Vanessa had shifted her whole body in her chair so she was facing the wall on her left, seemingly lost in studying Klee's mask on the wall. Michelle realized she'd forgotten to get out coffee mugs.

She stood, grateful for the extra time it gave her to think out her strategy. As she lifted them off the shelf, she saw an opening: Get her talking about Langley. With luck she'll reveal the subterranean demons that hold sway over her. Maybe, just maybe, she'd manage to find them for herself in the process.

"Tell me about Jon Langley." Michelle set the heavy mugs on the table with thud. The steel office furniture resonated like a bass drum. "I can't help but be fascinated."

Vanessa continued to stare at the poster for a few seconds before speaking. "He's a couple of years older than the other students. He went to Peninsula College in Port Angeles where he grew up."

"The community college?"

"Yeah, a two-year program." Vanessa turned back to face Michelle. "He's been fascinated by photography since he was a kid. Sold his first photos when he was still in high school. Landscapes from the mountains and beaches all around where he lived—and the farmlands near Sequim. The people, too—loggers, Native Americans, townspeople and tourists. And women—the girls in his high school loved the portraits he shot of them. And the women he met at the college."

Michelle poured coffee. She wished she could take notes. She saw a trend already. Did Vanessa realize it was her father she was seeing in Langley?

"So he left school after two years." Vanessa was ignoring the coffee mug with its aromatic wisps of vapor rising from it. "He was making a good living already selling his photos to tourists—and local people, too. Why should he get a bachelor's degree?

"The thing was, he was spending all his free time reading. He loved learning about new subjects. He read books in history, psychology, economics, religion—biographies of every kind of person you can imagine. He learned chemistry, physics and biology from college textbooks. He delved into art and culture. He pursued the great philosophers… And all the while he was traipsing around the Olympic Peninsula with his camera."

"Nobody was guiding or mentoring his reading?" Michelle was impressed.

"Only the books he was reading. One would get him interested in another one. Novels, too. They're full of ideas for nonfiction reading."

"I'm getting the drift. He came to the UW to learn more? To get some guidance?'

"Plus Seattle's turned out to be a whole new domain to take photos tourists will buy. Tuition was never an issue for him."

"Is he in the art school?"

"He's not interested in a professional degree."

Michelle had a hypothesis. "I'm sure it doesn't matter much to you, Vanessa. But tell me about his looks. Is he—?"

"Handsome? Yes. In this case, it made a difference. He reminds me of my father."

Bingo! Michelle had a feeling it wasn't just the fact that Langley was a photographer.

"I know where you're going with this, Michelle. But I saw the resemblance at our first meeting. From that moment, I've been telling myself that's why he has such a powerful effect on me. But there are so many other reasons I love him. He's the kind of man I can imagine being married to. I decided early on that if I tried to keep my distance, make our relationship professional—until the end of the quarter… I might lose him."

Vanessa finally picked up her mug and, after sipping gingerly, drank greedily. She was so typically herself. Even when she saw clearly where her behavior might lead, she could reason her way to a justification.

A new tack occurred to Michelle. "Does he like math?"

"He's only taken algebra courses up to now. That's how I got started tutoring him—would you believe?"

"Yes. It makes perfect sense." Michelle wondered if Vanessa was as good at explaining elementary mathematical concepts as she was with complex analysis or Lebesgue integration. Maybe she should look into getting a joint degree with math so she could teach math courses.

"Jon didn't need my help with psychology. He'd already learned most of what's covered in introductory psychology on his own."

There was one very delicate facet of Vanessa's relationship to Langley that Michelle hesitated to bring up. But she decided to risk asking. "If you don't mind my asking, has he taken photos of you?"

"He has such an incredible gift for coaxing facial expressions and poses out of people, how could I refuse when he asked?"

"Did you pose—?"

"Nude? Of course! That's the only way I know how to pose for a camera."

They both laughed, Michelle in spite of herself.

"You know, Michelle, Jon's taken some incredible photos of me. But he tried for a long time to take a portrait of me. There was nothing wrong with them. They were perfectly good professional portraits. But he wasn't satisfied. Then one day, he said to me, 'Vanessa, take off your clothes.'

"He'd been trying to get an unposed portrait by following me around his apartment with his camera and wasn't getting what he wanted. So I took off my clothes, and he started shooting.

"Out of fifty frames, he got six he was happy with. He's already sold two of those, so that tells you—he knows what he's doing."

"Has he photographed other women nude?" The question was out of Michelle's mouth before she realized she asked it.

"Oh, sure. He's as good or better than my dad was. But he's never done erotic stuff. He had a big show of his photos of me in a gallery downtown. I almost invited you to come see it with me. But I knew—"

"I'm no prude, Vanessa. The history of art's full of naked women. And I think photography is as valid a form of visual art as painting and sculpture. I wish you'd asked me."

"Jon's still got the files. I'll ask him if he could show them to you on his big flatscreen TV. We'll have you and your husband over. You'd come, wouldn't you?"

Michelle chuckled. "I'm sure Karl would enjoy seeing them."

"So there you have it, Michelle. Love conquers all. Even my future."

"No. Let's pick up the pieces and get you back on track. There are plenty of research positions out there, jobs that don't involve teaching. Many of them are even in academia—full-fledged faculty appointments, if you can support yourself with grants."

"That's the norm in med schools, I gather."

"Exactly. That's probably where you belong anyway. Given the direction you're taking. Now..." Michelle had already decided she was going to let Stan sort out Vanessa's options for the immediate future. "You're going to keep Stan as your sponsor."

"Whether I want to or not? Is that a question, or an order?"

"Whatever happened between the two of you, Vanessa, you can't afford to drop him from your committee. He's on the books as your sponsor, but he's agreed not to make any major decisions or sign anything for you without my approval, and Paul's. The three of us have formed a decision-making subcommittee, which will—"

"Plan my future?"

"No. Manage your academic career, so you finish your dissertation in time for spring commencement."

"What's to manage? I have two papers in press."

"Stan's already filled us in on them, but—"

"So, that isn't enough?"

"Vanessa! Stop interrupting."

"Isn't *Nature* good enough?" Vanessa jumped to her feet, pointedly ignoring Michelle as she stalked to the window and looked out. "I read somewhere it's the most prestigious scientific journal in the *world*."

Don't lose your temper, Michelle told herself. *You'll only make things worse.*

"Who or what do I have to convince that I know how to do research?" Vanessa was addressing Michelle's reflection in the window. "I must have chosen a problem that the editors and referees of *Nature* and *Psychological Science* think is important. They agreed I can design studies and analyze—"

"Stop acting like a child, Vanessa!"

"Tell that to the graduate dean, or whoever it is that's treating my research like it isn't good enough for this university."

Michelle slumped in her chair. "That's what we're trying to do. But we can't do it without your cooperation. Okay?"

"Okay." Vanessa finally turned around. "What do these idiots want me to do?"

Michelle knew Vanessa didn't mean her, but still Vanessa's behavior irked her. "Go see Stan. Get your committee signed up. File your application with the grad school."

"I'm not writing a stupid proposal. The only paper I'm handing out to some committee is a draft of a long paper I'm going to send to *Science*—or whoever will take it. If the graduate school won't take that and two published papers, screw it! I'm out of here."

Michelle gasped. "You can't mean that."

"Jon wants to travel. Maybe I'll tag along. See if someone in Europe or New Zealand will give me a degree—or better, a job."

How did I manage to stir up this hornet's nest? Michelle asked herself. "I surrender. Just don't leave until we've tried to do this on your terms."

"Thank you." Vanessa picked up her backpack. "I'll go see Stan. Right now, if he's in."

"He will be. I told him I'd send you on to him."

"Good." She started to leave, then turned back. "I understood what you said, and I appreciate what you're trying to do."

Michelle nodded.

"I also promise you that I'll come say good-bye if we decide to leave." She left so quickly Michelle didn't have a chance to respond.

Only when she was alone did Michelle realize what had happened. What had started as a conversation about Vanessa's emotional life had plunged into a battle over her academic career.

Was it all a defense against an unresolved conflict about her father's exploitation of her? The woman was much too complicated for an amateur to untangle. What could a friend do to prevent the hidden, unhealthy forces in her life from pulling her apart?

"I hear you're the speaker for the triumvirate," Vanessa said as she walked in Stan's office. "Can I find out what it's decided my future will be?"

She plopped into a chair across the table from him. Her backpack received gentler treatment as she lowered it to the floor beside her. He couldn't quite figure out her mood.

"I'm the spokesperson only because I'm still listed as your sponsor. If you want to change, I'll do everything I can—"

"Michelle told me the reason." She smiled. "It makes sense to me, Stan. I'm here to find out what the three of you have in mind."

"The problem is that your case doesn't fit the model."

"You mean it doesn't fit the rules of the graduate program?" Her tone was snippy but she continued to smile.

"Yes and no. The difficulty as we see it is that there are no precedents. No one has ever heard of a student who has published two papers in major journals during the third year of her program."

"Without jumping through the appropriate hoops, yes?"

"Exactly. So our idea is—"

"Stan, I'm tired of this paternalism. It isn't you and Paul and Michelle. It's the damn rules. Why does someone need permission to conduct research and publish it? Institutional ethics reviews, I understand. I've followed those rules because they make sense. But I thought science was broader than a single graduate program, bigger than a university.

"If a committee of your peers reviews my work and says it's good enough to publish, why should Brooks or the graduate committee or the graduate dean—" Her fury was gathering power. "Why should they sit around saying my work is inferior to theirs because I didn't file the proper papers or didn't tell them what I was doing?"

Stan raised his hands to ward off the torrent of words. The cute little tiger of her thesis defense was growing into a hungry tigress on the prowl.

"I agree with the content of what you're saying, Vanessa. But not the vehemence. Relax, and let me explain how to dodge exactly the people you're talking about."

"Look." She leaned forward ready to pounce, fingers like claws on the tabletop. "I hate wasting my time on these games. I've been asking myself whether I even want a PhD. Do I care enough to sacrifice my best ideas to please the gatekeepers?"

He took advantage of a moment's lull in her onslaught. "The three of us can help you do just that." He paused, expecting another threatening growl.

Instead, she grabbed her backpack and unzipped it in her lap. "Let's hear it." She yanked out the inevitable quadrille ruled yellow pad and flattened the pack on her lap with it. "What's my part in this plot?"

"You've talked to Kashiba—he'll serve on your committee?"

"Yes, he's been going over my derivations for me. He told me he'd be happy to join the conspiracy... I mean, committee."

He couldn't help smiling. "Good. And Lin Xuan?"

"He's fine. He'll be advising me anyway." She leaned forward, more in earnest than attack. "Stan, he's the only one who sees the whole picture. Do you believe that?"

"I'll take your word for it."

"Good. What's the protocol? I need their signatures on some piece of paper, right?" She riffled through some sheets of paper in her backpack.

"This?" She held out the form the department used to request the graduate school establish a dissertation committee and select a graduate faculty member to represent the dean on it. Technically, it was called an application for candidacy for the PhD.

He took the sheet of paper from her. "That's it." He saw that she'd already filled in the applicant's section at the top. "May I call Kashiba and Lin? I want to meet with them, along with Michelle and Paul, so we can agree on a plan. The 'triumvirate,' as you call us, wants to have a united front when we meet with the outside member."

"So then I'll have a united 'pentumvirate' I suppose?"

It took him a second to unpack the neologism. "Yes, a coalition of five on a six-member committee—a super majority."

"What's the big deal with this sixth person? Does the dean have a corps of ogres he sends out to trap unwary students?"

"Rarely. In my—"

"Or are we called 'candidates' now? I just can't keep all this nomenclature straight."

"Listen to me, Vanessa." He realized he sounded like he used to when he was trying to deal with his teenage kids. "You asked a question. Give me a chance to answer it."

He waited until he was sure she wouldn't interrupt him again. "Most outside members are very reasonable in my experience. The best selections add to the combined expertise of the committee—like Kashiba, or your friend, Lin. They read the dissertation carefully and ask good questions."

"Like someone in artificial intelligence, for example?"

"Maybe, or another mathematician or neuroscientist. Others have no idea what the research is about and either sit quietly or ask if the research has any practical applications they might be able to understand. The worst think they're experts, but aren't. They ask stupid questions. and won't admit they don't understand perfectly good answers."

"All right." She poised her pencil above the yellow pad. "I'm ready. What am I supposed to do here?"

"As soon as you can, bring me five hard copies of your published papers—"

"I just received reprints of the *Nature* paper." Seeing him nod with approval, she went on. "What about the one in *PS*?"

"Xerox the manuscript."

"How about page proofs?"

"Better." She could be such a delight when she wanted to be. "Xerox your copy of them," he added.

"And…?"

"And an outline of your theory paper in proposal form. A page or two's enough, but—"

"In proposal form?"

"Future tense. Make it sound like the final version isn't written yet."

"Why? It's already nearly complete."

"So we can pretend that—"

"Pretend?" She sneered. "You mean I'm supposed to lie?"

"It will make it easier to—"

"I won't lie. This is science, Stan. Lying is the worst crime a scientist can commit."

He sighed. "Okay, I'll tell them you want to do things the hardest way possible—as usual."

"The right way," she corrected him. "The grown-up way."

"And that would be?"

"I have a manuscript almost ready to send to the editor of Science. The one thing I am not going to do is waste time rewriting it in a form I can't submit to a journal. That's bullshit!"

"Okay. I didn't expect any cooperation from you on that. But we don't want whoever looks at this to think there's a possibility the paper will be accepted before we can have a meeting." He shook his head in despair. "If it is, then we'll deal with that problem."

"So what am I supposed to do?" She positioned the pad and pencil again.

He cleared his throat. "I want to see if I can set up this meeting next week. Before anyone can leave for Christmas break. Can you spare the time to put together an outline of your current paper with a note saying it's still being revised? How about that?"

"Closer to the truth. I guess I can say that without deceiving anyone."

Finally! "Can you have it to me in a couple of days?"

"Tomorrow morning."

He knew she would say that. "With your permission, then, I'll send the three papers to Kashiba and Lin after I talk to them on the phone."

"Lin already has the two papers. I'll run a copy of the outline by him in the morning before I make copies." She gave him a sidelong glance. "He'll accept electronic copies. And he already knows everything that's in the two published papers." She stood and rested the backpack on the chair while she slid the pad in and pulled the zippers up. "Call Lin after three-thirty. After he finishes his work in the clinic."

He made a sticky note.

"Thanks, Stan." Her smile seemed to light up his dreary office. "We can still be friends, I hope? Even if I act like an obstreperous kid a lot of the time?"

He was overwhelmed. "Yes," he stammered, "of course."

She shot out of his office like an arrow leaving a bow.

CHAPTER 26

True to her word, Vanessa had a stack of papers, neatly piled and sorted for Stan the next morning. The "pentumvirate" met during finals week in the conference room on the second floor of Guthrie Hall.

White-haired and slightly stooped, Misao Kashiba was deferential to a fault when he joined Michelle and Paul and Stan. "Thank you so much for asking me to join you."

Michelle knew him from the math colloquium series. He dipped his head repeatedly as she introduced him to the other two.

Lin was the last to arrive. Though less formal than Misao, he shared a combination of precise English tinged with just enough accent to suggest Asian roots. He was tall and trim with a lustrous domed forehead and an engaging smile. Stan was careful not to show undue curiosity about this man who Vanessa admired so much and whose judgment she trusted.

As they took their seats, Stan launched the meeting. "I hope all of you had a chance to look over Vanessa's three papers." Seeing nods around the table, he turned to what he hoped would be obvious to everyone.

"The reason I thought we should meet is that Vanessa's case is so unusual. Michelle and Paul and I have worked with her over the past two years or so, and to be quite frank, none of us has been able to keep her from rushing ahead, recklessly ignoring the rules and procedures of our graduate program."

"She's been an exception to every rule almost from the beginning." Michelle spoke, as Stan had, exclusively to Misao and Lin. "She had no need for my first-year statistics course, nor for my advanced courses and seminars in statistics. I fed her voracious appetite for applied statistics, and—to be perfectly honest, Misao—she taught me the fundamental principles underlying them."

"Yes," Misao said, nodding vigorously, "she is a talented teacher." He included all of them in his gaze. "She is also a brilliant mathematician. With a little direction, I believe she could do original work in my field."

"I sponsored her when she started in our program." Paul smiled at Stan. "And I can attest to Stan's summary of her graduate career. I made my lab available to her. She figured out how to make it run the experiments she wanted to run and went ahead and did them… without asking for help, advice or indeed permission." He laughed.

"I was fit to be tied when my heart attack ended my role as her sponsor. But I was so frustrated with her, I was thinking of telling her to find somebody else. Poor Stan here caught her on the ricochet."

They all laughed. His admission gave Stan new respect for Paul's professional integrity.

"My experience with her is similar to Paul's." Stan acknowledged him with a friendly glance. "I managed to persuade her to slow down long enough to complete a master's degree. But she turned around and quite explicitly tested the value of my advice about publishing it. If I hadn't been right, I doubt she would have listened to me again—ever."

Lin leaned toward the others, his face both earnest and puzzled. "So, is the problem here that her published research doesn't conform to some university rule?"

"I think you've hit the nail squarely on the head, Lin," Stan said. "She's taken all the necessary coursework and passed the department's comprehensive exams with flying colors. The next step would be for her to write a proposal and have it ready to distribute to her supervisory committee when the graduate school adds its representative.

"Instead of following our departmental guidelines, she went ahead and published two papers in prestigious journals. The research in either one of them would more than qualify as her dissertation. The hitch is that the psych department has a policy that previously published research doesn't qualify as 'original,' as specified in the university's graduate policy."

Misao raised his hand to shoulder height and waited for Stan to acknowledge him, although the rest of them had dispensed with this formality from the beginning. "Isn't there some way to appeal for an exception?"

"That's one option the three of us in psychology have discussed, Misao," Stan said. "We thought, however, that we should include you and Lin in that decision before we are joined by the outside member."

"And with your concurrence," Paul said, picking up the line of reasoning, "we thought it would be wise to agree in advance on a fallback plan—in case either the dean's representative or the graduate school won't permit us to go ahead with a final defense."

"Moreover," Michelle added, "we need to formulate the exact nature of the exception and support it."

"I see," Lin said. Misao nodded.

"May I outline our thinking on both issues?" Stan continued to direct himself to Misao and Lin, hoping they wouldn't bring up the six or seven alternatives Vanessa's triumvirate had kicked around.

This time Lin nodded and Misao spoke. "Please. That would certainly help me."

"We propose to ask that Vanessa be permitted to defend her two published papers in a public forum in lieu of all other formal requirements for candidacy and that she be awarded a degree following a successful defense."

Misao began speaking at the same time he raised his hand. "That would be a daunting challenge for any student."

"Any student except Vanessa." The lines around Michelle's blue eyes crinkled with laughter. "She's already functioning as an independent researcher. And her two publications are a credit to the university."

"So you would ask her to limit herself to her special theory of consciousness?" Lin asked. "And not discuss her general theory of the mind-brain?"

"Yes," Stan answered for the triumvirate. "We knew this would come up. We simply want to make her challenge a little less daunting. Her nearly complete manuscript notwithstanding, we thought it would be wise not even to mention it in our petition to the dean."

"I'm sure she will want to include it," Lin said with conviction.

"I'm sure she will." Michelle sighed. "That will be up to her, I suppose. If we give her an hour to make her formal presentation, we all know she'd give an excellent talk that includes her general theory, especially if she knows her audience represents many disciplines."

"That's why I asked her to include an outline of her general theory paper," Stan said.

"You realize, Dr. Har—" Lin looked flustered. "Sorry. Stan. She has a manuscript ready to send to *Science*?"

"Again," Stan said, "we know that, and like Michelle said, she'll do whatever she wants, and almost certainly do it well."

"Stan," Paul said, "as her sponsor, you should tell her to organize the speech in chronological order. That is, leave the general theory to the end, and cover the published papers first. Try to persuade her that she has an obligation to describe the historical development of her work as a student."

"A good idea, Dr. Kovick," Misao said. "She is such an orderly thinker, that otherwise she will begin with first principles and leave the empirical support until the very end."

"And confuse everyone except you," Paul joked.

"I agree," Stan said, "but remember, this will only apply if we get our exception. We aren't the final arbiters."

"That's right, Stan." Michelle had raised her hand as she spoke, but Stan realized she wasn't imitating Misao. It was a clever way to emphasize the point she was making. "But let's be clear about option one. We must state explicitly that the criterion guiding the committee's judgment is the one given in the university's *General Catalogue*."

She had one in front of her with a plain white strip of paper stuck in it. She opened to the marker and read. "'…a dissertation that is a significant contribution to knowledge and clearly indicates training in research.'—page forty-four, bottom of column three."

"There's more detail on page forty-five." Stan passed out Xerox copies to everyone. "Column two on page forty-five states, 'The candidate must submit a dissertation demonstrating original and independent investigation and achievement. The dissertation should reflect not only mastery of research techniques but also ability to select an important problem for investigation and to deal with it competently."

"That certainly covers Vanessa's work." Misao seemed to be speaking to himself.

"That's what we all think," Paul said. "Do you agree, Lin?"

"Yes." He nodded vigorously. "But may I offer a suggestion?"

"Of course," Stan said.

"My chairman…" Lin looked around the table. "Larry Nietz? He and I have already decided to ask Vanessa to present a research colloquium to our department. Perhaps we could piggyback on her defense. That is, if it's going to be open to all."

Stan made a quick note. "I'll call him tomorrow." He glanced around the table. "I've checked all the graduate school and department rules, and there seems to be nothing that prevents us from opening the meeting to the public."

"It's traditional to do that in European universities," Paul interjected.

Misao nodded. "I'm sure many of my colleagues would be interested in hearing her talk about the mathematical developments in her work."

Stan cleared his throat. "It's beginning to sound like we'll need a good-sized auditorium for this. Does anyone think Vanessa will have problems talking to a hundred people or more?"

"I doubt it." Michelle chuckled. "She told me last week that we should stop treating her like a child. If this scares her, it will serve her right."

There was a murmur of laughter. Stan waited until it died down and everyone's gaze returned to him. "I take it we're agreed on a preferred course of action," he went on. "Let me summarize: We'll recommend to the outside member that he or she join us in requesting the graduate dean to waive Vanessa's general exam and issue a warrant authorizing her final exam."

Lin shook his head. "I had no idea the process was so formal here. A 'warrant' for her exam? What a peculiar choice of words."

"It's in the catalogue," Michelle said amid another round of laughter.

Again Stan waited for their attention to return. "I would like us to also agree on an alternative strategy, in case either the dean or his representative won't permit a deviation from protocol."

"In our discussions here in the department," Paul said, "the three of us concluded that the best course of action is to accept a warrant for Vanessa's general exam, hold the meeting, and approve her for candidacy. This is catalogue gobbledygook for declaring her eligible to sit for the final oral."

"Why not proceed without the waiver?" Lin asked.

"Very simple, Lin," Michelle explained. "Page forty-five, bottom of column one—we can't have a general exam and a final oral in the same quarter."

"And beyond the unimportant detail of a month or two's delay," Stan went on, "her theory paper will very likely be published by the time of her oral."

"I see," Lin said softly.

Misao nodded sagely at Lin. "You psychologists are a good deal more clever than we mathematicians. We would have organized the final oral and passed the student—especially one as brilliant as Vanessa—and then informed the dean that he should sort out the paperwork." He chortled.

"Ninety percent of the time they just throw up their hands and let us get away with it. But sometimes our incompetence hurts the unfortunate student."

"Stan?" Lin asked amid the laughter, "do you really expect problems from the dean's representative?"

"In my experience," Stan replied, "they're generally quite cooperative. Many bring an added dimension of expertise to the discussion."

"But they can be a pain in the ass sometimes." Paul snorted. "I had a damn linguist who thought he knew more about psychology than anyone else in the room. Unfortunately, the student was a weak one, and we nearly had a train wreck in the general exam."

Michelle giggled. "The only wreck in Vanessa's case would have been the linguist."

During the ensuing merriment, the form to be sent to the dean circled the table collecting signatures.

When Michelle returned to her office after meeting the first graduate statistics class of winter quarter, Vanessa was standing in the hall waiting. Michelle broke into a broad smile that faded as she saw Vanessa's face more clearly.

It looked puffy even from a distance, and her otherwise unblemished skin was marred with red blotches. Michelle was one of the few people who had seen Vanessa cry recently, but she'd never seen her after an extended period of grieving.

Her mother? Had something happened over the break? An accident during their trip to Tierra del Fuego?

"I need to talk to someone," Vanessa said tonelessly.

"Of course." Michelle unlocked her office and held the door open for Vanessa. "What's wrong?" She closed the door.

"Jon left."

"Jon?" Michelle regretted the hint of surprise—or was it relief?—that had unintentionally colored her question.

"I told you he was going off on a photo expedition to Kenya, didn't I?"

"No, I don't think you did." Without thinking about it, Michelle had begun making coffee. "Kenya's a pretty big trip."

"Yeah, he'd never been to Africa, so it was a very big deal. A good friend of his organized a group of photographers who are all climbers. They walked all the way around Mt. Kenya getting acclimated and then climbed several peaks."

"A great opportunity for him. I hope nothing bad happened to him."

"Not to him. He came back last night. I went to the airport to pick him up with his car." Vanessa's voice broke.

Michelle interrupted the last stages of preparing coffee to get out her box of tissues. Vanessa had started crying.

"He didn't even wait until we got back to his place… He told m…" She wiped her cheeks and blew her nose. Tossing away the first tissue, she blotted her cheeks with a second one. "He met a woman who…" She dabbed her eyes. "He says she's just like he is… serious climber, photographer, spends her whole life traveling, living out of a pack… Doesn't even have an apartment…"

She threw the tissue away and covered her face with both hands. "I'm sorry to bother you like this but…"

Michelle came around her worktable and sat down in the chair next to Vanessa. "It isn't a problem, Vanessa." When she put her arms around her, Vanessa buried her face in Michelle's shoulder.

What was it about Vanessa and men? Some deep-rooted ambivalence that made her involvement wax and wane? Or was it the men who were first attracted to her and then repelled?

"You know what he said, Michelle?" Vanessa sobbed. "If he stays here with me, it'll stunt his growth—'stunt his artistic development'—those were his exact words."

When Vanessa leaned back and reached for another tissue, Michelle released her. She was teary eyed herself. They both pulled out tissues. Vanessa blew her nose again and shook her head.

"But the real reason is, he's in love with this woman." She balled up the tissue in one fist and pressed them both against her eyes. "At least he was honest with me."

Vanessa let her head fall lightly on Michelle's chest. Michelle encircled Vanessa with her arms and patted her back.

"I just don't get it, Michelle. What's wrong with me?" She straightened up. "I always screw up the relationship somehow."

"These things are never one-sided, Vanessa." Michelle stood to take care of the coffee.

Vanessa blew her nose several times. Between that and wiping her face, she consumed half a dozen more tissues by Michelle's count.

Should she point out that each of Vanessa's last three relationships had ended differently? Maybe what had happened with Stan was similar. Michelle sensed, however, that Vanessa had left Stan, so Paul, Stan, and now Jon seemed unlikely to be the same problem with Vanessa.

"I thought Jon was different."

As Michelle pushed a mug of coffee toward Vanessa, she saw that her eyes were dry. She looked terrible, but the wave of tears seemed to have passed for the moment.

"We weren't in the same field. We weren't working together every day. In fact, it seemed perfect. I stayed in my apartment most of the time and worked on campus, just the way I wanted to. He stayed in his place so he could go to class and out on shoots whenever he felt like it. We had marvelous weekends together. And a couple of wonderful four-day getaways on the Olympic Peninsula. We had our separate careers, and we supported and encouraged each other. We weren't arguing all the time like I did with Paul and Stan. I guess…"

When she didn't continue, Michelle nodded toward their coffee mugs. "Let's have some coffee before it gets cold."

"It was so harmonious with Jon. This thing came like a thunderclap with no lightning. I think the problem's with me. I'm too willing to throw my mind away along with my clothes."

Michelle couldn't keep herself from laughing. Her stifled giggle brought a smile to Vanessa's face.

"Captured two problems with one analogy, huh?" Vanessa emitted a squeak of a laugh. "How's that for psychoanalysis?"

"Freud would disown you."

"That's okay. I disowned *him* before I'd finished *The Interpretation of Dreams*."

"Clinical assessments aside, I don't think the problem is yours." Michelle wasn't sure she believed that, but it probably wasn't helpful for Vanessa to blame herself.

"It would be nice to think it was the men." Vanessa thought for a moment. "Or maybe my poor judgment. Either way…"

"It's probably neither. Do you want to know what I think?"

"You're the only person whose assessment I trust when it comes to me."

Michelle smiled, even as her confidence was sinking. "I think the problem is you, but only because you're so much smarter than the rest of us—"

"The rest of *you*? That's nonsense!"

"No. Listen to me. You're a statistician. You understand sampling. It's a problem in conditional sampling, okay?"

Vanessa folded her arms over her breasts and got her just-try-to-convince-me expression. "Okay."

"Let's assume you need a very intelligent partner to be happy, all right? Let's use IQ as a measure, just for the sake of this argument."

"Sure. Why not? IQs are fundamentally statistical measures anyway."

"So let's say you should definitely consider only men with IQs greater than 133."

"One man in fifty. So you're saying my only problem is that the odds are against me?"

Michelle wondered if Vanessa had the Gaussian probability tables memorized. "No. You came to graduate school where the mean IQ is, say 125."

"A skewed distribution, but for the sake of your argument, the probability is one in five? There aren't that many guys—"

"Ah, but more than half of them are married."

"Two in three, maybe? My odds are reduced to one in fifteen."

"And half of those guys are untrustworthy."

"I see. One in thirty. So that means if I limit myself to guys around the psych department, they're all risky bets?"

"It means you have to be patient, for one thing."

"And not jump into bed with the first man over 133?"

"That too."

Vanessa was smiling now. She checked her watch. "Good grief, Michelle. It's ten thirty."

"And you've barely touched your coffee. Sit back and finish it while I tell you what the pentumvirate decided."

Vanessa still didn't look the best, but she acted receptive.

CHAPTER 27

> 2010-01-07 15:23:19:
> [Fwd: Paper in Press]
> Lin, I just received the attached paper. It looks like my theory wasn't as original as we thought. Would you please take a look at it? Then let me know when we can meet to talk about it. Vanessa
>
> [Vanessa, I thought you might be interested in this paper that was just accepted by the *Journal of Cognitive Neuroscience*. Yours sincerely, Søren Vestergaard, Københavns Universitet]

Lin didn't have dreams, or at any rate, didn't usually remember them when he awakened in the morning. So why was he waking up recently with vivid memories of dreams involving Vanessa?

He'd see her in the neurosurgery ward, sometimes wearing scrubs, but always leaving just as he arrived and the dream ended. Or he'd spot her in the cafeteria line, but when he tried to catch up with her, people would block his way and he'd wake up just as she disappeared into the main dining room.

Occasionally, she'd even show up in a clinical conference and ask odd questions that made him cringe because the others knew he was working with her. But she'd always get up and excuse herself before the conference was over. Oddest of all, when he tried to look at her face in a dream, it was always blurred or obscured by a spectral vapor.

When he tried to picture her face in his mind, he realized he'd never really looked at it carefully. He could vividly hear her voice in his head when he read her drafts. She had even broken into his thoughts, speaking to him as though she were behind him—"I don't think that follows, Lin" or "That isn't the purpose of the control group."

It was uncanny. He knew it was affecting his objectivity when he critiqued her papers or the sections of the grant proposal they were collaborating on.

Reading through the paper she'd forwarded to him, he grew increasingly incensed. How could this Dane have hit on one of Vanessa's most original ideas while seeming to arrive at it from an entirely different set of assumptions?

Without taking the derivations apart, he thought he smelled a rat. There were leaps from postulates to functions over logical chasms that seemed impossible. A shift from the discrete mathematics of combinatorial topology to continuous surfaces seemed contradictory to him.

When he reached the paper's review of the neurological literature, however, he found one problem after another—unwarranted implications, misinterpretations, and outright errors. He bookmarked a long list of problematic journal articles cited in the paper.

He was too busy in the clinic to follow up on Vestergaard's paper. All he was able to do was read through it again before his meeting with Vanessa the following week. As always she was in his office before he looked up in response to the two little taps she made on his open door as she entered.

"Hi!" She slung her backpack on the chair next to his desk and unzipped the main compartment.

"Hello, Vanessa." He tried to look at her face, but she was turned slightly away from him as she pulled out a stapled stack of yellow quadrille-ruled paper. "Listen, I haven't had a chance to—"

"That's all right." She shoved the papers in front of him. "I've been working on the derivations." Her pointing finger pulled his eyes to the first page. "Here's my logic; I want you to check it for me. I worked backward from his predictions for my data on faces, okay?"

She began flipping over papers as she spoke. "So, at every stage I bring in Søren's own assumptions when I need them."

"Clever." He would never have thought of checking Vestergaard's logic that way. "What did you find?"

"A contradiction, I think." She had made her way through five pages. "The key is to define the first mental dimension so it passes through the origin of the three physical ones, that is, through the origin of the brain in space.

"I'm pretty sure you can't do it if you start with binary features. I tried to start from feature theory and derive discrete dimensions but even in the limit, no one feature can constrain the system adequately."

She turned over the next sheet. "So, here I started the forward derivation." His eyes struggled to keep up with her finger as it raced down the page. "The first part is straightforward, but I've tried half a dozen ways to get beyond here…"

On the last page, her finger finally came to rest half way down. Everything below it had been crossed out. "When you get a chance, would you be willing to—"

"Of course. I knew there was an important step missing, but—"

She lifted her papers to lay them back into a pile. "I don't see how he got the paper accepted. Saying 'It follows that…' isn't enough to go on."

"My intuitions told me it was suspicious. It's pretty amazing you were able to prove his derivation was wrong." He pulled her work toward him so he could look at the first page. "I'll go over your proof…"

"Do it first. I want you to look at it without the bias I had after banging my head against a stone wall for two days trying to figure out how he got from features to functions."

"I've been busy, too." He swung around to his computer screen and brought it to life. "I've pulled out eight of the papers he cites and checked them against his review."

"Me too." She pulled her chair around so she could look at the screen with him.

Lin brought up a list of references set up as hyperlinks to the articles themselves. "I think Vestergaard has made one kind of mistake or another in every one of these."

She studied the screen for a moment. "I don't have any of these. They're—"

"They're in the neurological literature."

"That explains it. Mine are all cognitive research. Same story though. He's got five or six of them screwed up. Or doesn't understand them at all."

They suddenly turned to each other and began to laugh.

"Perfect!" Lin retrieved a copy he'd made of Vestergaard's paper. "Who do you suppose reviewed this thing?"

"It's pretty sloppy, isn't it?"

"And why did he send you his paper?"

"I talked to him at APS. He asked a lot of questions and—"

"About your special theory, or—?"

"Mostly clarification. But I told him I was working on generalizing it."

"So he knew, and didn't acknowledge you? Not even—?"

"All he had to go on was a copy of my poster. He didn't know that my two papers would be published."

"He could have cited your convention paper, Vanessa."

"If he had tried to predict my results, he would have realized…" She stopped abruptly. "Lin, do you suppose he knew and deliberately left it out?"

Lin met her eyes. "Vanessa, I suspected from the beginning there was something fishy going on." He tried to look at her face, but her eyes had his gaze imprisoned in their fiery cerulean depths.

"Stan told me on the way home from the meetings that Søren has a reputation for borrowing people's ideas without crediting them."

When she looked down, he tried to take in her face, struggling to etch the details in memory, but without her eyes anchoring her features, they wouldn't cohere as a face.

"I promised him I'd send him a copy of my manuscript, but…"

"Your general theory paper?"

"Yeah. But Stan said, 'No, you're too busy. You will forget to send it.'" Her eyes were back on his with their overpowering intensity. "It seemed dishonest after I said I would. Anyway, I let it slide, figuring I'd decide what to do when he emailed me about it. Maybe, I thought, he wasn't all that interested."

"But he didn't?"

She shook her head. As always, her waving ponytail distracted him. "Never. I'd almost forgotten about it until his email showed up with the manuscript."

"You're going to publish a comment. This kind of careless work needs to be exposed for what it is."

"I've never seen comment papers in the *Journal of Cognitive Neuroscience*. I don't think they'll even consider it."

"They can hardly publish a slapdash paper like this and not accept a critique that exposes its ramshackle construction." Now that he understood the full extent of the paper's flaws, his original outrage had returned.

"Maybe it only looks that way to us, Lin."

"Definitely not. He knew about your work. The fact that he omitted any mention of your poster reveals the hollowness of what he's doing." He raised his fist and shook it. "It will be easy to show he stole your ideas."

"I'm not sure I see how. Will you help me write it, Lin?"

"Absolutely." He picked up the sheaf of yellow paper. "I'll check this out and help with the citations."

"Could you write the section on the neurological research?"

"Yes, but I'm so buried in clinical work, I'm afraid you'll have to pull it all together."

"Fine. But we're doing this together."

He felt pinioned by her eyes. "Are we discussing authorship?" It bothered him that he had to push most of the work onto her.

"What is there to discuss?"

"If you write the majority of the first draft, you should be first author." It seemed obvious to him, if indeed he should have his name on the paper at all.

"Not the way I see it." She leaned closer to him than she ever had before. "You're the only one who can get financial support for brain imaging studies of my theory."

"That's just an accident. You don't have a faculty position yet. But it's your theory."

"It's yours too, Lin. If Søren's theory gains currency, your chances of getting funding to test my unpublished one are nil." She stabbed a forefinger in his chest. "You have to be the one who knocks down Søren's theory."

The jab of her finger sent a shock wave of jumbled sensation coursing through his whole body. "I can't let you write a paper for me."

"For us." She laughed. "I want that grant as much as you do, Lin. I'm going to do everything I can to get it approved. And you being first author on this paper is the best—no, the only way—to do it."

The direction this was taking made him dizzy. He'd never been first author. In his field the author list always began with the senior investigator, the person with the grant, who decided who the other authors would be and in what order they'd appear. And if the senior scientist judged that the paper wasn't important enough for him or her to draft, one of the other authors got assigned to write the first draft for the first author's approval and editing.

On top of that was the reality that comment papers critiquing published articles were like slapping a colleague in the face with a glove. Was he willing to walk into a duel with Vestergaard—even with a marksman like Vanessa at his side?

"All right." His voice almost failed him. "Let's see what it looks like." He searched her face for some sign of her feelings.

"I'll email it to you in a couple of days." She stood and looked him full in the face.

As an impish smile took shape on her lips, the cerebral corona that had veiled her countenance in his dreams parted, and he saw for the first time the elegant symmetry of her features. He was awestruck by the most perfectly proportioned physiognomy he had ever seen.

"I don't know about you," she said, "but I think we make a great team. I'm loving this partnership!"

"Yes." He was overtaken by elation unlike anything he'd experienced before. "Yes, you're the best collaborator any scientist could ever hope for."

"I can hardly wait till our next meeting." Without taking her eyes off his, she gave him a little wave before leaving so quickly it seemed she'd said good-bye as she was on her way out the door.

Only when she was gone did he pause to wonder whether he'd be able to work with this ball of fiery plasma that electrified everything it touched, if and when they began working on the research project outlined in the proposal they were writing.

DATE: January 20, 2010

TO: Prof. Harte (Chair), Davidson, Kovick, Lin (Neurology),
& Kashiba (Mathematics)

CC: Vanessa Trippett

FROM: Psychology Department Graduate Committee:
Brooks (graduate program coordinator & chair), Cavanaugh, Forrester

SUBJECT: Doctoral Supervisory Committee for Vanessa Trippett

The graduate committee met on January 19, 2010, and decided to recommend to the Dean of the Graduate School, Harold Jacoby, that he appoint Professor Janet Tierney of the Department of History as the Graduate School Representative to Vanessa Trippett's doctoral supervisory committee (DSC).

We have also recommended that he appoint Dr. James Forrester of the Department of Psychology to her committee. The graduate committee is of the opinion that the latter addition will insure a more balanced range of expertise in the discipline of psychology for Ms. Trippett's DSC in light of the broad scope of her proposed doctoral research project.

A copy of our formal request for Ms. Trippett's DSC is attached. If you have any questions, please do not hesitate to contact me.

Floyd D. Brooks, Graduate Program Coordinator

Michelle and Paul appeared in Stan's door together.

"Have you seen this letter from the graduate committee?" Michelle held up the letter they had all just received.

"Not only seen it but talked to Brooks about it this morning," Stan replied.

"Have you ever heard of the graduate committee adding a faculty member to a supervisory committee?" Paul's chin was thrust forward and his fists were clenched. After a mellow period following his heart attack, his earlier temperament had reasserted itself.

"No," Stan said, "but apparently it's allowed. Brooks claims it was done five or six years ago."

"Did Floyd tell you anything more about what the justification was, Stan?" Michelle, as always, was calm and problem-oriented. She first wanted all the information she could get.

Stan leaned back in his chair and laced his fingers behind his head. "You want to hear what Brooks said?"

"Yeah, what's this bureaucratic bullshit about 'range of expertise in psychology'?" Paul demanded.

"They decided that because Vanessa's research has become more interdisciplinary than earlier—a reference to Misao and Lin joining the committee—there was a bias toward cognitive psychology on her committee—that refers to the three of us, presumably. They felt her committee needed more departmental balance of expertise in the direction of neuroscience."

"But Jim's on the graduate committee," Michelle said. "Surely Hank and Floyd didn't ignore the fact that he's biased."

"In more ways than one." Stan shrugged. "Apparently they let him talk them into it."

"The guy has a huge chip on his shoulder," Paul grumbled. "He feels left out of the graduate program. Thinks there should be a neuroscientist on every student's committee. He's got this damn reductionist thing about psychology being nothing but the study of the brain. According to him, we're all wasting our time on the mind. Our mental lives are just epiphenomena—completely superfluous to science."

"Vanessa's theory certainly challenges his deep-seated scientific convictions." Michelle put her hands on her hips. "Did Floyd say anything about why the committee specifically recommended Jim for her committee?"

"Yeah. Get this—and I'm quoting Brooks here: 'Jim is already acquainted with Vanessa's work'."

Paul let loose with a Bronx cheer. "Already biased against her work is more like it."

"Oh, yes," Stan added, "and Jim is willing to serve on her committee."

"I'll bet he is." Paul sneered. "I can't believe Floyd said that to you."

Stan nodded.

"Shit!" Paul stalked to the window, turned, and came back muttering, "What a bunch of knuckleheads."

"Have you thought about what we should do, Stan?" Michelle was moving into the decision phase of her problem-solving process.

Stan blew out the deep breath he had taken. "I'm guessing Jim wants to grill Vanessa at great length, ask her about the obscurest research he can think of. And he'll nitpick to death every administrative shortcut we try to take."

"That's what I was thinking." Michelle looked dejected. "Should we give up and plan on two meetings?"

"After talking to both Lin and Misao this morning, I still don't think we should have to. They agree with me that our graduate committee is out of line and that we should contest their recommendations."

"You mean take it to our weak-kneed dean?" Paul raised his eyebrows.

"Exactly," Stan said. "We should ask him for waivers of both the general exam and proposal at the same time. Vanessa's impatient enough now. More wrangling among the faculty is just going to make it worse."

Both men noticed for the first time that Michelle had grabbed one of Stan's pads of lined yellow paper and begun writing.

"Michelle?" Stan said.

"Just a minute more." She held up her hand while continuing to write.

The two men looked at each other. Stan shrugged. Paul broke into a broad smile. They moved to look over her shoulder.

"Way to go, Michelle!" Paul pumped his fist in the air.

"Wait, wait," Stan said as Michelle whirled around in her chair, pulling the pad off the table and out of Stan's view.

She ignored him. "Okay," she said breathlessly. "Listen to this: It's a letter addressed to the Dean of the Graduate School—"

"—signed by the pentumvirate—" Stan interrupted.

"The what?" Paul asked.

"The five of us," Stan said.

"Including Lin and Misao," Michelle said to Paul. "Vanessa's word."

Paul chuckled. "Figures."

"What are you going to say?" Stan pointed to the pad.

"We're asking for a meeting chaired by the dean to discuss the membership of Vanessa's committee that will—quote—best serve the needs of a student in an unusual situation —unquote."

"And challenge the addition of that doofus, Forrester." Paul stabbed his finger in the direction of Forrester's office.

"That too." Michelle made a note on the pad she was now holding on her knee.

"The best committee would be the one she already has." Paul pulled out another chair and started to sit down.

When Michelle turned herself back to the table with the pad, Paul turned so he was at her side.

"The dean isn't going to let us choose his representative." Stan rolled his chair to his computer. "Let's take a look at this Janet Tierney." He sat in front of the monitor and began working with the mouse and keyboard.

"All the critical documents are part of Vanessa's application for candidacy," Michelle said. "I'm thinking they should be attached to the letter, so we can point the dean toward the most relevant."

"And her publications," Paul added. "The *Nature* paper is out, you know."

"Right." Michelle studied the sheet of notes she'd been taking. "Why don't I go back to my office and draft this. I'll send it to both of you as well as Lin and Misao. Does that make sense?"

"Hey, get this." Stan was staring at the computer screen. "Tierney lists her specialty as the history of science, but she hasn't published anything since 2000."

"It makes a certain amount of sense, given the revolutionary nature of Vanessa's work," Michelle said.

"But do you really think the graduate committee appreciates what Vanessa is doing?" Paul asked.

"There's more," Stan said from his computer. "She served on the Graduate Advisory Committee and was part of the task force that rewrote the grad school guidelines back in 2000."

"Great! Just what we need. An expert on the rules we want to break." Paul threw up his hands. "I say we question the committee's authority to suggest anyone for any position on her committee. That's the prerogative of the candidate, her advisor, and her committee."

"I suggest we add that," Stan said.

"Thank you for offering to put this together," Paul said to Michelle.

"Okay, here's my list: Straight As, passed comprehensive exam with distinction—"

"With distinction—put that in boldface." Paul stood and started to pace.

"Brilliant defense of her master's thesis," Michelle continued, tracing with her finger the points she'd written.

"Now published," Stan added.

"And another paper in press." Michelle looked up. "Anything else?"

"Prestigious journals, both." Stan pointed to the yellow pad. "Plus a poster at the national meetings of an important scientific society."

Michelle added it. "What about her teaching innovations and student comments on it?"

Paul shook his had vociferously. "God! Stay away from her teaching. It's not relevant to her research anyway."

Stan nodded. "Agreed."

"Good." Michelle stood. "That was my thought, too. She tore off the sheet and looked at the other two. "I'll try to make it short and sweet."

"Short, sour, and bitter is better." Paul guffawed.

"That's why she should write it," Stan said to him as Michelle hurried out.

Paul started for the door but turned just short of it. "Do you have another minute, Stan?"

"What's up?"

Paul closed the door and turned to face him. "I didn't want to say anything about this while we were working on that memo."

"Something about Vanessa?" Stan had a sense of impending bad news.

"Afraid so."

CHAPTER 28

"One of my students told me he'd seen Vanessa stripping at a frat party recently."

Stan's heart froze. "God!"

"Yeah, I know. I can't believe it's lucrative enough she'd even consider it."

"You knew Langley dumped her?" Stan said.

"Michelle told me this morning." He grimaced. "What a bastard—just like you and me." He smiled feebly at Stan. "I never told you I physically shoved her out of my office one time. Nearly knocked her down."

"No shit?" Vanessa hadn't described it quite so violently, that he could remember.

"Gave me a heart attack, right?" Paul barked a sharp laugh. "Nearly killed me."

"You're sure she's doing it for the money?"

"No. With Vanessa, you never know what's going on."

"Would she accept a loan?" Stan had thought about doing it since she'd lost her assistantship, but he didn't know how to approach her—and still didn't.

"Michelle promised to talk to her about it. I guess Vanessa drops by her office once in a while."

"Maybe she'd take it for working for one of us privately. Any one of us has a ton of stuff she could do pretty much without supervision."

"And do it better than you or I would." Paul smiled ruefully. "But you know Stan, long story short, I'd just give it to her, no strings attached."

"I'm sure we all would," Stan said.

"Yeah, but you and I also know she'd refuse it in a heartbeat."

They agreed to let Michelle know that whatever the price, the two of them were ready to pay it—split it between them. It felt like a feeble atonement for what the two of them had done to her.

Stan decided not to wait until the full committee—the pentumvirate—had signed off on Michelle's draft. He called Vanessa's cellphone. She was in the building and came to his office a few minutes later.

"Stan," she began as she walked in without knocking, "what is this letter supposed to mean?"

Stan spun around in his chair. "For the moment you can ignore it."

"Ignore it?" The change in her tone of voice reflected the bafflement in her face.

"Your committee is drafting a letter to the dean of the graduate school, Hal Jacoby, requesting a meeting to challenge the graduate committee's standing regarding the make-up of your committee."

"What is that administrative gobbledygook supposed to mean?"

"If you really want to know, sit down." He pointed to his chairs.

She yanked a chair to the end of the table, swung it around, and sat down. "I'm not sure I do, but try me."

"The rules say you can suggest a graduate faculty member to the dean. So can I, as your advisor, and the other members of your predoctoral committee can, as well. The dean is supposed to consider them in that order—"

"But he has the final say—obviously."

"Obviously. So our memo notes—and we'll argue—that the department committee was simply out of order. We're the content experts; we decide who's qualified and able to make a contribution."

"I don't really care whether he's on or off. In fact…" She chuckled. "I would like a fair argument with him."

"But he's just an extra person to slow things down and get in the way."

"What I mean, Stan, is that in a faculty member's office or in his class, he can get away with any kind of challenge he wants—on his terms. But in a committee meeting, other people can judge what he's doing. A student has a fair chance of winning an argument in a meeting."

"Fine, Vanessa. I admit Forrester isn't the big issue here. The crux of the battle is our request for two waivers, one for a so-called general exam and the other for a dissertation proposal."

"Leaving only a thesis defense."

"Leaving only the dissertation defense. One big pass-or-fail event. And to make it more palatable for the dean, we're requesting it to be public, giving Jim and his ilk a chance to ask you anything they please."

"In other words, giving me even more protection against bullies. Sounds good."

"I agree, and so does everyone else who knows you. But I can't promise you that our weak-kneed dean, as Paul calls him, will go along with us. In that case—"

"In that case, I quit!" She exhaled noisily. "Stan, I'm sick of this." She flopped back in her chair. "I'd be happy to defend everything I've written about the mind-brain continuum before a committee of a dozen experts—no, a hundred super-smart, knowledgeable people—neuroscientists, psychologists, cognitive scientists, molecular biologists, neurologists—"."

"Vanessa, stop it!"

"—computational molecular biologists, mathematicians, anthropologists, philosophers, and Renaissance men and women of the Academy—anybody!"

Stan leaned back in his chair, waiting for her to stop.

"Anytime, any number of times. Just don't waste my time filling out forms and getting them signed." She took a deep breath. "Please. Just give me a chance to prove I can do science."

Stan waited.

"Sorry, Stan. I've had it with this political shit. It's wasting everybody's time."

"I couldn't agree more, Vanessa. But I don't know how else to approach this."

"Well, I do." She stood up and began pacing back and forth as she continued. "I'm thinking of calling Neil Sussex or Ben Steinberg." She paused to look out the window for several seconds.

"Why? How can they help you?"

"Maybe the people at Harvard or Princeton aren't so hung up on bullshit rules."

"Ask them to call Jacoby and tell him he'll make a jackass of himself if he insists on following the UW's rules. He'll ruin Washington's academic reputation."

"Huh-uh, Stan. I'm thinking about myself. There *has* to be a graduate program that will recognize the value of two papers like mine. Places that would take my thesis without a proposal, don't you think?"

"Sadly, Washington isn't one of them." He buried his head in his hands. "I'd give anything to put a UW doctoral hood over your head in June. But you're so special to me, I'd also write a letter to anyone you ask me to, explaining what's happened here and praising your work in the best words I can find."

Instead of going to the window this time, she came over to him and put her hand on his shoulder. "Thanks, Stan," she said, as she bent to kiss the top of his head.

It lasted five seconds, but something inside him snapped like a rubber band breaking in his hands. The sting brought tears to his eyes.

She went back to pacing. "The only thing that's keeping me here is Lin. I told you we're working on an NIH proposal, didn't I?"

He nodded. He noticed for the first time how tired she looked. He had ignored it earlier, assuming it reflected her disappointment.

"The trouble is, I need a degree. And going off someplace else to get it—Harvard, Stanford, or whatever—would cost me at least a year." She stopped at the window. After a moment, she resumed talking, but more to herself than to him. "If Lin gets the seed grant, he'll need me to test subjects and analyze data."

She turned and leaned back with her hands on the window ledge. Her shirt fell open, exposing the contours of her lovely breasts beneath her T-shirt. "I've got an idea for a long-shot experiment. Something like it will need to be done eventually to test the near-far dimension of my theory."

"Can you write it up as a proposal?"

"I could throw something together in a couple hours."

He leaned back and laced his fingers behind his head. "How much does it depend on understanding your theory, really understanding it?"

"Some." She looked at him sharply. "What are you smiling about?"

"Nothing. I'd just like to see Jim squirm when he's faced with evaluating a cognitive thesis requiring him to read and really understand your theory."

She laughed at him. "The motive isn't revenge."

"What makes you think that? But seriously, if you could be patient enough to wait until we can pull your committee together again…"

"There's no hurry on this one. Lin and I are shooting for a June five deadline. If I had the data in hand by mid-May, we could add another experiment to the proposal."

"Would you write the proposal for me, and give me a few days to line up the troops? I'll let you tell Lin what's going on."

She nervously glanced at her wristwatch. "It'll be a few days."

Her expression suggested she wouldn't tell him why, even if he asked. He had a premonition that it had something to do with the rumor she was stripping at frat parties. All he could do is hope she'd talk to Michelle soon.

She stood in the doorframe at the end of another yo-yo trip across his office. "Thanks again, Stan."

"Stay in touch, Vanessa." It was an involuntary plea.

Then she was gone. Emotionally drained, he went home and drowned himself in cheap merlot.

Michelle, Paul, and Stan had all been notified by phone that Dean Jacoby would finally meet with them, two weeks after the pentumvirate had submitted their request for a meeting. They agreed to meet at Stan's office on Friday after lunch and walk over to the Graduate School Dean's office together. It was a gloomy February afternoon with a soaking mist hanging in the canyons between buildings as they crossed the short distance between Guthrie and Gerberding halls.

Michelle was the first to voice what had been on all their minds for the past two weeks. No one had seen Vanessa since the day they had all received a copy of the letter from the graduate committee. All of them had sent her a string of emails describing what was happening, but none of them had heard back from her. She wasn't answering her cell phone. Stan couldn't find her in the lab, and they had all tried her office repeatedly.

Nobody else had seen her or talked to her either, and among the three of them, they had asked half the people in the department. It didn't really square with their previous experience with her. She'd had disappointments and setbacks before, but she had never withdrawn from the situation, even for more than a day.

When the dean's receptionist ushered them into his wood-paneled conference room, they were greeted by Roger Zhrudsky, Floyd Brooks, and Jim Forrester, who were already seated at the expansive rosewood conference table.

In front of each chair, there was a pad of paper and pencil, a glass turned upside down on a coaster with the university's seal on it, and an upside-down cup on a saucer. A pitcher of ice water on a tray, also bearing the university's seal, completed the pathetic attempt at opulence.

"Hello there," Roger said with artificial cheerfulness. "Pour yourselves some coffee and join us, won't you?"

Michelle and Paul filed around the table and pulled out chairs opposite the three already seated. Stan claimed the one at the end of the table assuming that as chair, people would expect him to sit there. All three went to the polished coffee urn on the sideboard and brought back half-full cups balanced on their saucers.

"What are you doing here, Roger?" Paul said as he sat down. "I thought this was a meeting between Vanessa's committee and the dean."

"It's a question of whether the committee followed rules established for the graduate program by the department." Jim Forrester was at his insufferable worst.

"And that's why I'm here, Paul." Brooks's thin reedy voice made him seem like an ineffectual apologist for the department compared to Jim's guttural bark.

Roger cleared his throat, although his windpipe sounded perfectly clear to Stan. "Floyd brings not only the most encyclopedic knowledge of the rules of anyone in the department, but also a practical understanding of how they have been applied and interpreted in the past."

Forrester slid a paper across the table on a thin cushion of air, but it stalled like a glider losing an updraft.

Brooks pushed it on to Stan. "As Vanessa's chair, you should take a look at Jim's proposed agenda for Vanessa's general exam."

Stan scanned the two-page memo, prepared for the seven signatures of the supervisory committee. Forrester was asking that the general exam be limited to Vanessa's background and preparation for doctoral research. The memo stipulated that she was expected "…to present, following a successful general exam, a proposal for a dissertation on a topic for which the data have not yet been collected," although it could be related.

"I might have known." Stan shoved it over to Michelle as though it had a foul smell.

Forrester was on his feet with several more copies, which he handed to Paul and to Stan, since Michelle had the one intended for him. He continued around the table, carefully laying one at each of the remaining places at the table. When he was nearly finished, a stout woman in her fifties was ushered in. Her graying hair was cropped short and shaped so her stern, unsmiling face looked less square.

Forrester rushed to hand the woman one of his proposals. "Hi, Janet. Nice to see you again." He laid the rest of the proposals at his place. "Oh." He turned back to Tierney. "The psychologists are all sitting here." He swept his arm around the room. "This is Janet Tierney, in case you don't know her."

Stan was annoyed. Obviously, Forrester didn't consider himself one of them.

Roger stepped into the breach left by Forrester's boorish behavior. "Hello, Janet. How are you?"

"Good, Roger. And how are things with you?"

Roger introduced the rest of the people at the table.

Tierney took the vacant place next to the head of the table where a somewhat larger wingback office chair clearly marked where the dean was going to sit. "Well, we have an interesting agenda today, don't we?"

There was no response.

She picked up Forrester's proposal but didn't look at it. "I understand we have a real firecracker student to discuss."

"More like an incendiary bomb, Janet," Forrester growled. "She sets everything in sight on fire when she lands."

"In my experience, students who make a splash with their coursework and exams go on to have mediocre careers." Tierney glanced around the room looking for confirmation.

Stan wondered whether this was intended as a challenge. Hadn't she read Vanessa's credentials? They had been attached to his memo to the dean.

Paul picked up the gauntlet. "You have lots of students in your program who publish two papers in major journals before the end of their third year, Janet?"

"History is different, Dr. Kovick." Stan couldn't believe she actually raised her nose and sniffed as she said this. "Books are the only publications we take seriously."

"I appreciate that," Paul said quietly. "In the sciences, revolutions are started by papers less than thirty pages long. I recall that was about the length of Einstein's special theory of relativity paper."

"It was quite short," she replied tartly.

"And thousands of pages of books on the history of physics, I think." Paul sat back, ostentatiously gloating.

The door opened again, and Misao Kashiba's white-haired visage appeared, commanding an instant respectful courtesy from everyone. "Am I late?" He slipped into the empty chair next to Michelle with decorous apology.

Stan glanced at his watch. "You're right on time, Misao. And in thirty seconds, our distinguished leader will be tardy."

Misao studied Forrester's proposal for a moment. "Is this what we're here to discuss?" His sincere incredulity made Stan laugh.

"I'm afraid it is, Misao." Everyone turned to Michelle, as though they had forgotten she was there.

The door opened again, and Lin rushed in out of breath. "Sorry, sorry. My shift ended an hour ago, but I was working on a head trauma case and needed to brief the on-call for the next shift."

The silence that followed had the reverberating solemnity of the contest between life and death from which Lin had come, in sharp contrast to the jingling triviality of their agenda.

Roger burst the bubble. "There's coffee… and tea." He looked at the newcomers, but there were no takers.

Stan noticed that Michelle had barely touched her cup of coffee. Obviously, the dean's coffee beans didn't measure up. It really wasn't that great. The whole room had a kind of ersatz gentility that struck Stan as a botched attempt to emulate a corporate board room—the huge table of dark, expensive wood, the thick carpeting, the unused pads of paper and freshly sharpened pencils, the glassware, and china.

What the hell does this have to do with Vanessa's effort to unify the mind and the brain in a single, explicit formulation? Yet we're sitting around this pretentious table chattering like squirrels about the meaning of half a dozen words in a university catalogue.

The seating arrangements people fall into when none is specified always fascinated Stan. He had landed at the end opposite the dean, not as a deliberate gesture of opposition but a choice dictated by his role as committee chair. The original triumvirate formed an equilateral triangle, while the pentumvirate was arrayed along one side of the long table.

When the dean arrived, he and Tierney, his representative to the committee, would occupy the opposite corner of the room, with his faculty allies lined up across the table from the pentumvirate like a medieval army facing another on the field of battle.

Stan's palms had begun to sweat. He felt a rising uneasiness about the way this meeting was shaping up. It was becoming increasingly clear to him that their memo had hit a raw nerve someplace between Roger's office and the president's.

Vanessa had five allies, equal to the administrative forces aligned against her, but one of those members, the dean, had all the power. His was the final decision. Among the other four, Forrester and Tierney had made their positions clear. Brooks would probably also be aligned with them, since he would be defensive about a decision made by the committee he chaired.

Roger Zhrudsky was the real enigma. He would side with the administration if it was better for the department, but his past dealings with Vanessa had clearly left him with a great deal of respect for her unusual accomplishments.

Harold Jacoby would try to strike a compromise. If the committee wanted only a single public final defense and the administrators stuck to the rules and insisted on three—general exam, proposal, and final defense, Jacoby would go for an agreement on two meetings by framing the question of whether the first one was called an oral general exam or a proposal meeting.

Stan had seen this kind of semantic compromise emerge on important issues all too often. And meanwhile Vanessa would go her own way, refusing to compromise her integrity in the name of upholding the literal meaning of words they chose for another meeting. While the clock ticked, she would be readying still another paper for publication.

CHAPTER 29

The dean kept them waiting for a full three minutes, while they exchanged half-hearted trifles about the weather, city politics, and the fortunes of Seattle's professional athletic teams. When the dean's short, pudgy figure appeared suddenly in the doorway, the tension created by the artificial small talk vanished briefly. He was followed by an attractive young woman they had all seen in the outer office. The latter was too young to be a faculty member; the laptop clutched under her arm made it clear her role was secretarial.

"My apologies. My staff schedules my appointments much more tightly than I really want." He paused at the head of the table while the young woman sat down next to him and opened her laptop on the table.

"Thank you for your patience. Is everyone here?" He turned to his left. "Roger. Thank you for making time to meet with us." They shook hands.

The dean proceeded around the table, greeting each person by name. One of Jacoby's best tools for resolving disputes was his ability to remember names. Even so, Stan found the whole thing ridiculous.

When Jacoby reached the end of the table, Stan put out his hand. "It seems," he said, "Ms. Vanessa Trippett has attracted attention outside the field of cognitive neuroscience." That earned him the frowns of both Forrester and Tierney. He could have sworn he saw the dean's secretary scowl at him, too.

Jacoby recovered from his momentary confusion enough to mumble. "Indeed." But he held on to Stan's hand. "Thank you for requesting this meeting, Stan. I always appreciate it when faculty recognize the role my office can play in academic disputes."

"Thanks for arranging it, Hal." Stan didn't like the tone of Jacoby's remark. It made his ultimate authority all too clear.

When the dean reached Lin, he said, "By elimination you must be Dr. Xuan of Neurology."

Lin seemed used to the confusion about first and last names in Chinese. "Please call me Lin."

"Yes, indeed, Dr. Lin. I've been looking forward to this meeting. I have some very good news for you."

Still holding Lin's hand, Jacoby looked at each of the others in turn as he continued speaking. "Now, this won't be made public until tomorrow, so I don't want any leaks, understood?" He turned back to Lin. "I was on the phone to your chairman this morning to let Larry know that your seed grant has been funded."

He dropped Lin's hand and raised both of his in the manner of emcees and administrators. Everyone joined in his applause and repeated his congratulations in murmurs. While they were still clapping, he suddenly grabbed Lin's hand and shook it again.

The gesture was typical of Jacoby, who in his dual role as vice provost was nominally in charge of awarding the university seed grants for faculty research. It was another subtle reminder of the power of his office.

On his way back to the head of the table, he paused briefly behind the woman with the laptop. "Kim here will be taking notes, and we'll see to it that all of you receive a copy of the minutes of this meeting." Finally Jacoby sat in the wingback chair and opened the manila folder he had brought in.

There was an ominous tone to all this formality. Stan couldn't shake the sense of impending doom.

"Now, I propose to follow the agenda implied by your memo, Stan." Jacoby's round face made his rapid survey of the room especially condescending. "Let's consider the role of the departmental graduate committee in an application for candidacy, which is, as I understand it, to verify that the student has met the requirements of the graduate school and any others unique to the department. Am I correct, Floyd?"

Brooks squirmed and answered timidly, "Yes… um…"

"But this was an unusual application, so to speak." Forrester's harsh voice cut into Brooks's indecision. "She was asking for special treatment. Exceptions from requirements."

"That's apparent, Jim." Jacoby nodded in Forrester's direction but didn't give him a chance to interrupt. "But a strict reading of the rules makes it clear, the departmental graduate committee has no role in influencing the composition of a student's doctoral committee."

"We fully understand the circumstances—" Floyd began.

"Well, of course I appreciate any relevant input. But…" Jacoby paused while he made eye contact with Forrester, then Brooks, and finally Tierney. "…in this case, the supervisory committee is already larger than normal. I see no justification for adding Dr. Forrester."

It was a victory for Vanessa, but Stan understood better than the others how little it meant to her. And it might be the dean's only concession to her committee.

"Now then." Jacoby raised his hand and frowned when Forrester appeared about to object. "So far as I know neither the student nor her committee requested a specific faculty member to serve as the graduate school's representative. Is that correct, Stan?"

Stan hadn't expected such a quick decision and prompt move to another topic. "Um, no," he said while he collected his thoughts. "We already have an unusually interdisciplinary and multi-college committee with Misao from math and Lin from the Medical School."

He paused to consider mentioning the physicist who had been impressed with Vanessa's term paper for Forrester. But he decided there was no point in fighting Tierney's appointment. "Obviously, Vanessa and I will accept your choice of a representative."

"May I suggest, Hal," Paul said, "that since the graduate committee had no standing in proposing someone as your representative, accepting their choice might not be the most felicitous decision on your part."

From the way Forrester nearly jumped to his feet, Paul must have hit a sore spot. *Where does Paul get his knack for backhanded jibes?*

"That's an insult to our committee's role," Forrester burst out.

"Jim, please. 'Insult' is much too strong," Jacoby said. "Paul is raising a worthwhile point."

"Janet is already involved, Hal." Until now Michelle's voice had been missing from the debate. "That will save time, and I'm sure she will recognize the philosophical and historical significance of Vanessa's work better than most in the humanities."

Stan could only marvel at Michelle's finesse. In one sentence, she'd mollified the dean and put Tierney on notice that Vanessa's committee, and she in particular, wouldn't tolerate superficial criticisms or requirements.

"Let's move on to the thorniest issue." Jacoby spoke more loudly than he had been. "That would be the request for waivers of the general exam and proposal." His voice sounded strained. "The argument her committee is making is that this young woman's academic performance—"

"Dean Jacoby?" Michelle's calm voice was just loud enough to require him to acknowledge her.

"Yes, Michelle?"

"I respectfully request that when you refer to Ms. Trippett in her role as a graduate student..." She cast a hostile glance at Tierney, then let her eyes drift past Zhrudsky and Brooks and finally come to rest on Forrester. "...please use one of three nouns. Between 'student' and 'scientist,' the latter more accurately describes her achievements, although 'scholar' would be equally applicable, if a little less precise."

"Amen!" Paul's spoken punctuation obviously annoyed Forrester.

Stan could see that the dean was squirming. Brooks was finding his doodles intensely absorbing. And their other two opponents from the department had lowered their heads, too.

"Point well taken, Michelle." The dean didn't meet her fierce blue eyes, and Stan didn't blame him.

"The argument is that Ms. Trippett's academic performance is so extraordinary that... What?" Jacoby looked at Stan. "She doesn't need to have her competence tested? That she should be left to her own devices to plan and carry out her dissertation?"

This was a question Stan had prepared for. "Not exactly. We are proposing that all those evaluations be folded into one very demanding examination: a public defense of her published papers, those in preparation and her current work in progress."

"Her published work should be background for new and original dissertation research," Tierney said. Her raspy voice seemed especially cantankerous.

"Let me address that, Hal," Stan said. "Vanessa's master's thesis was at first blush rather bizarre. She had spent six weeks during summer collecting data only on herself."

"She did this," Paul put it, "not only independently—from the design and execution of the research to the write-up—with no input from me except a heroic effort to stop her."

"But that's absurd, Dr. Kovick," Janet blurted out. "Why would a student ignore a faculty member's advice?"

"Exactly," Paul retorted. "Because Vanessa was so sure she knew what she was doing, she decided—correctly, it turned out—that I was giving her bad advice."

"That's preposterous! How can you know your advice was—"

"Because her research is now published, Janet. I'm surprised you didn't see her paper. You subscribe to *Nature*, don't you?"

"Published?" Tierney clearly didn't believe what she'd heard.

"The research," Michelle added, "represents three hundred hours of data collection and a completely original statistical procedure for the analysis."

Misao raised his hand and waited until Jacoby acknowledged him. "Yes, I showed the procedure to my colleague, Dick Hamilton, whose specialty is statistical theory. It is his opinion that Ms. Trippett would be able to publish it as an independent contribution."

"She had no help from anyone," Michelle went on. "She first explained it to me during one of our weekly conferences."

Tierney crossed her arms over her chest as if to prevent any more preposterous ideas from reaching her. "Well, I'll admit this is all quite unusual, if a little hard to believe."

"We've gotten a bit off the track of my account," Paul said diffidently. "For reasons irrelevant to Vanessa's work, Stan took over as her advisor and chaired her master's defense." He turned to Stan.

"I agreed, with some reservations, to chair her committee," Stan jumped in. "She rewrote what was to become her paper in *Nature* as a thesis and gave the best performance Michelle, Roger, and I have ever seen during her defense." He glanced at Michelle.

"Quickest committee decision any of us had ever seen," she said.

"And I learned a great deal from her," Roger added.

"But I'm confused, Stan," Jacoby said, looking back and forth at the speakers. "Why didn't you schedule her general exam after the thesis defense?"

"Because by the time she had her master's defense, she already had a dissertation proposal."

"And handed out a précis of it at the defense," Michelle said.

"That's bizarre," Tierney said.

"She'd actually collected almost a third of the data in her proposal by then."

"What? What's this woman's hurry?" Tierney said petulantly.

"Student's," Michelle corrected her. Tierney glared at her.

"Please, Janet," Stan said. "I know Vanessa's story is hard to believe. But if you'll be patient, I think the picture will come into focus."

Whether she realized it or not, Tierney was the perfect foil for Stan to unfold an account of Vanessa's career. He was feeling more confident, because he was ready for Tierney's question. It was exactly the point he wanted to make next.

"Vanessa's empirical research is a perfect example of good science: A very simple modification of equipment and software everyone around the world has in cognitive research labs these days. But one nobody thought to try. And… this one small methodological change opened a window on one of the central issues of cognitive neuroscience. Vanessa found an objective way to measure conscious thought."

"Surely you can't be serious, Stan." Tierney snapped. "That's a problem no one has—"

Stan smiled. "That's not what my colleagues around the country—around the world, actually—are saying. They've repeated her findings for just the reason I gave you."

"Stan's exaggeration is absurd, Hal." It was Forrester. "I certainly don't agree, and I'm—"

"Dean Jacoby?" Lin hardly raised his voice, but it stopped Forrester, his mouth already forming the next word. "I and my colleagues respectfully disagree with Dr. Forrester. All of us in the Neurology Department believe that Vanessa's procedure, combined with the theory she's developing, promises to revolutionize the treatment of unconscious patients. Anesthesiologists who have heard of it are already discussing how it might be used in their specialty." He glanced around the table, half smiling. "For obvious reasons. And psychiatrists have told me it could be a key tool in understanding schizophrenia, allowing them to understand the relationship between brain abnormalities and pathological thought patterns."

Perfect! Stan hadn't heard this before, and it was exactly the right bit of news to stop Forrester in his tracks and pin Tierney to the wall. Looking around the table, the expressions he saw on everyone's faces left little doubt Lin's comment had had a dramatic impact and turned the tide of the discussion completely.

Stan jumped back in to continue his story. "To come back to the sense of urgency Vanessa felt, she understood the need to claim credit for her discovery. She had submitted her master's thesis to *Science*, which turned it down, so at least a handful of people had heard about her work.

"Not long afterward, she presented a poster at the annual national meetings of the Association for Psychological Science. There she saw firsthand how easily others could repeat her experiments and rush into print ahead of her. When I told her to wait and have a proposal meeting, she ignored me. She quickly finished the three experiments she'd proposed and sent the paper to the most prestigious journal in cognitive science. It has been accepted and will be published shortly."

"As the lead article in the issue, Vanessa tells me," Michelle added.

"That is really quite astonishing," Jacoby said vacantly.

"To sum up," Stan continued, "at every stage where a cautious graduate student, interested first of all in a PhD, would have dutifully dotted the i's and crossed the t's for the faculty, Vanessa behaved like a working scientist, a brilliant one, pushing ahead her research, knowing she was on to something of enormous importance, and rushing it into print, aware of the hounds on her heels. All of our staid advice to slow down, jump the hurdles, and get a degree, she rightly dismissed. If she isn't qualified to carry out independent research, none of us are."

"But Hal." Tierney conspicuously turned her back on the rest of them to face him. "If she's as great as all this, why can't she propose something else?"

"It does seem—" he began.

"If I may answer Dr. Tierney's question?" Lin said in that placid voice that demanded attention. He waited for Jacoby to nod. "She is already at work on a theory that will change the way we think about the brain and mind. It's that work she would be able to describe to all interested faculty at a public dissertation defense."

"Without a proposal?" Tierney had spun around to look at Lin.

"Janet!" Paul had finally lost all patience with Janet Tierney. "You clearly haven't the least idea what the nature of scientific theory is. A proposal at this stage would be ludicrous."

Michelle picked up the thread. "A proposal would be the same as the present version of Vanessa's theory, don't you see?"

A thrill ran through Stan's body like the tsunami that was racing to engulf their opposition. It seemed possible they would walk out of this room with everything they had hoped for. "Hal, I hope you're beginning to see the point of the waivers we're asking for."

"Hal?" Tierney's face had gradually turned livid. "You asked your task force to revise the policies governing the granting of graduate degrees, and we did. You told us to strengthen them, make them more rigorous. I think we succeeded. You signed off on our work and argued for them until they were approved." She turned and glowered at Stan. "Don't let those people get away with—"

"Now, now, Janet. I have to confess to you that our Ms. Trippett doesn't fit the prototypic student our policies had in mind. I think, perhaps, her committee is right; a single dissertation defense, open to the university community does seem an excellent way to examine Ms. Trippett's accomplishments."

With a loud crack the wooden pencil that had been laid out for Forrester broke between his thumb and fingers. "I don't know why you invited me to this meeting, Hal." He tossed the two pieces of the broken pencil on the table, stood, and headed for the door. Just as he was reaching for the knob, the door opened and Forrester found himself confronting the considerable bulk of Provost Theodore Hilborn's enormous belly.

"What the fu—?" Forrester caught himself a split second too late.

"Jim!" Hilborn said, stepping back into a defensive crouch.

For an instant they stood like two male gorillas about to engage in combat. Then Hilborn asked Forrester, "Is the meeting over?"

"Nuh… I… I was just leaving."

Hilborn collected his wits and peered into the room. "Ah. All here." He put his hand on Forrester's shoulder. "Come on back in, Jim. I want you to hear the news, too."

CHAPTER 30

Looking abashed, Forrester made his way back to his seat.

Jacoby jumped to his feet. "Ted! What's happening? Why—?"

"Sorry to barge in like this, Hal." Hilborn refused the wingback chair Jacoby offered him. "No, no. Sit down, Hal. This will only take a few minutes."

"Of course. Of course." Jacoby slipped back into the chair where in the context of Hilborn's bulk he looked even smaller than before.

"Hal has kept me apprised of the controversy about Ms. Vanessa Trippett," Hilborn began. "And it pains me a great deal to have to tell a committee that's spent a considerable amount of time deciding a difficult set of issues that their work is moot."

"Huh?" Paul sounded like he'd been punched in the stomach.

"However, there has been a radical new development in Ms. Trippett's case."

"What?" It was Stan's turn to respond involuntarily.

"I just learned about it a few minutes ago, and knowing many of the people who know her would be here, I rushed down to let you all know the facts. I hope this will reduce the number of false rumors about Ms. Trippett."

"Ted," Michelle said. "What are you talking about?" She was half standing and leaning forward across the table toward Hilborn.

"Please sit down, Michelle," Hilborn said. "Vanessa is not in any physical danger."

"Well then, what?" Lin was leaning forward across the table like Michelle.

Stan was struck by the similarity. The relationship between Lin and Vanessa appeared to be stronger than he thought. But was he truly surprised? On reflection, not really. She did that to smart men.

"You all know that Ms. Trippett admitted to having an affair with an undergraduate student last quarter," Hilborn said.

"What!" Tierney's voice rose to a screech. "Why wasn't I informed about this?"

"Because it's irrelevant to her research," Paul said.

"It is not!" Tierney yelled at Paul.

"Please, Janet, wait until I've finished." Hilborn looked Stan in the eye. "What I doubt many of you know is that she was taking off her clothes for money at several of our fraternities."

Paul hit the table with his fist. "That's mere rumor, Ted."

"Her name appears in a police report. Paul. She wasn't arrested; what she was doing was legal. But the police contacted my office."

"Is that legal?"

"I'm not sure, Michelle. This is the first time we've done anything with the information. And you're hereby on notice that it is confidential. Is that clear?"

The silence was more from the shock of the announcement than a lack of answer to Hilborn's question.

"For your information, Ms. Trippett is now stripping professionally at a strip joint north of Ballard, under her first name. She's billed as 'The Girl from Outer CyberSpace,' a reference to her appearances as a *Playboy* model, I assume."

Stan grimaced. He felt nauseous. The rumor Paul had passed along was true, then. And even if it could be shown to be irrelevant to her status as a candidate for the doctorate, Stan was physically ill thinking of raunchy men ogling the body he could not get out of his mind, the image of which momentarily erased everything in the room.

"She should be expelled from the university," Tierney grumbled. "Immediately."

"Excuse me, Ted." Michelle's steely calm voice was under absolute control. "This news, while shocking, especially in light of the Vanessa I know, is not really relevant to this committee's deliberations. The fact is that academically, very little of what Ms. Trippett does on her own time is the university's business.

"I'm sure there have been other students, even graduate students, who have made ends meet by stripping in various local venues without any university sanctions. And the fact that the department and university reduced Vanessa's income by taking away her assistantship, may have forced her to seek the most lucrative part-time employment she could find."

Hilborn nodded his agreement. "Sadly, Michelle, I haven't told you the worst yet." Hilborn looked as though delivering this news made him uncomfortable.

Stan felt numb. His guts writhed, and he felt like any moment he might have to rush to the bathroom for a bowel movement.

"Some of you know," Hilborn said, "that Ms. Trippett's dismissal from a teaching assistantship began with a complaint filed by three women in the section she was teaching. In response, Ms. Trippett admitted having an affair with an undergraduate student in her class.

"One of the students who signed the complaint is the daughter of the prominent Seattle lawyer, Frank Holmes. Frank also happens to be a very generous financial supporter of the university."

"Oh, no!" Hal buried his head in his hands. "Not Holmes."

"Yes, Hal. A strong supporter of the liberal arts."

"God help us!" Hal moaned.

"Regrettably, Frank also learned of a rumor that Ms. Trippett has had affairs with two faculty members in the psychology department." Hilborn looked directly at Stan. "As a lawyer, he took pains to confirm the rumors." He gave Paul a cursory glance. "Frankly, I myself was shocked and outraged."

Stan's bowels were seething. In his imagination he saw a tornado of public hearings and the humiliation of being dismissed from the university bearing down on him, tearing to shreds the happiest year of his life.

"The upshot was that Frank took his daughter's complaint, along with the other information he'd confirmed, directly to the president and demanded we not only terminate Ms. Trippett's assistantship, which we'd already done, but also expel her from graduate school, bar her from any future association with the university, and hold a press conference to announce it."

"What's the daughter's name?" Paul asked curtly.

"It doesn't matter."

"Are you officially withholding her name, Ted?"

"No, I fail to see the relevance of it."

"We had another graduate student," Paul said, "whose last name is Holmes. He has a little sister named Brittany, who's a freshman."

"I believe that's the daughter's name," Hilborn said. "I'd have to check it to be sure."

"It is, Ted." The dean had been paging through the papers in his folder.

"How is this relevant?" Hilborn sounded less combative.

"The graduate student, Brad Holmes, has had several confrontations with Van— Ms. Trippett," Paul went on. "In one instance, she humiliated him. In another, she slapped him—"

"I personally observed evidence that he tried to assault her—sexually."

Everyone in the room turned incredulous eyes on Jim Forrester.

Everyone except Michelle. "She told me that he stuck his finger in her vagina."

There were slack faces around the table and looks of horror on Lin's face and Misao's.

"She told me the same story the day it happened," Stan added.

"But there were no witnesses." Roger had regained his composure.

"Did you notify the—?" Hilborn began.

"No, Ted. In the absence of witnesses, Ms. Trippett refused to file a formal complaint."

"Incidents of this kind should be reported through official channels, Roger," Hilborn said, "even when there are no charges or a hearing."

"Yes, I see that in this case." Roger looked thoroughly chastened.

Forrester spoke up again. "Ted, if I may put in my two cents' worth?"

"Yes, go ahead." Hilborn seemed honestly curious.

Forrester picked up one of the broken halves of his pencil and began twirling it. "I think this meeting should confine itself to adopting my suggested agenda for Vanessa's general exam.

"This lawyer's bullshit about barring her from university employment and calling a press conference to announce the actions taken against her... Who is this vindictive son of a bitch? He's both cruel and childish. Vanessa's already been stripped of her assistantship. Enough is enough. Tell Pete to bug the hell off."

Peter Henshaw was the president of the university. Apparently, Forrester played racquetball with him, too, if he could call him "Pete" in this setting. But Forrester's defense of Vanessa surprised Stan a lot more than his acquaintance with the president.

"You tell him, Jim." Hilborn looked amused. "Holmes is giving the university a great deal of money. You don't blow off a benefactor like him."

"Provost Hilborn?" Misao had actually raised his hand requesting the floor.

"Yes, Misao?"

"Does this mean that if the daughter of a wealthy donor complains to the president about the difficulty of my course or my teaching methods, you'd be forced to fire me and call a press conference?"

"Dr. Kashiba, you know that's completely different." Hilborn sounded like a parent scolding his son.

"The similarity lies in the fact that the father is a wealthy donor to the university."

Stan was astounded. Retiring, gentlemanly Misao had turned out to be another invaluable resource in their defense of Vanessa.

Hilborn seemed to suck up Einstein's curved space in the room like a massive star. "I interrupted this meeting to *inform* you of what I plan to do in Vanessa's case. This meeting has no bearing on that decision. I regret that you've wasted your time. But the timing was such that it was unavoidable."

Paul drew his pencil across his doodles like a knife, cutting the paper until the lead broke. "Can we leave now, Ted?"

"Not yet, Paul." Stan stood up. "I have a message I wish you would convey to President Henshaw personally, Ted." His voice was now level and steady. He was wasting his time. But he wanted to be seen going down in flames with Vanessa.

"I will put my thoughts in writing and send them to Dr. Henshaw. However, as the only administrator who represents the university's scholarly reputation, it's your responsibility to point out to him the academic consequences of his action."

Jacoby offered Hilborn his chair again. This time Hilborn accepted. "If you'll send your thoughts to me, Stan, we will be able to convey them to him more expeditiously. I'll be happy to talk to Pete on your behalf."

"Then I'll copy you when I send them to Dr. Henshaw. But you should be able to infer what his concerns should be after you hear what I intend to say in my letter."

"Then you have the floor, Stan."

"In 1905, Albert Einstein submitted a dissertation consisting of a collection of several of his published papers to a doctoral supervisory committee in the physics department of the University of Zürich. It was rejected because he hadn't written a dissertation. One of those publications was his first statement in print of the special theory of relativity. Another earned him the 1921 Nobel Prize in Physics.

"I suggest that before the president authorizes any action on Ms. Trippett's case, he solicit some qualified opinions about her work from outside the university. He may be at risk of leaving as his legacy to the university the distinction of having fired a future Nobel laureate." The burned out shell of Stan's body, charred by emotion, collapsed in his chair.

"I hate to burst the drama of your little story about Einstein." Janet had virtually disappeared until that moment. "However, I think you have your facts a bit askew. His doctoral dissertation was accepted at Zürich with little fuss in 1906, as far as I know from the historical research I've read."

Stan realized he was about to get buried by a history scholar, whose formal language included the German pronunciation of "Einstein." *Shit!*

"You're right in one respect," she continued. "In 1901, Einstein did submit a different dissertation draft—on molecular forces in gases, if I recall correctly. His advisor at the University of Zürich, Alfred Kleiner, didn't like it and made him withdraw it. He submitted a dissertation on the size of molecules four years later in 1905, and it was accepted. Because of its practical implications, it was widely cited when it was published later on, but it isn't the one that won him the Nobel Prize in 1921. So your story contains a kernel of truth about his struggles to get a PhD."

Everyone was listening raptly. At heart, they were a gathering of scholars, fascinated by any a tidbit of knowledge someone tossed their way. Even Hilborn and Jacoby couldn't put aside their earlier years of education, teaching, and research.

"I believe you're thinking of a later event in Einstein's life, which may be more relevant." Janet looked at Hilborn for permission to go on. Seeing he showed signs of interest, she continued.

"In 1907, he applied for a *Privatdozent* position at the University of Bern. In support of his application, he submitted his seventeen published papers, including the one on special relativity and the addendum deriving the famous $E = mc^2$. He was turned down because he had not submitted a Habilitation These, which is not unlike our PhD dissertation today, as far as academic employment was concerned in early twentieth century Europe.

"Apparently, he was highly amused, but in 1908 he wrote the required thesis, reapplied, and was given the post. So perhaps the University of Bern is the best parallel to the embarrassment UW might suffer if Ms. Trippett someday wins a Nobel Prize."

Stan could tell that the ending of Janet's story wasn't quite the one Hilborn had expected.

"Dr. Hilborn?" Lin, whose previous silence suddenly became apparent, had the earnest sincerity that marked almost everything Stan had heard him say.

"Yes, Doctor… ah?"

"Lin Xuan."

"Ah, yes. Dr. Xuan, you had a question?"

"No, a request. Please call Dr. Nietz before you talk to the president. He has already said publicly almost exactly what Dr. Harte just said. Indeed, he is planning to have Vanessa address the Medical School next month to describe her work. The interest in the life sciences departments of Arts and Sciences and several faculty in Engineering indicates an attendance of at least three hundred. He's having trouble finding a large enough auditorium."

"Most of my department plan to attend, Dr. Hilborn," Misao said deferentially.

Hilborn gaped first at Lin, then at Misao, and then back at Lin. "Thanks for the heads-up," he said to them finally. Then to the dean, "It sounds like we'd better talk to Pete."

"Yes," the dean said. "He will need to have the appropriate papers and a letter from Dr. Nietz, for sure."

"Can we leave now?" Forrester didn't wait for an answer. He stood and made for the door. The rest followed his lead as quickly as they could.

> 2010-03-03 16:22:31:
> Vanessa, We just met with the dean. We need to talk to you. If you aren't comfortable talking to me, call Michelle or Lin. And PLEASE—tell whoever you call to let Paul, Michelle, Lin and me know that you're not sick or in trouble. All of us are willing to do anything we can to help you. Stan

Stan went by her apartment on the way home that evening. The trouble was, there was no outside bell or buzzer for her apartment, and she couldn't hear someone knocking on the locked door at the bottom of the enclosed stairway to her third-floor apartment. He thought about standing out front and shouting her name, but the windows were dark. If she were sleeping, she wouldn't hear a voice outside.

The next morning he checked *The Stranger* online. A strip club called The Jungle Gym was running an ad for their featured act, "Vanessa, the Girl from Outer CyberSpace." It seemed an obvious way to advertise a *Playboy* CyberGirl without stepping on any trademarks.

He began a serious debate with himself that lasted most of the day. If he went to the club, which wasn't too far from where he lived, and caught the late show, he might be able to "pick up" Vanessa and talk to her. If it was the kind of club where the girls worked the tables, he might also be able to pay to talk just long enough to find out what was going on. But the idea of visiting a strip club that close to campus scared him.

Someone could see him there, and he wouldn't even know he was in trouble until he was asked about the rumor. It could easily be a student he wouldn't recognize. Hell! One of the dancers could be another grad student in psychology.

There had been raids of the city's strip clubs not more than three months ago, too. Getting picked up by the police would be a *real* disaster for him. He checked his email one more time, but there were no new messages. He clicked on Vanessa's name in the address panel and hit "To:"

2010-03-04 15:38:06:
Vanessa, Whatever it is that is keeping you away, it doesn't matter. Please let one of your friends help you. I know you've always regarded Michelle as your best friend. And it's true, she's the most reliable of us. Please get in touch with her? She's leaving her cellphone on 24/7. She said you can even call her in the middle of the night. You can count on her. But please don't drop off the face of the earth, whatever you've heard about what's happened. In spite of my role in your life—and I'm filled with remorse for it—I'm your (desperate) friend. Stan

He hit send, and sat for five minutes wiping his eyes with his handkerchief and blowing his nose.

After his two o'clock class, Stan returned to his office, still mulling over his options. There were no email messages from Vanessa. There was an email from Larry Nietz, the chair of the Neurology Department of the Medical School asking Stan to call him as soon as possible. It took an hour of phone tag before he and Nietz actually connected.

"Lin told me what happened yesterday at the meeting on Vanessa," Nietz began.

"I'm pretty much in shock," Stan said. "I have no idea what to do. The thing from the president's office completely blind-sided us."

"That's why I called. Lin said he told you about my plans for Vanessa to give a lecture in the Medical School."

"Yes. I was amazed to hear it. Things were so chaotic I forgot to thank him for contributing that bit of information. In fact, he was tipping the balance toward Vanessa until Hilborn showed up with the stuff from the presi—"

"I know, I know. What a crock. And that's one of the reasons I called. I assume that you'd be willing to chair a university-wide interdisciplinary committee to supervise Vanessa's doctoral program."

Stan chuckled. "That's what I thought we had until—"

"I know, but this one is going to be bigger… a *lot* bigger. Even though our criterion for membership is graduate faculty who have read at least two of Vanessa's papers.

"I've already talked to Misao Kashiba. Turns out two of his colleagues know her papers and have worked through the math. They'd be on the committee. And of course, those of us in neurology who have been following her work from the beginning. So, assuming the five of you—I mean, you and Davidson, Misao and Kovitch—"

"Kovick. Paul Kovick."

"Right, right. And of course, Lin. Oh, I forgot to mention—do you know Penny Whitford?"

"I know the name. Isn't she the dean of—"

"The Med School. She's read everything Vanessa's written. Lin's seed grant proposal went through her office, and she was blown away. She wanted to see anything else Vanessa had done."

"I have to say, my head is spinning," Stan said. "I didn't have an inkling something like this was happening."

"By the way, you should know that Penny has already called Henshaw. He's not committing himself… yet. But Penny really laid it on thick. I gather she told him the Med School thinks that Vanessa is to neuroscience what Einstein was to physics."

"Really. That's a coincidence. I told Hilborn to tell Henshaw the same thing."

"So I gather you think the committee is a good idea, and—"

"I couldn't have dreamed of an idea as brilliant as this." Stan wondered whether he should mention the fact that Vanessa had disappeared. It might complicate things unnecessarily—if he could find her within a day or two.

"So we can count on you as chair? I'll take care of getting a formal petition together for the thirty or forty I already—"

"Thirty!" Stan found the number staggering. "Who—?"

"At least. There are ten of us from neurology, anesthesiology, and psychiatry—that I know of at the moment. And of course, Penny. Naturally, there's a gaggle of neurobiologists—I counted at least seven the last time I looked at the list. Then there are three from the bioengineering department, a computational molecular biologist, and five or six so far from biology…"

"I'm overwhelmed." Stan sat back in his chair. The reality of acting as spokesperson for such a large, diverse group of scientists was just beginning to dawn on him.

"There'll be more, Stan. Her papers are circulating all over campus. I'm getting two or three calls an hour." There was a ten second silence. "Oh, did I mention that we're demanding that Vanessa defend her dissertation with no additional requirements? No other orals or proposals. With the super-committee having the final authority. That's okay with you and the rest of the committee, isn't it?"

"That's what we were asking from Jacoby."

"That's what I thought. So… I'll send you a copy of the petition later today. If it meets with your approval, call me and we can talk about how to collect the signatures."

"Thanks for taking the bull by the horns," Stan said, still mentally reeling from the heady conversation.

"Thanks for lending your name. Talk to you soon."

After he hung up, Stan sat and stared out the window at the fir tree for a dozen minutes, reviewing his conversation with Nietz. The way things were shaping up made it even more imperative that they find Vanessa and tell her.

CHAPTER 31

By now it was almost four in the afternoon. What time would she have to leave her apartment to get to work? He looked up the club's phone number on the Web and called to find out when the dancing began, a plausible enough question.

"What about your featured dancer, Vanessa?"

"She's hot, man. Did you know she was a *Playboy* CyberGirl?"

"Bingo! Is she dancing in your late show?"

"Last act of the evening, sir."

"And when's that?" Stan's palms were sweating and his stomach was doing somersaults.

"Around one-thirty. But if you want to get in to see her, I'd try to come before the last show starts. We've had full houses for *all* her shows."

"Okay, so when would you recommend I come in?"

"Listen. I'll give you a tip. If I were in your shoes…?"

"Yeah?" His arm was shaking so much he was having trouble holding the phone to his ear.

"I'd plan to hit the door around midnight, okay?"

"Great! Thanks for the—"

"Now, I'll be working the ticket booth. Or if I'm not, ask for Jerry, okay?"

"Right. What do you have in mind, Jerry?" In spite of his nerves, he was already thinking about how much cash he was going to need. He knew that was the way these places operated.

"I'll find a seat for you for her show. And, I might even be able to get you a lap dance with her."

"Perfect! And hey, thanks for your help."

"Don't mention it. See you around midnight."

His hands were still sweaty and shaking several minutes after he hung up. And his bowels were queasy with anxiety. Then he realized he might need to talk to a bank officer if he was going to withdraw… what? A thousand dollars? Would that be enough? Could he afford to carry, say, two thousand into a club like that? It had to be in what, fifties and hundreds?

He thought again about asking Paul to go with him. But he couldn't predict what Vanessa's reaction would be, especially if they showed up together. He considered Michelle for the first time. There were several problems, including the practical one that by now she was probably at home in Bellevue.

She'd have to make the trip back, and Stan really didn't know whether he should be taking her to a strip club, no matter how serious things were. He decided that if they hadn't found Vanessa by tomorrow morning, he'd float the idea for her to consider.

By the time he got to the bank, he'd decided on ten twenties, ten fifties, and ten hundreds. It took only fifteen minutes to get the cash. He was on his way to buy himself a cheap money clip at Bartell's drugstore, when his phone rang. It was Lin.

"Have you seen Vanessa in the last week?" Lin sounded frantic.

"I'm afraid not," Stan replied. "I guess you haven't either."

"I've been trying to reach her since her committee met, but she's just disappeared. And now that my grant is funded, I need her to get things going. There's a technician's slot in the budget we created just for her. It pays more than an assistantship."

"I've tried everything I could think of—even staking out her apartment." One of the people coming toward him on the sidewalk gave him a double take. "Look, can I call you back in a few minutes?"

He gave Stan his private cell phone number. Stan needed a few minutes to think out what he was going to say to Lin. After he left the drugstore, he headed straight for her apartment. He was going to hang around until time to go to the club, walking up and down the street, watching. As soon as he was out of the business district, he called Lin back.

"You said you 'staked out' Vanessa's apartment?" Lin asked.

"Yeah. I went by there around seven-thirty, but there were no lights in her apartment, and—"

"Really? I was there earlier. We must have missed each other."

"I'm walking by her place right now. Could you come over? I'm thinking of yelling her name, but I need a witness, in case someone calls the police." He was thinking, too, that Lin's relationship to Vanessa was likely to be completely different from his and Paul's. She might be more willing to talk to him than to either Stan or Paul.

"If the police do show up, we can file a missing person's report," Lin said. "That might be worth a try. I was getting ready to do it, anyway."

"Good thought."

"Listen, I'm on my way. I'm driving a maroon Buick sedan."

"Perfect. I'm here without a car anywhere close." Stan hated to drag Lin into accompanying him that evening, but if they succeeded, Lin probably wouldn't resent his asking. Come to think of it, even if they failed, he was sure Lin would understand.

When they were both standing in the front yard of the old house she lived in, they tried calling her name, softly and self-consciously at first, then with increasing volume.

An woman in a sari emerged from the first floor. "You're looking for Vanessa Trippett?" Her Hindi accent was nearly unintelligible.

"Have you seen her?" Lin asked.

"She's maybe not here now. She's working late nights. Comes home three or four in the morning. I think, she sleeps till maybe noon. Not ever here in the afternoons or evenings that I see her."

"Thank you so much." Stan's voice didn't really reflect the gratitude for the information she'd given them. He was too worried about what Vanessa was involved in

The late nights made sense, if she was dancing at The Jungle Gym. But afternoons sounded ominous. The thought that she might be working as a call girl, or worse, left him nauseated. For some reason, scenes from the movie, *Belle de Jour* flashed through his head.

When they were alone on the sidewalk again, Lin asked, "Why would she be working nights?"

Stan told him about the ads he'd seen.

"So it's true, what the provost told us?"

Stan realized then that Lin probably knew little if anything about her nude modeling until Hilborn mentioned it in passing at the meeting. It broke Stan's heart when Lin said, "Stan, it just isn't like Vanessa. Not the Vanessa I know."

"Not the one I know either." Stan's statement was true as far as it went. "The nude modeling part is true. I guess you didn't know?"

He shook his head. Stan gave him an abbreviated version of the story, starting with the *Playboy* photos, and skimming over the photos taken during her childhood as lightly as possible. Lin listened grim-jawed.

"Her father?" Lin said for the third time. "Poor Vanessa. I had no idea."

"Lin, I'm going to that club tonight. If she's on the program, she has to be there. Would you consider joining me?"

"Yes, absolutely."

Stan heaved a sigh of relief. "Okay, let's at least one of us hang out here until around eleven-thirty. We can spell each other to get something to eat, and later on I can watch while you try to park closer." Stan told him about his phone conversation with Jerry. "I'm thinking we should arrive there around eleven-thirty. Have you ever been to a strip club?"

Lin laughed. "No, have you?"

"I hate to admit it, but I've been to enough different ones to know the rules. I've heard there are some new wrinkles since the last time I was in one. But I suspect you'll find the whole experience disgusting and degrading. And we'll probably be there long enough you'll be bored silly before we leave."

"Well, if we can rescue Vanessa, it will be worth it, Stan."

"My thought exactly."

They climbed into Lin's car at eleven. On the way up to the Whittier Heights neighborhood north of Ballard, Lin turned to Stan as they waited for a traffic light. "Do you believe her father abused her—physically?"

"Not for sure. But I don't think so."

"I hope you're right. Unfortunately, her pattern of behavior makes me wonder. She's too smart to react the way she has to what's happened… with cold calculation. She's not weighing the money she can make taking off her clothes in public against other part-time work she could get. Don't you think there has to be something else going on?"

"Michelle and I have both had the same thought."

"She doesn't have to do this, Stan. And I desperately need her to help me finish the NIH proposal by the end of next month."

The line for the ticket booth was in a vestibule with black walls and dim indirect lighting. The faces of the men in line ahead of them were largely lost in shadows, and everyone kept their heads down to avoid eye contact. The admission charge was fifteen dollars, so when Stan reached the window, he stripped a fifty from his new money clip and held it on the counter halfway through the semicircular hole in the glass. "Jerry said I should ask for him at the ticket window."

The bored girl in the booth studied the bill for a moment. "Jerry," she yelled, barely turning her head. A muffled voice said something unintelligible. The girl nodded. "Fifteen," she said without inflection. "He'll meet you at the end of the tunnel." She tipped her head toward the dark passageway on Stan's right.

"Actually there are two of us." He pushed the bill a little farther toward her but kept it under his fingertips.

"Thirty."

Stan took his hand away from the counter. "Thanks! Keep the change."

He turned to Lin. "Let's go." Stan led the way into the darkness. In about thirty feet, the unlit hallway ended in a black wall. Only when they reached it could they see that there was another short hallway that led toward a large, dimly lit room and the source of heavy metal music. Silhouetted against a spotlit stage was a man two inches shorter than Stan. It was difficult to make out the shadowed face, but the voice matched the one Stan talked to earlier. "Jerry?"

"Yeah. Hi man. You the one who wanted a lap dance with Vanessa?"

"Right. My buddy and I."

"Okay, she's comin' on in like five-ten minutes. You wait over here." He pointed to an area where several men were already standing against the wall. "I'll be back in five. I got ringside seats for you guys, okay?"

"Excellent! Thanks Jerry." Stan handed Jerry a hundred he'd stashed in his pocket. "Here. This is for your trouble."

"No prob', buddy." Jerry glanced at the bill and then quickly scanned the room. "Come to think, there's a table over there." He nodded. "C'mon, follow me."

He led them to a table in the far corner of the room. "You guys hang here for a couple. Give the girl who comes over —oh, say, twenty bucks, okay?" He waited for Stan to nod. "Tell her Jerry's going to get you some premier seating."

"Hey, Jerry. This is great!" Stan pointed Lin to one of the chairs and pulled out his money clip.

Jerry bent close to Stan, eyeing the bills as he stripped off another hundred. "So… I already talked to Vanessa. You'll be right behind me during the show, so afterward, you just hang there until I get my shit packed up, okay?"

Stan nodded and tried not to let his face show his stomach's reaction to Jerry's garlicky halitosis, which enveloped him like a fetid fog.

"Then I'll find a table for you gents in the VIP room," Jerry continued. "And tell Vanessa you're all set for your lap dances."

Stan held out a rolled up hundred at waist level. "This is a real treat, Jerry."

Not sure what to do, Jerry eyed Stan's hand.

"For you, Jerry."

"Okay, man." He smiled a toothy grin as he took the bill without looking at it.

As Stan sat down next to Lin, he noticed for the first time the frozen grimace on his face. Stan glanced at the stripper on stage. The woman was kneeling in front of a customer, who was sitting at the bar that encircled the stage.

She was completely naked with her legs spread open around his drink glass while her torso undulated with the music. She flung her hair in every direction, sometimes hitting the customer in the face. The latter ignored the hair and leaned forward, his eyes on her crotch. Did it remind Lin of his rotations in OB-GYN?

Stan bent to talk into Lin's ear. "Pretty gross, huh?" He still had to raise his voice to be heard over the music.

He looked at Stan in surprise. "Will Vanessa be doing *this*?" He jabbed his finger at the stage.

Stan had to lip-read most of what Lin said. "I'm afraid so, Lin." He was almost shouting. "It's what these places are all about."

"Good God!" Lin turned away with a face full of grief.

The woman on the bar finished her dance abruptly. Following desultory applause, the band members left their instruments.

In the lull, Lin said, "How can we get her out of here, Stan? Tonight?"

"If you tell her about all the new developments, I think this will be her last night."

Lin shook his head hopelessly. "So much is happening."

"Tell her about your grant first—and the technician's slot."

He nodded with sudden enthusiasm.

"Then describe the lecture Larry is planning, but don't tell her it'll also be her final defense—at least until you've explained the committee Larry's also setting up."

"Okay. That's the order I learned about them."

"Make sure she knows it's Larry who's doing it," Stan said urgently. "Mention anyone else you know on it, but leave me entirely out of the equation."

"But you're the chair, Stan."

"She needs to know that it isn't just the pentumvirate."

Lin smiled. "Just like Vanessa to come up with a neologism like that."

"We don't have a good track record." Stan was also thinking about his personal failure—and Paul's.

"I understand her so poorly. I'm worried she'll just dismiss what I say. I mean, I have so little experience advising graduate students, and you have so much, Stan."

"But look where my advice got her."

"I guess you'll be here to back up what I say?"

"Absolutely." Stan put his hand on Lin's shoulder. "She trusts you more than anyone else right now, except possibly Michelle. She'll listen to you. Just don't let what you see get to you."

The musicians returned ten minutes later and began warming up. The room tingled with the anticipation of fifty men.

Jerry returned carrying a small suitcase made of metal. "Okay gents, come with me."

He led Stan and Lin straight to the front of the room and up on stage where he pointed out two chairs set up behind a camera tripod. "Here you are, my friends. I told you ringside. You've got ringside."

As they slid into the chairs, Stan noted that they were partially hidden behind the folds of the open curtain. But they could see several tables on the opposite side. No one would notice them on the darkened stage, but what if a wandering spotlight hit them?

A booming voice blasted through the room. "And now, my friends… our featured act… Give it up for the world-renowned nude model, Va-nesss-a… the Girl from Outer Cyberspace."

Applause and cheers ricocheted around them. The spotlights still hadn't come on, but Stan could see a figure in high heels walking slowly toward a large circular bed that a stagehand had just pushed to center stage.

"Now, we got something special for you tonight, folks," the oversized voice continued. "Please direct your attention for a moment to the big screens all around you. Now… when the photographer takes a photo…" On cue a flash went off on stage, magnified by umbrella reflectors, so the entire front of the room was bathed in light. "…you'll get a lens-eye view of Vanessa."

On the screen they could see a full-length, still photo of Vanessa standing next to the bed wearing a business suit with a skirt so short it barely covered her buttocks. "There she is, my friends…" Suddenly blinding spotlights drenched the stage where Vanessa was standing. "And *here* she is… in the *flesh*, ladies and gentlemen!" A palpable pause was filled with the collective in-drawn breath of the audience. "Vaaaan-esss-aah!" The disembodied voice drowned in the heavy metal music that started up.

She cocked her hips to the left, then the right while flipping her hair with both hands. Stan had never seen her face hidden behind so much makeup. It transformed her demure features into a mask of licentious seduction.

For the first few minutes of her act, he was mesmerized by the mutation she had undergone. Then he gradually became aware of their surroundings again. The spotlights never wandered close enough to light up the area where they were sitting. He was grateful for that, although the possibility that a light would swerve their way hung over his head like the dust motes he could see in their beams.

From where they were sitting the angle of the big-screen distorted the image so everything looked squashed together. The photos being shown were all close-ups: the gauzy circles of her areolae covered by a diaphanous white blouse when the suit coat came off; with the blouse discarded, the camera zoomed in on her nipples; when the skirt and panties dropped, it zeroed in on her private lips, shorn again of the chaste triangle that he knew and cherished.

Vanessa wasn't so much dancing as moving gracefully from pose to pose. The latter were straight out of *Playboy*. Even the lascivious expressions on her face fit the image of the oversexed siren. Every movement contributed to exposing more of her body, yet with an elegance unlike anything he'd seen.

He'd become so absorbed in watching her at close range that for a moment he'd forgotten Lin was with him. When he remembered and stole a glance, he saw that Lin was holding his head in his hands and looking at the floor. Seeing him in such obvious distress drove a stake into Stan's gut. He would never have subjected Lin to this if he hadn't been so desperate to contact Vanessa.

When she climbed on the bed and began writhing in fake ecstasy, Stan too turned away. But it did him no good. The big screen displayed a grotesquely thin Vanessa pulling her labia apart, sliding her fingers over her clitoris and hooking an index finger into her vagina.

The sight of it shredded the memories of what his fingers and tongue had learned. Her shrieks and groans were nothing he'd ever heard from her, even during their wildest lovemaking. It was as if the searing spotlights, the stabbing strobes, and the pummeling beat of deafening music were tearing apart the body he had loved and adored.

If he could have walked out unobserved, he would have. But the tiny stage offered no place to go but down the steps and into the audience.

"So, what do you think, man?" Jerry was whispering hoarsely to Stan. "Great, huh?"

"She's awesome!" Stan knew he didn't sound enthusiastic, but he felt obliged to at least add, "Thanks again." In the darkness he could see the smirk on Jerry's face before he turned back to his job behind the camera.

The entire six-minute performance failed to arouse Stan until the very end when Vanessa bent down and carefully collected her clothing piece by piece. The spotlights followed her as she walked down the steps from the stage and threaded her way through the tables wearing only three-inch pumps that made her buttocks rock and swing in a way that was new to him.

It was an inopportune moment to get an erection. Jerry had finished packing up his camera equipment and now stood in front of them. "Okay gents. Follow me."

Stan gently pushed Lin ahead of him. He wanted to watch for signs of physical distress. In the murky red darkness of the room, Lin looked pale green with nausea and on the verge of fleeing. And for his own protection, Stan didn't want Lin bolting for the men's room or out the front door

Jerry led them into a narrow room lit with more subdued red lights and red furnishings. They passed several lap dances in progress as they followed Jerry to the far end of the room. He waved them to a deep-cushioned sofa with a curve that created an enclosure facing the mirrored walls.

Stan peeled off another hundred to hold out as he sank into the plush upholstery. "What do the girls usually get for tips in here?" he whispered, handing Jerry the bill.

"Oh, they figure fifty to get the action started, maybe another fifty depending on the girl…" He winked at Stan "…and the guy, if you know what I mean?" He half-saluted them. "Enjoy."

CHAPTER 32

Vanessa came out wearing a miniscule black G-string and the same pumps she'd worn on stage. She walked into the space between them and the mirror. "What's this, Stan? Think you can buy a lap dance from me?" She wore the same manufactured smile as she had onstage. Stan wondered if it could possibly be painted on with makeup.

He'd rehearsed what he was going to say—concise and factual, with no apologies, no scolding and no recriminations—it came out mechanically. "I came here because I saw the ad in *The Stranger*. And I brought Lin along to tell you what was going on."

As Stan spoke, she bent over so she could hear him in the noisy room. It took absolutely every watt of concentration he had to keep his eyes from straying from her eyes to her bare breasts swaying like ripe fruit inches from his nose.

She turned to Lin. "What's this about?"

Lin seemed to have no problem keeping eye contact. "Vanessa, I've got the seed grant."

"Yes, I know but—"

"You *have* to come help me get our experiments going and put the NIH—"

She squatted by the end of our couch, steadying herself with one hand on it. "I wasn't going to send anything more to anybody until my theory paper was published. Especially not to—"

He leaned toward her ear. "Vanessa, we've been circulating your paper to everyone in the med school—"

She scowled. "Why? So a hundred more people can screw me over like Vestergaard did?"

"It's too late, Vanessa." Stan had to shout over the bass guitar and drums. "Your paper for Forrester is already all over campus."

"That bastard!"

"Please, Vanessa." Lin sounded frantic. "Don't—"

She shook her head angrily. "It's too noisy in here. I'll come over to your office tomorrow after lunch. One o'clock? Or are you on call?"

Lin vaulted off the couch. "I'll get someone to cover for me." He put his hand on her bare shoulder. "Come home with us, please? Right now?"

She gently pushed his hand away.

Stan jumped up and gripped both his shoulders. "You can't touch her in here, Lin. Not when she's working."

"And I work until two."

"Well, quit!" Lin said.

"I can't, Lin. If I skip out, I'll owe the club around three hundred dollars. Plus, they get a cut of all my tips." Something across the room caught her eye.

Stan followed her gaze. Three guys were waving at her to dance for them.

"They'll ding me for their slice of the tips I'd be getting if I were dancing right now," she said. "And the ones I'd make during next hour, which is the most lucrative all evening."

Stan pulled out his money clip. "I've got at least a thousand here. Will that cover it?"

She looked at him skeptically. "Five hundred ought to do it."

He counted out five of the remaining hundreds and held them out to her.

She shook her head. "Come backstage with me. Both of you."

They followed her out, pushing aside the moth-eaten velvet curtains that covered the entryway. Beyond it was a short grim passageway lit by two bare lightbulbs. Halfway to the end, she stopped in front of a day-glo yellow door. She rapped on it at the same time she pushed it open.

As the door swung open, a raspy male voice hollered, "Com'in."

"Hey, Harry." She waved Stan and Lin into a cramped office. "My Daddy Warbucks just showed up." She pointed at Stan with her thumb.

"Well, good for you, Orphan Annie." The speaker was overweight and swarthy. He was sitting with his feet up on a cluttered desk. A cigarette dangled out of the corner of his mouth.

"He's come to whisk me away to a South Sea island paradise," Vanessa went on. "He's taking me out of this hell-hole."

"Lucky you." Harry swung his feet off the desk and tilted his chair upright. Steadying the cigarette, he took a deep draught of smoke and grimaced as he held it in his lungs. Then in a theatrically prolonged sigh, he blew it out. "When'll you be leavin' us, baby?"

"Now, Harry."

"Whoa, whoa, whoa!" He stubbed the cigarette in an ashtray already overflowing with butts and ashes. "There's a little matter of say eight hundred in fees and tips…" He looked up with a sneering smile. "You can't fuckin' run off in the middle of the evening… without settlin' up with me, that is."

"Don't exaggerate, Harry. It's three for the stage—"

"And the house cut of the tips. Don't forget them."

"Check the till," she said. "There's less than two-fifty."

Vanessa barely raised her voice. With a jolt Stan was suddenly aware that she was standing in a tiny room with only her crotch covered and three fully clothed men, all close enough to reach out and fondle her breasts.

"Don't fuck around with me, honey. I know you're always good for five, six hundred—"

"On a hopping Saturday night, maybe five. But take a peek out there. Definitely not hopping out there this particular Thursday."

He frowned at her breasts. "Short notice here, Vanessa."

"I could have called in sick and vanished into thin air. Hell, I could have walked out with Daddy Warbucks here after the show—what could you have done? Huh, Harry? Don't accuse me of being a crook."

Stan stepped forward. "Eight?" He counted the bills out on his desk.

"Too much, Daddy." She picked them up, handed three to Stan and held the others out to Harry. "You think there's five hundred in my tip box. Keep it! I'm out of here."

"No way to treat your buddy, Vanessa." He took the money. "Been like a father to you, girl."

She spun around and pushed Stan and Lin out the door. "Good luck, Harry."

"Say hello to Tahiti for me as you sail by," he said as she pulled the door closed.

Out in the hallway, she said to Lin and Stan, "Wait here. I'm going to change. Don't let anyone try to kick you out. Yell for me. Then Harry, if necessary." She took off down the seedy corridor.

She was back in five long minutes and led them out the back door.

"Would you be willing to drive, Stan?" Lin said. "You said that I should be the one who talked to her. I'll be distracted if—"

"Perfect!"

Lin opened the back door for Vanessa, and then climbed into the front seat. "Are you sure you're okay with driving, Stan?"

"I'm fine with it." He started the engine. "You have the most recent information for her."

"Whose idea was this?" she said as they pulled out of the parking place.

"Mine," Stan answered. "We were all scared shitless something awful had happened to you. Why didn't you at least answer our emails or return our calls?"

She yawned. "I've been too busy. I've been working in the afternoons posing for amateurs in Jerry's studio downtown. A mindless job—follow their instructions, wiggle around naked for a half hour or an hour, no pawing allowed, then split fifty to a hundred with Jerry. Then head for The Jungle Gym around eight."

"Didn't you get my messages about the grant?" There was an edge of desperation in Lin's voice.

She flopped back in her seat. "I'm sorry, Lin. I should have called back, but I've been working from one in the afternoon until two in the morning. I've been so exhausted that I've slept until noon every day."

"But you knew we'd all been calling you?" Stan asked.

"Yes, but I guess I'd given up on this place. I was making so much money in such a short time, I figured I could save up enough in a couple months to live on for six months or a year, if I had to.

"In a few weeks, I planned to start calling some of the people I met at APS. I was pretty sure there was a graduate program somewhere that would be interested in taking a student who already had three publications and a transcript full of As. There had to be one with a fast-track PhD program, right?"

She laughed. "I was planning to start with Neil Sussex at Harvard. How's that for hubris? But I assume even they don't have too many applicants with recent papers in *Nature* and *Psychological Science*. Maybe a prestigious department would know how to work things out for an upstart like me."

Lin had twisted himself around in his seat to look at her. "Did you say *three* publications?"

"Yes. I had an email yesterday from the editor of *Science*. He's going to publish my theory paper."

"Congratulations!" Stan shouted. "What a coup. And a major scientific journal—amazing!"

"Well then," Lin said excitedly, "you now have *four* publications."

"You mean—?"

Lin's head bobbed up and down. "Our comment paper in the *Journal of Cognitive Neuroscience* was accepted, too."

Vanessa's arms flew up, fists clenched. She threw herself backward into the seat cushions. "I can't believe it!" she shouted. "*Now*, it's safe to send in that NIH proposal."

Stan saw her arms drop as quickly as they'd gone up. It was as if all of the energy had drained out of her body at once.

"It's not possible," she said softly, almost to herself.

"Not only possible, Vanessa," Lin said. "It's happened. And you *don't* have to go anywhere else. Larry's setting up a new committee for you."

"A big one," Stan added.

"But how can he chair my committee? I've never taken a course in neurology."

"It isn't really a committee in neurology," Lin said. "He's already lined up forty people or more, all regular members of the graduate faculty. There are four or five people I introduced you to in neurology, and several more in anesthesiology and psychiatry."

"Lots of people in Arts and Sciences," Stan said, "from biology, chemistry, physics, math…"

"Even several faculty in bioengineering and computer science," Lin added.

She knitted her brow. "You mean I start all over, with another proposal?"

"No, no," Lin said. "He sent out copies of your two papers, our comment on Vestergaard and the manuscript you sent to *Science*."

"Wait! I have to satisfy forty faculty members that my papers are—?"

"No, the whole committee signed a letter to the president demanding that you receive a PhD with honors at spring commencement."

"That's ridiculous!"

"Vanessa, listen," Stan said. "These people don't think you're a student anymore. They don't want you to *defend* your dissertation. They want you to tell them about your work."

"The only thing Larry's asking you to do is give a talk about your work," Lin said. "He thinks there are at least three hundred faculty and grad students on campus who want to hear about it."

"And I know you could do it tomorrow afternoon, Vanessa." Stan was convinced he wasn't exaggerating.

"No, I'm too tired." She yawned noisily, but Stan had caught a glimpse of her smile in the mirror.

"I still don't understand why you wanted to disappear—drop out of program," Stan said.

Vanessa blew out her breath. "You know, there have been times when I didn't care anymore whether I got a degree or not. If I died right now, somebody else would do the rest of the work for me."

For a moment the only sound inside the car was the whoosh of tires on the wet pavement of Fiftieth Street. "The theory's out there now. Other people will figure out what it predicts and test it."

"But *I* can't do it," Lin said. "Not without you, I can't. Don't you want to get our *f*MRI research going? We can't let someone with better facilities beat us into print."

"For your sake, Lin—yes. But I don't need a degree to help you out."

"Tomorrow. With you running things, we'll have the first paper out in six months. Less, maybe."

"I know I promised you I'd help, Lin. But I also knew that unless we could point to a published theory, there wasn't much hope of getting our work funded. That's why I was waiting to hear if *Science* would publish it as a major article. And hedging my bets by squirreling away every penny of my stripping money for changing schools."

They drove the next ten blocks without speaking. As they pulled up in front of the apartment house where Stan and Lin began the evening together, Stan almost expected she'd be asleep in the back seat. But when he shut off the engine, he saw in the rearview mirror that she'd pulled herself up close behind them.

"I'm more exhausted tonight than if I'd danced for another two hours." She planted a sloppy kiss on the back of Stan's head. "Thanks, Stan. You were a true friend tonight. And I'll pay you back soon for your Daddy Warbucks act."

"Forget it," Stan said.

Lin had turned again to look at her. With mercurial speed, she planted another juicy kiss on his lips.

"And thanks for doing this for me, Lin." She pulled her cloth shopping bag full of clothes across the seat. "I know just watching me tonight wounded you."

She scooched toward the door and opened it. "I'll try to make it up to you both somehow." She was out of the car and had closed the door before either of them could speak. They watched her unlock the outside door and disappear into the enclosed stairway.

Stan called Lin two days later to find out if Vanessa had shown up as she promised.

"She's talking to the *f*MRI technical staff now," Lin told him. "Do you want me to have her call you when she gets back?"

"No, no. Just wanted to be sure she's okay. How is she…?"

"She's her old self, if that's what you're asking." Lin chuckled. "She'll be testing our first subjects as soon as there's time available in the lab."

"Good. I'm glad to hear it."

"Should I tell her to call you, Stan?"

He hesitated. "No…"

"I'd be happy to."

"No," Stan said decisively. "As long as she's… herself, as you said." Still he wavered. He really should let go, make his exit from her life, much as he hated the idea. "No, in fact, don't even mention I called."

"Are you sure?"

"I think…" Knowing in his heart he and Vanessa would never be close again, he finally said. "Yes, I'm sure. If she wants to talk to me, she knows how to reach me." Then he remembered the other reason he'd called. "Oh, and by the way, Lin. Thanks for going along the other night. I hated to drag you into that place."

"No apologies required. Thank *you* for finding her and getting her out of there."

"Right." Stan felt awkward now. He wished them good luck with their research and ended the call.

On a rare sunny afternoon in mid-April, Stan, Michelle, and Paul again left Guthrie Hall together, this time headed for Kane Hall on Red Square.

"How many seats are there in 130 Kane?" Michelle asked Stan as they started across the brick plaza toward the university's largest lecture hall.

"Larry mentioned seven hundred, but with all the grad students coming, it may be standing room only."

Paul repeated the number. "God, I can't imagine myself talking to that many people about my dissertation when I was a grad student, can you?"

Michelle giggled. "You didn't have over seventy faculty on your committee either, did you?"

Stan couldn't suppress a snicker. "There weren't that many people in the whole *world* interested in my doctoral research. If Janet doesn't think this is a big enough hurdle for a PhD, she—"

"She shouldn't have one," Paul broke in.

They laughed merrily.

"She resigned from the committee, you know?" Michelle said.

"Maybe she decided to return her degree, too." Paul opened the door for Michelle.

They entered the lobby of Kane Hall, laughing loudly enough to draw stares.

"I'm meeting Vanessa, Lin, and Larry in the Green Room," Stan said. "I guess all four of us are supposed to sit on stage. "Did Larry mention that there are places reserved for you in the first row?"

They nodded and waved to Stan as he split off and headed down the hallway.

Vanessa and Lin were already there chatting quietly when Stan opened the door. She was wearing the suit she'd bought for San Francisco with the skirt that both advertised and understated her shapely legs. Lin wore a tailored navy suit with a white shirt and dark red tie. It occurred to Stan that Lin's introduction of Vanessa was probably the first time he'd addressed this large an audience.

Vanessa crossed the room with open arms. "Hey, it's great to see you." She hugged him enthusiastically but with a difference that made him think of Elise instead of his time with Vanessa. "I'm ashamed of myself for not coming to see you, or even calling, since you plotted my escape from The Jungle Gym."

"It's great to see you." He held her shoulders at arms length. "You look absolutely ravishing."

She kept her hands lightly on his shoulders. "Thanks!" Her smile faded. "But about not coming—we've been up to our ears getting the *f*MRI study going."

"Any results?"

"Absolutely!" She bounced on her toes and clapped her hands. "And guess what? It looks like everyone has a unique mental space with its own shape and size—its own set of curvatures."

"Does that mean you can't read someone's mind from brain images after all?"

"Not until you map their minds." She seemed to bubble with energy the way he remembered she had the afternoon she told him about making love to the universe with Beethoven. "The mapping process is like teaching transcription software your accent, only a thousand times more complicated."

"But," Lin interjected, "we're pretty sure Vanessa has the right geometry to map the curves of everyone's mental space." Lin sounded as jubilant as she did. They reminded Stan of two kids who have just discovered a new playground.

"I wish I could talk about our data today." She seemed even more irrepressible than before. "All the answers to the big questions and their implications are pouring out of our first three subjects, but there's not enough data to be sure."

"But here's the thing, Stan." Lin was serious in spite of the faint smile on his lips. "Vanessa's been testing herself, and even she can't untangle the curves of her own mind. The manifold defies dissection."

"That's not really true, Lin," Vanessa said. "I just happen to have *two* black holes." She turned to Stan. "You know, not just a single addiction."

Stan threw back his head in a guffaw. "Why am I not surprised?"

"No, no, Stan. This is an important discovery. Apparently, it's possible to have two very different addictions at the same time and in constant competition."

"Fascinating," Stan said chuckling now. "I assume one of them is your geometry of the mind-brain continuum. The other must be…" He suddenly felt his face catch fire. *You idiot! Why'd you say that?*

Vanessa and Lin eyed each other for a moment before bursting into hysterical laughter.

Larry Nietz interrupted them with a knock at the door. "You guys are having way too much fun in here. You have to come share your wit with the world, Vanessa." He held the door for her, and the three of them followed Vanessa into the lecture hall and onto the stage.

ACKNOWLEDGMENTS

In the sixteen years that it has taken me to turn a retirement hobby into a published novel, many people have read earlier versions. Their comments and suggestions have transformed my prose, heavily influenced by scientific style at the start, into what I hope is something closer to an engaging fictional narrative. Those individuals, to whom I am deeply indebted, include Abby Polus, Ian Mynatt, Jack Mynatt, Ken Shemberg, Sheryl Wilson, Martha Rogers, Peter Jekel, Birte Rau, Jessica Stapleton, and Sara Stamey. My copy editor, Virginia Herrick, went far beyond what we had agreed was to be her task of turning the present effort into a presentable text. My son, Jeffrey read the first version and has recently assisted in countless ways, and my daughter-in-law, Christine Smith, helped me turn a manuscript into a book.

Carl Brown was a beginning writer's ideal reader, cheerfully evaluating every version up to the last two, commenting extensively, and offering assessments that have goaded me to throw away cherished passages that did not advance the story and improve others that were awkward or ill-formed. The text is immeasurably better because of his tutelage.

Above all others, my wife, Ann, has been infinitely patient with me and a constant source of encouragement from beginning to end. She has suffered through virtually all the major revisions, lending her sure sense of authenticity to Vanessa's story.

ABOUT THE AUTHOR

Kirk Smith was born in Des Moines, Iowa and grew up there. Following high school, he moved to Seattle where he graduated from the University of Washington. He received a PhD in psychology from the University of Minnesota in 1963. After two years in the Army as a research psychologist, he moved to Bell Laboratories where he pursued research in memory and language. In 1971, he joined the faculty of Bowling Green State University in Ohio and, during the next twenty-three years, taught both undergraduate and graduate students and pursued research in thinking and memory with the support of the National Science Foundation. Following retirement, he returned to the natural attractions of the Puget Sound area he had discovered as a college student. He and his wife now live in Bellingham, Washington.

KirkSmith-Novelist.com
FictionAboutScience.com

19006863R00198

Made in the USA
Charleston, SC
02 May 2013